PRAISE FOR
PRELUDE FOR LOST SOULS

"Small-town staples—no-frills restaurants and chattering busybodies—blend with the supernatural to create a unique backdrop for this paranormal mystery. Small touches, such as a haunted piano, enhance the atmosphere and are regarded with a normalcy that makes the spiritualism-steeped streets of St. Hilaire feel as American as apple pie. Working to unravel the mysteries that drew them together, three teenagers find unexpected answers in a town where not only the dead are haunted."

—*Foreword Reviews*

"*Prelude for Lost Souls* is a charming novel perfect for a lazy weekend. It's moody and melodramatic, the kind of story that makes you think of falling leaves and cozy sweaters and waning friendships and new lovers and finally learning to let go."

—Tor.com

"Ghost story, love story, and mystery in equal measure, Helene Dunbar's *Prelude for Lost Souls* is filled with unforgettable characters who reveal the many ways a life can be haunted. Perfect for fans of *The Raven Boys*."

—Lisa Maxwell, *New York Times* bestselling author
of the Last Magician series

"Dunbar invokes small-town intrigue and plentiful atmosphere with this haunting, romantic tale."

—*Publishers Weekly*

"Mesmerizing and haunting, Dunbar invites readers into a world of family secrets, anxious ghosts, and a society's ruthless grasp for power that will leave you wanting more."

—*The Nerd Daily*

"Michael's journey of growth and self-acceptance, with all its drama, confusion, and raw emotion, is one that many teens will be able to identify with…regardless of sexuality or gender."

—*Booklist*

"Dunbar painstakingly populates the narrative with 1980s references—particularly to music—creating a vivid historical setting… A painful but ultimately empowering queer history lesson."

—*Kirkus Reviews*

"Dunbar paints a broad and accurate portrait of the pain of the times through a series of emotional snapshots."

—*Bulletin of the Center for Children's Books*

"This YA novel provides an interesting way for youth of all backgrounds to explore a dark history that is rarely discussed."

—*Washington Blade*

"In haunting and lyrical prose Dunbar beautifully and accurately captures a generation."

—Tom Wilinsky, coauthor of *Snowsisters*

"With staggeringly gorgeous, experimental prose, Dunbar delivers a critical story about love, heartbreak, the manifestation of fear, and hope."

—Mia Siegert, author of *Jerkbait*

PRELUDE FOR LOST SOULS

ALSO BY HELENE DUNBAR

We Are Lost and Found
Boomerang
What Remains
These Gentle Wounds
The Promise of Lost Things

PRELUDE *for* LOST SOULS

HELENE DUNBAR

sourcebooks
fire

Published by Sourcebooks Fire, an imprint of Sourcebooks
P.O. Box 4410, Naperville, Illinois 60567-4410
(630) 961-3900
sourcebooks.com

The Library of Congress has cataloged the hardcover edition as follows:

Names: Dunbar, Helene, author.
Title: Prelude for lost souls / Helene Dunbar.
Description: Naperville, IL : Sourcebooks Fire, [2020] | Audience: Ages
  14-18. | Audience: Grades 10-12. | Summary: In St. Hilaire, where most
  residents talk to the dead, Dec, who yearns for a fresh start, Russ, who
  plans to run his town, and piano prodigy Annie Krylova meet and find
  their lives transformed. Told from multiple viewpoints.
Identifiers: LCCN 2020005378
Subjects: CYAC: Mediums--Fiction. | Ghosts--Fiction. | Best
  friends--Fiction. | Friendship--Fiction. | Musicians--Fiction. |
  Orphans--Fiction.
Classification: LCC PZ7.D79428 Pre 2020 | DDC [Fic]--dc23
LC record available at https://lccn.loc.gov/2020005378

Printed and bound in the United States of America.
KP 10 9 8 7 6 5 4 3 2 1

To Lauren MacLeod,

WHO LOVED THIS FIRST

One need not be a chamber to be haunted.

—Emily Dickinson

GLENDOWER: I can call spirits from the vasty deep.
HOTSPUR: Why, so can I, or so can any man; But will they come when you do call for them?

—Shakespeare, *Henry IV, Part 1*, 3.1

RULES OF CONDUCT FOR MEDIUMS

NEVER CHANGE THE COURSE OF THE FUTURE
through the sharing of information.
~~This includes scenarios of life and death.~~

MEDIUMS PASS ALONG MESSAGES FROM THE DEPARTED.
We do not read minds and any attempt to insinuate otherwise
will be met with censure by the Guild.

NEVER READ A FELLOW MEDIUM OR SUMMON A SPIRIT
to that end without their permission. Mediums who have
passed on may only be contacted with explicit Guild approval.

NEVER USE YOUR GIFTS FOR SELFISH GAIN.

NEVER MISLEAD THOSE YOU COULD HELP.

ALL WISHING TO MOVE TO ST. HILAIRE WILL BE TESTED.
A full half of any family must be able to pass tests as certified
mediums and be able to support themselves as such.

ALL HIGH SCHOOL SENIORS WILL SERVE IN THE GUILD'S
Youth Corps during that school year. In the likelihood that
a student shows special promise, there exists the option for a
one-year position as Student Leader within the Corps, leading
naturally to a permanent Guild position upon completion.

HAVE A NICE DAY.

THE GUILD, GOVERNING BODY OF ST. HILAIRE,
NEW YORK, ESTABLISHED 1870.

DEC

Everyone in St. Hilaire talked to the dead.

Every summer, our town opened its doors to the inquisitive and the desperate, those in mourning and those overcome by guilt. The summer tourists who took the private midday train from New York City called themselves "seekers of the truth" or "the curious." We called them *customers*. Or worse.

I'd played along my whole life. Casting runes. Turning over cards. Participating in séances. But being forced to spend my final day of summer as part of a community-wide assembly to raise the ghost of Ian Mackenzie was pushing me over the edge.

Living or dead, Ian annoyed the shit out of me. He'd been an egotistical ass, a pretentious jerk, and as talented a medium as St. Hilaire—a town whose sole business was to contact the "dearly departed"—had ever seen. Bigger than life, he'd died of unknown causes at eighteen, and everyone, particularly the Guild, St. Hilaire's psycho elitist town council, wanted to know why. And it was just like him to avoid everyone's attempts at contact. Ian Mackenzie was a prima donna even in death.

Today, all the registered mediums in town, which was damned near all of the 367 year-round residents, had been required to gather in the brick square near the weathered statues of the town's founders. A cloud of incense smoke hung over the humming and swaying crowd. Some of the kids banged on tambourines. A group of healers focused on an empty chair in the middle of the square, hoping to convince Ian's spirit that his return to this plane wouldn't be a painful one.

I lurked in the back, as far from the spectacle as I could park myself and still be considered present, trying not to be annoyed that my best friend, Russ Griffin, was taking it all a little too seriously.

Russ was wearing the long, black coat he'd barely taken off since he bought it over a year ago, arms uncharacteristically relaxed at his sides, breathing in synchronization with the other mediums. "Ian," he whispered, loud enough for me to hear, reverentially enough to set my teeth on edge.

"Are you seriously playing along with this?" I hissed back.

Russ's eyelids fluttered open as he readjusted his focus. He licked his lips and rubbed the owl-winged tattoo on his wrist—the ink was so white it was almost invisible if you didn't know it was there. "Well, I thought…you know," he said, and looked away.

Unfortunately, I *did* know. And what I knew was this: While

I was planning to leave St. Hilaire and all of this paranormal weirdness in precisely thirteen days, four hours, and fifteen minutes (give or take), Russ was equally determined to prove his worth as a medium and become a Guild member.

It used to be easy for Russ and me to avoid even talking about the Guild, but now that our senior year at St. Hilaire High loomed—and along with it, the expectation that we'd join the Guild's Youth Corps along with every other senior—the tension was tearing a fissure in our friendship.

I looked at the clouds, giving myself a minute to embrace the anger I always felt when thinking about the organization that ran our town. My rage settled into a burning in my stomach that sought a focal point. When I couldn't stand it anymore, I forced myself to try to relax by fingering piano scales on the legs of my too-hot suit pants, speeding up and slowing down, hoping to lose myself in the notes. It might have worked had my phone not started to ring. Once. Twice. Three times. Each louder than the one before.

The chanting around me stopped as hundreds of pairs of eyes turned to stare at the person who had ruined their chance to summon Ian's ghost by forgetting to silence their phone.

I stared at the ground while I reached into my pocket. My phone had been ringing off and on for days...with **Unknown number** showing on the screen and no one there when I answered.

The smell of incense, something I'd loved as a kid and that reminded me of my parents, was making me nauseous. In truth, everything in my stupid town was making me sick, so instead of silencing the phone, I turned and threw it as hard as I could into the neighboring park. Then I stalked off after it, all of St. Hilaire's eyes weighing heavily on my back.

I squirmed in my stiff shirt. My skin was already damp with sweat, and all I wanted was to be able to hold it together until the end of the night when the tourist season officially ended and we could get our lives back.

The sun moved slowly through the trees, giving the leaves an eerie glow. It was hard to know if anyone from town would come to the park after me to make sure I was okay. If anyone did, it would be either my younger sister, Laura, or on Russ. No chance of it being my older sister, Harriet. She despised me, and I'd just given her more reason to.

The chanting resumed, re-creating the rhythmic song that had been my lullaby as a kid. The smoky smell of incense enveloped me again, but then morphed into one of lemon, crisp and clean.

"Hello, Daniel," said a shadow.

My stomach clenched. Aside from my parents, and Harriet, who did it to get under my skin, there was only one person who had ever called me Daniel.

"It's been a while," the shadow continued. The voice was clipped. Formal. British. A good match for the vintage velvet jacket and silk scarf Tristan had always worn and was still wearing as he stepped into the light. He was in his late teens, as he'd always been. Anyone who saw us would think we were the same age. That being said, no one else had ever admitted being able to see or hear him.

4

"Go away," I mumbled. Tristan was *my* nightmare alone. And he was the last person…ghost…whatever, I had any interest in talking to now.

"Daniel, I understand this might not be the most opportune of times. But I need you to listen to me," Tristan insisted.

I took a deep breath. Spirits were far more frightened of the living than the living were of them. The dead needed to be questioned carefully. Coddled, if you were trying to avoid scaring them away. "Think of them as cats," my dad used to say.

But that assumed I wanted to be welcoming.

"Daniel," he said urgently. "Don't open the door. Whatever you do, remember not to open the door."

My pulse raced. "I see you haven't gotten any less cryptic since I saw you last time. Besides, I'm in the freaking park," I said, and waved at the trees around me. "Do you see any doors here?"

Twigs snapped behind me, and I turned to see Russ striding toward me. I should have known that it would be Russ who would follow; Russ was always there when I needed him.

He scooped up my phone and handed it to me without a word, not even a question about who I'd been yelling at. The phone's screen flashed. At least that was still working.

I jammed the phone in my pocket and looked to see if Tristan had stuck around, but there were only trees where he'd been. "Sorry for back there," I said to Russ, even though we both knew my words were only half-true.

"You don't owe me an apology," he said. "But Clive Rice might have other ideas."

My anger surged back stronger than before. Clive Rice, Guild

5

President, was everything I hated about the whole organization. Smug. Secretive. Power hungry. "Rice and his Guild can take a flying leap as far as I'm concerned. And as for Ian Mackenzie..." The tensing of Russ's jaw stopped me. "Seriously?"

"If I can accept that you hate the Guild, can't you accept that for me, they're the only game in town?" Russ asked. I was sure he was as sick of having this argument as I was.

I waited to see if he was going to reply to my mention of Ian, but of course, he didn't. If we couldn't discuss the Guild, then the topic of Ian was definitely off limits.

"There are other towns, you know." I said.

"Not for me, there aren't," he replied, holding his ground.

And this was it. This was *always* it. Russ was certain he would serve his time as a member of the Youth Corps, which was mandatory for everyone in their senior year of high school. But that wasn't enough for him. No, *he* was jockeying to be named Student Leader of the Corps despite the fact that there hadn't been a Student Leader since Ian had done it his senior year. Then Russ planned to earn a full-time job with the Guild and eventually run St. Hilaire. No one had ever accused him of lacking ambition.

I stretched my shoulders, willing my muscles to loosen, my anger to dissolve. I hated fighting with Russ. "Can we not talk about this right now?"

He shrugged and thankfully changed the subject. "Are you coming to the festival tomorrow?"

"Yeah," I said. "Laura would kill me if I weren't there." The year-end festival was St. Hilaire's biggest annual party and my younger sister's favorite day of the year.

"Good," said Russ. "I'll meet you there. I have something I promised to take care of first."

I started to ask what he had to do that was so important, but from his determined expression, I could tell it had something to do with the Guild, and I knew not to ask, if I wanted to avoid a fight.

I kept to the side streets on the way home. The volunteers who worked at the Healing Pavilion were folding up prayer shawls and packing them away for the winter. Other workers were cleaning up the fairy gardens, collecting the wishes and charms left by the tourists. News traveled fast in St. Hilaire, and even here, I heard grumbling about how "that Hampton boy" had ruined the séance, and how my parents would be "so disappointed if they were still alive."

I did my best to ignore the comments and somehow made it home without a confrontation. As I walked through the house and up the creaky stairs to the second floor, past frame after frame of Hampton family photos dating back generations, Laura called out, "Are you okay?"

No, I thought. *I'm nothing like okay.* But Laura worried, and I didn't want to add to her stress. She had to know that it was my phone going off at the séance, but I knew she wouldn't bring it up unless I did first. So, when I poked my head into her room, I simply said, "I'm glad it's the end of the season."

She smiled, looking very much like our mom, with dimples in her cheeks. "I'm so happy you're coming to the festival.

Really. You'll see. You'll feel better once the last of the tourists leave."

I moved to the door before I said something stupid to ruin her good mood.

"Hey," she said. "There's a letter for you downstairs."

A letter. No one I knew would send me a real letter. It was probably just some junk about how to increase your "marketing dollars" or one of those "I've heard you're a psychic, and I'm hoping you can help me" notes that poured through our mailboxes.

"I'll check it out later," I said. "Right now, I've got to change." I pointed to my now-wrinkled and still-uncomfortable suit.

"Dec," she said, her brown eyes softening. "I know it's been a hard couple of years, but…Mom and Dad would be proud of you."

I opened my mouth, hoping the right words would find their way out, but they wouldn't come.

Without answering, I went to my room and started to undress. My anxiety lessened with every item of "Hey, I'm a medium; hire me" clothing I removed: stiff shirt, heavy jacket, worn belt. And everything I put on, ripped jeans, crumpled gray T-shirt, made me feel more myself and less the standard-bearer of the Hampton line that everyone in St. Hilaire expected me to be.

When I tossed the pile of clothing to the back of the closet, my eyes caught on the two pictures I'd hung on the inside of the door.

The first was of my parents on their honeymoon. Even now, I had a hard time understanding how they'd made it all the way to Jamaica and still had come back to St. Hilaire to hold séances and talk to people's dead relatives.

My parents were only nineteen in the photo, two years older than me, but they were already in love and *somehow* already comfortable with their futures. The photographer caught them draped around each other, drinks in hand, bright smiles pasted on their faces as if they couldn't believe their good fortune.

I'd been bugged by the whole "medium" thing for as long as I could remember, but the last straw came two years ago when my parents and I had been driving home from a movie one night and our car rolled into a ditch.

Why, in a town full of people who claimed to talk to ghosts—ghosts who often predicted people's futures—had no one warned Mom and Dad they were going to die that night? Why didn't they know what would happen for themselves? Why was I found bloodied and disoriented, but alive, a block from the accident, while my parents had died? Why didn't I remember the damned accident?

In school, we were taught that everyone was on Earth to learn their own lessons, so you didn't warn another medium about anything, even in a life-or-death situation. But that seemed like a particularly senseless rule now that my parents were dead.

On top of it, Guild law said no one could contact a dead medium without official approval. Kind of like getting a warrant. Lately, they were hammering the old laws home more, slipping reminders in people's mailboxes and such. And though I had questions for my parents, *so many questions*, I couldn't bring myself to try to reach them. Not because of the rules, really, but because ghosts were never the same as the people they'd been when they were alive.

Someday, I'd look at photos of my parents, miss them, and maybe laugh. But seeing their faces still made my stomach knot with the idea that no one had tried to save their lives.

So I had no answers. I only knew I had to get the hell out of St. Hilaire. And I had to do it before school started and I got stuck as a Guild puppet in the Corps.

"I hate this place," I said, although there was no one else in the room to hear.

Indulgently, I allowed myself a glance at the other photo. The edges of the printer paper were fraying, and the Blu Tack I'd used to stick it to the door was starting to bleed through, making tiny sky-colored circles in each of the corners.

Now Appearing it said in large letters. Carnegie Hall, it said below that. Then a photo of Anastasia Krylova, piano prodigy.

I'd found her first CD in the consignment shop in Buchanan, the town next to St. Hilaire, right after my parents died. For a year, hers was the only music I could listen to. The sharps and flats hadn't taken away my pain, but it had made it more manageable. And despite the fact that I'd memorized every note on every single one of her albums, my interest in her was something I didn't quite have a name for, couldn't ever put my finger on.

While I was trapped in a ridiculous upstate New York town that preyed on grief and guilt and greed, she was traveling the world, playing music with symphonies and accepting standing ovations with her tightly wound dark curls bobbing up and down. No one expected *her* to spend senior year helping to plan the next summer's community events, taking appointment requests, and serving as backup to the Guild members during their sessions.

My discarded clothes lurked in the back of the closet like a large, black dog, and I knew Harriet would be pissed if we had to scrape together the money to have them cleaned. *Whatever.* Since I wasn't going to be here next year, I'd never need to look at, much less wear, them again.

As I closed the door, I caught the scent of lemons, and my skin prickled. It couldn't be happening again, this sickness or hallucination that had plagued me most of my childhood. Aside from what happened at the park, I'd been free of it, free of *him*, for two years now. They'd been two depressing, lonely, boring years, but they'd been years when I hadn't had to doubt my sanity.

"Tristan?" I called, my heart racing.

I waited in the silent room. But I wasn't sure whether to be relieved or annoyed when no answer came.

2

ANNIE

"Dmitry Petrov." "Dmitry Petrov." "Dmitry Petrov."
The wheels of the lovely antique train chanted his name over
and over against the tracks, as if there were any way I could have
forgotten what I had lost. As if that could be possible when each
syllable of his name stabbed so painfully at my heart.

My hands caressed the sheet music in my lap, and I imagined I could feel each note. Tchaikovsky's Piano Concerto no. 1
in B-flat Major. I should have been in New York practicing
it for the Hull Competition, one of the most prestigious and
lucrative for musicians under eighteen. I had come in second
last year and gracefully accepted the statue—which lay buried
in Dmitry's storage unit—and the nominal check, which I had
sent to my parents.

I had spent my entire year preparing to win it this time. Dmitry had wanted me to compete with my signature piece, the Prelude, but my manager Viktor put his foot down after the infuriating review in *The Times* that began: "Though a brilliant musician, it is almost impossible to believe that Anastasia Krylova could be awarded the Hull Prize with a piece its unknown composer never completed."

"Hey, that was pretty hot." The boy across the aisle wore a blue cotton T-shirt that was too tight in a "notice me" kind of way. He looked as though he was around my age, despite his nicotine-stained fingers, which he used to twist and untwist the cap of a dented silver flask.

"Excuse me?" I asked.

How could I possibly live without Dmitry? More than a teacher, he had been my best friend. My mentor. My family, given that I was only six when he took me on as a scared child who could play an instrument, and turned me into an internationally competitive pianist.

He had been the only one to talk to me as if I were more than a commodity, more than a marionette who could play music on command. And he had listened to me as if my words mattered as much as my music.

Now he was gone.

"You. *You* playing that piano." The boy took a drink from the flask and wiped his mouth on the back of his hand.

Ah. Right. He must have seen me play.

Had I been performing anywhere but in the atrium of Union Station in Washington, DC, when Viktor's call came in, I would have done what was expected and flown to Montreal

13

for Dmitry's funeral. I would have arrived tired and sad, and been collected from the airport by someone hired to collect me. I would have tried to look pleasant for the photographers lined up behind their velvet ropes, and I would have hated every single second of it.

But Dmitry's death had changed everything. And the sound of the trains had called to me.

"Thanks," I mumbled to the boy, because it would be bad publicity to slap him, and I knew better than to court bad publicity. My headphones were in my bag. If I could find a way to put them on and block this boy out...

"So, do you do that a lot? I mean, for fun?" he asked.

I closed my eyes and said a silent prayer. When I opened them, the boy was, unfortunately, still there. "I am a concert pianist," I said. "It is my..." What was it? My life? My passion? My reason for existing? The only thing I was good at? This boy was never going to understand any of those, so I settled on, "job."

"Wicked," he said, and grinned. "You want some?" He pushed the flask across the aisle, brown liquid sloshing onto the worn carpeted aisle between us.

I glanced around to see if I could move to an open seat, but the small train was packed. I'd been lucky to get a ticket at the last minute.

"Suit yourself." He took the container back. "So, don't you guys have your own planes or something?"

I could feel my cheeks grow hot. It always went one way or the other. People either thought I had endless money or that I could not possibly make a living playing *classical* music. The truth, of course, was somewhere in the middle. I made enough to send to my parents back in Russia so that they and my little brother could live in a house that would not come crashing down around them, but not enough for my own plane.

Dmitry had been a different story. A star both in and out of the classical world, he had performed with rock bands and at the Olympics, on late-night TV shows and at world-class sporting events. He had been invited to openings and parties as much for his wit and movie-star good looks as for his musical talent.

Until he could no longer play. Then he learned who his real friends were.

"I usually fly," I admitted. "Not in my own plane or any-thing…but this is…" I searched for the right word. "Quieter."

It was only after I had stopped playing in the station that I checked my phone and listened to Viktor's message. He was very, very sorry to be leaving this on voicemail, but he was boarding a plane. Dmitry. Dead in New York. Circumstances being investigated, although an empty bottle of pain meds had been found clutched in his hand. I was expected in Montreal and the funeral would take place in three days. Avoid the press. There was a first-class plane ticket waiting for me at Dulles.

"Yeah," the boy said, misunderstanding. "The quiet sucks. And this train is something from the dark ages. It's like watch-ing paint dry. Nothing but damned trees and corn."

Outside the window, the trees and corn formed a beautiful mosaic as they sped past. Dmitry had always loved trains, and now I saw why. This was so much better than planes where you only saw the insides of clouds, white, vast, and dizzying.

"So, where are you going?" the boy asked, shoving the flask between his knees and cracking his knuckles.

15

The words stuck in my mouth like those peanuts they give you on a plane. I did not want to share my grief, share Dmitry, with this stranger.

Instead of answering, I returned the question. I did not care about his answer, but Viktor had always told me that people loved to talk about themselves. It worked for trustees and benefactors, so I was betting it would work with half-drunk teenage boys. Not that I had much experience with boys, drunk or otherwise.

Proving Viktor right, the boy laughed and then hiccupped. "State pen," he said. "Penitentiary. My mom got nabbed again for selling pills."

I rubbed at my eyes, feeling as if I were a hundred years old.

In the train station, I had done something I had not been able to since I was a child in our small, cold house in Russia. Without consulting Viktor, or my finance people, or my publicist, or my record label's marketing department, I made a decision.

I sent Viktor a text explaining that I would not be taking the plane. Then I had turned off my phone and bought the train ticket to Montreal, wanting nothing more than time, quiet, and most impossibly, a way to get Dmitry back.

Now, I was going to make another decision. I bent down and sorted through my bag until my fingers locked around a cord. I pulled my headphones out, gave the boy across the aisle a nod, and stuck them over my ears. Even if that meant I was being rude. And even if that meant I would never learn to speak to boys my own age and was destined to spend the rest of my life alone with only music for company.

After all, there had only been two things in my life that I could ever count on, Dmitry and music. And now Dmitry was dead.

How much more did I really have to lose?

3

RUSS

There was something both terrifying and seductive about the silver needle sticking out of my arm.

It had gone in gentle as a kiss, sharp as a scalpel. Heat crackled and stumbled its way through my veins while I waited for the knowledge promised in my grandmother's flaking blue notebook. She'd been legendary for her ability to speak to the dead without the need for séances and all the drama that came with them. *She'd* never had to say "I'm sorry, ma'am, your cousin doesn't want to talk to you right now" when the spirits decided they weren't in the mood to communicate.

Being a medium usually resembled being a radio with no dial—you might get signals, but they weren't always the ones you wanted. In comparison, my grandmother was like an on-demand service. She could tune in to anything she wanted at any time, and I was determined to learn her secrets.

I watched the liquid as it continued to trickle slowly, green as summer and thin as river water, into my veins and waited. Waited. Waited.

Five minutes in, my vision was still clear. The room was still empty. My hearing was normal and not picking anything up that I wouldn't have, had there not been a needle in my arm.

This isn't going to work.

I pulled the needle out of my arm and disposed of it in the bloodred Sharps container I'd swiped from the doctor's office in neighboring Buchanan. The container sat next to a small, black zippered pack that held two larger needles and four vials of a clear substance thicker than anything shot into an arm should be.

Over the summer, I'd followed my grandmother's shaky script as I brewed, reduced, strained, and aged various plants from the back garden near the woods, some unidentifiable by name, but dead ringers for the drawings in her notebook.

That it wasn't always clear what the mixtures would do made the whole thing a little risky, but also a little exciting. The recipes at the beginning of the book had been marked by my grandmother with checks and stars, and so far they seemed pretty safe.

It was the stuff in the back, the recipes that followed a series of blank pages, that really captured my attention. That was where the thicker serums had come from. The herbs were rare and hard to find, the directions difficult to read, as if my grandmother was putting in safeguards as she wrote the notes, reminding herself of the possibly nefarious purposes for the concoctions.

My future rested on my ability to catch the attention of the Guild. Somewhere in this book was my best chance to convince them to take me on, and I had to find it. I had nothing else.

I rubbed my arm, tossed the pack on my desk, and, head spinning, lowered myself to the bed. Without planning to, I fell into a fast sleep, dreaming of today's community-wide séance, only this time, the square was deserted. Mostly.

"Oh look, it's Sleeping Beauty," Ian said, breaking the silence and sitting on the bench next to me. I took in his still-muscled arms, his still-pressed tight white shirt, his still perfectly curled hair sitting still seductively on his collar, and I swallowed hard.

Then, I took a deep breath and tried to wake myself up through sheer will. No luck.

"I'm not talking to you," I said, looking away.

"Why not?" he asked, bumping his shoulder into mine.

I glanced back before I could stop myself. His eyes were the same piercing blue I remembered. He looked unnervingly solid. "First of all, because I'm dreaming." Dreams mattered in St. Hilaire, but I didn't want this one to.

Ian smirked. "You sure about that?"

"Yes." I raked a hand through my hair. *Wake up,* I ordered myself, but nothing changed.

"Well then," Ian said. "You might want to be careful about your diet. Too much coffee can give you nightmares."

My pulse quickened. *Don't take the bait.*

"Second," I said. "Because you're dead."

"Really? Because I seem to remember you talking to ghosts all the time."

"Is that what you are?" I asked, sucked in by him as always. "A ghost?"

"No, I'm an angel. I'm just waiting for my wings to come back from the dry cleaner's. Lord, Griffin. Don't be an idiot."

Sparring with Ian was always a type of verbal vortex. He managed to disarm his opponents through a dizzying combination of arrogance and charm, which was one of the reasons I hadn't spoken to him for months before he died.

However, not for the first time, I had a niggling sense of guilt that maybe I should have been a better…not friend, but whatever. Maybe then, things would have ended differently; maybe he'd still be alive.

Ian stared at me, a challenge in his eyes. Getting a straight answer from him had always been difficult. Getting a straight answer from a ghost could be impossible. Given that combination, if I believed, for even a second, that I wasn't asleep, then direct-as-hell was really my only option.

"Fine," I said. "You're here, so I'll ask. I've heard rumors… Did you really kill yourself?"

Ian made a "humph" sound, then stood and knotted his hands behind his neck, a gesture I recognized. I'd hit a nerve. *Interesting.*

He turned, and I watched his lips as he said, "Don't drink the Kool-Aid, Griffin. You know better."

A year's worth of defense mechanisms threatened to come crashing down around me. My subconscious obviously didn't believe the rumors. All well and good. Still, I wasn't going to stick around to let him drag me down this rabbit hole again. "I'm waking up now," I said.

Then, with a disorienting jolt, I did.

The room was quiet. I was alone, but as always, Ian, even dream Ian, seemed to leave some energy behind.

I picked up the pack of syringes again. In dying, Ian had lost everything I wanted. He'd led the Corps. Had the opportunity to make a good living as a Guild member without having to hang a shingle outside his door. If I followed his example, I could do the same. I'd have enough money that my father wouldn't have to work sixty hours a week at the train yard. I could be who I wanted to be. The only difference; I would stay alive.

I saw the future laid out in front of me as clearly as I felt the syringes, heavy in my hand. Unfortunately for now, both would have to wait.

Instead, I tried to conjure some anticipation for the festival. Dec had been distant this summer, distracted. He was always running off on secretive errands and staring blankly at walls. I hoped the absence of the tourists might bring some of the old Dec back.

And I needed to shake off this dream.

I glanced at the clock, gathered my forever-unruly hair, and grabbed a large pair of scissors. It was time to put an end to summer.

DEC

I had a couple of hours to kill before the festival, so I did the same thing I always did on the last day of the season. I sat at the old piano in our music room, took a deep breath, and focused on the feel of the cool keys on my fingertips, the pressure of my feet on the pedals.

Like everything in St. Hilaire, the piano was strange. For one thing, it was always in tune, which was good because it wasn't like Harriet was going to approve of me paying someone to tune it. Also, it had an unusual rounded keyboard, a three-panel upright carved back, and a bizarre backstory. My great-grandfather had been paid a literal fortune to take it in after some rich New York society woman claimed it was haunted. It belonged in St. Hilaire more than I did.

Yet, I was the only one who had ever learned to play it, and, even so, Harriet threw a fit if I played during the summer when tourists were in and out of the house. Not like I sucked. It just gave her one more thing to be pissed about.

I cracked my knuckles and limbered up with some easy scales. Lost myself in the music and the repetition of my hands on the keys. I thought of winter. Of freedom.

Then my phone vibrated.

I hoped it was Russ, but no, when I pulled it out of my pocket, it said **Unknown number.**

"Who is this?" I demanded. I'd tried to be nice. I'd tried threatening the caller with reports to the phone company and the police. But it never made any difference; there was only silence on the other end.

I switched it off. Once I got to the festival, I wouldn't be able to hear the ring over the noise, anyhow.

"Are you ready?" Laura asked as she bounced into the room. Her face was lit up in a way that made my chest ache.

I nodded and walked with her to the town square, listening to her excited chatter about the upcoming school year. I still hadn't made peace with the fact that leaving St. Hilaire meant leaving her. I hoped she wouldn't hate me for it. I hoped she'd be okay.

"Come stand by the stage with me," she begged when we got there. It was the town square of every old movie: green grass, ice cream vendors, signs directing people to the fairy trail. Except normal towns didn't have fairy trails.

A band was just setting up, and the scents of beer and incense melded into a smoke that was colored by the twinkling lights hung on each and every tree.

I grabbed my sister and spun her around in the one and only dance move I'd ever learned.

"You go," I said. "I'm waiting for Russ."

She pouted, but kissed my cheek. "Fine, spoilsport. Have fun." Then she was gone.

I moved a strand of lights and leaned against a tree. I'd wondered whether knowing this was my final end-of-summer festival would make me appreciate it more. But the only thing I felt was impatience.

Later tonight, the commuter residents, those who only came to St. Hilaire to work the summer season, would shutter their doors, pack their cars, and head back to their real lives in Ohio, Vermont, or Seattle. The rest of us would wait out the winter and pretend our lives were normal.

It didn't matter. I was out of here as soon as I passed my GEDs and figured out how to tell my sisters I was leaving.

And Russ. I'm not sure there were the right words for deserting a best friend.

Across the grounds, the band played. People danced. Someone was handing out glow sticks, making it look like a million multicolored fireflies had invaded St. Hilaire. Then Clive Rice took the mic to talk about the great services the people of St. Hilaire gave to the world. The way we used our talents to offer hope to all mankind. *Blah, blah, blah.* It was possible he gave precisely the same speech every year. By this point in the evening, I had usually already tuned him out.

A roar of applause went up in the crowd as the air shimmered next to Rice. Little by little, the ghost of Melody Thorne appeared next to him. One of the town founders, there was a statue of her with a huge parasol just a few yards from the stage, in the center of the square. It was her name that was invoked before all citywide readings, asking that our contacts with the dead and interpretations of the messages we received were fair and accurate. Apparently, she loved pomp and circumstance as much now as she had when she was alive.

Like all ghosts, she was less than solid, more the idea of Melody Thorne than a person. If you tried to focus on her edges too hard, they seemed to flicker and fade into their surroundings. It took a great deal of effort for a ghost to interact with us in any noticeable way, and they usually only mustered enough energy to get the attention of the living by slamming doors or whispering in the dark or moving stuff around the house.

Melody was stronger than most spirits, and probably had been resting up for a while. So she could make herself mostly visible while she spoke about her great joy at being able to bring another summer season to a close.

My head began to swim just as a fan of playing cards appeared in front of my face.

"Tonight. Poker. I'm getting a car this year," Russ whispered in my ear.

"You should have been gouging the tourists," I said. "Who exactly do you think you're going to win that much from?"

"Better not let the Guild hear you," Russ replied in a stage whisper. "Winning money from customers is illegal, you know." His mock warning might have been funnier had he not been doing everything possible to join that same Guild. "I tried to call you, but it went to voicemail. David Sheridan and Alex Mackenzie are apparently feeling flush. What about it?"

I turned and looked at him. Russ had screwed with his hair again. It was normally jet-black, but he'd given it a violet tint, and it sat mop-like on top in defiance of gravity. He'd also shaved the sides, which made his pale skin look even paler against his long black coat and dark jeans. He obviously hadn't wasted a second after the tourists had left, this year, to ditch his Guild-approved appearance and turn back into himself.

As Russ reached around to stash the cards in his backpack, I caught a glimpse of his owl tattoo, wrapped around his wrist as if it were hanging on for dear life.

"Impressive," I said pointing to Russ's hair. But really, I was talking about all of it. The hair, the tattoo, the metal bolt that sat in his ear, his dark and somewhat forbidding clothing, and most of all, his commitment to being himself in St. Hilaire, which didn't embrace rebellion.

Russ turned away. He never could take a compliment.

"So, why do Sheridan and Mackenzie want to play with *us* anyhow?" I asked. Playing cards with a bunch of mediums always brought its own challenges. Beyond that, while Sheridan was loaded and probably just looking for a recreational game, Mackenzie was a con artist. And it wasn't like we were friends with them.

Russ shrugged. "Sheridan wasn't exactly forthcoming, but man, I need a car."

Money always flowed freely for the first couple of weeks after a busy summer season. Playing poker, drinking a few clandestine beers. It sounded so normal. More than that, it sounded like an evening that could further my goal of escaping if I played my literal cards right.

I'd managed to squirrel a small amount of money away during the summer. With luck, I could add a couple of hundred to it tonight. The Griffins definitely didn't have cash to burn. Russ wouldn't be taking the risk if he weren't sure he would win.

"I'm in," I said, smiling, but it felt like I was using muscles that were out of shape.

"You know," Russ started. "I have the strangest feeling that this is going to be a…an important year." My shoulders tensed. I knew better than to question Russ's "feelings," but I wished he'd said "a great year" or "a fun year." "Important" sounded too ominous.

He continued, "You never know when someone interesting is actually going to walk through those gates."

We both looked up at the high, spiked, iron gates that would be locked in another hour—not to keep us in—all St. Hilaire residents had pass cards—but to keep the tourists out. There just weren't enough mediums here in the off-season to keep the businesses open. Some mediums did phone or web séances to pay the rent, but it was looked down upon by the Guild, who felt it was too "gimmicky." As if this whole freaking town weren't one big gimmick.

"*Interesting?* Here? Dream on," I said. We'd gotten boring, strange, skeptical, curious, and bat-shit crazy before, but as far as I was concerned, Russ was the last interesting person I'd known to move to St. Hilaire.

Up on the stage, Rice, alone once more, was still droning on about the coming year and an upcoming fundraiser to overcome some town financial crisis. Typical stuff.

"Please, make it stop," I whispered to the sky.

But then, Rice changed topics and caught my attention. "As you all know, St. Hilaire was founded by an accomplished and selfless community of spiritualists. But over the ensuing generations, we have found ourselves weakened by disbelief and external influences. In the coming year, we will be taking measures to once again strengthen our town's commitment to our mutual calling, as well as to the bloodlines of those who carry on the traditions that our founders set forth."

The crowd went quiet. Russ and I stared at each other.

"Bloodlines?" I asked. "What the hell does *that* mean?"

Russ shook his head. "I have no idea."

Rice continued. "We are in the process of putting in place some new parameters in order to tighten the bonds that hold us together. Starting with a more rigorous method of training the coming year's Youth Corps, we will be enforcing some of the regulations that served St. Hilaire so well in its storied past."

Everyone stood watching Rice with matching expressions of confusion.

"This program will begin as some of our past Corps members distribute Guild flags as our gift to you. All we require is that, as members of our community, you will fly these flags outside of your homes year-round. And while we don't wish to cause concern, it seems like a prudent time to inform you that the Executive Council has been tasked with examining the long-held policy of grandfathered families and whether that has set a precedence of allowing our talents to be diluted."

"Now," he continued. "If everyone will please rise."

Those who had been sitting stood, and the fireworks began.

I watched Laura, alone in a crowd of people, looking at the sky as if the fireworks were magic. I was jealous of her, actually. I barely remembered the time when the sound of the gunpowder exploding made me think of color and light and not regret and loss.

Rice's words echoed off the sides of my brain. There was something twisted in them and not quite right. However much I hated St. Hilaire, however much I wanted nothing more than to leave, Laura was going to be here. Russ was going to be here. I didn't want my hometown to turn into some sort of creepy dystopian town. Even Harriet didn't deserve that.

When the fireworks stopped, the entire town turned in unison to watch the ceremony of the locking of the gates. I couldn't take it anymore; the pressure was too much.

"I'm out," I said to Russ. "Catch you at the game."

I dug out my ID card as I walked to the gate and waved it at the security guard, who mumbled something under his breath at me for making him open the gate he'd just locked.

Then I stepped out into Buchanan.

Given that the towns butted up against each other and that Buchanan's commercial district was as close as St. Hilaire came to having a real one of its own—if you were looking for useful things like pens and craft supplies and dog food, and not ridiculous things like crystal balls or cases of candles—there was a surprising amount of animosity between the two.

To the people of Buchanan, St. Hilaire residents were freaks, out of touch with the real world while they fixated on ghosts. To those in St. Hilaire, the people of Buchanan were unenlightened and only interested in the money they made off St. Hilaire's tourists. Neither one was entirely wrong.

But I found Buchanan useful because it had a library, and I had a standing reservation for one of their computers. At home, Laura and I shared a computer, which was fine for school and checking email and all of that. Not so good for what I was about to do. There were things that I didn't even share with her.

I mentally added *buy a laptop* to my leaving to-do list, but since it followed things like *clear out bank account, buy train ticket to the city,* and *get a job,* it was probably going to be a while before I had one. If I was going to be indulgent, now was the time.

The library smelled like old books and escape; I felt the tension in my shoulders ease.

St. Hilaire had restrictions against electronic communications during the summer (to stifle those who accused the mediums of using cell phones and computers instead of actually talking to ghosts), but the library—firmly tethered outside the town gates—stayed wired. Along with the train station, it formed our town's only constant connection to the outside world, which might have been why it was my sanctuary, the place I always went when I needed to calm down. And after all of Rice's talk about bloodlines and mutual callings, I needed it more than ever.

I ducked into the cubicle, slipped on the worn headphones, and typed in the same URL as always.

It didn't matter how many times I watched Anastasia's performance at Carnegie Hall—and I'd guess that I'd watched it thousands of times—I never stopped being fascinated with the furrow in her brow when she was playing the Unfinished Prelude, her fingers moving lightning-fast over the polished keys.

And it didn't matter how many times I watched it, my memory could never quite pin down her smile. It was the smile she gave as she finished the glissando with a sense of accomplishment and relief. It was a secretive smile, one too small and too subtle, I guessed, to be seen by the audience. One I liked to imagine she meant for me, though we'd never met and probably never would.

The music drew me in, and the hour always passed too quickly. When the librarian knocked on the door to tell me they were closing for the night, I erased my history and logged off.

A train whistle blew as I stepped outside, and I felt a strange kind of pull to walk the mile to the station and buy a ticket to somewhere I'd never heard of and leave St. Hilaire behind.

I couldn't do that today. Not to Laura. Or to Russ. And even if I wanted to, Russ's father was the stationmaster and as much as Donald Griffin might like me, he'd never sell me a ticket without checking with Harriet first. Also, trains rarely stopped in St. Hilaire after summer season. There was nothing here for outsiders once the weather changed and the gates closed. I had to stick to my plan.

My chest squeezed as I flashed my ID at the gate.

"Back so soon?" the guard on duty said.

I poked my head into the guard station to see Colin, the middle of the Mackenzie brothers, sitting next to creepy Willow Rogers, a medium a few years older than me who had basically been raised by the Guild. They were an unlikely pair.

"Well, you know what they say. Home is wherever *you* are," I quipped.

"Dick," Colin said, but laughed. Next to him Willow glared at me. She wasn't known for having a sense of humor.

Colin pressed the button to unlock the gate, and I passed back through into St. Hilaire. The lawn signs advertising READINGS: TWO FOR ONE and BEST PSYCHIC IN TOWN were still up in front of most houses, but, thankfully, that wouldn't last long. I passed them, and instead of going home, I went straight through the town square to the back door of what passed for St. Hilaire's community center, Eaton Hall. A cracked plaque with the town rules was pinned on the door, and underneath the official rules, multiple people had written in a bunch of their own:

× *Don't admit to making things up (better to go down in flames swearing you are the real thing than to call everyone else in town into question.)*

× *Don't use your powers to seduce those who are in a vulnerable state because morality and state law still applies here, and Buchanan's police force is always looking for an excuse to come charging into St. Hilaire.*

× *Learn to keep a straight face, because, while some of your customers might be whack jobs, their money is still legal tender.*

I let myself in. The old door creaked, the plaque slapping against the wood, as it swung closed.

Thirty or forty teens sat at round tables scattered around the basement. The floor was sticky and the room smelled like what it was, a bunch of kids on their way to being drunk and stupid. Music blared; someone had cranked the bass up to eleven. Louder were the hundred or so conversations taking place at once, everyone trying to shout over the thumping.

"Dec." Russ stood and waved from the far corner.

I pushed my way through the crowd, ducking out of the

33

way of a beer bottle tossed from one laughing girl to another. Eaton Hall's party room was supposed to be alcohol-free, but no one really cared on the last night of season.

The dim light shone off a mountain of blue chips in front of Russ.

"You sure you really need my help?" I yelled over the music.

"More fun with two," Russ said, a sly grin on his face, gesturing to a rusty metal chair.

I sat and nodded to the boys on the other side of the table. David Sheridan was as wiry and jittery as a Pekinese on caffeine. He looked even more wiry and skittish next to Alex Mackenzie, Ian and Colin's erratic youngest brother.

Alex glared at me, his fists clenched, pupils dilated and black. *Yeah, this will be fun.*

"Are we going to play or do you want to ogle me some more, Hampton?" Alex asked. A whine came from beneath the table. I poked my head down to see Alex's ever-present dog, a huge disheveled Irish wolfhound named Garmer, drooling at his feet.

I stared at the dog and the dog stared back, ears twitching, until I had to look away. That dog had always made me uneasy. I pulled my head up. "Not used to you being so anxious to lose your money, Alex. Or is Sheridan bankrolling you again?"

Everyone knew the Sheridan family had more money than ability. For the past fifty years or so, anyone wanting to move to St. Hilaire had to pass a test administered by the Guild. At least half the members of any new family moving in had to prove they could earn a living as a medium or some sort of service worker or else they couldn't live here. The Sheridans probably wouldn't pass that test if they tried to move to town now. But some great-great-great-grandmother of David's had been one of the super-wealthy town founders and had invested well. No one wanted to lose the family's money, so they were grandfathered into the rules and allowed to stay.

If what Rice said was true, the rules were changing. I wonder what was going to happen to David and his family.

I couldn't work up the same concern for any of the Mackenzies, though. Some of them, like Ian, had abilities, but no common sense. Others, like Colin and Alex, lacked both. None of them had money. The family had moved to St. Hilaire when Alex was little and had been creating one sort of scandal after another ever since. Last year, his uncle was kicked out of St. Hilaire for secretly running a signal to a satellite outside of town and betting on horse races during the supposedly "disconnected" summer season.

Russ handed me a stack of multicolored chips and dealt the cards. It wasn't a bad draw. "Palms on the table," I said.

"Seriously?" Mackenzie rolled his eyes. "You don't trust us?"

"There you go using that immense mental power of yours, Alex. Just do it."

Sheridan and Mackenzie put their hands on the table. Sheridan's nails were bitten down. Mackenzie's middle fingers were extended.

Russ and I spread our own hands wide on the table to prove we weren't doing anything illicit. It was never about counting cards in St. Hilaire, but about reading your opponents, or reading the energy off the physical cards, or contacting someone on the other side. You never knew when someone's grandfather had

35

been a card shark and would be more than happy to come back from the beyond and help them win a hand.

In St. Hilaire, ghosts were everywhere.

There was always the option of having a Guild member oversee the game, but no one wanted Guild members around on the closing night of the season. Thankfully, not even Russ.

Sheridan and Mackenzie won the first hand, but we won the next five. I could see Russ adding up his chips, upgrading his car options with every win. It made me wish I had a more concrete plan for my winnings; leaving St. Hilaire didn't have a specific price tag.

"What do you say we up the stakes?" Sheridan said, looking nervously at Mackenzie for approval.

"To what?" Russ shuffled a bunch of twenty-dollar chips in his hand. They probably added up to more money than he'd seen in one place. He and his dad were always just scraping to get by.

Sheridan's eyes washed over me and then away and back. And instantly I *knew* what improbable thing Sheridan wanted me to wager.

"No," I said, fighting to keep from laughing.

"Dec?" Russ asked.

"One minute." I grabbed a handful of Russ's coat and pulled him over to the corner where we could talk without having to yell.

"Sheridan wants my piano," I explained.

The look on Russ's face was priceless and rare in its aston-ishment. "*The* piano?"

"Yup."

"That's absurd. Plus we've won five hands in a row."

"This is Sheridan and Mackenzie," I reminded him. "They could have thrown the games."

Russ closed his eyes and took a deep, even breath. I waited while Russ felt for vibrations. I never quite understood how that worked, and Russ was always apologetic that he couldn't explain it better, but everyone had their own method of reading things, and if Russ's was vibrations, that was okay with me.

"I don't think so," Russ said confidently.

"So, they're serious?"

Sheridan had lusted after the piano in the past despite the fact that he didn't play and had no real interest in music. All David Sheridan wanted was to belong. And the piano, with its eerie history, was rich in the currency of St. Hilaire: secrets and mysteries.

But as for Alex, his motivation could be anything. Most likely, he wanted to dismantle it, strip it down, and dissect its pieces. Ian had been legendary for collecting things and co-opting them for his own uses. People too. Russ specifically. It was one of the reasons I hated Ian, and it wouldn't surprise me if Alex was following in his brother's footsteps.

"Yeah, but one remaining question," Russ said, running his thumb over his wrist. "What are they putting on the table in return?"

"I don't know." Sheridan and Mackenzie both knew there was no way I'd ever give up the piano, so they must have had something big that they were prepared to lose; something so big that they thought it would change my mind. "Let's go find out."

"Not saying we're in. But out of curiosity, what the hell are you willing to wager?" Russ asked them.

Mackenzie chewed on his bottom lip before answering. "The 'Stang." His voice was surprisingly calm, but his face, tense and tight, betrayed him.

Even I had to be impressed at Alex's gall. Alex Mackenzie's Mustang was Ian's masterpiece. Created from pieces Ian had found, stole, and bribed out of the collections of the older families—some parts, it was said, were dug up from the town cemeteries—the car was notorious and unpredictable. Some said it couldn't be clocked on police radar and that it could drive itself. But I was pretty sure those were rumors or just wishful thinking. Still, where the Mackenzies were involved, you could never be sure.

The car was the only *thing* I'd ever known Russ to want. And that alone was enough to make me want to help him win it.

"I don't know. We need time to think," I said, although there was nothing to think about. We either played or walked away.

I tried to picture the music room without the piano. From the look on his face, Russ was trying to imagine the iridescent silver Mustang shining lustily and growling noisily in his carport.

Across from us, Alex Mackenzie hummed the theme to *Jeopardy* irritatingly off-key, and then said, "Come on, David. It's clear they don't have the balls for real stakes." He stood with a squeaking of chair and a groaning of dog.

"Wait," I said and took a sharp breath.

I pictured Russ driving the Mustang out of the Mackenzies' drive, and I pictured Colin beating the ever-living crap out of Alex for losing the car. Those were both visions I could get behind.

Then I closed my eyes, said a prayer of apology to my dead father, pushed the cards toward Alex Mackenzie as if saying "yes" was the easiest thing in the world instead of the most difficult, and said, "You deal."

I cracked my neck to try to loosen it and stared at my cards, which hadn't gotten any better since the last time I'd stared at them. Next to me, Russ was clenching his teeth. This wasn't going well.

Across from us, David was coughing as he had been through the whole game. Alex seemed oblivious, and neither looked as happy as they should have, given that they were wiping the floor with us.

How was that even possible?

"Okay, I'm taking pity on you," Alex said. "I call."

I looked down at my hand again. The cards still hadn't changed. "I fold," I mumbled, afraid to even glance at Russ.

"Oh, me too," David said, coughing into his hand again.

"Okay, guess that leaves just you and me," said Alex, looking at Russ.

I felt Russ shift in his chair next to me. He sighed in a way that sounded desperate, and it made my stomach tighten. I knew before he even flipped his cards over—a measly pair of fours and an even measlier pair of twos—that we'd lost. Lost the piano, lost the Mustang. Lost any hope I had that in gaining Russ the car of his dreams, I could assuage my guilt about leaving. Now, I would have to face it all. Plus the wrath of Harriet and Laura's disappointment. There was nothing left for me to hide behind.

"See ya' soon," Alex said flippantly as he and the dog and David got up and turned to leave. Neither of us replied, and when I looked over at Russ, he looked pale and empty, and I couldn't shake the feeling that it was all my fault.

5

ANNIE

"That'll be two dollars and sixteen cents," the man behind the counter said. I dug into my favorite flowered bag, which I had purchased at a San Francisco street fair. Or maybe it was New York. Or London. Yes, it was London. *Maybe.*

Well, wherever I got it, there was no chance it contained money. I had been traveling internationally since I was six, and exchanging cash took time, and converting it with fluctuating rates and countries merging and seceding and joining and leaving unions, took more. Time, Dmitry taught me, was not something to be wasted.

I pulled a credit card out from one of the bag's many hidden pockets and handed it over as payment for the tea.

"Sorry, our card reader has been off-line all day," the man

said, wiping down an espresso machine in rhythm to the music of the wheels. The train lurched and a good inch of tea sloshed over the edge of my cup. I watched, shocked, as hot water burned its way across my hand and the skin began to redden. My first thought was that my hands were insured for a massive fifty million dollars. Was it possible that each hand was then worth half that amount? If so, was I liable to someone for all that money?

The man behind the counter held out a cool cloth for me to place against the burn. "I'm sorry about the tea," I said. "But I don't have any cash on me. Is there somewhere I can mail a check, maybe?"

The man grinned and patted my unburnt hand. "That's okay," he said, winking. "I've got you this time."

I thanked him and took the tea and cloth back to my seat.

The train that ran between Washington, New York, and the Canadian border was an old black antique, wider than modern-day trains, which necessitated special tracks. The ticket salesman told me this was the only route that could accommodate it.

My seat resembled all the others on the train, with black armrests and red and beige cloth-covered seats. That fact made me happy in a way that flying first class never had. There, I was grateful for the chairs that became beds, and the endless supply of magazines, and the chance to catch up on the latest movies. But I always felt a pang of guilt watching families with children, elderly women, and people on crutches creep by on their way to the crowded coach section of the plane.

The train was far more democratic. Far more interesting.

Far more relaxing now that the boy across the aisle had left. Outside, the green of the fields of corn gave way to the brown of the wheat, and the red of the summer-weary grapevines. I indulged in listening to the lengthy conversation between the girls across the aisle about a party and the photos that surfaced online afterward, and watch the older couple in the seats diagonal to me who had fallen asleep, heads leaning together, hands intertwined. I wondered if I would ever be able to stay in one place long enough to put down roots, fall in love, and find someone to ride a train with when I was eighty.

I sipped what was left of my tea while the conductor announced the name of a stop in the crackly garbled way of train conductors everywhere. There were hours and hours left in my trip, and, never having been to a funeral, I needed to prepare myself for what lay ahead.

Dmitry's death wasn't completely unexpected. He had threatened suicide in dark and angry moments and had never hidden the overwhelming physical pain his arthritis caused and the equally overwhelming emotional scars that resulted from his slow descent out of the public eye. Dmitry was someone who needed to be loved, not by one person, but by millions. Easy to do when you are on the cover of *Rolling Stone*, being interviewed on all the late-night shows, and photographed with starlets on red carpets. More difficult when you are in constant pain and unable to do the one thing that you love: play the piano.

He always told me that he wanted more for me and hoped that someday I might find one person to love. Possibly, I could build a family of my own, even if I could not seem to connect with my own parents, who were still in the same small town in Russia where I had been born and where I sent them monthly checks to supplement their salaries.

But I loved Dmitry. He had been my teacher since I was six and my legal guardian since I was eight, so his death left me not only teacher-less and friendless, but guardian-less. I was sure that, at seventeen, I might not need a new guardian. I had my agent, manager, and publicist. Someone would step up to be the one to tell me what to do and where to be, but it would not be the same.

As the sky began to darken and fill with stars, I pulled out my electronic keyboard and headphones and played the opening of the Prelude.

In the dark, I allowed tears to well up in my eyes. For once, no one was watching me. No one was reviewing my performance, or taking my photo, or expecting anything. For once, I was allowed to be nothing more than a sad girl on a train.

When I got to the end of the Prelude, I switched to "When You Wish Upon a Star." Oddly, it had been Dmitry's favorite song. The one he used to teach me English. As I played, I tried to figure out what I could wish for. I could not undo Dmitry's death, which was all I really wanted. So, instead of wishing for something frivolous, I wished for things that were thrillingly intangible. Peace of mind. A sign. Love.

Then, with my hands on the keyboard and Dmitry's face in my mind, I closed my eyes and wished myself asleep.

The train lurched and screamed in a grinding of gears hitting things they were not supposed to. I woke, perplexed, as it came to a stop.

When I raised the window shade, all I saw was thick, gray smoke billowing from the belly of the train. The other people were already streaming onto the platform.

The man from the café came running up the aisle. "You'll have to get out here. Something's wrong."

I rubbed my stinging eyes. "Where is *here*?"

The man looked outside into the smoke. "Buchanan, New York," he said. "Someone in the station can tell you what to do."

I nodded, grabbed my keyboard and bag from the overhead bin, and headed to the door. Outside, the morning sunlight peeked through the clouds of smoke.

"Miss. Miss." A tall man with glasses ran out of the station and toward me. "It's going to take some time to get this damned antique repaired. Days, perhaps, while we wait for someone to examine the train and then bring in the parts or even make them," he said. "Sometimes it takes a while to get things here. Sometimes things go missing." He instructed me to write down my phone number, then handed me a pamphlet from the train company, which explained how to get compensation for a hotel and a refund on my ticket.

I looked around. The train station was at the end of a block of businesses and behind those sat rows and rows of suburban houses. The other side of the street held a park and beyond that, peaked spires that reminded me of Oxford and Paris. The sun glittered off the steeples. It was strangely calming. If I was going to be stuck somewhere, there were worse options.

I started to walk past the houses and through the park, passing a number of increasingly ornate wrought-iron signs with arrows pointing to a place called St. Hilaire. Most of the stores were closed, and while I was looking longingly in a bakery window, I noticed a beat-up blue Chevy reflected in the window. Its bumper stickers said LET PLUTO BE A PLANET and MUSIC GIVES A SOUL TO THE UNIVERSE. I had a feeling that I would like the person who put both of those on their car.

In the distance, a clock tower chimed. Had the train been running, I would be close to Canada by now. Viktor must be furious not to have heard from me. Out of guilt, I stopped and powered on my phone. Seven text messages and notifications for ten additional calls were waiting for me. A quick look at the log showed they were all from Viktor and my publicist Ginger, who I am sure had already issued a statement in my name, saying how saddened and shocked I was by Dmitry's death, and how we would all carry on in his memory. *Blah, blah, blah.*

Dmitry would have hated this. The way our management bowed down to the press and public opinion, trying to make everyone happy regardless of what that meant for the *art*, angered him like nothing else.

Then I opened my email. The first message in my inbox was from Dmitry. The letters swam in front of my eyes. I put my bag and keyboard down on a stretch of grass and counted to ten before walking to a nearby bench. My legs felt like they were giving out.

There was no doubt he had sent it on time delay. He had loved being able to send things and have them show up when he was on a plane or otherwise unreachable for a response. Better to ask for forgiveness than permission, he liked to say.

I hesitated, terrified it was a suicide note. But it was from him, and there was no way I could avoid reading it. I scanned the words and realized the note both was and was not a good-bye. In truth, it was a request for a favor, the kind of favor you asked when you had given up everything else. The kind of favor he knew I could not say no to.

Find the rest of the Prelude, the email begged. **I believe, as I have always believed, that it is out there and that it's destined for you to play, to be a part of you. You will bring great joy to the world with that music, Annie. Everyone will know, as I do, how special you are. If I have failed to redeem my miserable life by finding it, then you must do it. For both of us.**

DEC

Pinned to the bulletin board on my bedroom wall was a collection of ticket stubs from train trips I'd never taken, receipts from stores I'd never shopped in, a passport I'd never used. Aside from the passport, which I applied for on my sixteenth birthday by forging Harriet's signature, none of the items were actually mine. They were pieces of someone else's life—many someones—found outside on the street, tucked into library books, and nestled in the pockets of a distressed leather jacket I'd bought in Buchanan's vintage clothing store.

The bulletin board was my attempt to distract myself from the view of my parents' headstones, which sat square in the middle of my window, looking like they were framed. I thought if I could keep my eyes on the board long enough, I wouldn't notice the graves and the bare patches of ground next to them. It was either that or block off the window and deal with Harriet's tirade about defacing a historic property.

But it didn't matter how many hours I'd spent this past year imagining I was the one on a train heading to Oregon, or shopping for turtle-shaped bookends in Maine, or buying chocolate in Pennsylvania. When I followed the receipts and stubs from one end to the other, they told the story of a life, but it wasn't mine, and if I didn't get out of here soon, it never would be.

Outside, a truck squealed to a stop, and it felt like my heart did too. It didn't even feel real.

The doorbell sputtered to life.

"Daniel," Harriet's voice shrieked up the stairs.

My bedroom door opened softly as Laura came in and wordlessly pulled me into a hug I didn't deserve.

This nameless cocktail of loss and guilt reminded me of how I'd felt a few weeks after my parents died when the numbness finally went away, leaving everything to come crashing down around me.

"How could I have been so stupid?" I muttered.

Laura sat on the bed, smoothing the blanket next to her. "I'm sorry. I'm really, really sorry."

If there was one upside to my losing the piano, it was that I proved I didn't really deserve her love. I'd been a shitty brother.

"Dad would kill me," I said.

Laura shook her head. "No, he'd be upset, but then he'd probably tell you it was okay. That you could win the piano back, or that instead of playing it, you could spend your time on something more productive. School maybe?"

I tried to laugh, but it felt like I was choking. "Yeah. I guess."

"Daniel," Harriet shouted again. She was in the middle of studying for some online degree, convinced she could finish what she'd started before she was forced to move back to St. Hilaire to take care of me and Laura, and hated to be disturbed.

I really had no choice anyhow but to go downstairs and "pay the piper" as Dad would have said. Each stair led me closer to my punishment. From their homes on the wall, photo after photo of Hamptons seemed to sneer at me for losing a treasured family heirloom.

I opened the door.

"You can come play it whenever you want," David Sheridan said instead of hello. "I know it was, *is*, important to you."

I couldn't answer. Instead, I backed up against the wall and watched as the front door opened farther. Alex Mackenzie and his dog stormed into the house, followed by Colin and three burly guys from the Buchanan auto shop who carried piles of blankets and a couple of bundles of ratchet straps. They began wrapping up the piano like a burrito.

I fought to catch my breath. It felt like I'd been punched in the stomach, and I could only begin to breathe again when Russ came in. I hadn't called him. But just like Russ always knew whether it would rain, whether our calc test would be canceled, or whether the customer walking in the door actually wanted to contact their dead aunt or was trying to make fun of the whole thing, he knew when I needed him. Most importantly, he always knew *that*.

Russ had been the first to arrive at the hospital after the accident. The first to show up on my doorstep with a burger after a séance that left me shaken and starving. Russ was more than a best friend; he was a brother. And *that* made me feel guilty because I wasn't sure I'd given enough back over the past two years. *I don't know if I have anything left that anyone would want.*

Two wooden dollies were wheeled through the large front doors of Hampton House. Alex's dog growled and snapped at the dolly's tires. My tongue felt thick and useless.

"Hey, Mackenzie," Russ called out. "You might want to put that dog outside before he eats someone."

Alex Mackenzie marched over. His black boots left dusty footprints on the wood floor, which in this room was patterned with interlocking puzzle pieces. Harriet would be in a snit about that later.

"He's a therapy dog," Alex shot back, but I knew better.

"Remind me." Russ's voice was a deliberate study in disinterest. "What is it again that you're in therapy for?"

Alex broke out a creepy grin. "Frustration since Hampton's sister won't put out."

Russ grabbed my arm before I could think of throwing a punch. "Not worth it. Those goons will flatten you."

Mackenzie laughed and went back to the piano, the dog settling against the wall with a loud thump.

"The dog was Ian's, you know," Russ said under his breath.

The dog looked sideways at us as if he knew he was being talked about. "That explains a lot, I guess," I said, only I wasn't sure what it explained aside from the fact that Alex seemed to take it everywhere.

The team finished wrapping the piano. "On the count of

three," Colin said. The dog whined. Russ put his hand on my shoulder. I closed my eyes. I couldn't watch. "One. Two. Three."

I waited for the sound of the dolly's wheels across the floor, but there was nothing except the frustrated grunts of four guys finding it impossible to move a piano.

"What the hell, Hampton?" Alex exclaimed. "You better not be screwing with us."

I opened my eyes to see all of the guys red-faced and sweating. I knew the piano was movable because I'd had to do it on my own when I was ten and dropped the moon card from Mom's favorite tarot deck underneath it. Looking back, I wasn't sure I *should* have been able to move it; after all, it was a large piano and I'd been a small boy.

"I haven't done anything," I said.

"Well, get your ass over here and help us, then," Alex said. "And bring goth-boy too," he added, pointing to Russ.

A strange sort of lightness filled me. There was no way I was going to help them. "Bite me."

Alex's dark eyes scanned me like an X-ray. "Maybe next time, dickhead."

The crew examined the piano from every angle and readjusted the blankets and straps and the dolly, going so far as to rotate the wheels to make sure they weren't locked or stuck. Nothing worked.

The crew packed their stuff, shaking their heads.

"I know you just want an excuse to ask me back," Alex said as he stalked off.

Only Colin hung back. "I assume you've read the new regulations, right? I mean, a non-movable instrument seems to

52

fall under the Guild's 'unexplained occurrences' category. That means they're going to have jurisdiction here."

"But it's just a piano," I stammered.

"Rules are rules. They were fine with me overseeing the initial collection of the piano. But now that there are complications, I'd prepare for an official visit if I were you," he said, and as he turned to go, I caught the silver flash of a Guild pin on his collar and tried to draw Russ's attention to it, but he'd missed it.

I locked the door behind them, relieved when Russ and I were the only ones in the large room. "Well, that was..." I started and then stopped when I couldn't find a word to finish the sentence.

Russ nodded. "I know. Keep your head down. I'm going to make some inquiries, see if I can find out what Alex's plan for the piano is," he said. I didn't ask if he intended to inquire of the living or the dead and didn't really want to know.

"Hey, while you're at it, see what you can find out about Colin," I said instead. "He was working the guard booth with Willow Rogers yesterday. And did you catch a glimpse of his collar?"

"I saw the badge. I wonder when that happened. Also, why would Willow be working the gate? And why with *him*?"

I shook my head. Willow was St. Hilaire royalty. She'd been abandoned at the town gate by her grandparents when she was five. Pinned to her shirt was a note explaining that she could talk to the dead and that her family had no interest in raising her. No one had ever been able to find her relatives, so the Guild members worked together to bring her up in an apartment in

Eaton Hall. She was powerful, intense, and creepy, and it didn't make sense she'd waste her time with Colin.

"Wish I knew," I said. "I don't really understand anything that's going on around here at the moment."

"Well, I'll see if I can find anything out," Russ said.

After he left, I walked over to the piano and ran my hand across the deeply carved panels.

Then, as if the seed of hope in my heart had a snowball's chance of blooming into a living thing, I knelt down and pushed it gently. The piano rolled a couple of inches. I rolled it back easily and smiled.

DEC

I grabbed some polish and started cleaning the fin-gerprint smudges off the piano just as Laura settled into the window seat to finish her summer reading.

As I rubbed, I felt her eyes on me. "What?"

"School starts soon. Have you finished all of your assignments?"

No, because I won't be here, I thought. "Most of them."

"Well, I've heard senior year is rough, since you'll spend all that time in the Corps after school."

My chest ached. I had to tell her, but I didn't know how. I made a noncommittal noise, and she said, "Oh, and don't forget about that letter."

Before I could ask why she was so invested in the mail, the

doorbell rang again. Doorbells simply didn't ring at Hampton House in the off-season. Harriet never had visitors. She was usually out in the evenings or holed up in some dusty corner of the house. She never shared what she was doing or where she went, and I was usually too glad she was gone to force the issue. Laura's few friends were too wary of the house to come over, and, knowing that we rarely locked the door, Russ usually walked right in, which annoyed Harriet to no end, so of course it was a habit I encouraged at every opportunity.

But Russ was probably camping out in the restricted section of the library, trying to figure out what Sheridan and Mackenzie were up to, and even if they *had* launched some sort of investigation with the Guild, it wouldn't happen this fast.

Laura and I listened as Harriet answered the door.

"Well…I don't know," Harriet said. "This is highly unusual. How did you get in here?"

The visitor answered. The voice was female, but I couldn't make out her words, just the same pleading tone of desperation that filled St. Hilaire every summer.

When Harriet groaned loudly, my chest tightened. When she called for us, my head started to throb in dread and anticipation.

Laura pulled on my sleeve, and I followed her to the reading room while attempting to come up with an excuse that would work with my older sister. *I'm sick. Studying in preparation for the start of school. A spirit has possessed me. Who am I again?*

The room was dark, shut down for the off-season. I threw myself into a chair, closed my eyes, and leaned my head on my arms on the old wood table while Laura went around the perimeter, lighting candles and incense.

The beginning of a séance always included a request for help from any available spirits. Now I offered my own. "If you freaking spirits want to prove your worth, then get me the hell out of here."

I waited, but of course nothing happened. Nothing aside from Harriet and the customer entering the room.

Two chairs were pulled out. Sat in. A low drumming started on the table that made my heart beat too quickly.

The chair next to me scraped as Laura sat.

"Daniel," she said in an airy voice.

"I don't want to do this," I whined, knowing I sounded more like I was seven than seventeen.

"Daniel," Laura said again, and this time I got that she was using my *full* name.

I looked up, and what I saw made me pretty sure I'd finally lost my mind once and for all.

Anastasia Krylova was even more striking in person than she was on my computer screen, but it was her fingers that held my attention. I could almost hear music as she laid them on the corner of the worn tablecloth and gave them free rein to play a silent sonata against the wood.

"Mozart," I blurted out. I couldn't help myself.

She opened her eyes wide. "How did you know?"

For all the hours I'd spent watching her videos, I'd only heard her speak on scratchy audio taken with people's cell phones and posted online. Her voice was deeper and softer than I'd expected. It was surreal to think she was sitting in my house, talking directly to me.

"I play," I croaked out. "Piano, I mean."

Harriet cleared her throat. I'd never told her about the reason for my trips to the library, not like she'd care. She didn't know who Anastasia was, or what she meant to me. She only saw a well-dressed girl who looked like she could pay for whatever information she wanted. "Look, you know we're closed, right?" Harriet said. "The whole town is closed."

Anastasia's face hardened. "As I said, I just walked in through the gates."

"That's impossible," Harriet said.

I bit my tongue to keep from reminding Harriet that nothing in St. Hilaire is impossible, only improbable.

"What can we do for you?" Laura asked. "Miss…"

"Krylova," Anastasia finished. "Anastasia. Well, Annie… Krylova."

Annie? All of her posters and videos only ever had Anastasia on them. *Annie Krylova.*

"I was on the train," Annie answered. "The antique one. And it broke down. They said it was going to take time to fix and a week or maybe two, to get the parts." She shrugged self-consciously. "I could rent a car, but I am not old enough."

"It's the off-season, and there aren't enough passengers to keep the train route running more than once a week in the winter," Laura explained, glancing at me. "Even when it works."

The look Laura gave me was full of meaning. I knew what my sister was thinking. St. Hilaire was a town that believed in synchronicity and things happening for a reason. If that was true, then Annie was supposed to be sitting at our table. We were supposed to be helping her. It was the way things were supposed to be.

Annie Krylova was in my town. Stuck here for at least a week.

Harriet broke my reverie, of course. "We aren't a hotel, Miss Krylova."

The fluttering of Annie's fingers picked up against the table. "I know. I did not mean... I passed a hotel, but the sign said they were closed for the season and... It probably sounds ridiculous. I just started walking from the station, and this is where I ended up. I will sort something else out. I do not want to be a bother."

"I don't know what you know about St. Hilaire..." Harriet started, but I knew I had to cut her off.

"No. It doesn't sound silly at all," I said. Our entire town was founded on more ridiculous twists of fate.

Laura walked over to a metal rack in the corner and grabbed a brochure. It had a photo of Hampton House on the cover and a brief history of the town. Part of Harriet's "marketing efforts," I thought it made us sound like a bunch of freaks, but not surprisingly, no one had ever asked my opinion about marketing.

Annie flipped through it, and I watched the blood slowly drain from her face. "Oh."

Her skin began to take on a green tint, and I knew what that meant.

"The bathroom is over there." I pointed through the kitchen.

Annie looked apologetic as she got up and ran in the direction of my finger.

I followed, ignoring Harriet's eye rolls. Then I ran the water in the kitchen sink on full blast to drown out the sound of retching that came through the door and filled a glass.

Laura's hand landed lightly on my shoulder. "Dec, are you okay?" As she moved to take the glass from my hand, I realized I was shaking.

There was no point in trying to lie to Laura. "I just…"

The bathroom door opened and Annie stood there looking flushed and sheepish as Laura handed her the glass. Annie took a deep sip of water, keeping her hazel eyes on me. They looked blue in the afternoon light rather than the emerald green her posters accentuated.

"I am sorry," she said. "I can only imagine what you think."

It's impossible, I thought, *that you could have any idea.*

"Are you okay?" I asked. "Where were you heading? Your train, I mean."

"Montreal. I have a… I am meant to be on my way to Montreal."

"What's in Montreal?" I asked, forgetting for a second that I wasn't supposed to know the tour section of her website said she would be playing Cleveland next.

She sat and under her breath, said, "I was on my way to a funeral."

Icy fingers caressed my neck. I was used to spending the summer around loss. Parents who had lost children. Children who had lost parents. Lovers who had lost each other. Each one reminded me of my own parents and how much I missed them and how the way we'd lost them had damaged all of us. Harriet became bitter. Laura worried about me twice as much as my mother ever had. I was still trying to figure out all the ways I'd been changed.

Anastasia. Annie had been my fantasy—the dream of escape

60

that I held onto through it all. I didn't need her wrapped up in the whole "contacting the dead" thing too.

"Dec." Laura shook my arm.

I cracked my knuckles, needing a physical "something" to make me focus. "Sorry," I said. "I'm really sorry."

Annie smiled and my pulse raced. I needed to get out of the house.

"Do you want a tour of St. Hilaire?" I blurted before I could chicken out. Laura's eyes went wide, but Annie nodded.

I gave my sister a hopeful glance. "You'll deal with Harriet?"

"Don't I always?" she replied.

I pulled back, struck again by the reality that I was really going to leave St. Hilaire without Laura.

I needed to find a way to apologize to Laura, to the memory of our parents, to the whole freaking universe. But here was Annie Krylova waiting at the door for me. For *me*. And so I simply mouthed "thank you" to Laura and hightailed it out the back door with the girl whose picture was hanging on the inside of my closet door.

8

RUSS

I rubbed my eyes. Trying to decipher my grandmother's notes was a challenge. The paper was brittle and the ink was fading, and her notes were obviously meant as reminders to herself and not as instructions to her desperate grandson.

"I need a break," I said to my empty bedroom, proving that I really did need one.

I headed out. The chilly air carried the scents of wintergreen and clove, jasmine and sage. The garden was a cacophony of fragrances, a congruence of potential magic and possibility.

But no amount of herbs was going to stop the chilling cut of the wind. It sliced through my ragged wool coat, making me feel like I'd jumped in the Chicago River in the middle of December.

When I was a kid and complained about the Chicago deep freeze, my mother would roll her eyes and say I had "thin blood." She should have known better. She'd grown up in St. Hilaire and had spent her entire early life trying to leave. It had only taken her a couple of hours, once she'd been forced to accept that I'd inherited her family's abilities, to decide to deposit me and my father in her childhood home and disappear with only an annual Christmas letter from the Virgin Islands to remind me I'd ever had a mother.

Only after my father and I moved to St. Hilaire did I make the connection that I was always freezing when spirits were around; and here, they were *always* around, even now in August.

It was hard not to think about the warmth of the Mustang. Had we won, I wouldn't be trekking through the backwoods of St. Hilaire in a threadbare coat, trying to force the incompatible ideas of Dec's non-moving piano, the poker game, and the freaking Mackenzie brothers into a box and still get it to close.

I'd broken my own rule when I allowed myself to hope for the car. When I'd given up hope of my mother returning to St. Hilaire, I vowed to give up hoping.

But that car. *That freaking car.*

Dad and I had been working on an old Vespa, but we rarely had time to make any progress on it. Besides, it was too undependable even when it *did* work and the weather was warm enough to ride it. Next year, if the Guild chose me as Student Leader, I would need to be ready to respond. I wouldn't have time to slog through the woods, hoping not to trip in the mud or freeze to death.

Those were the practical reasons for my interest in Ian's car.

The other side was that the thing fascinated me. I had a spreadsheet that listed every detail I could collect about the car: each part, its origin, and the associated rumors. It had been stupid of me not to ask Ian more about it when I'd had the chance, but talking about cars hadn't really been how Ian and I had spent our time.

With Ian gone, St. Hilaire was left to deal with not only the untamed car, but with the even more feral younger Mackenzie brothers. The fiasco of a poker game had Alex's grimy signature all over it. Regardless of the reasons for the piano not budging, there was still the issue of why Alex and David Sheridan wanted it in the first place.

And Colin. He'd already graduated from high school and was working gate security, but, thinking about it, he'd been milling about Guild offices more and more. My dad said he'd seen Colin and Willow in deep conversation outside Eaton Hall as he was heading to work the other morning. It didn't make sense. The two of them couldn't be more different. There had been talk recently about the Guild moving in a "new direction," but I couldn't imagine "just-this-side-of-psychopath" as the direction they'd choose.

As I walked, I felt for the pack of vials in my bag, the weight a comfortable reminder of potential and still unfound answers.

Then, I stepped into the woods.

In my head, the scent of herbs grew overwhelming, and the sun blazed down burning hot.

I focused on putting one foot in front of the other.

Even in the heat, my teeth chattered, and I swore I heard the sound of rain falling around me. There was a tear in my memories—a slippery place in my mind, I couldn't grasp on to long enough to make sense of. A night I couldn't remember except for flickering images that made me think Ian and I had been in these woods back when we were still talking. Back when he was alive.

I tried to lasso my thoughts. I focused on Dec. I knew he wanted to leave, and it would take just one more thing to push him over the edge. Losing the piano would probably do it. I hated that he'd risked it just so I could have Ian's stupid, wonderful, mysterious car.

My whole life in Chicago had been about hiding my abilities. Flying under the radar. Friendship wasn't something I could afford to risk. Moving to St. Hilaire and meeting Dec had changed everything. I knew if I let myself, I'd fall half in love with him. Half in love with his snarky anger and his overwhelming grief and his unwavering loyalty and his family who had given me back so much of what I'd lost along with my mother.

I needed to make things right.

"Russ Griffin."

I looked up just in time to avoid walking straight into Willow Rogers, who was kneeling on the ground casting tarot cards on a stump. "Sorry," I said, but my voice was eaten by the wind.

Willow smoothed her long skirt, but didn't reply. Then she turned over another card. Interesting because the Guild frowned upon cards as a rule, and I never thought of Willow as someone to cross the Guild.

"Three of swords. Heartbreak and loss," she said in the

same tone someone else might use to order a pizza. "Take a step back. You're emoting all over my reading."

I stared at the card, and at the swords impaling a boy through the heart. Willow used a particularly detailed deck. I could almost smell the coppery scent of blood in the air. I didn't know how to respond.

She looked at me and narrowed her eyes. Then she scooped up her cards and started to shuffle them. "Well, you've already ruined my reading, so you might as well sit."

It was hard to get any vibes off Willow. Ever since she'd graduated from high school, I'd seen her tutoring the Youth Corps and leaving students in tears. She was tougher than any teacher we had. Tougher than most of the Guild members, honestly. It was odd to think she was only a couple of years older than me. There was something almost otherworldly about her, anyhow. And this place always gave me the creeps. The combination was a little too much. But I knew better than to argue, so I sat on the ground, the damp from the soil seeping into my jeans.

"What are you looking for?" she asked, rubbing the Guild pin on her collar.

I thought about the ingredients called for in my grandmother's book. Most of them shouldn't have been able to survive New York winters much less the unattended year between when my grandmother died and when I moved here. But it was St. Hilaire, so anything was possible. I began to list them, "Sage, lavender, ver…"

"No," she insisted. "What are you *looking* for?"

I settled on, "My friend. Dec Hampton. Something is going on…"

"I know." She looked back down at her deck of cards and her shuffling sped up. Of course, Colin would have told her, but I didn't know what he would have said. I needed to be careful. I went over everything I'd learned in the past four years about speaking to the dead. Wording was important. There was a difference between "could" and "will," and between "should" and "might."

I rubbed the tattoo on my wrist, and the owl's beak somehow caught the tip of my finger. Shocked, I held out my hand and stared at the perfectly formed drop of blood on my skin. I smelled patchouli and something floral as Willow took my finger in her hand, which was almost unbearably hot against my clammy skin. As she turned my finger over, the drop of blood elongated into a tear and held that shape for an insurmountable time before falling. And falling. And falling. She grabbed at a card. The three of swords again, and the blood landed in the middle of the boy's heart. She waved it in the air and then plunged the card back into the center of the deck.

Then she spread the deck out on the stump. "Pick one," she ordered.

I picked one and turned it over. The graphic was of an angel blowing a trumpet. JUDGMENT written underneath. It wasn't the same style at all as the three of swords and looking at the card backs, I suddenly realized why. "Each card is from a different deck?" I said. I'd never seen anyone do that before.

Willow looked at me but didn't reply. She wasn't one to answer obvious questions. "I shouldn't have to interpret the cards for you. I know you can read them. I've heard the stories about you."

"Judgment means a spiritual awakening. A call to action,"

I recited from memory, ignoring what really disturbed me—the fact that anyone, anywhere was discussing me. And with Willow, no less.

"One more."

I ran my hand across the cards and chose another just as the wind whipped up and handed it to her.

She laughed, deep and throaty. "The moon. Well, of course it is. Intuition and illusion, and all of that."

She was silent long enough that I wasn't sure if I'd been dismissed or if she had more to say, so I stood. But then, before I turned to go, I thought better of it. It wasn't as if Willow Rogers and I sat around and had coffee. This felt like a unique opportunity.

"About the piano..." I started.

Willow put down her cards and stood, shaking out her long, spiraled hair and leaning back against an oak tree. "Which part didn't you listen to? What's the point of doing readings or even of being a medium if you aren't going to pay attention?"

For a minute, I thought she'd just leave me here without the answers she obviously thought she had. But then she scowled at me in a knowing way and said, "Fine. What do you do? You follow the cards. You listen to your intuition or your heart or whatever. And for god's sake, Russ, stop hiding behind"—she looked me up and down—"all of that."

I glanced at my coat and could feel the metal bolt in my ear. *I'm not hiding.*

My grandmother had written me a letter before she died. I'd found it in the mostly empty house after my father and I had moved in. In her spindly writing, she told me to be true to myself, and I had tried to be. I didn't really worry about what other people thought. I'd followed my own path, sacrificed for those I cared about.

I was determined to make Willow see that. *I'm not hiding.* The words were on the tip of my tongue, and yet I couldn't form them. And my heart? My heart was a caged animal. I hadn't been on speaking terms with it since my mother left.

"Willow…"

"Look," she said, picking up her cards and depositing them into a leather bag. "Stop playing around and pretending to be a shitty medium. We have enough of those around here. You want a place in St. Hilaire? Earn it. Don't turn your back on the things you already have."

Then, as if for emphasis, she turned her back on me and stalked off, leaving me alone in the woods.

9

ANNIE

I was used to being in places I didn't belong. Cities where I did not speak the language, could not recognize the currency. Places where the local customs were baffling. I was never sure what foods you should not eat in India or whether you were supposed to walk with your eyes down in Japan. I had spent my life living out of a suitcase in hotel rooms without real friends or family, just the artificial grouping of my road crew. I always had someone to rely on to tell me what to do; my management company had even hired a consultant to make sure there were no gaffes when I traveled internationally.

But no one had prepared me for St. Hilaire, and it was already clear that this was someplace that did not embrace outsiders. *That* was not in the brochure Laura had given me, but it might as well have been. Every odd item I saw in Dec's house—tambourines, glass balls, *so many* candles—told me this was not a place I knew how to navigate. Also, I was not sure what belonging somewhere would actually feel like, or if I would even recognize the feeling if I came across it.

"Old Man Morris lives there," Dec said, pointing to a dilapidated ranch house that didn't fit in with the beautiful Victorians I had seen when I arrived in town. He was pointing out all the local landmarks as we walked.

"The Guild, the town leaders, banned him from practicing as a medium after his wife died. He was just spending all day in the house drinking and trying to talk to her ghost. It was super sad."

It *was* sad, so I nodded and tried to pretend it all made sense. But selfishly, I wondered whether he could tell me if I would win the Hull Prize. If I should even bother to try for it, given Dmitry's death. My parents were counting on the money. They might not understand music, but the cash prize that came with the Hull was more money than they would make in years. Plus, it would solidify my career as it had done for Dmitry and so many others.

I could also ask Dec what would happen if I tried to honor Dmitry's last wish to find the rest of the Prelude. Would I end up as frustrated and out of control as he had been?

Or I could ask if I would ever feel as though I was a member of my family instead of an outsider who simply paid the bills. Or if I would ever kiss a boy I really, *really* wanted to kiss instead of the cheeks of old men who funded orchestra halls and handed out trophies.

There seemed to be so many possibilities.

Dec continued. "And that house belongs to the Saeeds. Their daughter is five, and they already think she might grow up to be one the strongest mediums in town. I feel sorry for her."

"Why?" I asked. "This does not seem like such a bad place."

"It's a freak show," he said. "Once they get ahold of her, she'll be stuck here until she grows old and dies."

"Does everyone just stay here forever?" I asked. The concept was so unlike my life, I found it fascinating.

Dec stopped and looked up at the sky. "The Guild doesn't really like it when people leave."

We began walking again and as we passed St. Hilaire High School, Dec pointed out a sign, No readings, séances, or circles within fifty yards of the school.

"Like I said, this place is just..." He left the sentence unfinished.

I felt sorry for him. It was easy to imagine that I might feel similarly out of place, had I stayed in Russia with my family. However, I could not quite put my finger on the reason for his discomfort, and I was not sure how to ask.

All my life, Dmitry had warned me about the boys who waited outside the stage door in their shiny cars and with their expensive Swiss watches. I had never been on a date because I had never had the time, and even if I had the time, I probably would not have been allowed to go. And that was fine, because what would I really talk about to a normal boy? My weeks involved flights that left late, rehearsals that began early, and greenroom meetings with local dignitaries. Not much that boys my age would be interested in or understand.

I watched our legs move in unison as we walked—Dec's in black jeans strategically ripped at the knee, mine bare in a navy skirt layered with inches of gauze that I had picked up at my favorite boutique in New York—and I had the strangest thought. *I will pretend this is my first date.*

All my life I had heard, "Focus, Anastasia. Pay attention, Anastasia. You are a professional; you don't have time for games." I had tried to do my best and had pretty much succeeded at avoiding any sort of frivolous relationships that might take time or energy away from my music.

Now, no one knew where I was. And for the first time, I was standing next to someone who had nothing to do with music, who had no idea who I was, but who I wanted to get to know.

Dec pointed out a statue of one of the town founders who everyone believed could turn rocks into gold. Next to the statue was a wishing well, and Dec handed me a coin, saying, "I don't really believe that it works, but since you're here, you might as well." I knew there was no way to wish Dmitry back and so I wished again, for a way to make some sort of sense of it all.

Then I followed Dec wordlessly along a back road that snaked through a wood and ended at a waterfall.

"This was my mother's favorite place in St. Hilaire," Dec said in a way that made it clear he did not normally talk about things like his mother or favorite places. Then he added, "It's one of the few places I'm going to miss."

It took me a minute to process his words. "Miss?"

I studied his guarded expression as he said, "Well, St. Hilaire isn't the kind of place someone like me can stay forever."

His words danced in and out of the sound of the waterfall. It

73

was indeed beautiful. Not as large as one I had seen in Argentina last year, or Niagara Falls, but there was a dry space underneath where he led me to sit and watch the water flow from places unseen right above us, and that made it better somehow. It actually felt like *just* the kind of place someone could stay forever.

"What do you mean someone like you?" I asked, feeling brave. "Are you not a psychic like everyone else here?"

Dec stood and threw a pebble into the water, and we watched it skip along the surface before it sank. "Didn't you read the brochure? We aren't psychics. I mean, we don't read minds and all that crap. We're just 'mediums' here in good ol' St. Hilaire. We talk to the dead and hope we can bring people closure."

I began to apologize and blame my obviously insensitive question on a lack of social skills. But then Dec looked at me with pained eyes. A voice in my head said, *truth*, and I closed my mouth. I didn't want to take his honesty for granted.

"But to answer your question. Would you believe me if I said I wasn't sure if I can actually do it anymore?" he asked. His voice was different, softer. Whatever he had been trying to hide under his anger had torn its way out.

"Is that not something you would know?"

Dec shook his head. "It's like the mob. You grow up in the family business. I'm not sure there's a lot of effort made to figure out who's genuine and who's just faking."

"Do you?" I asked carefully. "Do you fake it?"

He bit his lip, and said, "You're pretty direct."

"Oh…I am sorry," I sputtered.

He laughed. "No, it's actually nice. I've had to bend the

74

truth at times. You know, like someone has driven seven hundred miles to say goodbye to their mom because they'd had a fight the last time they spoke before she died. But then we hold the séance and nothing happens. I mean"—he looked down—"sometimes there really isn't a choice."

"So, how does it all work?" I asked. My grandmother had adhered to certain superstitions; mostly things meant to ward off bad luck or curses. So while I did not exactly believe in the supernatural, I did not disbelieve in it either.

"Like I said, it's all about talking to the dead. Sometimes *they* know stuff. Then again, you can't always trust them. But people can be weird here. My mom could always tell what someone was feeling, even if they were hiding it from themselves," Dec explained. "My dad was more into bigger-picture things. He could see patterns of action. It's hard to describe. In the end, it didn't matter."

I kept my eyes on the water. I already recognized the sting in his words. "What do you mean it did not matter?"

"They died," Dec said. That was all. *They died.* I waited for him to say more, but all he added was, "Two years ago."

I felt the pain in his words. "I am so sorry," I said.

"Me too," he answered. Then quickly, as if it had been on his mind all this time, he asked, "Whose funeral were you going to?"

The water surged below us. I had not had to say the words out loud before, and when I was able to say, "My teacher's," the wind seemed to blow them back to me. I did not want them, but once words were said, they took on a life of their own.

I considered trying to explain Dmitry's meteoric rise to fame, his rock star–like standing amongst classical fans, the arthritis that claimed his ability to play more than a few measures. But in the end, I was not sure any of that mattered. "Dmitry taught me everything I know about playing the piano and most of everything else. He was my only real friend."

Dec nodded, knowingly. Of course, he had been dealing with death all of his life. My grief was nothing special.

"So, you don't just play on table edges?" he asked and gave me an honest smile that made my heart leap.

"I have been playing professionally since I was six," I said. "That was all my parents ever wanted. Competitions then concerts. Now I headline. With orchestras mainly." I could hear the exhaustion in my voice, product of the five to ten hours of practice a day, the never-ending tours, and the isolation. This was why Dmitry had always urged me to take time off when I had the opportunity. I got it now. But I never had anything that I wanted to do with my "free" time; music was my life.

"Most people who come here are trying to reach someone who has passed away," Dec said gently. "Is there something you need to talk to your teacher about? Maybe I can… I mean, maybe *we* can help you."

"Can you really do that?" It was a generous offer. I pictured Dmitry's email again. I could hear his voice making the request. He had to know what he was asking.

Dec made a steeple of his fingers. "Maybe. I mean, I'd try. I used to be okay, but I've been kind of crap at it ever since my parents died. But, I know someone who isn't. Crap, I mean. You need to meet my friend Russ."

Before I could answer, a low groan came from my coat

pocket. The universal buzz of a phone on vibrate, demanding to be answered.

"Do you need to get that?" Dec pointed to my pocket.

I crossed my arms in front of me as if I could make the outside world go away. "I know who it is," I said.

Then I realized that my evasiveness might make Dec wonder if I had a boyfriend somewhere trying to reach me, so I answered the question before he could ask it. "It's my publicist or my manager. Or the record label. I'm supposed to be in Canada. I have not checked in since I got here."

"Won't they be worried? I mean, 'pianist goes missing' and all of that?"

Guilt waged war with my newly found sense of freedom. "Probably. I know I need to call in, it is just…"

"What?"

"It is the first time I can remember—in my entire life—that I have been out on my own. I am going to answer, and Ginger or someone is going to tell me they will send a limo and take me to some airport or that someone is going to show up here to drive me to Montreal or…" I ran out of steam, suddenly exhausted. "Something."

"And you don't want to go?"

I looked around at the waterfall and the trees, which were just beginning to change into their fall colors. My fingers drummed lightly on my lap, the same reaction I always had when I was stressed. Music calmed my head. "I have been *going* since I was four. From the minute my parents realized I could play, they barely allowed me to do anything else. Had Dmitry not taken me on…"

Dec's face was interestingly expressionless. Not as if he did not care, but as if he magically understood where I was coming from, so I continued. "Well, with Dmitry gone…I do not know. *He* never went to funerals. Anyhow, after all that *going*, I think I would enjoy finding out how *staying* feels."

Dec looked puzzled. I did not know how to have conversations like other girls. Flirting. Even just talking suddenly seemed as hard as playing the Rach 3, which was near impossible. I swore in Russian under my breath and then gave in. "But I guess I do need to speak with them, right?"

Dec nodded with a look of regret on his face that I did not quite understand.

"Yes, I know," I said for the fifth time. "I understand I cannot cancel the whole tour. I am just asking for…" I stopped because I was not sure exactly what I was asking for. Some sort of normal life? *That* wasn't anything my manager Viktor would offer me.

"You are tired, *zvyozdochka*. I understand this." Viktor was trying to be sympathetic. He only called me *zvyozdochka*, or "little star" when he was trying to be parental. But I knew his head would be spinning with the idea of how much money we would lose if we canceled two weeks of shows.

I had only missed shows twice. Once, I had to be rushed to the hospital when I broke my foot after tripping over a violin bow backstage in Glasgow, and once when my mother had given birth to my little brother and I flew to Russia to meet him. Although even then, taking up the space of another person in my parents' house simply made me feel as though I was in the way.

"But you will come out here, and you will practice, and you will rest," Viktor said, hopefully. "You only need to play the next shows, and then there is a break in the schedule. And you will have time to focus on preparing for the Hull, yes?"

I glanced back at Dec, who was watching the waterfall. He had said he knew someone who might be able to speak to Dmitry; perhaps they could also find lost items. Going to Dmitry's funeral was not an action that would honor my teacher's memory. But following his last request would honor him in the most dramatic way I could imagine.

I took a deep breath. "I am sorry, Viktor. I am truly sorry, but no. I cannot do this. Not yet. I need to mourn Dmitry in my own way."

I told Viktor how grief-stricken I was and how my hands shook uncontrollably every time I tried to play. That second part was a necessary lie. Viktor would never want me to go on stage if I were less than perfect. It would ruin my image and everything "the team" had worked for so many years to achieve.

"If you insist on telling me that you are safe, I will believe you and run interference with the others if I must. You are seventeen now. And I trust you. You have earned that. But you are certain that you will be at the Dublin shows?"

I nodded, though Viktor would not be able to hear it. The shows, which took place in just over three weeks, had sold out; and the money was going to benefit a children's charity. I could not bail on them. "I promise I will be there."

On the other end of the phone, Viktor made a sound of

relief that reminded me the money I brought in not only supported my own family, but the crew and their families as well.

Now that the big issue was out of the way, Viktor began to fill me in on the other business deals my team had signed or discussed in my absence.

I let my mind wander as I turned to watch Dec again. He was attractive in a way that made it clear that attractiveness was not a goal he found important. His dark brown hair had just enough wave in it to catch the sunlight, and his eyes had the tired look of someone who spent too much time thinking. There was a complexity about him that reminded me of a set of *matryoshka*, Russian stacking dolls, I had as a child. Every time you opened one, there was a smaller one inside.

As I watched, Dec picked up a handful of pebbles and held them tight in his hand before tossing them into the water one by one.

"Anastasia!" Viktor barked on the phone when it became obvious I hadn't been paying attention.

"Sorry. I am…tired. Could I call you back in a few days, Viktor? Please. Just tell everyone I am well."

I spat on the ground for luck. It was an old superstition. One of my grandmother's. Like throwing a coin in the wishing well, I was not above looking foolish if it meant that everyone would give me these few days off.

It paid off, because Viktor took a deep breath and said, "Under the circumstances, I will do this. Just remember your commitments and stay safe. I will let you know how the 'event' goes."

"Is everything okay?" Dec asked when I hung up.

His concern was obviously genuine, and it was amazing, for the first time, to feel like someone was actually interested in *me* and not my career.

Was everything okay? I was alone in a town I did not know. Dmitry was gone. But the air was fresh with falling water, and I felt like I was making a friend for the first time. I had time to myself to decide if I would continue my grueling schedule beyond this year or whether I would honor Dmitry's request to find the rest of the Prelude.

Dec's face was open and eager for my answer. "I believe it *is* okay," I said to Dec, enjoying the sudden weightlessness of my shoulders. "I truly do."

10

RUSS

I thought back to Willow's words. There was only one thing I "have" and that was the notebook of my grandmother's. The writing was dense and the pages were old and it wasn't as if there was an index or anything. I couldn't just look up "unmoving piano" or "assholes who cheat at poker."

Still, I had no choice but to try.

Starting at the beginning, I deciphered pages that, near as I could tell, held the secrets to caring for wounds and giving yourself strength for longer than average séances. I whipped up a solution from a note on page seven, titled "archival tips" and used it to carefully pry apart pages that were stuck together with mildew and age.

Then, I admitted defeat and tried to sleep. After another

hour or two of failing at *that*, I got up and, despite it being the middle of the night, quiet except for the sounds of crickets and other nocturnal creatures, I let myself out of the house and walked.

This time, I avoided the woods. There was a place near the town square I'd always liked. A small fountain surrounded by some old brick benches near a statue of Sarahlyn Beck, one of St. Hilaire's founders. She was an alchemist, we learned in school, and the story was she had turned enough metal into gold that she was able to fund the creation of the town.

There was nothing overly remarkable about the fountain itself, except the only memory I had of St. Hilaire from my childhood was of this place.

When I was little, my teachers complained that I was dazed at times, distracted, almost as if I were somewhere else. As I got older, I improved at ignoring the voices I sometimes heard and the movements I saw in the shadows.

I knew my mother could see the ghosts as clearly as I could. Knew she understood why I was cold *all the time*. But she refused to talk about it or, aside from that one time, to bring me to St. Hilaire.

I remember the sound of the water, the cold spray on my face, and the music being played by some older kids nearby. It was hot, and I'd danced in the water while my mother and grandmother had argued about how to deal with my abilities, but the memory was removed as if I were watching a movie. I was such a different person now.

A breeze picked up and blew a flyer into my leg. It was for the Guild's failed community séance to summon Ian's ghost.

What a crock. Ian had never done anything simply because anyone else demanded it. They were fooling themselves if they thought he'd start now that he was dead.

Looking at the flyer, I admitted to myself that part of me missed the push and pull of our banter, the incredible sense of possibility I'd always felt when Ian was around, the rare feeling of being part of something, instead of on the outside looking in.

Two years older, he'd taught me everything I needed to know about St. Hilaire and probably more than I wanted to know about myself. He had an intense and almost overwhelming way of making me feel as if I were wanted. That was something I missed too, even if Ian had seemingly wanted everyone and everything at the same time.

But it sucked that no matter what I tried, I'd never been able to negotiate a peace between Ian and Dec. Where Dec was skeptical and steady, Ian was a constant explosion of personality and expectation. There was no middle ground between them and no way to cultivate both friendships. Mostly, Dec could barely stand to be in the same room as Ian.

Time with Ian always felt transient, and too much like something I wanted only because it was forbidden, and complicated, and loud. He'd always had a unique way of leaving me feeling empty when he left a room, as if he'd taken something that would be impossible for anyone else to replace.

Alternatively, my relationship with Dec and his family was real. Solid. Comforting. The Hamptons were a household of mediums, a *family* of mediums. It was all so different from what I had with my hardworking, normal father and my missing mother, and I found I craved the warmth of it all.

Ian might have put up with Dec, but the problem was Ian wasn't something you did halfway. He was all or nothing, and "nothing" had seemed like the right choice at the time, so when I had to choose, I chose Dec.

The Guild, made up of the most powerful mediums in St. Hilaire, couldn't contact Ian. However, my dream had me wondering if I would be able to. Still, "able to" wasn't the same as "should," and it certainly wasn't the same as "want to." I had bigger things to focus on.

I crumpled the flyer into a tight ball and threw it at the garbage can that sat to the left of the fountain.

It bounced off the rim and landed still, back at my feet. I stared at it and felt a familiar otherworldly chill. Then I turned around and headed home.

DEC

My dad used to say that only the guilty suffered from insomnia. Actually, he'd been full of sayings: "Mistakes are doorways to discovery," "A beautiful thing is never perfect," and "When the moon is full, it begins to wane" had all been his favorites.

I think the guilt thing was right, though. Usually, I slept like the dead. Now, I was awake, unable to get over the fact that I'd managed to spend all day with Annie without telling her how much she and her music meant to me.

I was pretty sure it was too late to say that without sounding creepy.

Miraculously, Laura had convinced Harriet to let Annie stay with us. For a fee, of course. Still, that bought me some time, and I was trying to figure out how to make things right when the curtains rustled, just enough light to catch my attention. Footsteps crossed my floor as I heard the unmistakable yet familiar sounds of a flint being struck and a cigarette being lit. The room smelled like lemons.

I tried to fool myself into thinking I was dreaming of the frozen lemonade my mom used to make for the tourists, but I knew better.

"Tristan?" I called into the darkness.

"I told you not to open the door," the darkness replied.

Reluctantly, I pulled myself up against the pillows and rubbed my eyes, hoping that would make this ghost from my childhood disappear. But when my vision cleared, Tristan was there, all blond hair and heavy-lidded green eyes.

"What the hell is going on? I thought you were gone this time," I said, suddenly awake and choking on anger that tasted of citrus. It was a peculiar type of anger, one that I'd had the better part of two years to turn over and examine. It was both irrational and overwhelming, a memory of a feeling I could never shake, but also never fully understand.

"Really?" Tristan stared at me. "Did you?"

"I'd assumed…" I started. Aside from the park, the last time I'd seen Tristan was at my parents' funeral. He'd shown up and paced around our family plot, wearing a path in the dusty ground behind the house. Two years later, that grass still hadn't grown back.

"You know what is said about those who assume, Daniel. They just make an ass out of you and me." Tristan took a drag, and the room filled again with the scent of thin Indian cigarettes, called bidis, I'd rarely seen him without. He was close enough that I could see the thin band around the top of the cigarette, decorated with a parade of elephants.

I fixated on Tristan's fingers, which were as long as Anastasia's but broader. They were musician's hands, but as far as I knew, Tristan had never been musical. To the contrary, he seemed almost repelled when I'd had learned to play the piano and always tried to distract me with games, plots, and trips to the creek that ran alongside the edge of our property.

"So, what can I do for you?" I asked politely, trying not to cough. I really didn't have the energy for a fight.

Tristan leaned forward and blew a perfectly irritating smoke ring toward my face. "Well, it's really more about what I can do for you, isn't it?"

I waved the fumes away and wondered, not for the first time, why everyone else's imaginary playmates disappeared as they grew up, while mine stuck around to torment me.

"What do you want, Tristan?" It was a simple question, but he looked jittery as he stood and went to the window, his blue velvet coat appearing black in the moonlight.

"The girl," Tristan said.

First, I heard Tristan's words, and then I heard them repeated in a rush of blood to my head. Tristan couldn't possibly mean Annie.

He got up and stubbed out his cigarette on my windowsill. Lit from behind by the moon, Tristan resembled a painting of a teenaged romantic poet and it had always annoyed the crap out of me that I could never quite figure out what he *was*. He couldn't be a ghost, because no one else could see or hear him—not even Russ—and in St. Hilaire, it would be more likely for a pink unicorn to walk down Main Street undetected than a ghost.

Tristan linked his hands together and sat on the edge of my bed again, which barely registered his weight. "I *told* you not to open the door, but you did, and now...something's wrong, Daniel."

Oddly curious, I reined in my anger. "What?"

"Well," Tristan drew the word out, "she isn't meant to be here, is she?"

"Neither are you," I muttered.

Tristan laughed. "That's debatable." His laughter faded as quickly as it came, and a cloud passed across his face as he ran a hand anxiously through his long blond bangs. "This doesn't feel right."

"And just what is it you want me to do?"

Tristan's green eyes opened wide. "Why, I want you to make her leave, of course."

I blinked hard and then glanced at the clock on my nightstand. 2:22 a.m. Triple digits were important, but I couldn't remember why. I just knew I wanted this conversation to be over.

"Go away, Tristan. I'm not sending her away, and I'm not staying up to do this with you either. I'm going back to sleep."

I pulled the covers over my head and waited, though I could still smell Tristan in the room. Lemon, and the must of mothballed clothes, and something else I couldn't place that reminded me of old flowers. I could almost feel him in the chill in the air and in the abnormally fast beat of my heart.

"I wouldn't ask you to do this if it weren't important," Tristan said petulantly.

I pulled the covers back. "You mean like when you suggested I push Harriet in the lake as a joke that summer? Or when you told me my father would be down with me skipping school and taking the train into the city for that comic book convention I really wanted to go to? I was grounded for a week that time."

A hundred different memories flooded my mind; I was surprised to realize that Tristan had been a part of so many of them.

"Those were pranks," Tristan replied. "This is different."

I bolted up. "Why should I believe anything you say? Why should I believe you exist?"

Tristan dimmed like a light bulb during a brownout. "I'm sorry I don't have the answers you need, Daniel. But I'm obviously here."

"Really? So why can't anyone else see you?" I reached out a hand toward Tristan and pulled it back. It wasn't that Tristan wasn't solid. Mostly. It was that he shouldn't be—only the most powerful of ghosts had substance—and the thought of Tristan being a powerful *anything* was mind-boggling.

"We don't choose who we are," Tristan answered, softly. "What we are. What happens to us."

I fought against feeling sorry for him. As a kid, I'd been grateful for the company, although Tristan always managed to get me into trouble. When I told my parents who the real culprit of the pranks was, my mother took me to local doctors, doctors who could read lumps in your skull or the lines in your hand. One actually suggested they foster me out to a family in

90

Buchanan. When we returned home, my parents told me never to mention Tristan again. And I was so scared that I never did.

"Where do you go when you aren't here?" I asked, suddenly consumed by anger. I knew the definition of insanity was doing the same thing over and over and expecting a different outcome. If that was the truth, then asking this question for a gazillionth time probably confirmed I was certifiable. "Where have you been for the last two years?"

"I..." Tristan paled and looked away.

So many of our conversations had ended this same way. "What's your last name?" "What are you?" Everything added up to frustrated confusion.

Tristan sighed. "You're thinking of leaving St. Hilaire again."

"I *am* leaving," I snapped back. "But I'm not going to throw Annie Krylova out of my house just because some whatever-it-is-you-are says I should."

Tristan stared back with wounded eyes. It was so easy to hurt him. Too easy. Too tempting. He was a bruise I couldn't resist poking; everything I hated about this place rolled up into one.

"Be careful what you wish for, Daniel," Tristan said and faded away.

The room was colder after he left and more than a little empty. Although I lay back down, I knew I wouldn't sleep. I just tried to figure out what my wishes had to do with anything.

12

DEC

I woke up angry.

My phone showed another missed call from "no number." The coffee wasn't strong enough. The breakfast table was crowded. Harriet crunched her toast as if she wanted to hurt someone. Laura chattered uncharacteristically about some story she'd read online about a group of California psychics who were predicting the end of the world.

Across the table, Annie was taking it all in, her hand wrapped around a charm that hung from a chain around her neck. I wondered if I'd missed it yesterday or if she hadn't been wearing it. Then I wondered what Tristan's problem was. *Then* I wondered if I was going to be able to stay awake.

Somehow I'd managed to forget how disoriented I always

was after Tristan's visits. When your life was filled with mysteries, one more shouldn't make a difference, but Tristan was my secret alone, and that feeling of isolation always ended up making it harder.

I bit down on a piece of bacon, and it shattered in my hand. Laura always liked her bacon crispy. "Damn it. Does everything here have to be burnt?"

Harriet glared at me, and Laura stopped her story in the middle of a sentence. "Sorry," I mumbled and got up to pour another cup of coffee.

Laura joined me in front of the coffeepot on the sideboard, a half-empty cup in her hand. "You look tired."

I considered telling her I'd seen Tristan, but she hovered over me enough, and I didn't want to give her one more reason to worry.

"I'm fine," I lied and turned around to watch Annie nibbling at the corners of her toast. It didn't make sense for Tristan to consider her a threat to anything. Also, it didn't feel like there was any sort of disturbance in the house, not that I was particularly sensitive to that sort of thing. Still, Laura and Harriet didn't seem abnormally bent out of shape either, and Harriet was always looking for trouble.

I couldn't shake Tristan's warning. *Be careful what you wish for?* Was he serious? Was it a threat?

I decided to try something I hadn't in a long time. I excused myself and went back up to my room with only weak coffee as a crutch.

"Tristan," I called to the empty room. "Look, I'm sorry." The apology stuck in my throat. "Just tell me what the hell you're talking about."

The air flickered. One minute I was alone, the next Tristan was there, standing by the window, pouting.

"You aren't sorry," Tristan said into the cool window. Defying physics, his breath did nothing to mark the condensation.

My chest tightened. "I'm sorry enough to call you back here. It's what I'm offering. Take it or leave it."

Tristan raised an eyebrow. "You drive a hard bargain, Daniel."

I almost laughed. "It would help if you weren't so cryptic all the time."

"You can't fault me for not knowing what I don't know." Tristan reached out a finger and drew a lazy spiral in the moisture on the window. "Perhaps you're simply asking the wrong questions."

"So what are the *right* questions?" I asked, feeling my anger rise again. Standing next to Tristan, the smell of citrus was almost overwhelming, but it was a scent I found irritatingly comforting. "Fine. I'm listening. Tell me what you *do* know."

Tristan turned and sat on the corner of the desk, pulling up the tails of his jacket and swinging his black boots forward and back.

"This house," he said, waving his long hands around, "This house…"

Tristan's voice dropped off as we realized that we were both staring at the edge of the hill of the family cemetery. My grandparents were buried there. And my great-grandparents. And generation before generation of Hamptons. But only two headstones could be seen from my room, and those belonged to my parents.

Tristan's voice was soft when he said, "This is the place I've felt the safest. It's my home as much as it is yours. It doesn't feel safe now, Daniel. Don't you sense it? The unease. *Something* is happening."

I looked at him and tried to feel for vibrations like Russ did. It didn't work, but there was something. A strange prickling on the back of my neck, a whisper in my ear.

"I don't," I said, and then, "Well, maybe," before deciding on, "I'm not being a jerk. I just don't get what you think Annie has to do with anything. And seriously, are you telling me *the house* is unhappy?"

Tristan nodded gravely. He looked ancient in the bright sunlight.

I shook my head to clear it. "You realize that a house is a thing, right? I mean, it can't really *feel.*"

Instead of answering right away, Tristan lowered himself to the floor, crossed his legs, and started picking rhythmically at tufts of carpet.

"How do you know?" Tristan asked eventually, looking up. His eyes were a hundred unnatural shades of green. "How do you know that a thing can't feel? Everything is alive in its own way. Everything has a collected history and a reason for being. Everything has a way of fighting back when its balance is forced out of kilter."

His words made me shiver and think of the piano. "Why can't we ever stick to the topic?" I asked uncomfortably. "Why does everything always come back to you?"

"You're projecting," Tristan said almost playfully.

"You're a figment of my imagination," I replied. When Tristan's hands froze, hovering over the now fluffy carpeting, and he dimmed the same way he had the previous night, I felt a jolt of fear that he might disappear for another two years without explanation. "But, I'm glad you're here," I added, trying to salvage things. It wasn't entirely untrue. It just wasn't a statement I felt comfortable saying out loud.

Tristan looked up with an eager, trusting expression. "What are you going to do, Daniel?"

"I'm not going to do anything," I said, unable to keep the exasperation out of my voice. "I'm just going to—"

Suddenly there was a knock on the door.

Then the door opened.

Then Annie Krylova walked in, looked right at Tristan, who no one else had ever been able to see, and said, "Oh. Sorry. I didn't realize you had company."

13

ANNIE

Dec stuttered something I was unable to make out. Then he closed his mouth tight. When he opened it again, he said simply, "Tristan. Anastasia."

I looked from one boy to the other. In contrast to Dec, who was dark and energized, Tristan was fair and ethereal. He reminded me of the drawings of Peter Pan in the ornately illustrated hardcover book Dmitry had given me when I was eight and still learning to read.

I waited for Dec to explain, but instead, the boy said, "She can see me, Daniel."

"Yeah," Dec said. "I get that."

The silence in the room grew oppressive, and I had a sudden feeling that I was intruding, so I began to back out.

Dec began to walk toward the door too, but Tristan said, "Please don't go."

I was not sure which of us he was addressing.

Dec narrowed his eyes. "You *can* see him, right?" he asked.

I nodded. "Yes. I should not be able to?"

Dec said, "No" and Tristan said, "Yes." Only they sounded like the same thing.

Dec spun around. "Tristan was just leaving. Isn't that right?"

Tristan leaned back against the window as if he could be absorbed into the sunlight and crossed his arms. "Actually," he said to Dec, "I thought you wanted to talk to me."

"I did. I mean, I do. But maybe now isn't the time," Dec said. "Why don't you hang out and I'll be back in a bit?"

Tristan nodded and bit his lip. "Well, maybe if you put the TV on. There's a football match…"

Dec put his cup down on the far end of the desk, clicked on the remote, and said, "Do you want me to tuck you in too?"

Tristan looked like he was going to reply, but Dec pushed me out the door before he had a chance to say anything at all.

14

DEC

If I didn't have the words to tell Annie how I'd been listening to her play online for years, I definitely had no way to explain Tristan. I didn't understand him myself.

We walked out back to the swing in the garden, and I wondered if seeing Tristan had frightened her. But as we settled in next to each other, Annie put a hand on my arm and said, "I will not say that I am not curious. But I understand if you prefer not to talk about it."

My brain was empty of lies and easy answers, so I went for the truth. "It isn't that I don't want to talk about it. I mean, I've never been in this situation before. All my life, no one could see him. I know you don't know a lot about St. Hilaire, but everyone here claims to have all of these strange visions, yet when something weird actually happened, it was only to me. I assumed there was something wrong with me for the longest time. Then I figured Tristan was some type of poltergeist. They aren't ghosts; you know that, right? Poltergeists are just emotional energy made physical. Stress. Anger. Love. I figured I just felt things too deeply or something."

I struggled to take a deep breath. Why had I just told her... well, everything? Bad enough that I was some freak who could see ghosts. Now, she probably figured I was some emo boy who couldn't control his emotions.

But when she answered, she simply said, "I am looking for something." Her expression was complicated. "Well, my teacher was, and now he is dead, so I guess that means *I am* looking for it."

I tried to tie her words to my confession. "What are you looking for?" I asked. The question *felt* larger than the words it was made of.

She wrapped her hand around the charm at her throat. "It is such a long story."

"Oh," I said, although I didn't really understand.

"Do you ever find lost things?" she asked, after a while.

I kicked at the ground, and the swing arced up and back hypnotically. There were plenty of lost things I wanted to find, but most of those were people, or times, or places. Nothing that lurked in a box or under a pile of laundry.

"Not me," I admitted. "But there are people here who do that." As much as I wanted to be the one to help her, the thought that I'd try and fail terrified me.

"What do you do?" she asked gently.

"I see weird ghost boys," I said, because at the moment, Tristan was all I could really count on. "So, tell what you're looking for."

She looked at me, her eyes shifting from green to blue and back again in the light that filtered through the breeze-blown trees. "Better than that," she said. "I was coming to your room to ask… If you do not mind me playing your piano, it would, perhaps, be clearer for me to show you."

RUSS

Eating breakfast alone was nothing new, since my dad was usually at work before my alarm even went off. So I'd developed my own rituals involving dry toast, lukewarm tea, and a bunch of books spread across the table, dog-eared, highlighted, and stickered.

Somewhere in today's mess was a note. My father was big on notes and started leaving them in my lunch bag well before we'd moved to St. Hilaire. I'm sure some kids would have been embarrassed by badly drawn dinosaurs, or motivational quotes in advance of their math tests. But I wasn't. My dad didn't have any ability as a medium, but he knew me, and he made sure that I never had a reason to doubt my importance to him.

I moved a stack of napkins, a handwoven rune mat, and

two books dissecting the Handel tarot, to find his latest offering. It read: *Regardless of what else you do, be true to yourself.*

The message was eerily similar to what Willow had hinted at. I thought about it as I twisted the bolt in my ear. I still felt I had that covered.

As I stacked my breakfast dishes in the sink and piled the books into a structure that vaguely reminded me of the Merchandise Mart, I ran through the discussion I was hoping to have with David Sheridan.

I wouldn't get any more of a straight answer from Alex about why they'd wanted Dec's piano than I had from Ian in my dream when I'd asked him how he'd died—evasiveness was a finely honed Mackenzie family trait—but David Sheridan was a weak link, one I wasn't going to hesitate to break.

When I found him near the town square, David Sheridan was cowering against a picnic table, staring into an egg sandwich as if it held the secrets to the universe.

"Hey," I said. And that was enough to startle David into flinging the sandwich into the dirt. A couple of St. Hilaire's resident squirrels, fat from summer feasting, waddled over and helped themselves to the remains.

David had to know why I was there, and so I waited to see if he was going to say anything. When he didn't, I cut to the chase. "The Guild will get to the bottom of things, you know."

I was sure that David was just the fall guy for whatever Alex had planned, so the idea of the Guild stepping in and learning the truth should have been comforting to him.

"Oh, goodie. I just love dealing with them," he replied, kicking the ground. "Look, I can't talk to you about this."

David wasn't a bad guy; he was just kind of spineless. "Alex is a bully. You know that, right? He's a coward. If you stood up to him, he'd back down," I advised, even though I knew that David had never stood up to anyone before. "David, do the right thing here."

A few feet away, the squirrels fought over the dropped sandwich.

David gave a strangled laugh, and the winning squirrel picked up its egg and hopped off. "Really glad we had this chat, Russ. You've been a big help. Thanks."

"I'm trying to help," I said and dug my hands into the pockets of my coat. This was just the kind of thing I'd face if I worked with the Guild. If I couldn't even get David Sheridan to open up, I was going to be in trouble.

David shook his head. "No offense, but you don't know anything about it. You don't know what it's like. What he can be like."

I opened my mouth to protest. After all, I knew a lot about the Mackenzies. And I knew a lot about feeling as if your life was out of control. And mostly, I knew more than I wanted to admit about the place where those two things intersected.

Then I shivered. The hair on my neck bristled. I didn't know what was happening, but I knew who it was happening *to*.

David Sheridan looked at me, puzzled.

"I have to go," I said. "Now."

David's brow wrinkled. He looked almost disappointed. "Sure. Great chatting with you."

I felt bad for him, but I didn't have time to stick around to express it.

Dec needed me.

16

DEC

I couldn't bring myself to sit next to Annie on the piano bench, so I hovered over her shoulder and watched her play. I knew the Unfinished Prelude. I could play it back note for note in my head and frequently did during boring lectures and séances and most of the time Harriet was speaking. None of that came close to hearing Annie play it on the piano—*my* piano.

The piece was alternatingly energizing and heartbreaking. I intellectually knew every one of the emotions it called upon, but watching her play brought them all to the surface at once.

I sank down in the window seat, afraid I might hyperventilate.

"Here it comes," Annie called out.

I winced and willed myself to pay attention to the individual notes as they hurtled and jumped over one another. I knew where the piece stopped, and it was at such an annoying place, I usually muted the sound on the video a measure or two before it came to the final notes.

Now, I had no choice but to listen. When Annie played the last measures, which ended on an unresolved chord, they made my teeth clench. The tension in the room resembled a coming storm. I waited for the windows to rattle with it.

"Irritating, right?" Annie asked. "Your ears cry out for the missing tone."

I struggled to open my jaw as she continued. "I read once that Mozart's wife used to play an unresolved chord to get him out of bed. He would have to get up to play the resolution, or it would bug him all day."

Annie tinkled the keys until the note resolved, the tension in the room withdrew, and I could breathe again. "Why would the composer write music that annoying?" I asked.

Annie's hands hovered over the keys, soundlessly. "I don't think he did."

"What?"

"I told you I was looking for something, and this is it," she explained. "My teacher discovered this piece. He found the original sheet music rolled up in a tube and shoved in a hollowed-out old umbrella in an antique shop on London's Portobello Road. Since then, it has been picked apart and analyzed by scholars all around the world. But there is something they did not have. Something Dmitry hid from them."

She closed her eyes as if she were making a wish and then reached up, pulled off her necklace, and held it out to me.

I rolled the box around on my palm. Slightly bigger than

my thumbnail, it was warm from being next to her skin. The sides were decorated with intricate swirls and tiny musical notes. In the middle of a half note was a small button, flush with the surface.

"Press it," Annie urged, when she saw that I'd found it.

I held the box between the fingers of my right hand and depressed the tiny button with my left. The music that came out was louder than I expected. The notes were thin, but still recognizable. I couldn't believe what I was hearing. "That's…"

"Yes. The next eight measures," she said.

"Where—"

She cut me off again. "Dmitry found *this* in Tunisia. He bought it for less than the gold it took to make the box was worth. The seller told him he needed to get rid of it because it was cursed." She took it back and draped the chain around her neck.

I walked over to the old leaded-glass window that gave everything a slight blur. It was like looking through water and made me slightly dizzy.

"I know it is odd," Annie continued. "There are a million pieces of music in the world. But Dmitry wanted to find *this* one. He wanted me to play it. The entire thing. I guess I want to play the entire thing too."

I turned and watched as she closed the piano lid. "I am not sure whether it was the music or the mystery behind it that interested Dmitry most," she said and hesitated. I badly wanted to ask about the mystery, about the music, about *her*. I was a box filled with unasked questions.

"There are stories about the composer too," Annie continued. "Mostly about how he was young when he wrote the

Prelude. They say that his father tried to imprison him in a mental hospital but disappeared before that could happen. Why would a father do that?" Annie's hand reached protectively around the charm.

I thought about my parents who were always supportive of our dreams, even when Harriet left and moved to New York to intern for a finance company on Wall Street. That was about as far from the life of St. Hilaire as possible. What would they think about my plans to bail?

I couldn't answer.

Annie ran her hands along the keys, not making a sound. "I have Dmitry's notes. He found pieces of the Prelude scattered throughout Europe, always with some curious story attached. But he found so little information about the composer. People say *he* was cursed too."

I took a deep breath and knew I was screwing myself in the worst possible way. I was leaving in less than two weeks, and I also knew, without question, that some part of this musical search was going to force me to do something I didn't want to do.

As I exhaled, I tried to let go of my hope that I'd ever have a life that didn't involve spirits, visions, or mediums. The word "curse" curdled in my stomach. Had it come out of the mouth of anyone other than Annie Krylova, I might have hit something, thrown something, even. As it was, all I could do was parrot it back. "Cursed."

Thankfully, Annie seemed oblivious to my distress. She said, "What is shocking is that the composer was supposedly our age. It is amazing that someone so young could have written a piece so heart-wrenching and exciting."

I pictured the Carnegie Hall poster in my room that announced Annie's show. At once, every single one of my failures came surging back. *I was the only one who hadn't done anything by seventeen. I was the only one still trying to figure out what I wanted to be when I grew up, or even where I wanted to live. I didn't even have the guts to tell Annie I knew who she was. I was a coward.*

"And the whole curse thing seems so cruel. I mean, if you believe in things like that," Annie continued.

I was about to point out the obvious, that a boy who lived in a town of mediums was more inclined to believe a story about a curse than just about anyone she could have told, when a loud roar surged up the drive.

St. Hilaire was a quiet town. A peaceful town. There was only one thing in it that sounded like a lion devouring a herd of terrified gazelles, and that was the Mackenzies' pieced-together Mustang.

"Shit," I said.

"What is it?"

"Either nothing or the end of the world, take your pick," I muttered, and then realized I wasn't making any sense. "I'm sorry. In advance, I'm sorry."

"For what?"

"For whatever is about to happen."

The front door burst open, and Alex Mackenzie's dog came rushing in. It circled Annie and then fell to the ground, looking up at her, a string of drool hanging from his mouth.

I really needed to start locking the freaking door.

Alex Mackenzie followed his dog. There was a hitch in his

step when he saw Annie, but then he looked at me and broke into a carnivorous leer. "You've been practicing your conjuring skills, right, Hampton? I mean that's the only way you're going to get a girl who isn't your sister."

I went for his throat while Annie said some things in Russian that I hoped she would teach me.

My punch was interrupted by a shout that started outside and carried through into the room. "Alex!"

I held onto Alex's shirt until Colin Mackenzie was in striking distance, and then I pushed Alex away with a shove that made him stumble backward. I wasn't sure if Colin would want to pick up the fight from there, but I almost didn't care, and was disappointed when Colin only wound up and slapped his brother in the head.

"Two minutes. You can't keep your mouth shut for two minutes, can you?" Where Alex was a pinless grenade, looking for an excuse to self-destruct, Colin was a nuclear core, hot as molten lava one minute and cold as dry ice the next. I might have had issues with Ian, but at least he'd kept his brothers in check.

Colin pulled back his shoulders and turned to me. "We're here about the piano," he said, all business. "Rice and Norton are on their way."

"Awesome," I said sarcastically.

"And I've got something for you." Colin handed me a package wrapped in brown paper.

"What is it?" I asked. I wasn't used to getting gifts from Mackenzies.

"Guild flag," Colin said. "Didn't you hear the new rules announced at the festival? Every house is supposed to fly one."

I waited for the punchline, but there was nothing. "Seriously? You're kidding, right?"

Colin was straight-faced when he said, "No. I'd suggest putting it up before school starts. There'll be fines beginning in September."

I wanted to tell him to take it back, but instead took the package and threw it in a side table drawer.

"And what's he here for?" I asked, pointing to Alex.

"He's here so that I can keep an eye on him," Colin said.

"Fuck off," Alex spat in his brother's direction.

"Whatever," Colin replied, sounding bored. It was easy to believe the two of them replayed this exact conversation three or four times a day.

They only stopped bickering when a number of car doors slammed in front of the house.

I went over to where Annie was standing, against the wall, eyes shining as if she were looking for a fight.

"Sorry," I said to her under my breath. "They have rules about outsiders being here for these things and really"—I glared back at Alex—"it's probably for the best."

She snarled at Alex in Russian again and nodded. As she headed upstairs, I pointed at Alex and said to Colin, "He's your responsibility."

"Story of my life. Let's just get to the bottom of this."

With that understanding reached, I nodded and hoped the piano and my teeth would both still be intact when it was all over.

The Guild was always cryptic about its structure at any given moment, but as far as I knew, there were fifteen active members and a couple of assistants this year. They could have sent any of them, but it was the top two officials who arrived to look at my piano.

We said our hellos, and by the time that was done, Russ had burst through the door.

Everyone naturally lined up according to our allegiances: Russ and me on one side. Alex and his dog, who was staring at Russ, on the other. In the middle, Clive Rice, Charlotte North, and Colin approached my piano.

It was hard to watch the Guild members run their hands over the wood I'd spent hours polishing. Russ put a hand on my shoulder and squeezed hard. I guess I was showing my stress more than I thought.

The room was silent, all of us waiting for answers.

"What is that infernal noise?" Clive Rice asked, head cocked toward the piano.

Russ and I looked at each other. I hadn't heard anything, and the dog hadn't even reacted.

Colin bent and put his ear to the dark wood.

"Oh for god's sake. Can we just try to move it already?" Alex exclaimed.

Colin jerked up and turned toward his brother. "Shut up or I'm going to tie you *and* that dog up in the yard."

There was a lot of deliberation as Guild members examined every inch of the piano. They loosened the locks on the wheels, poked and prodded it, and opened and closed the lid to the keyboard, but thankfully, it didn't move any farther this time than it had before.

"You say this was the prize in a poker game?" Charlotte North asked me.

My stomach churned.

"Yeah," Alex answered before I could. "And we just want to know why he isn't paying up."

"Well, the answer to that is twofold," Clive Rice said. "First"—he turned toward Alex—"we have it on good authority that you cheated."

The room went dead quiet. Then, surprisingly, Alex drew back his shoulders, looked Rice in the eye, and said, "I didn't cheat."

I waited for Russ to contradict him, but he just leaned toward me and said, "It's the damnedest thing, but I think he's telling the truth."

"No," Rice said to Alex after a beat. "Not technically you." He stroked his beard with one hand and ran the other over the keyboard. "But you weren't alone." His words didn't quite form a question, but they also weren't an accusation.

Alex nodded quickly. "David Sheridan," he said. "It was him."

"Way to throw your friend under the bus," Russ muttered next to me.

"Yes. Well. Be that as it may, you were a team," Charlotte North said. "What did you put up for your end of the bet?"

Next to me, Russ swallowed loudly.

Rice tapped the glass on his watch, trying to get the famously errant second hand to move. I never understood why he didn't just get the thing fixed.

Colin took a step toward Alex. It was just a step, but we all tensed. "Yeah, Alex. What *did* you put up for your end?"

The dog looked up and angled his head. I wondered if Alex had the nerve to give Colin an honest answer.

Alex looked his brother in the eye and said, "My car."

"The Mustang?" Colin barked.

"That's the only car I have."

"Had," Russ said under his breath.

I waited for the explosion. Instead, almost more frightening, Colin started laughing. "Oh, you can't be serious. The Mustang? *Ian's* Mustang?" With every word, his laughter turned more caustic.

I'd never had an issue with Colin, although I'd known those who did. Joey Gonzales, for instance, had never really been the same after Colin had finished with him and he was finally released from the hospital.

"Mine," Alex said forcefully. "My Mustang."

I knew the minute I heard the words that they would be the ones to set Colin off. His face sharpened so quickly that I could see the bones under the skin. His fists curled and uncurled. Next to me, Russ stiffened.

"You have nothing," Colin said to his brother. "You *are* nothing."

Before I knew it, Russ was between them, a hand stretched toward each boy's chest, holding them apart.

"Enough," Clive Rice said.

No one in the room was stupid enough to argue.

"You," Rice said, pointing toward Alex, "will deliver the car and its keys to Mr. Hampton by noon tomorrow. Your accomplice will come to the hall at one tomorrow afternoon. I trust you will inform him of this. And you will stay available should we need to speak to you."

Aside from the Buchanan police, who were rarely seen in town, there was no higher authority in St. Hilaire than the Guild. Their decisions were law, and this time it looked like the law had won.

"Ah, quiet," Clive Rice said, cupping his ear and turning to me. "Enjoy your piano, Mr. Hampton. It seems to be where it would choose to be." Then he leaned in and whispered, "Also, we look forward to meeting with you as discussed in our letter." He set his bowler hat back on his head and turned to leave.

The letter. That must have been what Laura had mentioned, although it would have been nice had she mentioned it was from the Guild.

"Wait," Russ called. "Didn't you say there were two reasons for the piano staying, sir?"

Clive Rice turned and looked back at us. "Well, yes. There is the matter of the cheating. But also, it's quite simple, really. You see, the instrument wasn't Mr. Hampton's to wager. Good day."

I watched as the Mackenzies followed the Guild members out the door with matching sneers. When the dog walked by, Russ held out his hand. The dog sniffed and then rubbed his waist-high head against Russ's fingers. Only when Alex turned back and called the dog did it follow.

I waited until the door shut. "What the hell did that mean?" I asked Russ. "How did they know Alex and David cheated, and whose piano does he think it is, then?"

"They probably have some old ghost spying in Eaton Hall. But does it matter?" Russ glanced at the instrument, his eyes shining with hope. "You heard him; it's where it wants to be. And…I believe that means we have a car."

Every tense muscle in my body relaxed. "The Mustang. *You* have the Mustang," I said, because I'd never once thought it would be mine, and I was so grateful to be the one to give it to Russ.

"The Mustang," Russ repeated, seemingly in shock. His dark eyes were glassy; no doubt, his head was swirling with thoughts of Ian's car.

"Hey, and there's something else," I said in a whisper. "Quiet, but you remember Anastasia Krylova?"

Russ blinked. "The piano girl?"

I laughed. What a strange simplistic way to sum up everything that went into making Annie Krylova. "Yeah. Well, she's kind of here. And staying with us."

"Here?" Russ snapped out of his car-fueled bliss.

I filled him in, excited to be sharing my good luck. But then Russ asked the same question Tristan had asked me, "What are you going to do?" and my shoulders stiffened as the tone of his voice sucked down the momentary joy of keeping both the piano *and* the car.

"Do?"

"Well, think. This can't be random. I mean, come on, it's the off-season. And you've been more-or-less obsessed with her."

"Russ. She's *here*. Ask your dad. That stupid old train broke down. She says she just walked into St. Hilaire. *And* she's in my house. She…" I was about to tell Russ that she could see Tristan, but Russ cut me off.

"The train? I want to meet her," Russ demanded.

"Yeah, sure," I replied. "Not today. Tomorrow or…" This, the speaking in broken, uncertain sentences, wasn't how we usually were with each other. Of course, I wanted Annie and

Russ to meet; I'd just assumed it would feel happier and more celebratory than this. "Soon, promise. Just don't say anything. About me, you know…"

Russ nodded, but the moment—the jubilant, triumphant moment of having beaten Sheridan and Mackenzie at their own game—had passed.

ANNIE

As soon as the awful boys left, Laura let out a huge breath. "Well, that was interesting."

I was not usually one for eavesdropping, but Laura had stopped me at the top of the stairs, where we listened to the whole conversation. "I am not even sure what just happened," I said.

"Alex has always been a little unglued. The thing is, David Sheridan is actually a nice guy. I can't believe he let Alex talk him into being a part of this," Laura said.

"But Dec gets to keep the piano, correct?" If I had to count, I would guess that I have played thousands of pianos, none of which had belonged to me, but to concert halls and rental companies. The closest I came to having a relationship with one was the showy transparent grand in Dmitry's New York loft. I could not imagine any piano had cared whether I played it or not.

But I felt an overwhelming sense of relief that *this* piano was going to stay where it was. In part, it was that I could not imagine the beautiful instrument being given to that horrid Alex Mackenzie. And in part it was something more. Some part of me that *felt* the words the Guild member had said. The piano was where it needed to be.

"I guess," Laura said, running a bitten nail along the stair rail. "But I'm not sure it's enough to get him to stay."

I thought back to Dec's comment at the waterfall about St. Hilaire not being a place you could stay in forever. "He is really planning to leave?"

Laura leaned over the edge of the stairs looking down into the music room and then gestured for me to follow. When we got to her room, she sat stiffly on the bed. In contrast to the well-lived-in look of the rest of the house, this room was as immaculate as a hotel. Even the books in the one bookcase were organized by color. It made me feel out of place, as if my long hair and patchwork bag of many colors were disturbing the organization of the space.

"It's been hard for him since Mom and Dad died. He and Harriet…" Laura started and then seemed to think better of it. "Well, I think he blames himself. And St. Hilaire, for what happened to them."

I felt a sudden pang of regret that I had never been at my parents' house long enough to form a relationship with my younger brother. It would be nice to have someone to care about the way that Laura and Dec obviously cared about each other.

"What happened?"

"Dec and my parents were going to see some movie," Laura said, smoothing out an invisible wrinkle in the quilt. "Harriet was on spring break, so she and I were home. I had a math test the next day. They were supposed to be home by ten. Harriet went to bed, but I knew something was wrong, so I stayed up reading, waiting for the phone to ring or for someone to show up at the door."

I rubbed my hand where only a shadow of the burn from the hot tea remained.

"The Buchanan police—they were around more often, then—said my parents' car went into a ditch after they tried to avoid some bobcat that had been roaming around. They'd just come through the West Gate and were killed on impact. Dec was found a block away. Unconscious against a tree. No one knows how he got there."

"How awful." I tried to picture the scene. Dec with his hair dark against the tree's dry brown bark. Him waking up and not knowing where he was or how he'd gotten there. It was a hard picture to bring to life, just as it had been hard for me to imagine Dmitry dead with a bottle of pills in his hand.

"Dec was in the hospital for a while, and he's been angry at everyone since," Laura said. "He used to be different."

Different. People used to say that about Dmitry too. That he had been "different" when he was still playing, still touring, still everyone's darling. Where everyone else saw anger, I just saw sadness. I guess it was much the same with Dec.

Laura continued. "All Dec ever talks about is how soon he can leave St. Hilaire. I don't want him to go, but I can't imagine what would happen if he stayed."

I asked, "What are you afraid would happen?" but all I could imagine was some parallel version of Dmitry's descent.

Laura looked away. "I don't know," she said.

"What about you?" I asked. "Are you happy here?"

She flushed. "I like St. Hilaire. It feels right. I've never thought of being somewhere else."

I envied her contentment. I had not stayed anywhere long enough to know what that would feel like. Laura made being a part of a place sound so simple.

I stood and wandered over to the wooden dresser. Hanging above it was a sign titled St. Hilaire Rules of Conduct. The first item read, *Never change the course of the future through the sharing of information. This includes scenarios of life and death.*

I stopped reading there. Life and death. If I had an "off" show, the customers might grumble or even ask for their money back, but no one would die. Could die. But Dec... I understood now why he would want to leave. The weight of that responsibility must be crushing.

Below the sign was a photo of Dec and Laura as kids, holding hands. Laura had not changed much, but it was Dec who caught my eye. His hair was blowing in a breeze, and it covered his eyes, but his grin was so large, it almost dominated the photo. It was hard to imagine the Dec I met looking so happy.

My parents would have no similar photos of my little brother and me. Andrei would grow up without knowing me at all. If I were lucky, my parents would play one of my albums, point, and say, "This is your big sister."

"Why does that photo make you sad?" Laura asked.

I turned away from it. "It should not. I have everything in the world anyone could want, right?" I plastered on my stage smile. "I am just feeling sorry for myself. Nothing more."

I did not know why I was holding back. Maybe it was that I had never had a female friend. There were the other musicians I toured with and the one time in London where the first-chair violinist had asked me to go shopping at Harrods so she could get a performance gown. We had lost track of time trying all the free samples in the food court and almost missed our rehearsal. After, I left for the airport, and we had exchanged one or two emails before one of us forgot to answer, and that was the end of it.

I considered telling Laura about Dmitry and his search for the Prelude, but then there was a knock on the door, and Dec walked into the room, wet-haired and obviously recently out of the shower. His gray sweatshirt stretched over his arms as if it had once belonged to someone larger; he had the cuffs folded up to his wrists. He looked a lot like the little boy in the photo.

My thoughts tangled. Or perhaps it was not my thoughts. Nothing so tangible. But something inside me twisted with desire for something I was not sure I was allowed to have.

We held each other's gaze.

I was the first to look away.

18

DEC

I woke up to the sound of Annie playing the Prelude. It seemed I'd been listening to it all night, chasing the notes throughout the house in my head.

As I came to, I felt for the letter on my nightstand. The envelope was the color of dead leaves, and the sealing wax (sealing wax!) was marked with the Guild's complicated logo made up of vines and the letters *SHG*. I switched on the light and reread the words, hoping they might have morphed during the night.

The letter should have contained information about my required year in the Youth Corps, which involved following Guild members around, sitting in on community-wide séances, typing up reports, and generally doing the Guild's grunt work after school for credit.

I knew the standard format of the Guild's "invitation" letters; I could see the text swimming on my eyelids. *As part of your graduation requirement, you will join the Youth Corps for the duration of your senior year and be assigned to a Guild member in order to complete your training so that you may be evaluated and **considered** for both legal status as a medium and a permanent role in the ranks of our esteemed organization. At that time, if you are deemed worthy, you will be officially welcomed into the historic ranks of St. Hilaire's ancestors.*

But when I'd opened the letter, there were other words at the top of the page. *Leadership. Legacy. Responsibility.*

I knew these words too, and if I was willing to risk the wrath of the Guild to leave town to avoid joining the Youth Corps, I was damned if I was going to stick around to audition for a position as Student Leader.

They *had* to know I wasn't good enough. My parents might have been talented, but ever since they died, I'd just taken up space at the séance table. Harriet thought I wasn't trying. Laura thought I was too distracted. Russ was probably closest when he said I was more than likely just too sad to open myself up to the spirit world.

It was Russ they wanted. Russ who had the talent and the interest. Russ who was going to be here.

And I'd remind them of that, except the Guild was historically "disappointed" in kids who grew up in St. Hilaire and then moved away. Although I doubted they could do anything to me if I left, there had been issues in the past. Some young mediums found their families' land unexpectedly taxed an outrageous amount, or their parents' licenses revoked. And there were rumors of worse. Much worse back in the town's early days.

That was all history, though. It had been a while since anyone had left permanently. It was difficult, I heard, to try to live a "normal" life, when you were aware of the ghosts surrounding you.

Even Ian Mackenzie had hung around enough to keep the Guild on his good side.

Still, it was one thing for me to hope they'd overlook some has-been medium ditching town to avoid the Youth Corps. It was far more unlikely for them to turn a blind eye when one of the students they offered a rare audition letter to skipped out.

I got up, tossed the letter on my desk, showered, dressed, checked my phone for messages, and checked the corners of my room in case Tristan had come back. Through it all, I could hear Annie playing the Prelude downstairs.

I grabbed two cups of coffee and headed to the music room. She didn't look up when I came in, so I stood and watched her.

Perhaps this was what it took to perform at her level, this single-minded focus, but to me, she didn't even look like she was enjoying herself.

"Do you want something to eat?" I asked, grateful as the final notes echoed in the room.

"No," she snapped, "I have to…" She looked up and flushed. I could see pale circles under her eyes. "I am so sorry. Wow. I am just. Yes. I could use a break."

I handed her the coffee. "How long have you been practicing?" I asked.

She hesitated. "Too long? I really am sorry. I did not mean to land on your doorstep and lay claim to your piano. But it *is* funny. Playing the Prelude on this piano, in this room, maybe in St. Hilaire. It feels very different."

"Yup, no one does 'different' as well as St. Hilaire."

She looked at me through her lashes, and I was overwhelmed with the reality of her being here in this room with me. Not only playing my family's piano, but that I was bringing her coffee and just…talking. I wanted it never to end.

"Thank you for this," she said. "For the coffee. For… everything."

"Anytime," I said and meant it. It struck me that she could have come to St. Hilaire two years ago before I knew who she was, or a month from now, when I'd be gone. It was the first time in a long while that I felt lucky.

She gave me a quick hug that set every nerve in my body buzzing, and said, "I think I need a shower. And maybe to lie down," and headed up the stairs.

Behind me, the door opened. "Hey, I'm guessing you didn't get my message?" Russ called. "Alex is on his way. I'm assuming you aren't inviting him in?"

"Hell, no," I said, still reeling from Annie's hug.

We stepped out on the porch. I knew I should tell him about the letter from the Guild. I'd never kept anything from Russ, but I wasn't sure where to begin.

I put the letter out of my mind when the bright sun and the smell of my mom's wildflower garden, now overgrown with weeds, took me somewhere else. Some*when* else. "You know what this reminds me of? Those dirt bikes."

Russ flushed. "I always knew your dad didn't get that second bike for free like he claimed."

"He wanted you to have one too," I said. It would have been nice to be able to turn back the clock to a time when we spent the bulk of our summers racing through the woods around town. None of the futures that I could imagine included the space and time for us to be able to do those kinds of things again. Russ would be in the Youth Corps and I'd be gone, or worse, here and miserable.

Our friendship felt impossibly complicated these days.

"Not putting your flag up, then?" Russ asked, shading his eyes and pointing toward the flag bracket on the front of the house.

I stared at him in shock. "Are you seriously telling me that you *have*?"

He shrugged. "It's a stupid rule, I agree, but it's just a flag. Could have been better designed, I guess."

My reply was thankfully cut off by the Mustang screaming up the road, followed by Colin's elderly rust-colored Nova.

When Alex got out of the car, he slammed the door hard enough to make me wince and made his way up the steps. Without a word, he held out the keys. I let Russ take them.

On the street, Colin sat in his car, waiting to drive Alex home and who knew what else. It was a bad day to be Alex Mackenzie.

"This isn't the end," Alex said. "It isn't over."

Russ held the keys in front of him. Clearly, they were heavier than they looked and as impossibly shiny as the car itself. Sunlight flew off the metal and reflected against the columns of the porch. I looked away from the lights, the way you'd look away from an eclipse. Staring at them felt dangerous.

Russ closed his hand around the keys and stuffed them into his pocket. "It seems pretty over to me," he said.

Alex knew better than to tangle with Russ, so he leaned in

to me. "We have unfinished business, Hampton. I'm planning to finish it. Consider yourself warned."

I nodded with a rush of anticipation that made me feel both guilty and alive. Alex Mackenzie hadn't killed my parents. But he was here and he was a pain in the ass. Those were enough for me to allow my anger to boil over. "Ian's dead, Alex. He's not coming back. You need to get over it."

I'd gone for the most painful target I could, and Alex didn't disappoint. He slammed me hard against the door frame, before I responded by barreling my fist into his face.

"Enough," Russ said quietly. Alex and I froze as if we had no other choice. "Enough."

I rubbed the back of my neck. I felt better after the release, but Russ was right. This wasn't the time or place. Alex swung his head, shaking a nice amount of blood over the wooden slats. Harriet was going to be furious.

As if she knew I was thinking about her, Harriet opened the screen door with a look of disgust on her pinched face.

"I don't want to know what this is about," she said. "But whatever it is, it's not going to happen on this porch."

I watched Russ settle into the Mustang's driver's seat through the curtains, then I went to join Harriet in the reading room. I was surprised to find Laura and Annie there, too, huddled over cups of tea, laughing like old friends.

I felt energized. On fire. Annie was here. Russ had the Mustang. I was…leaving.

Harriet said, "I've been thinking…"

There was little Harriet could say that wouldn't make me cringe, but these words were the worst of all. Harriet was always thinking. And usually she was thinking about ways to make me miserable.

"Hope you didn't pull anything," I said.

Harriet looked bored. "Sit down. I want to know what Clive Rice meant about the piano not being ours."

"Who knows, Harriet? Maybe great-grandpa never paid the bill."

Her eyes narrowed. "Do I need to remind you…?"

This time, I couldn't keep my mouth shut. "That you gave up hope of ever having the life you dreamed of so that you could serve as our super-reluctant legal guardian until we turn eighteen. No, I think we heard you the first ten million times."

"Sit down, Daniel," she repeated. "And watch your mouth. I also don't need to tell you that you don't want to get on my bad side."

"Oh, hell, Harriet. Really?" I hated that she was talking to me like a child in front of Annie. "Look," I said in the nicest tone I could muster, "I'm sorry. I really am, but I don't know anything more than you do. And frankly, I don't think I care."

I went upstairs, lucky to have escaped without more drama. Standing outside my bedroom door, I heard the soft drone of the soccer announcer's voice discuss a penalty for someone from Uruguay.

I opened the door cautiously, to find Tristan sitting at my desk where I'd left him yesterday. He was staring off into the distance looking concerned.

"How nice of you to visit," I said, mocking the formality of Tristan's accent. "I thought you would have waited up for me last night."

Tristan startled, as if he hadn't heard me come in. "I've been thinking," he said. "You realize, don't you, that the odds of Annie actually getting stranded here by accident are about... well, how many trains run through the U.S. daily? It seems quite unlikely..."

I put my hands up to quiet him. "You've been sitting here worrying about this for how long? Never mind. It doesn't matter. After you disappeared last night, I wasn't sure you'd be back."

Tristan cocked his head and said, "I'm always here."

I bit my tongue. Tristan had to know that he'd been gone for most of two years. "So, hit me. What have you figured out?"

Tristan's face lit up. "Well, nothing yet. But her showing up here must *mean* something."

I waited, hoping there was more to this "revelation." But when Tristan spoke, it was to say, "And she can see me," with a sense of awe.

I turned off the TV and sat. "Yes, she can see you," I said, wondering what it must be like to be seen by only one person. "So, how does that change anything?"

Tristan drummed his fingers silently on the desk. "Hmm... Of course. There must be some connection between her and this house."

"That doesn't make any sense. She's from somewhere in Russia. She's never been to St. Hilaire."

Tristan shook his head slowly and tugged on the ends of his scarf. "No, no, that's not it." Then his face lit up. "Houses

131

have many parts, Daniel. Many, many parts. There's the actual building material, and the objects inside, and the family."

"You think she's related to the bricks? The family? You think she has some connection to us? I mean, to me?"

"I don't really know. But I think we should find out." Tristan moved to the door; I beat him to it and blocked the way.

"What do you mean, 'find out'?"

"Really, Daniel. Must you be quite so difficult all the time? I just want to talk to her." He paused and then added, "And I want to take a walk through the house. There must be something here that is linked to her."

I thought about telling him there was nothing to find, but he had me curious. "Yeah. Fine. Lead the way." I hoped we wouldn't run into my sisters. Laura would understand, but Harriet would freak out if she saw me talking to empty air.

I stepped out to the top and realized two things. First, Annie was downstairs playing the Prelude again, and second, Tristan was frozen in the doorway.

"I thought you wanted to do this," I said to Tristan. But something was wrong. Tristan stood with his back pressed up against the wall. His face blank, his hands trembling.

"Okay," I asked. "What am I missing?"

Tristan closed his eyes and pushed his hands flat against the wall at his sides. His fingers moved against the plaster.

"Tristan?" I started.

"Shh." Tristan tilted his head back as Annie's music circled up the stairs around us.

The hallway grew cold with the kind of chill I'd felt at my

parents' séances when Mom was calling on very strong spirits for a client.

Behind me, I could hear Tristan panting for breath like a dog in the sun.

Annie was still playing, and she was nearing the place where the chords unraveled into their unresolved state. The tension was unfurling. The back of my neck began to itch. I turned to Tristan in an effort to break the pressure that was overtaking the hallway, but this time, when I looked back, Tristan was gone.

ANNIE

"You want to take a walk and get out of here?" Dec asked. I had no idea how long he had been standing there.

I nodded, but allowed myself a few more measures. The Prelude sounded different in this house. Fuller. More complete. More majestic and dynamic. I could not figure out if there was something in the way the piano was tuned, or built, or if maybe it was the acoustics in the room, but the piece had never sounded so alive.

"Annie." Dec leaned closer, his breath hot on my neck, though it made me shiver.

"Right," I said. "Sorry." I balled my fists and pulled them off the keys. My palms itched to go back to playing; my ears rang with the sudden silence.

Dec looked relieved as I stood and followed him outside. "I thought we might pop by Russ's. You two should meet, and he wants me to see the car up close."

We left the house and walked through some of the areas I had seen earlier and then through what Dec said was the older side of town where the buildings were smaller, in need of work, and flying more of the brown Guild flags. There were fewer signs reading MEDIUM FOR HIRE in this area than I had seen near Dec's house as well.

Eventually we came across a garden of…well, I did not know what. "What a complicated combination of plants," I said, taking in the flowers and herbs and green, brown, and purple things I did not recognize, which were corralled in wooden planters, almost as far as I could see.

I moved in closer to look, but Dec kept to an overgrown stone path, and I had no choice except to follow.

Russ's house itself was an intriguing shade of deep blue. Smoke rose welcomingly from the chimney. In front sat a planked porch with a display of rocking chairs that looked handmade. A brown Guild flag hung off the side of the porch.

"Check it out," Russ called as he came out from under the carport next to the house.

Dec gave a low wolf whistle as we approached the Mustang, but stopped short. I knew that good manners said I should hold back as well, but I could not keep myself from reaching out to touch the iridescent surface. Its curves melted into my hands, like a cat who appreciated being stroked. I blinked and reminded myself that cars did not melt.

"I half expected Alex to have tampered with it," Russ said,

behind me. "Put explosives in the doors or sand in the gas tank, but so far it's behaving."

"It is so beautiful," I said, unable to look away. I knew, as I said it, that I was talking about more than the car. I was talking about Dec and his grief, which matched my own, and Russ, who I saw was beautiful in an odd and intense way, with a guarded expression and questioning eyes, and St. Hilaire, which seemed to be a place of inexplicable possibilities.

Russ brushed the roof with an appreciative gloved hand and then turned to me. "I'm Russ Griffin."

"I guessed," I said. His eyes were warm, yet he stood, tense, as if he were preparing to be attacked. It made sense that he and Dec should be such close friends.

He held his arm out toward the door. "You guys should come in."

Russ's room sat in the back of the house and was more library than bedroom. Aside from some basic furniture, the room consisted of wall-to-wall shelves overflowing with well-worn books on spirits and the occult. Native American, Ancient Japan, modern-day Ireland.

"Have you read all of those?" I asked, looking through the impressive stacks.

Russ nodded as if the thought of having unread books was alien to him.

"Russ is an encyclopedia," Dec said and laughed.

I pulled out a dusty, leather-bound book on Russian folklore and flipped through it. "This could be my grandmother's story," I said. "She believed all of these things."

Russ leaned over to examine the book. He pointed to a

vivid illustration of an owl. "Many cultures believe that owls allow you to see through illusions and into the real meaning of someone's actions. Russia is one of them," he explained and pulled up his shirt cuff. At first, I saw nothing, but then I saw a series of white dots that formed the shape of an owl on his wrist. It was unlike anything I had ever seen.

"How gorgeous," I said. "And I actually knew that about owls."

"I didn't," said Dec from behind me. He sounded hurt and exchanged an odd look with Russ.

I moved over to the desk and picked up a deck of tarot cards illustrated in muted grays, dark blues, and greens. There was a foggy, haunted quality to the images that was unsettling and made me feel like I was going to fall into them or that the shadowy figures were going to come to life.

I drew one out. It felt cold in my hand. "This one. What is it?"

Russ took it from me, while Dec said, "Let me guess, she drew Death, just like what happens in all the movies."

Russ flipped the card. "Nope. Not this time." Then he handed Dec the card I had picked.

"Figures," Dec said. "My favorite card. Wheel of fortune. Grab ahold of your own future and make your own decisions, Annie." He replaced the card into the middle of the deck. "So, what do we do now?"

Russ put the cards back in the box and wrapped it in a red-and-black silk scarf. Then he picked up the keys from his desk, and the echo of a smile crawled across his face. "Now? Let's go for a drive."

On a second viewing, it was still impossible to pin the Mustang down to one color. The shade was somewhere between the reflection of a full moon in a deep black pool, and the blue of a cashmere sweater Dmitry had been given by a European princess who had fallen hopelessly in love with him.

"She's a beauty, right?" Russ asked. Then he turned to me. "Sorry, Annie. I always wonder why we do that—why are cars and boats always 'she'?"

"Language was created by men," I said. "They seem reluctant to give it back."

Russ laughed and waved me into the front seat. The car came to life with a hum that sounded more animal than machine.

"Hey, what's the bass in this thing like?" Dec asked, learning over from the back seat to fiddle with the radio.

Russ pushed Dec's hand away. "That's the funny thing. I can't seem to get it to play." He flipped some switches and hit some buttons to prove his point.

"Odd that Ian would have overlooked that," Dec said. "He always seemed to push things too far. I would have expected a disco ball and a smoke machine."

Russ twisted in his seat. "True. He wasn't exactly one to leave things unfinished." The engine revved as we exited the town gates and hit the edge of the highway.

Next to me, Dec quickly changed the subject. "Annie is trying to find a mythical piece of music," Dec said. "The whole story is right up your alley, and we could use your help."

Russ's eyes floated up to the rearview mirror. It felt like the two boys were having a conversation that went beyond words.

"Of course."

As Dec filled him in, the car floated along the highway. It wasn't really floating, I knew. It just felt like we were not quite touching the road.

Then, with one hand, Russ dug into the pocket of his jacket, pulled out a small bag, and held it out to me.

"Those are runes," Russ said. "Pick one."

"Only you would do a reading on I-81," Dec said, with a sort of awe in his voice.

I dug into the bag and pulled out a worn, gray stone. It was etched with something resembling the letter *R* and felt cool in my hand.

"Ah, a journey," Russ explained.

"You mean because we are riding in a car?" I asked.

Russ shook his head and changed lanes. A car behind us raced to get a good look at the Mustang, and Russ slowed down to allow it. The driver gave him a thumbs-up as he drove off. "No," he continued. "More like the progression of your life. You know, destiny."

I nodded. Destiny seemed like a dangerous concept. I had no idea what the future held anymore.

"Go on," Russ instructed. "Pick another."

I stuck my hand back into the bag. The noise of the stones running between my fingers sounded like rain. This time, the etching looked like a *Y* or a broom.

For a minute, Russ didn't say anything. Then he pulled the car over onto the shoulder. Outside the tinted window was a meandering lake.

"Pull a third," Russ said, his voice serious.

I shivered but followed his instructions. This time, I was afraid to look at the stone before I handed it over.

Dec leaned over the seat between us.

"*Raido, Algiz, Obila.*" Russ repeated the words, an incantation in another language. "You're on a journey," he said. "You're changing. From one thing into another. And you have help, but…" Here he picked up the middle stone and rubbed it with his gloved thumb. "Be careful, Annie. Some help comes with a cost. Make sure you know what the price is and make sure you want to pay it. Make sure you want the people around you to pay it as well."

We all stared at the final rune. "What *is* that one?" I asked.

Russ picked up the gray stone and tossed it into the air. It seemed to hang there for an impossibly long time before it found its way back to his gloved palm. "That's the end of your journey," he said softly. "That's your home."

The car went quiet and stayed that way until we were back. The whole time, I considered the possible meanings of "home." Did that mean I should stay in St. Hilaire, if such a thing were even possible? Did I need to go back to New York? Book a seat on the next plane to Russia? In some ways, Russ's words brought up more questions than they answered.

And the strangest thing was that I believed him implicitly. It was not like reading a vague horoscope in the newspaper and laughing over the many ways it could be interpreted. This felt real. And Russ felt like someone I could trust.

20

DEC

As soon as we got to the house, Annie headed upstairs to practice on her keyboard. "Do you want to…" I was going to ask if she wanted to watch a movie or grab something to eat or hang out with Laura, but she was gone before I could get a word out.

So instead, I stood at the bottom of the stairs, watching where she'd been. "Coming up?" I asked Russ.

Russ came up.

"Thanks for not saying anything about my being a fan of Annie's," I said. "I know I have to tell her. I just haven't figured out how."

"Well, you could always…" Russ started and them my phone rang. Like before, there was nothing on the screen except **Unknown number.**

"I'm going to have to change my number," I said. "This is ridiculous."

Russ took the cell from me and examined the screen. He stared at it for a while before handing it back.

"What?" I recognized Russ's expression; it wasn't one I particularly liked.

"Next time," Russ said. "Next time, answer and ask the caller what they want."

I tossed the phone onto the desk, and it tumbled before landing facedown. "It's a wrong number or a robocall. When I answer, there's only silence."

I turned and busied myself with straightening the already straight crap on my bulletin board.

When I spun back around, Russ was staring at me. His eyes seemed darker than usual. "Ask what they want."

I swallowed. Russ's words sounded less like a recommendation and more like an order.

The phone rang again, the vibrations moving it across the wood.

Russ narrowed his eyes, and I reluctantly picked up the phone.

"What?" I asked and then had to clear my throat. "What do you want?"

There was a pause. A loud intake of breath. Then, against everything that was real or possible or true, my father's voice saying, "Forgive me, Daniel. Please. Forgive me."

My legs wavered. It was only luck that I landed on the edge of the bed. "What?" I asked. I wasn't sure if I was asking the caller, or the universe, or Russ, whose expression was unreadable.

142

Somehow, I found the sense to put the phone on speaker.

In my father's voice and through tons of static, the phone said, "Tried to protect you...the truth...I didn't mean... Tristan...ask him..."

"What?" I asked again, my nerve endings sparking like broken fuses.

The phone stayed quiet, filled with silence as deep as I'd ever heard, then a click as it shut off.

I set it down on the bed, my mind churning with possible explanations and impossible ones. It was easy to believe someone was playing a trick on me.

But it was my father's voice.

But that was impossible.

But it had happened.

I picked up the phone again and looked at the incoming call log. There was nothing there from today. Nothing at all.

The phone felt like fire in my hand. I threw it across the room, where it clattered against the bottom of my bookcase.

I could feel Russ's eyes on my back, but I couldn't look at him. Tears were welling up in my eyes, and I tried to brush them away as an idea struck me.

Throughout all our discussions over the years, all of the times when Russ sat and listened to me rage against St. Hilaire for my parents' deaths, there was one thing I never asked of him or even seriously considered.

I spun around. Pretended I wasn't having a breakdown of sorts. My father was calling. *Fine*. Wasn't as if the dead didn't reach out to those in St. Hilaire all the time. The only thing that made this different was that it was *my* family. *My* grief.

"My parents." I hoped Russ would fill the rest in. But if he knew where I was headed, he didn't say.

I frowned at him.

"Don't," said Russ, quietly in the voice he used with clients. It was supposed to make him sound trustworthy, supposed to put me at ease. Instead, it pissed me off. This wasn't how we were with each other. The way Russ sat, with his left hand tight around his right wrist, telegraphed his tension. I knew any attempts he was making to look calm amounted to bullshit.

"You don't know what I was going to say."

"Don't I?" Russ clenched his jaw and leaned over to grab the phone. Put it down. Picked it up again.

"Fine. Tell me, then," I demanded.

Russ's face filtered through a slideshow of expressions. "Dec, don't. You don't want me to do this."

Okay. He *did* know. I opened my mouth and used every bit of control I had to stop and think. *Did* I want him to do it? I knew I didn't want to fight with Russ. At the same time, what good were Russ's talents if he wasn't going to use them to help his friends? I hated asking for favors, but this…this was different.

Russ didn't give me time to sort out his feelings. "I don't know if I can contact your parents. But even if I could, even if we could get the Guild's permission, even if you actually *wanted* me to…"

"What if I do want you to?"

"I would do anything you asked me to. *Anything*." Russ's expression was complicated. It contained every secret we'd ever shared, every angry outburst of mine he'd overlooked, every facade of his I'd fought to see through. It cut me to the core almost as much as Russ's next words. "But you'd regret this. They wouldn't be the same. You *know* that." I winced as he threw the phone down on the bed in uncharacteristic frustration. "You *know* that."

I *did* know. I knew how people changed when they died. How they became angrier, more narrowly focused. Obsessed. I'd had to explain to customers over and over that the person they were trying to contact was probably only contactable because they had a bug up their butt about something specific. One issue that they just couldn't break free from.

Rationally, I knew it wouldn't be any different in my case, and that I was asking Russ to break the Guild's laws and probably screw up his chances of becoming Student Leader. But I wasn't feeling particularly rational.

"Easy for you to say. Your mom might be gone, but she's still alive." I regretted the words before they catapulted themselves out of my mouth. "I'm sorry. That was a shitty thing to say."

I watched the public face that Russ wore fight with his private one. I knew about this as well. Russ wouldn't hesitate unless there was a reason. Unfortunately, reasons weren't enough this time.

"I'm sorry," I said again.

I wanted Russ to tell me it was okay, or that he understood. Instead, he just stared across the room, so I kept talking even if it meant no one was listening. "What if Dad is sticking around just because he knows you could contact him? I mean, he called me."

"He said what he had to say." Russ's voice was even, but I could tell these words were a gift created by years of friendship. Plus, Russ had his own bond with my parents. He'd mourned them too.

"But I didn't understand anything he said. And seriously? Tristan? Who cares about him?"

"It doesn't matter what you care about," Russ said. "It's what your *dad* cares about that's kept him here. You don't get to play twenty questions with the dead."

"I don't have twenty," I tried to joke. "Only ten."

Russ's expression didn't budge.

I changed gears and tried the truth. "Look, he's back. Tristan—he's back."

A flash of pity crossed Russ's face before he could hide it. He was the only one I'd talked to about Tristan in years. "Ask *him* then," Russ replied. "Do what your father suggested and ask Tristan."

It took me a second to realize what he was suggesting. "Seriously? Seriously? You only say that because you've never tried to ask him anything."

"I could," Russ offered quietly. Then again, more urgently, "I *could* ask him. You know, if I could actually see him."

My shoulders relaxed slightly. We were okay. Or we would be. Fine, Dad had called from "the great beyond," and fine, I'd have to have an actual discussion with Tristan next time he showed up. But Russ and I would be okay, and that meant I'd be able to somehow get through the rest of this mess.

"I guess I'm stuck doing it, then," I said.

"Are you going to tell Laura and Harriet?" he asked.

"About Dad calling?" I considered his question. Harriet would be pissed about Dad calling me and not her, and Laura would just be sad. Sadder. "Not a chance."

"Didn't think so." Russ stood, his coat billowing around his legs as if a sudden wind had blown through the room.

I leaned over to pick up my discarded phone and froze when I saw the Guild's letter lying on the floor.

Russ would recognize the Guild's signature stationery. Russ was obsessed with all things Guild, and there was no way I was going to be able to hide it now. I could lie and say I'd received the standard invite, but Russ would know it was a lie, and we'd never lied to each other before. It seemed like a stupid time to start.

Before he had to ask, I picked up the letter and took a final look at it, hoping the words had changed. But no, the Guild was still asking me to discuss the Student Leader position. I thrust the paper in Russ's direction and turned away, not wanting to see the pain I was sure would cross his face.

"Your parents would be proud," Russ said after a minute, his voice inappropriately calm.

I winced at the idea of us getting into another fight. "I didn't ask for this. You know I have no intention of joining the Guild, much less leading the freaking Youth Corps, right?"

Russ stared straight through me, his dark eyes blazing against his chalky pale skin. The letter was still clenched in his hand.

"*Russ*—come on." Anger clawed its way through me. We were okay, damn it. We had to be okay.

I'd hoped we'd laugh over the absolute *weirdness* of the

Guild contacting me for any possible reason. But Russ looked pissed, and *that* was something else altogether. Russ didn't show his feelings. Sometimes it seemed as though Russ's dark coat muffled all of his emotions. Except now…

"You know I'm not going to *do* it," I said, hoping to break the tension.

"That isn't the point."

I heard the pain in his voice and grasped at anything I could to make it go away. "Maybe they haven't sent out all the letters. Maybe after what happened with Ian, they've decided to take on more than one Student Leader at a time, just in case one of them disappears or something."

Russ clenched his jaw so tight, I could see it.

"Fine," I said. "Okay, fine. Tell me what you want me to say, because I don't know how to do this. I don't want to argue with you, and this is totally fucked up, and you're the one I always go to for this sort of stuff only I can't this time because the letter should have gone to you, and we both know that."

I gave up and sank into my bed. My eyes were still locked on the letter in Russ's hand.

"I know you wouldn't ask for this," Russ said, his voice weary and careful.

I took the opening he'd offered. "Oh, god, what am I going to do?"

Russ turned, and for a minute, there was something unguarded in his expression. I knew Russ better than anyone and still couldn't identify all of the feelings he kept walled up.

"Have you thought of meeting with them?" he asked.

I leaned up on my elbows. "The Guild? No."

Russ nodded. He knew that would never happen. "But you have to find a way to tell them."

"Dear Guild," I started. "I have no intention of being part of your creepy archaic organization. Please take your position and shove it."

Russ cracked a hint of a smile, and I knew I should leave it there, but I couldn't. I owed Russ more than that. "I might just ignore it anyhow. I'm not planning on being in St. Hilaire when school starts."

I waited for a reaction, but Russ was silent for a long time. Too long. Maybe I'd finally found his tipping point. Maybe he could deal with me being distant and angry so long as I was *here*. I'd wrestled with hurting Russ and Laura in the abstract, but seeing the blankness on Russ's face was another thing altogether. "Russ."

Russ took a deep breath. "I know. It isn't like you've hidden it. You've been studying. Even this summer. And squirreling away money. It's just..." He closed his eyes. "I need that spot. I need to convince the Guild I can do it."

I nodded. "I'm sure they'll figure it out eventually. They may be creepy as hell, but they aren't stupid."

"Do you trust me?" Russ asked.

The silence in the room took on a life of its own. "Of course."

"Then believe me when I say I have a feeling things are about to change. And I need to be a part of that change."

I shivered. Russ wasn't talking about a normal "feeling" but something *more*, something St. Hilaire. *Exactly why I need to leave.*

"I believe you," I said, although I wasn't sure what Russ was asking for, aside from my trust and, *of course*, he had that. He always had.

I couldn't say anything, didn't know what to promise. The only thing I had was my plan to leave St. Hilaire, and that wasn't negotiable. But neither was my friendship with Russ. So all I could do was nod a promise I couldn't pin down. And breathe a sigh of relief when Russ nodded back, a trace of hope on his otherwise expressionless face.

RUSS

The water in Morris Creek surged. My heartbeat echoed the sound, erratic and out of time.

I clenched and unclenched my fists. I hated fighting. Not the physical throw of a punch, or the menacing stand between two opposing forces. *Those* I could handle. What I hated was the emotional rip and tear of feelings I didn't know how to quiet.

I'd considered telling Dec about my dream with Ian, considered telling him about running into Willow and the extent of this feeling I couldn't shake that things were soon about to change so drastically, we wouldn't even recognize them.

Then we'd fought and I'd been blindsided by the Guild's letter, stung by the reminder that Dec was going to leave regardless of what else happened.

Something rustled behind me, and I turned, expecting to see an animal moving against the leaves. Instead, Alex Mackenzie burst through a copse of ash trees, red-faced. "Hanging out with all your friends, Griffin?"

Then the leaves rustled again. Garmer came through them, panting, and laid his giant head on my leg. I ran my hand through the dog's wiry coat and waited for Alex to say what he wanted.

"I don't suppose it would do any good to tell you to leave him alone?" Alex asked, pointing at the dog.

I looked up from the animal and narrowed my eyes at Alex until he sat on a rock, just far enough away that one of us would have to move to connect with a punch.

"He hates everyone, you know. I mean, except me." Alex stared at the dog. "He was Ian's," he added, his voice full of uncharacteristic emotion. Alex hauled himself to his feet and paced along the rocky edge of the cliff. The same sharp features that had arranged themselves so dangerously well in Ian were jumbled and complicated in his youngest brother. "Have you heard from him? Talked to him or anything?"

It was impossible to know how much Alex knew about my previous dealings with his brother. "Look, Alex, Ian and I were..." It was impossible to finish the sentence. I'd never figured out what precisely Ian and I had been. The dog flipped onto his side and let out a huge groan. Pretty much how I felt too. "Ian's dead," I said. Sometimes the truth was all there was.

"I know that, dickhead. Seriously. Do you think I haven't noticed?"

The speed of Alex's pacing increased. "You should sit," I suggested. He seemed even more edgy than normal.

"You should fuck off."

I stood and buttoned my coat. "How about this? I'm going to leave and go do my thinking somewhere else. You can have this whole cliff to yourself."

I made it four steps before Alex rushed up and stopped me by saying, "I need my car back."

My hands wrapped about the keys in my pocket. "Didn't Ian ever teach you not to bet anything you couldn't afford to lose?"

"I didn't lose it," Alex said. "I just... You have to help me." His eyes were wide and desperate.

Suddenly cold, I pulled the edges of my coat tighter. I didn't *want* to be intrigued. I didn't *want* to care at all. But Alex had piqued my curiosity. "Help you do what?"

"Don't be dense, Griffin. I need you to help me contact Ian."

I almost laughed. "Everyone has tried. It doesn't seem like he wants to be in touch. Besides, you know the rules." Even to me, the excuses sounded like excuses.

"The rules? *The rules?*" Alex exploded. "Do you think the freaking Guild gives a fuck whether or not you talk to my brother for me? Not like *they* don't want to use him."

I looked up, unsure about whether Alex's question demanded an answer. Pink clouds dotted the sky. *A painted sky,* that's what my mother would have called it. I didn't often miss her anymore. But now, I wondered if she could see this same sky, wherever-the-hell she was.

Alex grabbed at my sleeve, and I reacted without missing a beat, pinning him against a tree, feet dangling like a pendulum. "Are you done?"

153

"I…" Alex sputtered.

I counted to five in my head, and then gently placed him back on the ground.

"That's something else your brother never taught you," I said. "Don't piss off the people you're asking for help."

As I walked back into the woods, I allowed the smug expression I'd put on for Alex's benefit slide off my face. As always, talking about Ian left me feeling strangely empty and defeated, as if there was something I should have been doing that I'd overlooked.

I didn't even know where to begin to find it.

Instead of going straight home, I detoured through the gates and into Buchanan. The old gas streetlamps flickered as I made my way to the deserted train station. According to the big clock on the outside wall, the 11:42 to Penn Station should have been about to leave, but the tracks were silent. There was a sign on the office that read ALL TRAINS CANCELED UNTIL FURTHER NOTICE.

I went to the side employees-only door and pulled it open.

"Sorry, we're closed," a voice called, and then my father came out of the office. "Oh, it's you," he said, wiping his hands on a towel. "Everything okay?"

My father looked concerned, and I hated worrying him, so I lied and said, "I'm okay."

"Mm-hmm," my dad said, knowing better. While it wasn't the first time, I didn't habitually show up at the Buchanan train station in the middle of the night. He put the towel down on a sawhorse and opened the small fridge he kept under the work-bench. "Drink?"

I peered into the darkness. "Depends. Do you have any-thing in there that doesn't resemble lawn?"

My father laughed, a sound that made my heart ache with its rarity. "I have some less healthy options too." He rummaged around and came out with a bottle of iced coffee.

I popped it open and took a long swig. "How come you have to be at to work when the trains aren't running?"

My father leaned against the workbench, a thick green smoothie in his hand. It resembled the stuff from my grand-mother's recipe. Just looking at it made the place where the needle had gone into my arm pulse, hungry for more.

"Style over substance, like everything in St. Hilaire. They don't make anything like these old trains anymore. And this is one of a kind. So I thought I'd give it a shot, while we wait to hear if there is a part that can be shipped in."

Of course, my father would make whatever random part was missing. It was just like him to create a solution to a prob-lem if one didn't already exist.

Dad continued. "The normal trains are still running, but of course they can't use this track, so no one will be coming in or leaving through the station. Not a big deal. No one comes by train this time of year anyhow."

I twisted the cap off the bottle again and took a deep drink of bitter coffee. "There's a girl. She was on the train the other day. She's staying at Dec's."

My father looked at me with meaning. "Ah."

"No, it's not—" I took a sip of coffee and regrouped. This

had nothing to do with any feelings I may or may not have for my best friend. "Everything feels off. Like it's shifting."

When my father's eyes narrowed behind his glasses, I realized how much older he'd gotten since we moved to St. Hilaire and he'd taken on a job that sucked up all of his time and energy. Seeing him every day made the small changes hard to notice, but the shop's too-bright light accentuated the tiny wrinkles that now lined my father's face. It made me wonder what my mother looked like now, if she still wore her hair in one long blond braid like Rapunzel.

"Welcome to adulthood," Dad said.

Was this all just down to everyone growing up and apart? We *were* all thinking about our next steps. Stay. Leave. Maybe it was just that simple, but it felt like *more*.

"Do you miss Mom?" I wasn't sure why, out of everything that was troubling me, I'd latched onto that one.

"I was missing your mother long before she left. I guess I kind of got used to it."

"Do you ever regret…" I don't know why I asked. Staying in Chicago had never been a real option.

"Russell, mistakes aren't necessarily made up of the things you screw up. It's the things you do for the wrong reasons that end up hurting. Or the things you don't do at all."

My father didn't have a spiritualist bone in his body. But he knew me and knew there were a lot if things I hadn't done. Things that were only half-formed in my mind. Things that seemed too risky. And the small smile on my father's face was urging me onward. Offering promises without words, that I would always have his love and support.

I drank the rest of the coffee. Vines of caffeine raced through me. It was barely after midnight. The night was still young after all.

22

ANNIE

The cursor on the screen blinked as if it were yelling at me. It was ridiculous that I was having so many problems telling my parents about Dmitry's death. I was long past the point where they would have or would want to have any say over whether I returned home or continued with my tour. And they had no personal connection to Dmitry, so it was not as if they would grieve.

Still, nothing I wrote sounded right. I was trying to share my feelings of loss, my wonderment over arriving in St. Hilaire, and the crescendos of excitement I felt when I thought about taking over Dmitry's search for some lost measures of music.

The truth was, nothing I could write would make my parents—who each worked ten hours a day, my father as a tailor and my mother as a housekeeper—understand. To them, I led a charmed life of travel and frivolity. After all, what was music? You couldn't eat it or live under its protection. I had long ago given up trying to explain that it created jobs and made people happy and less stressed and therefore *had* to count. They only saw my music as something foreign and mystical, something that existed to pay the rent.

I hit delete, started over, and then hit delete again.

This time, without reading the thirty or so new emails already lined up in my inbox, I grabbed my phone and sent Viktor a text, even though it was late.

I miss him.

The phone rang, as I knew it would, even though I had never hidden my frustration with people who answered voice-mails with an email or text messages with a call.

"*Zvyozdochka.*" Viktor's voice was warm and familiar.

"Hi, Viktor. How is everyone?"

He made a number of "tsk" sounds. "It's what you'd expect. Weeping and wailing and whatnot from all those pretty people who thought they were his friends."

It was easy to picture the spectacle of the funeral. Tomorrow the paparazzi would sell all of their photos, and it would be impossible to turn on a computer without seeing the pictures of black-clad mourners attempting to cry without ruining their makeup.

"He loved them," I said. I had rarely commented when the topic turned to Dmitry's social life since I always felt too young and sheltered to be worthy of an opinion. Still, I knew him well enough to know Dmitry loved nothing more than to be in the center of a crowd of adoring fans. He had the ability to make them feel as if they were long-lost friends, even if he kept the important and vulnerable parts of himself hidden.

"This is true, this is true," Viktor said. "Do not quote me to anyone, but I think he would have been happy that you were not here to see this."

I exhaled. "I am also happy not to be there. Is that horrible?"

There was silence on the other end. "There is something I must tell you, Anastasia."

I braced myself and then relaxed. Dmitry was already dead. There was not much else Viktor could say. "Go on."

I waited.

"Li Yong has entered the Hull competition," he said.

Of course, he had. It had been too easy to think of the most important under-eighteen competition without my biggest rival.

"I thought he was hurt," I said. I had heard about a fracture in his arm or elbow or something.

"I hear, underground, that a medical team is working with him. This is not American football. There is no penalty for taking shots of steroids or whatever. He's practicing."

The unspoken meaning in Viktor's words was clear: *And you're not.*

"Strangely enough," I said, running a hand over the bedspread, my fingers playing the familiar Prelude notes. "I *have* been playing here." I omitted the fact that it had been the Prelude I was playing and not the Tchaikovsky.

"This is your last year. Your last chance. Your parents are relying on you."

My stomach turned over. I did not need Viktor to remind me that my parents were counting on me to win the competition, counting on the money that came with that honor so my mother could work shorter hours and spend more time with my little brother.

"Viktor, what would happen if…" I was not sure I wanted to start down this path, but I could not help myself.

"If?"

"I have decided how to honor Dmitry's memory." The phone grew hot in my hand. I could picture Viktor pacing around his hotel room, weaving circles in the plush carpet. "I am going to find it, Viktor. I am going to find the rest of the Prelude."

With each word, my enthusiasm grew. Saying it aloud made my goal a true and tangible thing. I felt responsible for assuming Dmitry's search now. In my head, I heard Russ saying, "home." Maybe home did not have to be the place you were born. Maybe it was a place you tripped across by accident when your train broke down. Or maybe it was not a place at all. Maybe home was an idea that existed inside yourself or one you claimed to make it your own.

Or maybe it was a boy who took you to his mother's favorite waterfall.

"This is madness, Anastasia. Madness." Viktor's voice exploded over the phone. "Do you want to end up like him? Nothing more than fodder for gossip? A could-have-been?"

The sharpness of Viktor's words surprised me. Sure, the less Dmitry had been able to play, the more he obsessed over finding the Prelude. He found a ripped sheet in a market in Turkey. An old man humming a tune his grandfather had taught him in India. Piece by piece, Dmitry had sewn the music together like a quilt. I understood now how such a search could easily turn into an obsession. Understood how wanting to find a thing could take over your life, so the wanting became more important than the thing you were seeking. I would not let that happen to me.

"Dmitry was *never* a could-have-been and you know it," I said sharply. "I *am* going to do it, Viktor. I am going to find the Prelude, and I am going to win the Hull with it. And I will do it in Dmitry's name." Those were the reasons I said to him. Another, *perhaps spending all of my time practicing and traveling and never staying anywhere long enough to get to know a place or person isn't the way I want to live*, wound around my heart and made it surge not unlike how it did during my first step onto a grand stage.

"The search for that ridiculous music made him reckless, Anastasia."

"No, not being able to play made him reckless." I remembered too many mornings when Dmitry could not muster the strength in his hands to open the door to his bathroom, much less play warm-up scales. Those were the days when Dmitry was at his worst.

"The Hull is in eight weeks. You are out of practice. You have previous engagements. He searched for years and only had a measure here, a measure there, to show for it."

I knew all of that. Still, not one of Viktor's reasons felt like an obstacle. "I am going to do it, Viktor," I said again.

"You will not win," he said, his voice dark and serious.

Something within me fluttered. My head spun with trills and possibility. I said, "Watch me," and hung up the phone.

DEC

My father's words of apology replayed in my head and woke me in the middle of the night. Why Tristan? What connection was there between him and my dad? What was Dad sorry for? He'd said something about a choice. What choice? What was it about all of this that was so important, that it kept him tethered here?

I needed answers.

I needed to leave.

Those needs seemed mutually exclusive.

I embraced the feeling of every second of time moving forward toward my escape. But I knew time wasn't my friend. I had to act quickly. If I entered the Youth Corps, I wasn't sure I could get out. If the Guild would be pissed about me leaving

St. Hilaire now—and I knew they would be—that was nothing like what their reaction would be once I started training. Once I started leading.

But answers meant Tristan, and, of course, now that I actually had to talk to him, he was nowhere to be found.

I grabbed my cell and dialed Russ who always had his phone, and who always knew when I had to talk to him.

The first time, I hung up when it went to voicemail. The second time, I left a message asking Russ to call me back. The third time, I went all in and asked for a favor I knew he might regret granting.

24

RUSS

Sunlight. My brain screamed with the full force of morning. My head throbbed as if I'd led a hundred simultaneous séances. Opening my eyes was too much of a commitment, so I stretched my arms wide and tried to figure out where I was.

The wood under my hands was worn and knotted, and the blue looped rug was just where it should be. I was in my room. A good sign.

The familiar ancient herby smell of my house was another good sign. I felt around on the floor and found a pair of dark glasses. I put them on, counted to three, opened my eyes, and forced myself upright. The room exploded in a burst of pain-filled stars, but at least it was *my* room—even if it embarrassingly resembled a drug den with bits of rubber tubing and needles and half-empty syringes littering the floor—and I was alone and alive to see it.

I scooted across the floor until I could lean back against the side of the bed. Then I grabbed a warm, half-drunk bottle of water and gulped down the remainder.

Somewhere in this mess was the pad of paper where I'd written down my thoughts. I searched around and found it under my discarded coat, but the paper was filled with incomprehensible scrawl. I squinted, hoping to make the text coalesce, but the blue ink moved in waves like water at the creek.

I sorted through the sequence of last night's events. I remembered slowly and painstakingly separating some of the pages at the back of the notebook. And I'd finally found what I was looking for. The explanation for how to use the serum to contact the dead.

It wasn't guaranteed to work. Not all the time, anyhow. There was risk. Apparently, a lot of risk. It needed a serum *and* an antidote, which explained why there were two different liquids.

But I had the serum.

I had the antidote.

And I had the time.

I'd tried it—twice—to see how much of the serum I could inject without needing the antidote shot, pushing further than I should have, caught up in my first near miss. Once I thought I'd seen my grandmother, but repeatedly the fear of, well, dying brought me back.

I rubbed my arm and reached for my phone. It was noon. I didn't really remember much after 3:00 a.m.

There was a missed call and two messages from Dec, and,

absurdly, one text from Alex Mackenzie. Alex's words were laughably hostile, but it was Dec's message that actually concerned me. I shook my head, sure I misunderstood what he was asking for.

I always knew if he truly needed me, and I hadn't felt anything. I was sure it was fine. I needed to call him back. But, first, I needed a shower. Then I needed coffee. Besides, how much could have happened in just twelve hours?

"Can we come in?" Dec asked.

"Yeah. Of course." I stepped out of the way as soon as I regained control of my limbs—it was like I was moving in slow motion while the rest of the world continued in normal speed—and watched Dec and Annie walk over to my grandmother's threadbare floral sofa and sit, legs pressed together.

I lowered myself carefully into the narrow armchair across from them. My hair was still wet. I should have put on something heavier than a T-shirt after I called and told Dec that he and Annie could come over. My bare arms felt too sensitive, my scattered emotions written all over them for anyone to see.

My memories of last night were still incomplete, but my body certainly had been through hell. My voice shattered when I said, "Do you want—"

"Tristan is gone," Dec interrupted. "He wanted to talk to Annie a couple of days ago. But when we stepped out of my room, he just vanished. I figured he'd be back, but I *need* to talk to him about my dad."

Dec rubbed his dark-circled eyes. He obviously hadn't been sleeping. And I recognized the expression on his face. It was waking up in a hospital bed and not knowing how you got there; finding out your parents had died; searching through your head for weeks of memories and finding only a suffocating emptiness. Alex might have wanted to talk to Ian, but Dec *needed* to find Tristan, so I had no choice but to help him. Even if my brain felt like pea soup. Even if we were about to break a ton of Guild rules.

I nodded; even *that* hurt. "Give me an hour, and I'll meet you at your place. See if Laura is free too."

Dec glanced at Annie and said, "Can we do it here? I'd rather not worry her."

I wanted to remind Dec that he hadn't actually been much use as a medium over the past couple of years, that Tristan was obviously at home in Hampton House, and that when it came to young mediums, more was always better than less. But the nervousness in Dec's voice stopped me.

Here it would be, then.

"Sure." I did a mental check of my room, making sure I'd cleaned up the evidence from last night. "Upstairs. I'm not sure when Dad is due home."

"Wait." Annie swung her head from Dec to me. "What's happening?"

I caught Dec's eyes and saw myself there. Saw the last three years. The ebbs and flows of our friendship that would need to sustain us once Dec left St. Hilaire. No, there was no way that I wouldn't help. I said, "We're going to hold a séance."

Dec and I sat across from each other on the floor, only a single candle between us. Given the choice, I always went for darkness.

Guild rules dictated that since we were both under eighteen, we could only participate in séances with adult family or Guild members, so we were taking a risk. I had to hope that no one would be looking for any sort of activity or disturbance since Tristan hadn't set off alarm bells yet. And, unlike some ghosts, he was unlikely to rat us out.

I handed Annie a rain stick. She tested it by turning it over a couple of times, and we listened to the beads inside rush around like music. Then she nodded from her place under the window.

St. Hilaire mediums had many ways of inducing a trance. I knew some who drank until they almost passed out. There was someone who used to hit his head against a wall until he hallucinated. Some went without food, played a drum, or stared into a flame. Most simply tried to relax and listen.

The goal of all rituals was to lose yourself. I always knew when it was working because I'd stop being aware of my physical body.

Dec and I joined hands on either side of the candle. With our fingers wrapped tight around each other's and the heat from Dec's skin distracting me, I had to fight hard to focus and remember why I was here.

We closed our eyes in unison as Annie began to move the rain stick slowly one way, then the other.

I tried to quiet my mind. I focused on my breathing. *In. Out. In.*

Dec whispered, "Tristan, Tristan."

Out. In. Out.

When it was this quiet, it was easy to hear your heart beating. Feel another's pulse where your index finger sat against his wrist. Notice the tension in your shoulders.

In. Out.

Time began to dart and weave in and out of my mind. Had it been a minute? Twenty? Tristan had to know we were trying to contact him. Ghosts weren't usually elusive; in fact, they were more often driven, obsessed with connection and whatever goal had kept them tethered to the living.

So, where was Tristan?

I opened my mind.

"Damn it," Dec said, pulling his hands back. "This is a fucking waste of time."

I opened my eyes and shivered.

Dec shook his head. "This isn't going to work."

"Dec," I said, watching his jaw clench. "There are other ways." Common sense said I should leave it alone. Recharge. Recover. But I couldn't deny the excitement of running an illicit séance.

I stretched, hoping to get my bearings and to assuage my guilt. I'd had a good year—a successful year—sitting in on a ton of Guild séances. Now, when my best friend needed me, I couldn't pull it off for him. It wasn't like any medium could draw spirits 100 percent of the time, but it was frustrating as hell to have failed now.

"What in the world is that?" Dec said, pointing to my arm.

I looked down to see my arm trickle green-tinged blood. It

had stopped aching, so I hadn't noticed this latest development. "Rough night," I said, swallowing hard.

Dec's eyes blazed. "Is this what you're doing when I can't find you? Is this your 'other ways'?" He reached out and grabbed my arm. I snatched it back. "You know what?" he said. "Never mind. You want to light candles and chant some stupid words over and over, that's fine. You want to call upon the spirit of your dead grandma, go for it. But if this is how you're getting stuff done, forget I asked for your help."

I closed my eyes. Tendrils of energy still crawled through my veins. I was tired and ever-so-slightly shaken, sure, but beneath that, I felt strong. Powerful. I could do this. *All* of this. Dec would realize that it was worth the risk. And so would the Guild.

I got up, pulled my desk chair over toward the bed, and sat on it backward, leaning my arms on the wood. Memories from last night started to surface. People. In this house. No, not people. Ghosts. I'd seen them. Not for long, but still. No séance. No stupid Halloween special effects. I had to make Dec understand the significance of what had happened. The potential. If I took a full dose…if I had someone to administer the second shot…

I licked my lips. "Dec, calm down. I know how to do this. I'll need your help. Both of yours, actually. And a day. Just give me a day. But I'm sure I can do it."

I stood, drew up my shoulders, and stepped over to Dec. So much was riding on this one conversation, I saw that now. Dec knew it too because he wasn't asking questions. Instead, he was spring-loaded. We were so close.

I knew everything in the world was riding on my next words, so I chose them carefully and spoke them softly for Dec alone. "Your dad loved you. He did this for a reason. Tristan is here for a reason. *Annie* is here for a reason. You can't just turn your back on them. You said you trusted me, so stop freaking out and let me help you."

There was a war playing out in Dec's eyes. What he wanted versus what he thought was right. I watched him, my arms tingling with hope.

Dec bit his lip and, after a while, said, "I need to know what Dad was talking about." His voice was quiet, painful in a way that made my heart ache.

"I know," I said. He had to understand I'd never put him at risk. This was all me.

"Fine," he said. And then again, "Fine. We'll try. Once. But we stop when I say to stop. You aren't turning yourself into some sort of psychic vegetable for me."

I'd done it. It was happening. And when it was over, somehow, someway, we'd let the Guild find out and my future would be clear.

25

RUSS

"Okay, so think back to what you remember from school," I told Dec the next day. "Ghosts are the leftover bits of a person. They leave a trail. They're usually focused on one thing: revenge, someone they loved, or guilt."

Dec drummed his fingers on his pants. I couldn't imagine what he'd told Annie about all of this. "Like Dad."

I nodded, determined to stay calm even though I was buzzing with unspent anticipation. "Usually that obsession is so strong, I can almost see it."

"But you don't see it?" Annie asked.

"No, where Tristan is concerned, I don't see anything." I grabbed my backpack and settled in on the floor. "That's why I think the… We failed yesterday." It wasn't as if I was worried the

Guild was bugging our houses, but where ghosts were involved, you couldn't be too careful.

I avoided Dec's wide eyes as I pulled out the black pack and then two prefilled syringes with lengthy needles. "Here's the plan." I peeled off my coat and pushed up my sleeve. Sparks of electricity raced through me, too eager for the shot. "I'm going to start with one of these." I pointed to the first syringe, which was filled with murky liquid. "Hopefully, I can find Tristan and convince him to show up and talk to you like he normally does. But I won't have a lot of time. Give it seven minutes or so, and then, one of you is going to have to stab me with this." I pointed to the other syringe.

Dec reached out and picked up the first syringe, shaking it. The fluid was greenish-white and thick, like it wasn't sure it wanted to be liquid and not a solid. "What the hell is in that?"

There would have been no harm in telling him. It was all herbal, after all. But plants had been used for medicinal purposes for centuries, and this wasn't the time for a history lesson. I took the needle back. "Old family recipe."

Dec went green. "Look, this isn't…" He paused. "The way."

I took the cap off the thin long needle. The longer Dec fixated on what I was about to do, the more freaked out he was going to get. I needed to get on with it. "Relax. I'm on top of this. My grandmother wrote about it in her book."

Dec gasped. "Well, forgive me if that doesn't exactly make me more comfortable with you becoming some sort of drug addict."

Next to him, Annie reached out and put a hand on Dec's back. Something about the two of them together was both comforting and unsettling. I swallowed down a complicated type of

174

jealousy that was as thick as the serum. Then I busied myself, prepping the other syringe. "Remember, seven minutes."

Dec lifted his hand for the syringe and froze. I knew this would be hard for him, but couldn't figure out how to make it any easier. He was just going to have to trust me.

"I'll do it," Annie said and took it from me. "Dmitry was on a ton of pain meds. I used to give him shots all the time."

"Wait," Dec said. He looked so scared, it made my head ache. "What happens if we don't give you the other shot after seven minutes?"

I downplayed the risk. "If you do it too soon, this probably won't work. And if you do it too late, it probably won't work in a different way."

I nodded at Annie. She nodded back. I only caught a glimpse of Dec's pale face before I said, "Well, there you go," and jammed the needle into my arm.

I jolted. Not awake, but something else.

I was still in Dec's room, only I wasn't. Dec and Annie were faded, moving slightly out of time as they hovered over my body, the needle still sticking out of my arm. It was the strangest thing I'd ever seen. I couldn't let myself get distracted by this either; If I understood my grandmother's notes, I only had seven minutes.

I mentally reached out and felt for the energy of the room. As I did, a small child skipped through the wall. An older woman rocked in a chair in the corner. A couple stared into each other's eyes and talked, their voices quiet, far away. I blinked. Then blinked again.

A boy my age sat in the window seat, worrying at the end of his velvet cuff with one hand. The other held an impossibly thin cigarette that gave off the scent of citrus.

"Hey," I said quietly.

The boy's eyes opened wide. They were the green of the twinkling fairy lights my mother used to hang on our fire escape in the summer. There was something almost bioluminescent about them. Dec had never mentioned how otherworldly he appeared. "Tristan, right?"

He nodded.

I wanted to race over and fire questions at him, but I knew that wouldn't work, so I approached slowly and gestured for Tristan to move over on the bench.

"Dec is looking for you," I said, sitting down.

"I know." We both turned to watch Dec and Annie staring at the timer on his phone, although we couldn't hear their conversation. "It's rather funny, isn't it?" Tristan said. "That he should be looking for me after all this time. He usually acts as if I'm a nuisance."

There was a lot of truth in his statement, but I had nothing useful to add. Dec was never going to embrace a spirit.

"I want to help," I said.

"I've seen you here, you know," Tristan said abruptly. "With Daniel. He trusts you. He's never trusted me. I wonder why that is."

I knew what he was saying was true. "Trust isn't really his thing."

Tristan stared at the glowing end of his cigarette. "I know what he wants to discuss with me, but I promised I'd never speak about it."

That wasn't something I was expecting to hear. "His father—" I began, but Tristan cut me off.

"Tell me what I am. I don't think I'm a ghost," he said, words tumbling over one another. "That's my price. Tell me what I am and I'll talk to Daniel."

My pulse raced. Back in the room, Dec and Annie moved to the floor, sitting next to my body, their eyes locked over my slowly rising and falling chest. I pulled my attention back to Tristan.

I thought a moment, then asked, "So, when you aren't here, what is it that you see?"

Tristan's green eyes rolled to the right the way people's do when they're trying to grasp onto a memory. "It's hard to sort out what's real and what's a dream sometimes." Then he closed his eyes. His voice dipped to a whisper. "It's dark. Even when I *do* open them. It's been dark for a very, very long time."

I weighed my words, sifted through specifics, and carefully asked, "Do you know what happened to you?"

"What happened to me?" Tristan's eyes snapped open, and in them was a steeliness that hadn't been there before. "Of course, I do. My father happened to me."

26

DEC

"He said he'd talk. So where the hell is he?"

Annie put a hand on my arm. "Perhaps this is difficult for him."

I wanted to be as forgiving as Annie, but truth was, I wasn't. I was pissed. I'd spent, no *wasted*, two whole days waiting for Tristan to show up to explain what Russ meant when he said that although Tristan hadn't shared much, he wouldn't be surprised to hear that Tristan had been cursed.

"The only rules that dictate how a curse will behave is the wording of *that* specific curse. Maybe something in the wording of the actual curse explains why no one else can see him besides you, your father, and Annie. Maybe it explains how he can interact with some things and not others. Maybe it also explains why he doesn't remember much." Russ had repeated in a number of different ways.

"What could be so difficult?" I mumbled to Annie. "All Russ did was talk to him." Then I glared at Russ. "That *was* all you did, right?"

Russ's head jerked up from the floor where he'd been stacking up rune tiles in random order. "Yeah. We just talked. But after all this time, Annie can see him. And I've just invaded his space. He's probably more used to solitude than he is to people giving him the third degree."

Damn Russ for making sense all the time. "Fine," I said. "But meanwhile, I'm still waiting. What do you suggest we do now?"

Russ gathered up the runes and looked at me as if he had all the answers, but before he could share them, Laura came flying into the room. "There's... I mean, Dec, you need to come with me," she insisted. "Fast."

Whatever I expected to find in the music room, it wasn't Alex Mackenzie holding a rusty hammer and trying to pry the back off my piano. "How did you get in here?"

He looked up at me with eyes that had the same wild, trapped look that characters had in the horrible black-and-white horror flicks my dad used to love.

"I'm feeling generous," he said, voice quivering. "I'm going to give you a second chance. That isn't what you want to ask. What do you really want to know?"

I hated when a Mackenzie was right. "Fine," I said, trying again. "What the hell are you doing?"

Alex stared at the hammer as if he were seeing it for the first time. "I'm not Colin," he said. "I'm not the smart one. And I'm not Ian. I'm nothing like Ian."

I froze, unsure of the correct response.

He can't see or hear me, said a voice in the corner. Tristan. I jumped slightly, and Alex swung the hammer around, missing the piano by inches.

Figures he'd show up now.

I held up my hands and took a small step forward. "Alex. Let's talk about this."

"Really? You just want to sit and chat like old friends? We aren't friends. Screw that."

That made the second time Alex had gotten it right. The third if you counted the fact that he had admitted he was nothing like his brothers, which I didn't, because it was just so damned obvious.

"You came here," I said warily, "for a reason."

"I need your piano. Just part of it, actually. But this damned piece of crap isn't working." Alex waved the hammer around the room.

My hand wandered to the cell phone in my pocket. I wanted Russ to come downstairs. Russ would know what to do. He would solve this whole thing.

The curtains in the corner rustled as Tristan moved and Alex spun at the noise. "I need to talk to my brother. The flipping Guild has crapped out on reaching him, so I just need one freaking part of your piano."

"Ian?" My mind spun. What the hell did Ian have to do with my piano? "Alex, look…"

"You and your friend. You both think you're such hot shit."

Right on cue, Russ descended the stairs. "I'll take that as a compliment," he said, eyes sliding over me. Then he walked up to Alex and stuck his hand out, waiting for the hammer.

I was sure there was no way Alex was ever going to hand over the only thing that was keeping Russ from beating the crap out of him. Yet after a wordless staring contest, Alex passed the tool over to Russ, who tossed it to me before grabbing a large amount of Alex's shirt, pulling him outside, and slamming the door.

27

RUSS

"You know what your problem is?" Alex tried to poke a finger into my chest, but when I narrowed my eyes, he wisely took his hand back.

Still, I was surprisingly curious about what he thought my problem was. I wasn't even sure *I* knew the answer to that. "This should be good," I said. "Please. Tell me."

Alex took a step forward. "Your problem is that you think you can do anything. Your problem is that there isn't one single thing you're afraid of."

I mulled that over. I didn't think I could do anything; but thanks to my dad, I was a firm believer in hard work. And there were definitely things I was afraid of, I just had no intention of sharing them with Alex. "Why do you care?"

"I'm right. Tell me I'm not right."

"You're not right," I answered.

Alex let his face slide into its usual sneer. "Name one thing, then."

I considered how other people I knew might have answered the question. Dec was afraid of being trapped in St. Hilaire. My father was afraid of lightning. A girl from school was afraid of germs. Virtually all of the summer visitors were afraid of dying. My fears weren't so tangible. "Wasting time," I said, deflecting. "I'm afraid of pointless conversations that go nowhere but around in circles."

Alex spun around in frustration. "Your arrogance is going to bite you in the ass someday."

I was glad I was getting to him. "Promise?" I grinned. Done correctly and at the right time, a grin always disarmed people.

Alex slapped the brick wall next to my head. I didn't move. "I know things about you, Griffin," he said. "I know your secrets."

The challenge in Alex's words excited me in a strange way, and I echoed his instruction. "Name one thing, then."

Alex scowled. "I know about your little drug cocktail. I know you need to shoot up to have any sort of contact. The great Russ Griffin is a fraud."

Okay, that's interesting. I wondered how Alex knew, but really, I'd been collecting and brewing herbs for the three years I'd been in St. Hilaire. And herbology had been my grandmother's specialty. Given what some people were into, our family's process wasn't *completely* unusual.

I waited a beat, then slipped under Alex's arm and walked

to the other side of the porch. "Okay, first off, that isn't entirely true. Though I know you don't care about truth, so what? You want some? Is that it?" The hungry expression on Alex's face said that I'd hit a nerve. "That *is* it. This is your way of asking me for a favor." I began to laugh and could tell it was the right reaction to get under Alex's skin. "Don't you ever learn?"

"Not a favor." Alex's face grew red. "It should be for everyone to use if it works. I'm going to tell the Guild. I have Ian's gun and next time I'm going to…"

Alex ran out of words, obviously unsure of *what* he was going to do. The only thing keeping me from laughing again was the idea of him having Ian's gun, an old family heirloom Ian loved to use to shoot targets in the woods behind his house. Ian said it relaxed him. I doubted it had the same effect on Alex.

I took a deep breath. "I doubt you'll go to the Guild. In case you haven't noticed, they aren't exactly happy with you at the moment."

Alex tried a new tactic, one that I'd never heard from one of the younger Mackenzies before. It teetered on the edge of honesty and looked like it took a great deal of hard work. "Look, man, I just need to talk to my brother."

Why did everything always come back to Ian? I decided to give Alex an equally honest response. "The drugs won't work for you," I said optimistically. "It's some weird family thing. My grandmother liked playing chemist in her free time. I couldn't share it with you even if I wanted to. Which I don't, by the way."

I wandered down the steps and Alex followed.

"Everything is so fucking easy for you," he said.

I turned to face him. There was no reason to tell him how

there was nothing easy about being deserted by your mother. Or about hearing the dead except when you really wanted to. Or about having feelings for your best friend. Alex had no idea.

"You're in a town full of mediums," I said. "I'm sure that any number of them would be happy to contact Ian for you. Given all the shit your brother was into, I'm sure some of them already have. Go ask them for help."

Alex ran a hand through his hair. "I'd rather it was you. I mean, I don't like you, and I know you don't like me. But at least I know you can pull this off." It was probably the nicest thing I'd ever heard Alex say until he added, "Even if you *do* need to get high or whatever first."

I was already bored of trying to explain. "What do you want to talk to him about anyhow? And what does that have to do with Dec's piano?"

Alex bounced on the balls of his feet. "I just need one freaking string from the piano. Ian told me I needed it to talk to him on my own. Look, it doesn't matter. There's just some family stuff. Okay?"

The desperation in his tone chilled me, and the whole string issue made no sense. But the thought of having an excuse to use the serum again, to explore whether I could actually contact Ian and succeed where the Guild had failed, was exciting as hell.

Ultimately, Alex Mackenzie had done the one other thing necessary to secure my help; he made me curious. I wanted to know what the heck Ian had told him. I said, "Tell you what. You stop breaking and entering Hampton House and you know, being a general pain in the ass, and I'll do it."

It was rare to be aware that you were standing on the edge of a precipice between your past and your future. Rarer to be in control of that process.

As I stood alone in my room, I felt my future calling to me. I felt all the energy that St. Hilaire had to offer swirling around me as I stirred it into a mixture of herbs and fluids, heated it according to my grandmother's recipe, and shot a measure of it into the pulsing vein in my arm.

28

DEC

"My room. Now." I started up the stairs, but had to turn around to make sure Tristan was following. He never made any sound when he walked.

I closed the door behind us. "I'm sure you already know my dad called on whatever ghost phone he has access to. *And* the connection sucked, *and* he said something about the truth *and* said he was sorry, *and* then he mentioned *you*." I held my stomach. I felt like I'd just been sick, with nothing left but a horrible taste in my mouth.

"Oh," Tristan said as he sank onto the floor. "*Oh*."

"Don't you dare freaking disappear on me again," I threatened.

Somewhere a clock ticked too quickly although the only

manual clock in the house was the grandfather clock down in the reading room, too far away to hear from my room. The sound made my head hurt.

"No," Tristan said. "No, I wouldn't."

I needed fresh air but froze in front of the window. I couldn't read my parents' gravestones from here, but I could picture every chiseled word, every chip of mica in the rock.

The accident, though, was just out of the reach of my memory. An empty space where the trauma should have been. It had been months after the accident before the memories of being in the car with them came back to me. Hearing my father's voice had shaken something else loose. Some fragment of recall I hoped was false and just my brain's way of putting the pieces of the puzzle together.

I cleared my throat, trying to make a path for the words. "Why did you save me and not them?"

Tristan pulled on the bottom of his jacket and looked away. "Someone very wise once told me that you shouldn't ask questions you don't want answers to."

It was true, then. I held my hands against the glass and traced the outlines of the unseen text. I didn't look at him because I was afraid he could read my anger. "I need you to tell me, Tristan. I need to know."

Surprisingly, Tristan agreed. "I suppose you do. *Now.* Just understand that I'm breaking a promise."

I glared at him. "Tell me."

Tristan stood and started running his hands over stuff on my desk. He played with a silver bookmark of my mom's. Then he picked up a book of Poe, put it down, and messed up a

Rubik's Cube it had taken me months to solve. Then he must have run out of things to touch because he spoke. "Years ago, there was a boy. I was honored to call him my friend. He asked me for a favor."

A new wave of anger washed over me. "You let my parents die because of some favor?"

"I didn't. I mean." Tristan rubbed at his eyes. "Please believe I never thought…"

"Thought *what*?"

"Daniel, your father was my friend." Tristan's voice was small, and when he turned, his eyes were wide and pleading.

My parents claimed not to be able to see Tristan. My mother took me to doctors, seers. *They were ashamed of me. They thought I was crazy.* That's what I'd believed, anyhow. And they had done nothing to convince me I was wrong aside from telling me I could never mention him.

"My father could see you? Why? Why can I see you, but Laura and Harriet can't? Why can Annie see you?"

"Daniel, I'm sorry, but I don't know."

Tristan ran his hands through his hair, and I worried he might vanish before I got the answers I needed. "So, what was the favor?"

"You have to know, Daniel, that everything I've done, I've done because your family is, was, in some ways, the only real one I've ever had."

I couldn't move. Couldn't really breathe. "Can we cut through the drama? Just tell me."

"Your father was the first one who ever said he could hear me. He was the first who spoke to me. Before that…" Tristan wrung his hands. I thought people only did that in books. "It was horrible. Truly horrible to be here, surrounded by people and yet be completely alone."

"To be here. You mean in *this* house?"

Tristan nodded but didn't speak.

"Just how long have you been in my house?" I asked. I wished Russ were still here. I wished I'd never started this conversation. Most of all, I wished my parents would have been honest with me.

"Being here is most of what I can remember. Everything before that is…" Tristan searched for a word, "…dark. But I remember your grandparents."

The room chilled and I shivered.

"And your great-grandparents," Tristan continued, wincing slightly. "It was a long time to go without anyone speaking to me."

"So no one could hear you until my dad. And what? You just started talking to him?"

Tristan took a drag on his cigarette and the room filled with lemon, the scent of my childhood in so many ways.

"He was just a boy when I realized he could hear me. Trust me, Daniel; you don't know how it feels to be invisible to everyone. You end up talking to yourself just to feel like you're actually there. I used to sing to him when he couldn't sleep." Tristan's large green eyes looked up at me and twinkled slightly. "And I did the same with you, only he actually appreciated it."

With Tristan's words came a memory. A song. One I used to ask Dad to sing. Usually, he'd make some excuse. His throat hurt. He couldn't think of the tune. Once he started, and I'd complained, "No, sing it the way you normally do," and Dad had stopped and rushed off to help Mom with some task.

Neither Laura nor Harriet admitted to remembering Dad ever singing to them.

Because he hadn't.

"That was you?"

Tristan nodded.

It was too much. "I don't get it. If Dad could hear you, why did he lie to me? Why did he make me think I was crazy?" As I said the words, I realized this was the issue at the heart of it all. I'd always felt broken and *wrong*. Worse, my parents had let me believe in my own wrongness. I was losing them all over again.

Tristan put his hand on my shoulder.

"He loved you, Daniel," Tristan said. "He loved you enough that he stopped speaking to me after he realized you could not only hear me but see me as well. You have to understand. The Guild was both disturbed and fascinated to learn your father could hear someone they could not. He was in his early teens when they began to study him, thinking he had some sort of untapped potential. It wasn't easy for him, Daniel. The tests were more invasive than you might imagine. And when they introduced him to your mother…"

"What?" I'd always been told my parents had met on a class trip taken by students at St. Hilaire High and a school in California where my mother had gone.

Tristan paled, if that were even possible. "Oh, I thought you knew, but I guess…"

I looked at him. Looked through him. He wasn't going to get out of sharing what he knew.

Tristan crossed his arms and looked sheepish. "Your parents were introduced to each other by the Guild. Matched, might be a better term. Even then the Guild was trying to strengthen medium talent by, pairing up, shall we say, mediums from strong families."

Everything I knew. Thought I knew. My entire history crumbled with Tristan's words. I sunk to the floor. *The fucking Guild. I should have known.*

"Daniel," Tristan continued. "Your parents truly did love each other. And you. They adored all of you. And that was the point, really. Your father's entire life was here. But rather than subject you to the same fate he'd suffered, the testing and all, your father committed himself to pretending he couldn't hear me either. It took a while, but eventually the Guild accepted that whatever spirit had been haunting your father had simply gone away. And thanks to your father, they never learned you could communicate with me."

I looked up, right into the blinding light of a full moon, unsure if I could take in any more information. "So what was the favor Dad asked you for? To save me?"

For two years I'd been burning with guilt and curiosity, anger and longing. Yet I'd never considered that Tristan held the answers to my questions. The moment surged and retracted; the wait for Tristan's response was impossibly long.

Tristan squeezed my shoulder, and I didn't need any of St. Hilaire's magic to know how much his next words were going to hurt. "There was no time to deliberate that night, Daniel. Your father hadn't spoken to me in years, but I was always there. Around. I can make it as far as the gates. Or well,

I could. Anyhow, when he called out and asked me to pull you from the car, to make sure you were safe, well, you see, I had no choice. He'd been my friend, after all."

My vision clouded. I started to recoil from Tristan's hand, but then leaned forward again, allowing it to stay, taking what comfort I could. Then I began to cry.

After I called Russ to fill him in on everything Tristan had told me, I sat at the piano and hammered the keys, hoping the chords would tell me how to forgive my parents.

How to forgive Tristan.

How to forgive myself.

ANNIE

There was a pressure in my chest and an *affrettando* pounding in my head that would not let me sleep.

The guest room did not have a clock, and I could not bring myself to turn my phone back on, but the high full moon was bright enough for me to pull out my keyboard, put on my headphones, and begin to play.

Dmitry had the keyboard made for me. The keys that were normally white were blue. The black keys, silver. They winked like a starry sky.

Scales came first. Then a couple of pop pieces that I had played at Union Station. But I gave in quickly to my urge to work on some of the most difficult sections of the Prelude. In truth, ever since I arrived in St. Hilaire, it had been the only thing I was interested in playing. Maybe that was due to Dmitry's message. The Prelude had been a link between us unlike any other. And there was the fact that finding the rest of it had been his dying wish after all.

No matter what I was playing, Dmitry had always insisted that each note needed to matter on its own. So, as I played, I tried to take stock of each tone, each pause. In a way, I became the music. *This is mine*, I thought. And it was. The music moved through me thicker than blood.

I was lost in the notes. My breath came faster and faster, this was the sensation that made all of the hard work and sacrifice worth it. This feeling of being alive, truly alive, and filled with passion and energy was what every artist yearned for. My vision tunneled. It was impossible to believe that the room could be misty, but I swore I felt a haze of water, smelled rain. The air was warm, fruity, and exotic.

Dmitry had equated music and sex often enough to pique my curiosity, but my basically friendless life meant that I had only experienced the first of those. It was more than a little terrifying to imagine that anything could possibly be as all-encompassing and intense as this.

I followed the music to its known conclusion. Then the conclusion that the necklace had given me. But the music did not stop. My hands did not stop.

I forced my eyes away from the keyboard. Musical notation appeared on the mirror in ghostly handwriting. I stared at it. Listened to it as my hands turned the script into music. The countermelody wasn't what I would have expected. Instead, it was better, brighter, so much more dynamic and filled with life and light and beauty than I could have dreamt. I played it again, and a third time, committing each note, each pause, to memory.

It was not the entirety of the Prelude, but it was more than I had previously. More than Dmitry had been able to find.

It was a new world.

Caution, I heard. Just the single word, but I felt nothing but joy.

Elated, I pulled my hands from the keyboard and rushed to Dec's room. I knocked twice, but no one answered, and as I turned to leave, the door swung open.

"Hello?" I called.

The door opened wider. I did not want to snoop, but I poked my head in. Lemon and smoke swirled in the air.

In answer, came the question, "What's the most beautiful sound you've ever heard?"

As my eyes adjusted to the semidarkness, I recognized Tristan, backlit against the window, his long fingers splayed on the desk.

I walked the rest of the way into the room. Dec's clock read well after two, but he was nowhere to be seen.

I considered Tristan's question, thought of the waves crashing against the shore of a beach in Bermuda, Dmitry saying, "You are one-of-a-kind and the world will recognize that," a nameless street performer in Venice expertly playing a mournful violin piece, the wind chimes outside my parents' house that my father had made from scraps of metal when I was a little girl, the music that I had just played. "I do not know how to narrow it down. How about you?"

Tristan smiled, looking both elegant and mischievous. "I

don't know either," he said, brushing long blond bangs out of his heavy-lidded eyes. "I'm sorry; I shouldn't have asked you that."

"Why?"

"You shouldn't ask people questions that you can't answer yourself."

That seemed like a good way to lead your life. "So, tell me something else," I asked. "Something you *can* tell me."

Tristan's eyes lit up. "I had an elephant."

"An elephant?"

"Yes, it was made of wood. One of my tutors carved it for me when I was small. It was the one thing I insisted on taking with me." Tristan's brow furrowed. "Oh, but I'd really rather not talk about that. Let's find another topic."

"How about music? Do you enjoy music?" He stared at me blankly, and I was out of ideas. "Do you know where Dec is?" His room was so *lived in*. I had a small suite of rooms off Dmitry's apartment, but I was not there very often, and Dmitry filled his space with showpieces and antiques that were not my style. He threw parties and entertained financial backers, but there was so little of him actually out on display. Only his piano room had any personal items, and they were so tightly wedged together—photos and books and trinkets from around the world—that there was barely a clear space aside from the keyboard.

A bulletin board near the window caught my eye, filled with an intriguing mess of ticket stubs and buttons, fortune cookie slips and photographs. There were so many tiny *things*—so many pieces of stories that together would form Dec. I wanted to somehow tie them up and get to know him.

"He's downstairs," Tristan said, behind me. "Can't you hear him?"

I moved to put my ear to the door. Strange that I had missed the music in my excitement. Then I turned back to Tristan, but it was the inside of the open closet door that caught my attention. At first, I was sure that my tired eyes were playing tricks. But as I stared, the reality of what I saw soured my stomach.

The poster on the wall was framed, ripped, and faded, but was obviously cherished.

The comfort I had felt since I got off the train evaporated in one strong gust. "He lied."

Tristan's face contorted in confusion until I pointed behind the door. At the poster with my face on it.

"Oh," Tristan sputtered. "Is that bad?"

I looked away and could not speak, so I just nodded. Then I rushed out. As the door closed, I heard Tristan say, "But, the bells of Notre-Dame. I remember now. That's my favorite sound. I remember."

I sat at the top of Dec Hampton's stairs, listening to him play the piano, anger lodged in my stomach, a stone forming in my heart.

30

DEC

"You don't have to go."

I'd said it at least four times, but it was the only thing I could think after Annie announced she was going to find somewhere else to stay until the train was fixed.

I stood in the doorway of the guest room, watching while she packed her keyboard and small backpack. Every muscle in my body ached in panic. She hadn't looked at me. She just stared down at a white shirt she kept folding and unfolding.

"I think I do," she said, holding the fabric still.

"But I don't want you to," I said, aware my needy response was the wrong one, but unable to stop myself. "I mean, you're welcome here. We want you to stay. All of us."

She took a deep breath and spread her fingers out on the

silk. I wanted to reach out and touch them, so I'd have that memory to hold on to when she was gone and St. Hilaire was back to being the same awful place it had always been.

Annie touched the charm at her neck and pressed the button. We listened together as it played the last few known measures of her piece.

"You could have told me," she said. "I thought…I do not know what I thought. But you seemed like someone different. Someone not like everyone else."

For a millisecond, I was happier than I'd remembered being in years. I *hadn't* been the only one to feel like there was something between us. Sure, maybe it was only friendship, but it wasn't like that was nothing.

But then the realization came crashing back on me. Of course, somehow, I'd fucked it up.

"What did I *do*?" I asked.

Frustration danced across her face as she told me how she'd been playing and how the notes had appeared and how she'd come to my room and found Tristan, well not only Tristan, but—

I got it. "The flyer. You saw the flyer."

Annie nodded.

I had nothing to lose, so I laid it on the line. "I admit to being a fan of yours. For a while now. More than a fan. Wait, that sounds wrong." I closed my eyes. Pictured the flyer. Remembered the stolen moments in the library, escaping to the tune of her piano. I forced myself to sit on the bed and look into her hurt eyes. I forced myself to be honest. "You saved me. You and your music. I'm not being melodramatic. The last few years have sucked. Listening to you play kept me from going off the deep end. Well, mostly. And then you show up at my door and ask for help, and there was nowhere in those conversations for me to tell you how much of my free time I've spent in the library listening to you play the Prelude."

Annie dropped her shirt to the bed. I couldn't read the look in her eyes.

"I'm sorry I didn't tell you, Annie. You can hate me if you want. But please don't go." I tuned out everything except for the quiet in the house, the beat of my own heart. I tried to feel what Russ always picked up on, the vibrations. I was a Hampton, after all, and had to have *some* ability running through my veins. "I think what you're looking for is here, in St. Hilaire," I said. "I don't think you would have gotten that message anywhere else."

My words sounded odd to my ears, but down deep, I knew Russ was right. *Something is happening.* And it was happening at least in part because Annie was here. And whatever it was, needed to happen and then get itself sorted-the-hell out so I could leave.

"Please?" It wasn't so much a question as it was a message to the universe. She had to stay, simply because I really wasn't sure what I'd do if she left. Not before I did.

Annie's expression melted into something more complicated as she moved closer to me.

I braced myself, knowing I deserved whatever came next. But she got closer, so close that I could feel her hair against my cheek when she gave me the smallest, most cautious, and most wonderful of kisses.

I waited, frozen, for her to explain, but all she did was give me a small smile, then turned, leaving all of her belongings unpacked, and walked out of the room.

31

RUSS

Alex Mackenzie paced around my room, sneered at my books, and glared out the window at the Mustang as if it were a misbehaving show dog.

He was already on my last nerve; now, I had to rely on him to stick a needle in my arm.

"There are no promises this will work," I reminded him.

"Way to cover your ass."

I drew myself up. "Watch it. I'm doing you a favor."

Alex made a face, but sat down and shut up.

I pulled the black bag out of my closet, feeling a familiar surge of anticipation. I took out the first vial, the one I hoped would allow me to contact Ian, and drained a third of the solution into the potted ivy next to my desk. The plant shook and shuddered with the knowledge of generations of Griffin seers. I shook and shuddered with the realization that my supplies were running low.

"What are you doing?" Alex asked.

No way was I going to tell Alex I was concerned he wouldn't bring me out of the fugue at the right time and was hoping a slightly smaller dose might do the trick. I lied and said, "I don't totally have the doses sorted out yet," then broke the top off the second glass vial and poured a quarter of it into the first, betting that might be enough to keep me from dying should Alex bail.

My arm pulsed. This was it. Contacting Ian would get Alex on my side, and Alex couldn't keep his mouth shut. Soon, everyone would know I was the one to contact Ian, that I was Guild material.

No use wasting time. I filled the syringe. "Here goes nothing." Then I plunged the needle into my arm.

The room blurred unpleasantly and then pulled itself together before starting to fade around the edges. The ache in my arm transformed into a rush of pleasant heat. I heard myself moan and felt my eyes shut.

A noise in the room pulled me back.

I was used to reading things and people, not summoning them. Tristan had already been present in Dec's room when I'd gone looking for him. This was different. I wasn't totally sure how I was going to go about finding Ian when everyone else had failed.

The room was suddenly crowded as I searched face after face. Time felt slippery, and so it seemed like less than a minute before Ian walked out of the wall near my closet, looking surprisingly alive for someone who had been dead for a year.

"About freaking time, Griffin," Ian said.

He looked exactly the same as he had in my dream. I forced myself to blink. "Death obviously suits you," I said. It was a confession I hoped would buy me some goodwill.

Ian bent forward, close enough that his cold breath caressed my cheek. "Good to see you too. Awake this time, I mean."

"Stop." I took a step back. "I'm here about your brother."

Ian folded his arms across his chest and smirked. Even dead, he was apparently unused to rejection. "Colin? I figured he'd be relieved I was gone."

Yeah, probably. "No. Alex."

"That makes more sense. I keep meaning to check on the little bastard, but"—Ian waved to the barely visible ghosts behind him—"I've been busy."

"You're dead," I reminded him.

"No shit, Sherlock. Doesn't mean I don't have things to *do.*"

I took a harder look around the room. It looked like the aftermath of one hell of a party, apparently that also hadn't changed for Ian since he had died.

"I don't get it. You could have done anything you wanted. Why bother..." I didn't finish the question. He hadn't shared the manner of his death before, and I didn't expect him to explain it this time either. But time was running out.

Ian cocked his head. "Curiosity, Griffin, curiosity. It's fucking real. All of it. And don't tell me you haven't lain awake in your little twin bed with the Batman sheets on it, wondering."

I clenched my teeth and got to the point. "Alex is out of control. He wants to talk to you."

"Yeah, man, well. The gene pool kind of ran out before it got to him, you know? He couldn't contact a dead rat. I told him the one way I thought he could get in touch with me, but he was never good at following directions."

"The Guild has been spinning their wheels trying to reach you, you know," I said while I replayed Ian's answer. *One way I thought he could get in touch. One way.* I was missing something. "I get you not talking to them, but any chance you could work a conversation with Alex into your schedule? Like now, perhaps?"

"I *told him* what to do. He's halfway there. I left him my freaking car."

I weighed the pluses and minuses of telling Ian I was the new owner of the Mustang and decided against it. Sometimes the key to dealing with Ian boiled down to simply having more information than he did. But I had to wonder. "The other half of your little plan wouldn't have to do with Dec Hampton's piano, would it?"

Ian smiled and reached out to run his fingers over the collar of my shirt. "You dressed up for me. Nice," he said. "So, let me guess. You're still stuck on Hampton, and he still has no clue, right?"

My head spun. Talk about places I was not going to let this conversation go. I snapped my fingers in front of Ian's face. "Focus. Your psycho little brother has your gun."

Ian's hand dropped. I had his attention now. "My gun? Shit. Mom should have locked that thing up."

"You need to do something."

"What? Haunt him?"

I glanced back from the shadow figures in the room to where Alex was sitting, agitated and looking at his watch repeatedly as if he thought I was trying to screw him over.

"Can you?"

"If you remember, I can do whatever you want me to," Ian said. I knew he wasn't talking about Alex, and when I didn't reply, he simply said, "Well, no. I don't know. As I said, I'm kind of busy."

The room shifted suddenly on the edge of my field of vision. Something else shifted inside, pulling and dragging me away.

"What's the one way Alex can contact you?" I asked as the room started to swim. "Tell me, Ian. What's the one way?"

Ian's words were garbled as everything went dark.

I shook my head. Then regretted it. I vowed to lie still until the waves of pain subsided. Only they didn't.

Alex stood above me, a dripping needle in his hand.

My arm hurt like hell. Hopefully Alex had no plans to go into medicine. The only upside was that the pain in my arm distracted me from the pounding in my head. I needed to cut back or take a couple of days off. Now that this was over, I was going to need to get my shit together for a while.

My mouth was as sore as if I'd had all of my teeth pulled without Novocain. "You cut that a bit close," I mumbled.

"Did you see him?" Alex waved the needle around.

"You can put that down now." Although at some level, I was pleasantly surprised Alex had followed my instructions, I still didn't enjoy seeing him with anything that could be used as a weapon.

Alex scratched his head and stared at the needle as if he'd forgotten he was holding it. He tossed it across the floor. "Did you *see* him? Did you talk to him? Stop stalling and tell me."

There were many things I could tell Alex about his older brother, but none Alex would appreciate hearing. Instead, I asked him the same question I'd asked Ian. "What does Dec's piano have to do with Ian's car?"

Alex shook his head. "No way. If he didn't tell you, I'm not going to."

I struggled to pull myself up, determined not to vomit. "I have the car, Alex. And I'm trying to help you."

"Ian said not to tell anyone."

I leaned over and felt the room spin. When it stopped, I grabbed the needle off the floor. "He started to tell me, but, you know what? Never mind." Against reason, I hauled myself to a standing position and held onto the desk. "This has been interesting. Fun, even."

Then I turned toward the door, faking stability, and gestured Alex out.

"Wait. That's it?" Alex's voice rose.

"Yes," I snapped. "That's it. I saw Ian and told him you wanted to talk to him. But I can't help you if you're not going to help yourself."

Instead of waiting for Alex to answer, I crawled into bed on top of the covers, closed my eyes, and waited for Alex to leave.

I dreamed of New York City. And of Ian. We toured the city, Ian playing tour guide and dragging me to see the hidden tunnels under Central Park, the view from the Empire State Building, an underground sake bar.

Then Ian, remarkably sober but still technically dead, looked at me and said, "Why didn't we do this earlier? You make a great travel companion."

I'd spent copious amounts of time building up my defenses against Ian. I wasn't keen on bringing them down now, particularly when I had work to do. "What use would Alex have for Dec's piano? How could he use that to talk to you?"

"He doesn't need the whole piano." Ian laughed. "Just the G string."

I looked past Ian's searing blue eyes, his carnivorous smile, and his overwhelming intensity, to notice that, unlike most ghosts, Ian was mostly opaque. I'd hovered over Laura's shoulder while she was designing Hampton House's latest marketing pieces and watched as she'd changed the images from 100 percent to 50 percent so the background could peek through. *That* was what most ghosts looked like, depending on the strength they'd had while living. Ian was an unnerving 90 percent, only his edges—and possibly his morals—were fuzzy and insubstantial.

"Pay attention, Griffin. Seriously; take notes if you need to," Ian said. "Talk your boyfriend into giving you the low G string from his piano. Then pull the stereo out of the Mustang and slot the string in. Somewhere. You're smart. You'll figure it out, not like *I* had an engineering degree or anything, and I built that whole damned car. Alex will just have to take it from there on his own. That was kind of the point."

I bolted up in bed, covered in sweat. The clock read three in the morning. Blue light bathed the room. I wasn't completely sure I was alone.

Unlike most dreams, this one didn't fade as my eyes adjusted to the sensation of "awake."

But I knew this. Alex wasn't going to stop until he talked to his brother. It didn't matter what the younger Mackenzie needed to discuss with Ian, I had to arrange a meeting. A real meeting, unless I was going to let him hack up the piano. The problem was going to be talking Dec into playing along and not killing myself in the process.

I grabbed my phone.

ANNIE

Insomnia and I were old friends. In truth, insomnia was a friend of all performers. But even when I had been deep in rehearsals, my sleep was rarely interrupted by a piece of music repeating in my head.

Now, ever since I arrived in St. Hilaire, I found myself falling asleep, but waking up an hour or two later, when I would hear the Prelude playing relentlessly.

I stretched, then regretted it. My arms had begun to ache with any movement, which meant I was only playing with my fingers instead of my whole body. Tense muscles were the penalty for bad form.

Still, I got out of bed and grabbed my keyboard and headphones. I stretched again. I would play. Not the Prelude and not the Tchaikovsky, but some of the show tunes I had learned for the Union Station performance.

I began the medley from *Porgy and Bess*, but my fingers slipped over the keys as if someone had greased them. Lightning flashed against the curtains, and I allowed myself a minute to sit and stare out the window.

Why had I kissed Dec? Where had the courage to do that come from? I had no regrets, but it felt like a kiss that only could have happened in a strange place like this. As if there was something in the air giving me permission, making me bold.

I tried the medley again.

The notes sounded wrong. My keyboard could not be out of tune, so it had to be my playing. I slowed down. Started over, with no luck. Slammed my hands on the keyboard and winced at the discordant mess that blasted into my ears.

In the back of my mind, the Prelude played on. I closed my eyes and tried to focus. Knowing I was going to find the rest of the Prelude and then hopefully win the Hull, made everything clearer. Weeks ago, I would have been appalled at the arrogance, the pure absurdity of the idea. But now, here, it felt right. It *was* right, in a way. I knew I would succeed as certainly as I knew my life was about to change. As certainly as I knew that kissing Dec was the right move. Russ said I would "find my home" or "go home" or something like that. I did not know where home would be, but St. Hilaire was the right place for now.

I hummed the last few measures of the Prelude's performance arrangement. Then I added on the measures from the necklace. Then the new measures from the mirror. I was not a proficient singer, but I could carry a tune if forced. Dmitry had even dragged me to karaoke a couple of times.

I repeated the measures, trying out different tempos. Neither the music in my charm nor the music from the window had been notated, and so I hummed at the same speed the known sheet music had ended on, a *rallentando*, a gradual decrease in speed.

But as I came to the end of a measure, I was sure I had heard a voice.

I hummed the notes again. Then I heard them repeated back as a soft echo.

"Who is there?" I asked.

There was no answer. Perhaps I should have been afraid, but I was not. I hummed the notes a third time. The response came quicker, stronger, and to my delight, kept going.

It carried through the notes I had seen on the mirror and *oh, allegro, of course*. I saw now, how the piece was coming together. And miraculously the humming continued. Around and around the music spun, the notes were almost tangible.

Sing with me. I'll show you.

The voice, vaguely familiar, but distorted, came from all sides of the room at once. It picked up the melody at a place I knew well, and I joined in, the two of us carrying on a duet. I noticed changes in phrasing now. Ever so slightly different from how I had been playing, but so much more meaningful.

I wished I could record it or at least write it down, but somehow, I knew I was going to be able to play this from memory. After all, this song had been flowing through me for years.

Dmitry, I thought. *Oh, how I wish you were here.*

As my first tear fell, the room went silent.

As the second tear fell, I realized that in spite of the gift I had been given, the music was still incomplete. I still had far to go.

As I wiped the third tear away, I gave into the ache in my stomach and the insomnia, and made my way to the piano downstairs.

33

DEC

"Why are we here again?" I asked. In truth, we weren't anywhere in particular. I'd been lying in bed, replaying the kiss with Annie over in my head, when Russ had called and begged me to meet him outside. He picked me up and drove outside the city gates, pulling over near the entrance to a deserted winery, which had closed after blight destroyed their crops last year. Served them right. Harriet had tried to warn the owners, but they'd laughed her off the property.

I glanced at the clock on the Mustang's dash. "You know it's three thirty-one in the morning, right?"

Russ turned in the driver's seat. "Were you sleeping?"

Yeah, I wish. "No, I kept thinking I heard Annie playing that damned Prelude, but…"

Russ raised an eyebrow. His intuition or vibrations or whatever no doubt told him I was awake.

"Fine. But seriously. Why *are* we here?"

Russ turned his face toward the fields of dead vines. The lightning flashed creepily in his eyes. "About six months before Ian died…"

"Ian *Mackenzie?*" The name alone made me itchy and uncomfortable. Russ seemed drawn to him in the same way he was drawn to his grandmother's book of recipes. Like it could either kill him or seduce him. Or kill him in the process of seducing him.

"Do you remember *that* summer?" Russ asked.

I stared at him. *Of course,* I remembered that summer.

When Russ first arrived in St. Hilaire, he'd immersed himself in every bit of mumbo jumbo the town had to offer. And then he'd…lost it. His father was working all hours, and Russ had started playing poker with Ian *a lot.* And one night, right before the gates closed for the season, my phone rang, and the only sound on the line was Russ's voice saying my name and that he was in the woods. I'd never run so fast. I found Russ alone and disoriented and, over Harriet's protests, brought him back to Hampton House.

I stayed silent. There was no reason for me to answer Russ's question. He already knew the answer.

"That night I lost…" Russ's voice cracked. He stopped a minute to regroup before finishing, "…a series of poker games to Ian."

"Go on."

Russ closed his eyes, and when he opened them again, he

was a study in control. "We hung out. That's what Ian wanted for winning. For me to hang out with him."

Of all the euphemisms Russ could have come up with, "hung out" was probably the stupidest. "Hung out? What? You built model airplanes together or baked cookies or…?"

Russ narrowed his eyes. "Do you want a play-by-play, because…"

"No. Stop."

The silence between us threatened to blow out the car windows.

"Look," Russ said eventually. "It wasn't like that. But you knew Ian and I had been dancing around things, and it was kind of a relief to be able to use the bet as an excuse. Anyhow, not that it matters, but we *were* just hanging out that night. Talking, mostly." I couldn't look at Russ's face, so I concentrated on his wrist where he was rubbing his tattoo so hard, I wondered if it would come off. "I know you didn't like him. I get that. But I actually did. Mostly. In small doses anyhow."

All the reasons why we never discussed Ian Mackenzie.

"We were in the woods the night you found me because I had some botany assignment for school. Honestly, Dec, that's the last thing I remember; I don't even remember calling you. The next thing I knew, I was at your house. Ian and I didn't talk much after—I couldn't figure out how to both spend time with you and spend time with him. You always got angry, and Ian was… too much. I had to make a choice. Then…then it was too late."

"Why are you telling me this now?" I didn't bother to keep the hurt out of my voice. And I wasn't even sure what the cause of it was. Anger? Jealousy? Nothing fit.

There was a glint of determination in Russ's eyes when he said, "Alex isn't going to stop. You know that, right? He's totally unhinged."

"He's a Mackenzie. It was bound to happen at some point."

"Well, I've had enough of it," Russ said. "And he's just going to keep coming after the piano until…"

"The piano? Until what?"

Russ ran a hand methodically over the stitching in the Mustang's upholstery and wouldn't meet my eyes. "Alex wants to talk to Ian. That's what all this is about. The piano is some weird part of that. So I tried to facilitate a meeting between him and Ian so he'd leave you and the piano alone."

I had to walk away before I did something I'd regret. The door opened soundlessly and the field's oppressive darkness enveloped me as soon as I was away from the car. My anger surged in a way that scared me. I balled my fists and waited for it to pass, but the rage just curled hard into my stomach.

Behind me, a car door opened and closed. "Dec?" Russ called.

I spun around. "Why are you doing this?"

Russ leaned his hands on the car's hood. "Because," he said softly, "you don't have a lock on grief."

His words stung. "No. Of course I don't. By all means, tell Alex freaking Mackenzie how sorry I am for his loss."

Russ charged around to my side of the car. "Do you think I don't understand how messed up you are about your parents? Do you think that I, of all people, don't understand that?"

I didn't answer, but I didn't walk away either. I wanted to forget that this was my best friend, but I couldn't. However angry and hurt I was, I knew what Russ meant to me as well as I knew anything. "Fine," I said. "You understand."

Russ paused, then said, "I'm not making excuses for him. For them. For any of them. But if I can stop Alex..."

"And cement your position with the Guild, right? That's really it. Because no one has figured out how to contact Ian, and if you do it, you'll be their golden boy." I reached out and grabbed Russ's hand, pushing his dark coat up his arm until the green-tinged puncture mark was exposed. "Is it worth this?"

Russ's eyes narrowed, and he pulled his arm back, but his voice stayed even. "It can't only be worth it when it's to help you. It's either right or not."

My jaw tightened. "See, that's where we differ. I told you I don't want you putting yourself at risk for me. Or for Annie. And certainly not for Tristan. And yes, I probably screwed up by asking you to help me. I'm sorry. Really, I am. But Alex Mackenzie doesn't give a shit whether you live or die. And neither does your beloved Guild, who, by the way, I just found out set my parents up in the hope they'd have little medium babies."

I watched as Russ's entire body tensed. "Bloodlines," he said. "That's what Rice was talking about at the festival. Strengthening the community through bloodlines."

I wanted him to condemn the idea, make the obvious connection to the racial and religious purity programs we'd discussed in history class, but he stayed silent, biting his lip and pissing me off. I filled him in on everything else I'd learned about my dad being able to hear Tristan and Tristan saving me after the accident. Then I said, "If they screwed my dad over, they'll do it to you, too. Why don't you see that?"

In measured words, Russ replied numbly, "Dec, there are bigger things at play here."

We were at a stalemate. The wind picked up and blew Russ's coat, black as the night, around until he resembled some old movie vampire. He was so, so still. I felt a flash of awe and fear, not necessarily fear *of* Russ, but *for* him.

"What bigger things?" I asked. "Is it about Ian Mackenzie?"

Russ turned, his mouth opening with an answer he swallowed and left unspoken. Instead, he said, "You're leaving, Dec. But my future is here in St. Hilaire. I have something I'm good at doing. But I could be great at it, and that means being hired by the Guild, because there *is* nothing else here. At least then, Dad wouldn't have to work himself to death every night."

"But the Guild? The Mackenzies? Is that what you want to be? Do you want to paired up with some girl to have super spawn?"

Russ pulled back as if I'd slapped him.

"Or," I whispered, "do you want to *be* the next Ian Mackenzie?"

Russ hesitated for an impossibly long time. "Of course not. I want to change it. All of it. Make it better. I agree with you that the Guild is out of touch. Disturbing even. Do you think I want what happened to you and your dad to happen to anyone else? Between this whole bloodlines thing and..." Russ shook his head, at a rare loss for words. "Look, to change the Guild, I need to work from the inside. And to do that, I need your help."

My chest constricted. Sure, I'd been there for Russ when he and his father had first moved to St. Hilaire. But Russ had always been there for me too. And in all that time, I'm not sure he'd ever asked me for anything. Not directly.

I reached out and grabbed his wrist. I could swear I felt the white owl tattoo flutter against my fingers, but perhaps it was just Russ's pulse racing. "Promise me. Promise me you're not going to get sucked in. That you're actually going to fight against this shit and not just become some Guild pawn."

Russ raised his eyes to mine. "I swear to you, Dec. I swear if I can get in, I will do my best to make sure that none of this happens to anyone else again."

I swallowed hard. I either needed to believe him or… There was no choice, really. "What do you need?"

Russ steadied himself against the car. "This is going to sound strange, but…I need to borrow a string from your piano. I'll replace it, I promise. And I'll tell you everything as soon as I sort things out. Please?"

The piano again. I wanted to know what was going on, but Russ was asking me to trust him. *Asking.* And so I said the only thing I possibly could to make the anger in my stomach uncoil. I said, "Fine."

34

DEC

"It isn't the house, Daniel. I realize that now," Tristan said.

I'd been fighting against my lack of sleep and running through some algebra equations for the GED, two things I pretty much hated, so Tristan's appearance wasn't entirely unwelcome.

I spun and leaned back against my desk, folding my arms across my chest in the posture that always seemed to work for Russ when he was trying to look both bored and intimidating. "So, what it is?"

Tristan swung his legs a little, clearly proud of himself. "Well, me actually. I think I'm the reason she's here."

If there were any part of my stomach that already didn't feel suspended on a tightrope, this pushed the last of it over the edge.

"What?"

"I think what I was feeling wasn't Annie, and it wasn't the house. It was the piano," Tristan said as if he was proud to have finally figured it out. "Well, the piano now that Annie is here."

"The piano?" *Again?*

"*My* piano. Yes," Tristan replied.

"*Your* piano?"

Tristan got up and went to the window. He turned, pulled a bidi out of his pocket and lit it. Then he went back to the photo of Annie and stared at it, eyes wide open and wanting.

I couldn't take it anymore. "Oh for god's sake, sit down."

Tristan sat on the edge of the bed. "I'm starting to remember more things, Daniel. From before."

"Before?"

"Well, I haven't *always* been here, have I?"

My shoulders tightened with a sense of foreboding. Or maybe it was fear. Somehow, growing up in St. Hilaire hadn't immunized me to either. "So, where were you?"

"Well, I remember camels. And monkeys. And there was a place where I used to walk through lemon trees," Tristan said, wearing a proud-of-himself grin. It was too much.

"What does this have to do with the piano?"

Tristan crossed his arms, his voice apologetic. "I'm not entirely sure. I'm not actually comfortable being in the same room with it. Have you noticed? I just realized *that* was the thing. Anyhow, it doesn't matter because I know it's important. And it's important to Annie."

The way Tristan said her name as if they had some secret connection was the final straw. "Well, *your* piano is about to lose a string. Russ needs it."

223

"A string?"

"Pianos have those, right?"

"Yes, but."

"Well, Russ needs the…" I racked my brain trying to remember which string Russ actually needed. It was possible he hadn't mentioned which one. "One of them. Something to do with Alex Mackenzie."

Tristan paled. "No. Daniel, no."

It was hard not to feel smug. "Sorry, it's a done deal."

"You have to let me speak with him," he pleaded.

"With Alex?"

"No." Tristan shook his head. "Russ. I mean, with all of you. Of course."

"I'm not stopping you. Go talk to him if you want. I doubt anything you say will make him change his mind. This *is* Russ we're talking about."

"What if he can't see me anymore?"

It was hard to imagine Russ not being able to do something. "We'll find out, I guess. I think he's coming by this afternoon to grab the string."

"Oh." Tristan's face fell. "Well, then."

It almost made me feel sorry for him.

35

RUSS

The steel string was cold. It was such a small thing, a bit of cable wrapped around an ivory piano key, but it was putting up a large fight. Once we pried off the back of the piano, it was easy to see the screws that needed to be turned in order to release the peg that held the string. A few turns, and it should have released.

The screwdriver slipped for the zillionth time. "Oh, hell." My hands were clammy. Just a couple of hours and I could go home. Have a shot. No, a tenth of a shot. Just enough to take the edge off.

I tried again. *It's a screw. How hard could it be to yank out?*

Behind me, Dec paced impatiently. I pulled my head out of the piano. "You okay?"

Dec startled as if he'd forgotten I was there. "Yeah, just thinking about something Tristan said to me, claiming the piano was his."

"You might have mentioned that earlier."

Dec shrugged apologetically. "I didn't want to believe him."

I stood and stretched. "Well, something doesn't want us to have that string." We both stared at the piano as if pure will-power would convince the string to fly out. "Should I try to find him again?"

My pulse quickened. My arm was sore, my head slightly dizzy. I knew I shouldn't take another full shot, but getting Tristan to agree to give the string to Alex and stopping Alex from harassing Dec while proving myself to the Guild added up to the best of all possible reasons to take the risk. I knew he wasn't going to stop at this, and I hated to think how far he'd take this obsession.

Annie and Laura walked in, laughing at some shared joke, but Annie's expression changed drastically when she saw the backless state of the piano.

"It's temporary," I said, even though I wasn't sure it was technically true. If we were able to get the string and install it in the car's radio, who knew if it would come back out? Conceivably any store-bought string should work in the piano, but it was unlikely that a store-bought item would work in Ian's car.

Annie glanced at me and then walked around to the front of the piano as if she couldn't stand to see the surgery taking place on its rear. I needed to get this over with.

"Okay," I said, "I'm going back in."

I ducked down, looking for another way to attack the offending screw, when Annie said, "Wait. Wait."

I stood back up to protest, but then, without warning, she sunk to her knees, her hands traveling over the old wood.

"What is it?" Dec asked.

She held her hand out to me, and I thought she wanted help up, but realized she was gesturing for the tool, so I handed it over.

The rest of us watched as she dug the metal point into a gap in the wood and worked it around. The panel bent as if it were fighting to stay on.

"I have read about pianos with false front pieces put in for smuggling." Annie stood and handed the screwdriver back. "Still, I cannot," she said. "I mean, I *can* do it, but I would rather not. Will you?"

I nodded and replaced the tool's tip into the gap of wood and pulled slightly. A gasp of stale air escaped. I pushed harder on the panel, which slid rather than pulled off. It stuck, but one good slap moved it enough to see inside.

I pulled hard on the door and then reached in and pulled out a wrapper of some sort, decorated with…elephants.

"Hey! I recognize that design from those bidis Tristan smokes. Tristan?" Dec called.

"I told you not to open the door," said a voice on the other side of the room. Tristan moved toward us slowly, his green eyes never leaving the door in the wood. I had wondered if I'd be able to see him now without a shot. I guess I had my answer. "I told you not to, Daniel," he repeated.

I followed the path of his eyes to the piano. "I don't understand."

Tristan swallowed. There were years, decades, centuries perhaps, of pain in his expression. "I've been…remembering."

Tristan sat hard on the floor next to Annie, who reached out and took his hand. He leaned his head on her shoulder.

This was a proving ground, the type of stuff I'd face with the Guild, and I knew I had to take charge. Everyone was waiting for me to tell them what to do.

I asked Tristan, "Are you able to talk about it?"

He nodded slowly and answered, "Since you came to see me, my memory has been coming back."

"What do you remember?"

He sat in silence so long, I wondered if he was going to be able to tell us anything useful.

"Tristan…" Dec implored.

"Oh, yes, right, I…" he answered sadly. "I remember a fight. With my father. I remember a curse."

And there we were. Had Tristan just realized this? Would he have shared it earlier had the drug not whisked me back? Is that what he meant by his father being the thing that happened to him?

"This might be a long shot, but I have to ask. The Prelude," Annie said. "Is it yours?"

"Of course." Tristan nodded. "And the piano. That, too. I wrote the Prelude on it, actually. Kind of ironic if you look at it the right way, isn't it?"

Across the table, Dec exploded. "Wait? When the hell were you going to tell me, us—tell us about that?"

The room held its breath as Tristan said, "Well, I didn't actually know, Daniel. I think I've been waiting."

"For what?" I asked.

"Well, first to remember. Obviously. But then, for someone who cared about the Prelude as much as I did." And then, looking at Annie, Tristan finished, "And now she's here."

36

RUSS

I'd failed.

On top of that, it was cold as hell as I walked back from the Hamptons', even though I had my coat pulled tight around me and borrowed a pair of Dec's gloves before I left.

I knew the chill had nothing to do with the weather. It was the type of cold that came from the inside, the type that came from not being sure where to turn next.

We didn't have the piano string, and we might never have it. Forcing it out of the piano would feel wrong now, and I didn't have the heart to ask Tristan for it.

I reached the town square and sat on one of the brick walls that served as benches.

I was alone. *Again.*

Sometimes I craved silence more than food, more than anything. But tonight I was lonely, and I didn't know what to do about it. I could visit my father, but he'd just tell me he loved me even if I never made it into the Guild. That wasn't going to help.

I rubbed my arm. My easiest option for company could be found at the other end of my grandmother's syringe, in that place where I knew I wouldn't care whether I was alone or not. It was the same slippery slope I'd rolled down three years ago when I was still adjusting to St. Hilaire, the spirits, and the truth that I was able to know the unknowable. Ian had been the only one around who understood and was more than eager to take me under his wing. The pull of that feeling—of being *understood*, of being *guided* instead of being the guide—was almost too much to walk away from.

It would be so easy to head home and take a shot despite the fact that I had no one to bring me back. There wasn't a snowball's chance that Dec would stick around for it again and less of one that I'd trust Alex a second time.

Perhaps it was possible that Ian, once summoned, could do it, but that solution was too convoluted, and even if I could find him, there was nothing safe about Ian Mackenzie. Which was actually the point. Ian, it seemed, existed simply to be dangerous. To be an option. Death hadn't changed that, but at least Ian was a temptation I knew and one I vaguely understood.

The vials were in my backpack, only inches away from my fingers. *Man, how I want another hit.* Perhaps the effects of the drugs were cumulative. The more you had, the more you craved.

That would be a problem eventually.

"Ian," I called out into the square. Maybe, like Tristan, I didn't need the shots to see him. But there was no response and while my brain was hungry for company, my arm wanted the serum.

Instead of heading home alone, I stumbled up and forced myself toward Eaton Hall. Like every high school student, I had a key to the town's archives, and there was always the chance that I could distract myself with knowledge.

Books had gotten me through worse than this. My mother disappearing, moving to St. Hilaire, the realization that no matter what I did, Dec was going to leave and I was going to stay, and that would be that. Books would get me through this.

I needed to research curses, anyhow. Needed to figure out a way to redeem myself and do what I could for Tristan.

I pulled out my skeleton key and opened the rusty door. Like a lot of St. Hilaire, the door was run-down, with wood that used to be beautifully decorated with metal filigree, but was now flaking with abandonment. These days, money for upkeep was diverted to tourist spots. When I was a member of the Guild, I'd change that. History needed to be treasured.

I headed to the archives and breathed in the glorious smell of the books. There was no specific section on curses. St. Hilaire was all about guiding the living through contact with the dead. We weren't witches. St. Hilaire High wasn't Hogwarts. I couldn't count the number of times those edicts had been drummed into us. We didn't cast spells, place curses, or otherwise overtly change the course of someone's life. We simply relayed the words of the dead to those who needed to hear them. What the living did with those words was their choice.

But somewhere in this vast array of pages, there had to be an answer for Tristan. And a way to corral Alex.

Something clacked behind me, and I ducked into a section on psychometric sciences.

"Just because they're all obsessed with talking to spirits doesn't mean the rest of us should have to take this stupid class, does it, David?"

I knew the voice all too well. I recognized the sound of a hundred-plus-pound dog slumping to the floor. I was familiar with the fear in David Sheridan's eyes as he came around the corner lit up by the glow from Alex Mackenzie's flashlight.

"Oh, look. It's Russ Griffin," Alex said.

I grabbed the first book I saw, one that sat on the bottom shelf under at least a decade's worth of dust. "Funny running into you in a library, Alex. I didn't think studying was your cup of tea." I was surprised to see David Sheridan in Alex's company again. Rumor had it, he'd been interviewed by the Guild for a full day about the poker game. David had never admitted anything and didn't implicate Alex, and now he was stuck doing eight hours a day of community service until school began.

Garmer sauntered over, and I rubbed him between his massive ears. The dog groaned and rolled onto his back. "Your dog is upside down," I said.

"Look, asshole. I'm running out of time. Did you get the wire or not?" Alex asked and pulled on the dog's leash. The dog looked at Alex, irritated, and then begrudgingly flipped over onto its belly.

Interesting that Alex was talking about this in front of David. I wondered how much he knew. And if that even mattered. "Getting that wire might be more difficult than I previously thought," I said. "The piano still seems to be using it."

Sheridan shifted uneasily. "I told you, Alex. What made you think it was just going to give up after all of this?"

Mackenzie kicked a stack of books in front of him. I winced. My mother had taught me that books were sacred. I could barely tolerate people who bent down page corners.

When Alex didn't answer, David Sheridan shifted and said, "We should go."

"Look," I said. "I know what you need the piano string for and how to use it."

Alex narrowed his eyes. "How?"

I looked from him to David and back again. As much as I wanted the Guild to know that I was in touch with Ian, this didn't seem to be the right way of getting the word out. "I just do, okay? But there's a problem."

The dog whined, and Alex's face animated. "You talked to him again. You talked to Ian, didn't you?"

Before I could respond, a voice behind me said, "Why would you do that? My brother was a dick."

I hadn't heard Colin come in and suddenly felt like the stacks were too small to hold this conversation and both Mackenzie brothers.

"Stay out of this, Colin," Alex said.

"Stop worshiping him and grow the fuck up," he said to Alex before turning to me. "Ian was a jerk. He used to rat me out to Dad every chance he got. 'Colin cheated on the algebra test.' 'Colin has the hots for Maria Foster.' He was in my business all the time. I think he bugged my room. And Dad would kick my ass while Ian just stood there grinning like the freaking Cheshire cat."

Yes, that sounded like Ian. I stifled a laugh.

"Ian was better than any of you," Alex sneered.

I stood by and watched Colin grab Alex by the shirt. "Your Saint Ian was a narcissistic ass, Alex. You think he wasn't, but you're lying to yourself. He went away. He left you. He cared about sex and the limelight and his parties and his fucking car more than he cared about you."

Alex went pale.

"Colin. Enough," I said. I didn't know if my words would hold any weight with Colin, but I put everything I had into them.

"Oh, please," Colin said, pushing his brother into a shelf. "It's about time he wised up."

For years, I'd wanted a brother or sister. But every minute I spent in the company of the Mackenzies made me grateful my parents never granted my request.

Colin shook his head and linked his thumbs into the front pockets of his jeans. The gold Guild pin gleamed on his collar. "Whatever. Listen, Griffin. I'm glad you're here. I have news for you. You're being summoned to try out for Student Leader."

"What?" I asked, waves of sensation running through me like current. I was sure I'd misheard. This wasn't how things happened. The Guild had a process and they kept to it. There were letters written. Signed. Sealed with wax and a stamp. Hand delivered. The Guild's summons weren't delivered by angry young men in dark library basements.

Colin slapped me on the side of my head. Coming from him, it was a surprisingly brotherly gesture. "Summoned, Griffin. They want to meet with you."

235

I pulled on the sleeves on my coat, appreciating the way the rough wool was so tangible, so grounding, in my hands. "Officially? Why?"

Colin gave me a half smile. "Yeah. I mean, the letter is coming and all. But Charlotte North told me herself. They want to get to you before school starts. Something about their new plans for this year and needing someone really good in place."

My breath caught. I stumbled back a step, examining Colin for any sign that he was screwing with me, but there was nothing. I swallowed hard. *Get ahold of yourself,* I thought. *You're more than this.* I crossed my arms and centered myself, and then reached out to *sense* Colin.

"Reel it in, Griffin. I'm not bullshitting." Colin leaned over and squeezed my shoulder hard. The thick wool was the only buffer between my skin and a bruise. "Welcome to the club."

37

DEC

A loud hum in the corner of my room woke me up. "Morning, Tristan," I said, eyes still closed.

"I love when it rains and the sun is shining," Tristan said. "It makes everything look so magical."

I forced myself awake. "You believe in magic?"

Tristan walked into the light and sat on the edge of my desk. "You mean, you don't? There are many things that can't be explained by pure science."

From anyone else, this would be an attempt at a bad joke, but Tristan looked as sincere as always. "You do remember you're in St. Hilaire, right? This whole town defies science."

Tristan beamed. "Doesn't that prove my point?" He looked wistfully toward the window. If there was one thing Tristan was an expert at, it was looking at things wistfully. He picked a snow globe off my desk that Harriet had brought back from the city with her; it had a miniature Empire State Building inside, and he was turning it over and over, making it snow.

I didn't really know what to do with my newfound appreciation for him. I didn't want to be the type of person who only valued things when he was afraid he'd lose them, but maybe that's just who I was.

"What do you dream about?" Tristan asked out of the blue.

I concocted a bunch of lies in my head, but then decided to be honest. "My parents, mostly. You?"

"Yes, although I'm not sure that I truly sleep." Tristan looked down at the globe in his hand. "But, me too. Sometimes." He raised his eyes to meet mine.

"You dream about my parents?" The words hurt as I said them. "Never mind. So, looks like I'm not the only one stuck here."

"I'm not sure that's true any longer," Tristan said. "I think... something is changing." He stuck his hands out, and now, if I squinted, I could almost see the bones beneath his skin. No, that wasn't right. It wasn't bones. It was the stripes of my carpet showing through where bones should be. I shook my head.

"Crap. I can't... Let me call Russ." I reached for my phone, dialed, and when Russ didn't answer, said "Crap" again.

My head was a mess of things I wanted to deny. My parents. Tristan. The image of Russ lying on the floor with a needle sticking out of his arm.

In a way, the last one was the worst because I should have stopped him. How selfish did it make me that I sat and watched

238

my best friend shoot who-knows-what into his body just for my benefit?

It terrified me that he might be doing it again right now.

Russ had always had a sort of restrained recklessness, and I suspected that was at the heart of his interest in Ian Mackenzie. There was little Ian wouldn't do, and if Russ wasn't stupid enough to participate, he at least wanted to be close enough to observe. I hadn't wished Ian dead, but I was glad he wasn't around. He wouldn't have mixed well with a bunch of syringes.

I turned my thoughts back to Tristan. "Can you stay put for a minute?"

When Tristan nodded, I threw a sweatshirt over my T-shirt, stepped into the hallway, and knocked on the door across the hall.

Annie answered, her headphones draped around her neck. Her hair was damp and lovely, and I wanted to lean in and return the kiss she'd given me. The kiss we hadn't even found time to discuss. Was it any wonder I wanted to get the hell out of here?

We stood there awkwardly, staring at each other. I said, "Something is happening with Tristan."

She removed the headphones and followed me back to my room, where Tristan sat on the floor with his arms wrapped around his legs. "I don't think it's an emergency," he said, "I mean, I don't think anything is going to happen right away."

"What do you mean 'happen'?" Annie asked.

Tristan held out his insubstantial hands and shrugged an apology.

Annie settled herself on the floor and took one of Tristan's barely there hands in her own. "Have you remembered anything else?" she asked.

"I've been thinking a lot about my father, actually." Tristan drew a deep breath before he continued. "My father had never worked a day in his life and had no desire to begin. That was why he married my mother. For her money. He never loved any of us. My mother had doted on me, piano lessons, music teachers, she'd been so proud of everything I'd accomplished— but my father was jealous. And after she died, he quickly drank through her whole fortune."

I watched Annie while we waited for Tristan to get to the point of his story; her face was lined with concern.

Tristan continued. "Anyhow, we had to live on something, so my father became a thief who represented himself as a type of mystic, telling fortunes and performing sleight of hand on the street. When he swindled the wrong people, we had to flee England. He told my brothers and me to keep to the shadows, but there was my music. I was seventeen and loved performing. I didn't *want* to stay in the shadows." He cleared his throat as if the words were awkward in his mouth. "Plus, I wasn't wholly unknown at the time. I had signatures, musical signatures."

It was chilling to hear Tristan tell us his story as if he were alive. Strange to think of him as seventeen, the same age as me and Annie.

Annie had other things on her mind. "The unfinished chords. The countermelodies," she said.

Tristan nodded. "My father wanted me to get a job on the docks. He was growing impatient with me sneaking out and playing. One of his parlor tricks involved burning a playing card only to find it whole again in the deck. When he drunk-enly threatened to set my sheet music ablaze instead of a card, I sold off the written part of the Prelude to a wealthy benefactor who promised to see it published. Then I used the profits to purchase the piano. Your piano, Daniel."

"Wait." Annie stopped him. "The written *part*? You mean it was not even finished?"

Tristan shook his head. "Well, it was sketched out in my head. I simply didn't have time to polish it and write it down. My father was on edge. I wasn't sure when he'd snap. And the parts I didn't have time to write down, I scribbled on scraps of paper and hid in old books and such. I asked some traders to carry some of those pages far away."

"So the piano really *is* yours?" I asked.

Tristan turned, the light catching in his suddenly serious eyes, and nodded.

"On the day after the piano was delivered to the house, my father was particularly drunk and particularly livid. He accused me of loving music more than I loved him, which wasn't incorrect. He was shaking with anger about my not giving him the money I'd received, and there was something not quite right about him. He smelled of herbs and reeked of whiskey. He said I was too headstrong. Too full of myself. That it was up to him to teach me a lesson. He said he had seen to it that I would never rest until I finished the Prelude. And that I could never finish it because it could not be com-pleted on any piano save this one. And *that* wasn't going to happen because he had already sold it and arranged for it to be shipped to America."

"What did he mean you could not finish it on any other piano?" Annie asked.

"Well, I thought it was preposterous. I was seething. I knew I had to get out of the house before I did or said something I regretted. So I stormed off. I went to the old music school, but…" Tristan looked down at his hands, turning them over and over.

"I tried to play the Prelude, and couldn't. I could barely play anything, really. But every time I tried to play the Prelude, my fingers would ache as if they were breaking. By the time I returned to the house, the piano was gone, and so was my father. I was absolutely frantic. I rushed down to the shipyard and made an impulsive decision."

"You stowed away in it." I could picture Tristan climbing into the piano's false side, pulling in his velvet coat and shutting the door without thinking the plan through. "That's how that scrap of wrapper got there, isn't it?"

He nodded. "Apparently this pronouncement was the one bit of real magic my father got right. I never even had the chance to say goodbye to my brothers," Tristan said. "And of course, I hadn't thought to prepare. And the voyage was far longer than I could have imagined."

I looked away, sensing what was coming next.

Tristan lowered his voice. "I also hadn't counted on not being able to open the door from the inside. The mechanism was built for things to be put in, not for things to let themselves out. And no amount of banging brought any assistance. The air grew thin quickly. Frankly, I thought I'd died, and while something happened, it simply wasn't what I expected death to be like."

Tristan pulled his hand out of Annie's, animated once again. "The piano changed owners a number of times, but oh, Daniel, I was so was grateful when it was delivered here. Although that's when I realized I was not quite whole. And not quite as trapped as I thought. But I was tired. That sounds odd even to my ears, yet it's the truth. I was emotionally worn out. Your great-grandfather played the piano regularly, and after a time, I realized I wasn't limited to that tiny space any longer. But it wasn't until your father was born that anyone ever spoke to me."

"Did he know?" I asked. "Did my father know everything you're telling us?"

Tristan's eyes grew misty, and he rubbed at them. "I didn't remember these things to tell him. I think that when Russ found me and I started remembering, and Annie…well, it all changed things."

My stomach soured.

"I was alone," Tristan whispered.

"You weren't," I said, thinking about my father's words.

"I was," Tristan insisted. The room chilled. It was the first time I'd ever heard Tristan angry. Strong. Perhaps this is what he was like *before*. It was a sobering thought. "I was. Until your father. And then you. I haven't been able to write. All this time. It was part of my father's pronouncement, I think. I have, not dreams precisely, but there are times when a melody wafts through my head like smoke. When I reach out to commit it to paper, it's gone. My father was apparently an effective curse maker."

Tristan rubbed his hands as if they were in pain. "He was not a strong man, my father. But he was a man of strong feelings. You see, it didn't just *feel* as though my hands were breaking when I tried to play, they *were*. I was in unbearable pain. I haven't tried to play since."

Annie snuffled. It must have been her worst nightmare, not to be able to play anymore.

The heavy sadness that filled the room was so oppressive, I had to fight to draw in air.

"You should try," I said quietly. "The piano is downstairs, waiting. Try it."

"That's very kind, Daniel, but I'm afraid it may be too late for that."

"Too late? Why?" Annie asked, her brows knitted together.

Tristan looked at Annie. Then at me. Instead of answering, he stood and walked over to the wall. His hands out in front of him, he went to push into the plaster, only his hands went right through. "I seem to be disappearing," he said to us sadly. "That would make it difficult to play the piano, don't you think?"

38

RUSS

The morning shadows moved along my closet door, dispersed, and then reassembled into a familiar, surprisingly solid, shape.

"I thought you couldn't haunt people," I said. The previous night had apparently been rough; my voice sounded like I hadn't used it in a year.

"What I *said* was I couldn't haunt Alex. His brain is a closed door. And I've been busy."

I twisted to watch Ian drape himself onto my bed, shaking his long hair out of his eyes. I wasn't going to point out that he was apparently not too busy to haunt *me*.

"Besides, you left the door open…" Ian continued and winked, "…psychically." Then he added, "And I had to check in on the 'Stang."

My heart betrayed me by racing. I was glad Ian couldn't hear it; he wasn't someone you wanted to hand an advantage. "Don't you have to be invited in?" I asked.

Ian smiled a smile filled with still-perfect teeth. "Nice try, Griffin. I'm not a vampire. But if you're looking to be bitten…"

I cut him off. This was already going badly. "Okay, what are you doing here?"

Ian picked up one of my pillows and hugged it pathetically to his chest. "Being bored. You would have thought that wouldn't be an issue for me now, right? But it turns out, people don't get more interesting just because they're dead."

It was amazing how much *space* Ian took up in my small room. He'd always been too over-the-top for St. Hilaire, too intense, too unrestrained, too dramatic. Death hadn't changed any of that. It was still too easy to become entangled in his web. I wanted to open the windows to let in more air, move stacks of books to create pockets of emptiness. Just do *something* to feel like I was in control.

Instead, I moved to the farthest corner of the room between the closet and a shelving unit filled with glass balls of air plants that only needed water every couple of months. "Well, I'm not your entertainment committee. I have work. Go talk to the Guild if you're that bored. They're wasting valuable energy trying to reach you."

The candles in the opposite corner of the room flickered as if a wind was blowing through the room. My heartbeat echoed in the crook of my arm in a way that should have been both uncomfortable and unfamiliar but was neither.

I'd worked so hard for the chance to sit and talk with

the dead without the help of other mediums and a séance. I deserved this. But fate had a shitty sense of humor. Ian showing up uninvited in my bedroom was the last thing I'd had in mind.

Ian bounced off the bed and over to the window. "You're taking care of her, right?"

I didn't have to ask to know he was scrutinizing the rain-kissed Mustang. The longing on his face said it all. "Why do you sound like you knew I was going to end up with your car?"

Ian didn't admit to anything. He just gave me the grin that had won over teachers and tourists alike.

I knew I should tell him to leave. Most ghosts would go if you were forceful enough. Not that Ian had ever listened to anyone before; it was a crapshoot as to whether he would now.

Before I could say anything, my phone vibrated with a text. Ian got to it first.

"You're needed," he said, looking at the screen with a cocky grin. I reached out for the phone just as Ian tossed it casually onto the desk. "But then that's the whole thing between you and Hampton, right? He calls and you come?"

I was definitely losing control. Ian. In my room. Picking up a book here. Fondling the leaf of a plant there. It was too much, too unreal and too paralyzing until Ian moved to the tall bookcase my father built right after we'd moved in. I watched in horror as his hand reached toward the tiny framed picture of my mother that sat, almost unnoticeable, on the top shelf.

"Stop," I said, finding my voice. There was a sharp stab of panic in my chest where my composure usually lived. "Come on, Ian," I pleaded.

Ian didn't reply. I waited for a searing comment. Instead, he squinted at the small photo—the only one in the room—and then at me. "You have her mouth," he said and replaced the photo.

I exhaled. Now that Ian was dead, I couldn't get any read off him. This was a whole other kind of unnerving. "Why are you so…solid?" I asked.

He barked out a laugh. "Oh, sometimes you make it too, too easy, but let's chalk it up to strength of character and leave it at that."

We stared at each other while I scrambled for a safe topic. One thing Ian had always been good at was navigating the system of the Guild. Somehow, he'd been talented enough to get the otherwise conservative and stuffy group to accept him, wildness and all. Maybe I could use that.

"Look, since you're here…" I rubbed my wrist, feeling pressured to ask my question before I lost the nerve. "Colin says I'm going to be summoned to audition for Student Leader. I need to know how you passed their tests."

"Easy," Ian said. "I gave them what they wanted. And congrats, by the way. Not that I'm surprised."

I turned away from the compliment. *We are not friends*, I reminded myself. *We have never been anything like friends.* "And what was it they wanted?"

Ian walked over and leaned in close, too close, but I was determined to hold my ground.

"Just what they've always wanted," Ian answered. "Power. Money. The chance to screw with people's lives. Anyhow, I'll walk you through it, just chill. You're making me tense."

My pulse became a jagged thing, sharp with dread and anticipation.

"I'm fine," I said, mostly to myself.

Ian chuckled. *Chuckled.* "Prove it. Take your coat off."

"Why?" I resisted the instinct to pull the fabric closer.

"Lord, Griffin. You're *inside*. In your own room. Besides, I'm not hitting on you. I'm dead."

I also resisted the urge to ask whether, in Ian's case, the two things were mutually exclusive. Instead, I gave in and slowly peeled off my coat and threw it on the bed. Then I crossed my arms and tried futilely to rub the ghost-chill away. "Now what?"

Ian circled me. "Now? Close your eyes."

Closing my eyes would put me in a defenseless position I'd always tried to avoid around Ian, but this time, I did what he wanted. I needed his information.

"After you dispense with all the pleasantries, they're going to put you in a room on your own with whatever you need to work your magic and ask you to contact a spirit to answer a question. It's a silly test." Ian's voice seemed to be coming from all sides of the room at once. I had a vision of birds circling around me, prickly beaks parted, ready to attack. "Hell," Ian offered jovially. "Give me a heads-up and maybe I'll be your 'plus-one.' I could give you *all* sorts of dirt on Charlotte North."

A chill ran up my back. I could do this without Ian. St. Hilaire ran through my blood. I might not be as dramatic as Ian, but who was? Plenty of spirits called St. Hilaire home. The Guild wouldn't be considering me if they didn't think I was ready.

"You still with me?" Ian asked.

I nodded. My head felt heavy and leaden.

"Good. The second thing they'll ask is for you to contact someone specific. Someone who will give you a prearranged password."

That was harder. I was certain I could pull it off on demand with the shots, but without it… My abilities were strong, but their appearance was never conveniently timed.

Ian seemed to be able to read my hesitation. "Whoever it is will be expecting you. Remember that. Sort out the energy in the room. That's your shtick, right? Energy? Whoever it is will probably be the strongest."

"Okay," I tried to say, only it came out as a cough.

"You can do it," Ian whispered into my ear.

"What's the third thing?" I asked.

Ian's prolonged silence was unnerving enough to tempt me to open my eyes, but I stayed still.

Against my closed eyelids, the sun seemed to shift. My head spun, and I reached out for the bookcase next to me, but all I touched was Ian's arm. Solid, warm, and disturbingly *alive*, which was impossible. I tried to pull my hand back, but Ian covered it with his own and held it there.

"Listen to me, Griffin," he said. "Winning over the Guild is easy. St. Hilaire is a joke. Nobody buys the whole spiritualist thing anymore. This town is hemorrhaging money. They need a sure thing. Marketing. Tourism. Blah, blah, blah. *That* is one of the reasons they're busting their asses to try to reach me. They think I'm their ace in the hole; that they can market me as their poster boy. Ghosts exist and all that crap. Just think of the Times Square billboard they could buy with my picture plastered all over it to advertise their freaking fundraiser. Get your shit together and give them an angle they haven't seen before, and they will eat you up."

With his last word, Ian pushed me backward into the bed. I opened my eyes. "What if I can't?" It wasn't as if I could go into Eaton Hall and ask a Guild member to inject me full of chemicals.

Ian leaned over and slapped me lightly on the face, leaving his hand there a beat too long. "Wrong question." He turned and reached for my backpack, and I froze when he pulled out my grandmother's notebook.

"Hey," I called out. "What's the right question?"

Ian tossed the book onto the bed. "They don't know what you have. Stop overthinking everything. Go in there and do what you do. Let them worry about picking up the pieces."

I glanced at the book. *Maybe.*

"So what...?" I started to ask Ian again what the right question was, but the room was empty.

I stood, staring at the book for an absurdly long time. Once again, I'd let Ian screw with my head. I shrugged back into my coat. Then I closed the window against a suddenly sleet-filled rain, sat down, opened the book, and began to read.

The letter that arrived the next morning was just as I expected: cream envelope, tangerine sealing wax, brown calligraphy. "The presence of your company is requested..."

It must have come in the middle of the night, because my father left it on the dining room table under a note that read,

"Not all who wander are lost." I didn't know why my dad would think of me as wandering. And I didn't know if he'd written the note before or after he'd seen the invitation from the Guild. He'd never been a huge Guild supporter, but he'd always wanted me to do what made me happy.

I put the summons in my bag, flat for safekeeping. I owed Dec a call; usually, I answered on the first ring. Ian's accusation had hit close to the mark.

While I knew Dec would agree our friendship was *supposed to* go beyond scorecards, and checks and balances, that didn't change the fact that Dec wasn't going to be thrilled about my Guild invite. It was safe to say Dec hated them. Would he hate me too once I joined?

I had to hope that Dec would come to terms with it eventually. Maybe he wouldn't love the idea, but he could learn to tolerate it. That was the best I could really hope for.

My phone rang again and this time I picked up.

"Are you okay?" Dec asked.

Something in my veins quieted at hearing his voice. "I'm good," I said, trying to choose my words carefully. "Sorry about not calling you back last night. I was reading and fell asleep. I was about to, actually. Call you."

The lies sat uneasily on my tongue. They tasted like my father's health shakes—bitter and green.

Dec was silent for a long time. The tension that hung between us was new and toxic, a quickly growing vine that would choke out all other living things.

"So this morning," I began. *Tell him.* I thought the words, mouthed them, *Ian Mackenzie showed up and told me how to win over the Guild and then I got my letter.* In my head, Dec exploded in anger.

No words would be able to deflate Dec's reaction. So instead, I finished with, "Sorry. Wasn't trying to blow you off."

Dec ignored my apology and said, "Something is happening with Tristan. Something bad."

I exhaled, my breath jagged. For Dec to sound so upset about Tristan, sad not angry, things must really be dire. "Do you want me to come over?"

Dec went silent on the line. We were both instantly aware of the oddity of the question. *I'll be right there.* That was what I would normally say if I hadn't been there already. Somewhere in the question existed the option for me to do nothing. That option had never existed before, and now it was too late to take that option off the table.

"He's remembering a lot more," Dec said, ignoring the question. "But he's less. Like fading. Physically. He says he's disappearing."

I fumbled with a pen on the table, flipping it over and over and over. From what I'd read about curses, I knew this might be a possibility. And I knew that the only chance he had of actually resting was to finish the Prelude. I was afraid to think about what the alternative might be. That was often how these things worked.

My hand tightened in a nervous twitch. I put the pen down. Whatever was happening to Tristan wasn't a problem I'd be able to make go away. Its existence would be one more log on the fire of Dec's anger. And that was *before* Dec knew about the Guild summons. Or about Ian.

"Never mind," Dec said. His voice sounded weary, all the fight gone out of him.

"Sorry," I said again. And I was. For everything I was saying, and more, for everything I wasn't. "Actually there are a couple of things I need to talk to you about," I spit out before I could stop myself.

Dec made a "huh" sound into the phone, and my jaw clenched. For someone who didn't believe in keeping secrets, I was suddenly overflowing with them.

I glanced outside the window to see rain still pouring down. "I could come over now," I offered. "If you want me to."

Dec sighed. "I don't know. I mean, I guess you could. But I promised Laura I'd help her drag some stuff down from the attic and sort through it before school starts, and we're running out of time. I don't think Tristan is going to fade away today, anyhow. I mean, maybe soon, but not today."

It was such an obvious lie that I stared at the phone long after Dec had hung up.

I'd gotten what I'd been wanting for years: a request from the Guild. Now I needed to respond. My heart wasn't in it, though; it felt empty and wrong, beating out of rhythm.

Going back to bed sounded like a strangely viable option, but instead, I pulled my coat tight around me and walked outside, hoping the rain would tell me how to fix things.

DEC

It wasn't often I went looking for Harriet. It wasn't often I needed to; she was always there, mixing up herbs in the kitchen, yelling at me for something I'd done or forgotten to do, rolling her eyes and muttering to her computer.

But now, when I actually wanted to speak to her, she was nowhere to be found. I checked the kitchen where everything was neatly put away, no sign of potions or candle wax or any other telltale signs that she'd been there. I knocked on the door to her room and was met with such stony silence that I couldn't bring myself to push it open. The basement was padlocked, and her bike was still in the yard, so I knew she was somewhere in the labyrinth of the house.

There was only one place I hadn't looked, had least wanted

to look, and that was our parents' room. I stood at the bottom of the stairs that led to the master suite and inhaled the scent of the cedar that lined the stairs, the walls, and the entire room. As a kid, I'd raced up and down these stairs, pretending they were taking me to the bridge of a starship or they were the way up to a massive pirate ship. Now, I was having trouble bringing myself to put my foot on the first step.

I called up. "Harriet?"

No answer came, but something in the air made me think she was there. I forced myself up the stairs.

The room hadn't changed much since I'd last seen it. Thick pillows, weapons thrown during family movie nights, littered the four-poster bed. One dresser held Mom's collection of tiny porcelain bells and the other held Dad's equally tiny framed quotes. It all looked the same as it always had, but the *feel* of the room was wrong and empty.

In a corner, Harriet sat facing Mom's desk, looking at an old photo album. I didn't need to look over her shoulder to see the pictures because they were burned into my brain. All of us Hampton kids had loved to see the old photos and hear about how our parents had fallen in love so young. I thought about sharing what I'd learned about the Guild's role in pairing them up but couldn't think of anything good that would come out of it. This way, I was the only one who had to be pissed off about it. Let Laura and Harriet live in the fantasy world where our parents had a say over their own lives.

From the way Harriet's shoulders tensed, she knew I was here. I thought I should say something, even something as inane as "what are you doing?" but I knew what she was doing.

It just wasn't something that I'd had the courage to do myself since they'd died.

"Go away, Daniel," she said after a while. Her usual forcefulness was missing.

Instead of snipping back like I normally would, I walked up and looked over her shoulder.

Here, Mom smiled out from the album. Holding a very young Laura in her arms, she looked impossibly innocent and unscathed. There, Dad, a baseball bat in his hand and a cap on his head, waited for four-year-old me to throw the ball. Next to those, our parents and a very young Harriet stood in front of the town's wishing well.

"You kind of look like her," I said, trying to be kind. "Now, I mean." What I meant was that as Harriet had gotten older, she'd grown into the bone structure that made Mom look almost delicate. Only recently, Harriet had worn those same bones like a badly fitting suit.

Harriet closed the album. Still, she didn't turn around. We were sailing in uncharted waters. I didn't remember when we'd last had a real conversation.

"It's okay to miss them," I said even though I wasn't sure I believed it. I mean, I knew it was okay to miss them in theory, but the pain was so great, I couldn't deal with it in reality.

"What do you want?" she asked, still not turning around. Her voice shook, and I saw why when I noticed the stain of tears on the old wood.

The truth was, I was out of ideas that might help Tristan, and she was my last hope. I said, "I wanted to see if you were okay." It was a blatant lie and we both knew it. Neither of us could remember the last time that I'd checked on her "just because."

"I'm..." The word was a defensive bark. But then she turned and I caught a glimpse of the sister I used to know. We'd never been close, not like me and Laura. But we used to be able to hang out without fighting. "I'm tired," she said after a while.

I opened my mouth, planning to tell her everything that was weighing on my mind, planning to prove to her, finally, that I wasn't a bad guy, not really. But instead, I knelt down beside the desk and looked up at her. "I'm sorry," I said, unsure what exactly I was covering in my blanket apology. Our parents dying, I guess. The fact that I didn't. All of the silence that had come in the years that followed. I knew I hadn't been an easy person to live with since the accident.

"You should leave, Daniel," she said, her words sharp.

An angry heat surged inside me. Of course, I'd tried to bridge the distance between us, and she'd thrown it back in my face.

Then she stood. "No," she said. "I didn't mean it like that. I mean. You should *leave*. St. Hilaire. Go and get as far away from here as you can."

I wasn't sure I'd heard right. "What?"

She turned and picked up a photo of our parents with all of us children. It had been taken at some community picnic that I didn't remember.

"Look, a couple of months before the car accident, I don't know. Something happened with Mom and Dad. Don't you remember? Dad never wanted to leave the house, and Mom was burning sage all over everything."

I tried to remember what she was talking about, but it was

as hard for me to remember the time right before the accident as it was to remember the time right after. I shook my head.

She threw the photos back on the desk. "I wasn't here except for the occasional weekend. I only came back for that week because they were being so squirrelly, and I thought they just needed a night out or something. I bought tickets for all of us to go to the opening night of that movie, but Laura had some test, and she asked me to stay and help her study."

Suddenly everything became slightly clearer. "You can't blame yourself. I mean, you didn't know."

"I keep trying," she said, almost to herself, "to get it all back. You know, I had a boyfriend in New York." She laughed at the shock that was obviously showing on my face. "Don't look so surprised. I had a life, a job. I had friends, an apartment."

"So why?" I asked without filling in the rest of the question. There were simply too many *whys* to list.

She looked up. "You. You and Laura. I mean, what was I supposed to do?"

I couldn't believe we were talking. Really talking. And it stung that we'd waited so long. "We could have come with you," I said, but as the words came out, I knew they weren't true. There was no way that Harriet, as a student, could have taken care of us in New York City.

Harriet grimaced. "Mom and Dad's will stipulated we had to stay in St. Hilaire. And what choice did I have? How would I have supported us in Manhattan?"

"We're old enough now," I said. "*You* can still leave."

"No, only one of us can. Unless, of course, we're going to sell the house and everything in it and give up." She stood, and

I could see both of us reflected in the freestanding mirror, look-ing so much like our parents. "I know you hate me for not being Mom, but I've done everything I can to keep us afloat."

I stared at her reflection in the mirror. "I don't hate you."

"Sure."

"No," I said, but we both knew I didn't mean it. "I hate that nothing is the way it used to be," I explained, and we both knew I meant *that*.

I considered what she'd said about one of us staying in St. Hilaire to keep the house running. Even to me, the idea of the old house falling into disarray was repulsive. When I dreamed of leaving St. Hilaire, I also dreamed of coming back to visit armed with stories of my life in the real world. I never thought of the house going to new owners who we'd have to rely on to maintain our parents' graves. That had never been the plan. "What about Laura?"

Harriet rolled her eyes, and although it was hard to keep from reacting, I knew she was right. Laura would be miserable trying to run this house on her own. As much as I hated all of the business stuff that came with our work, I understood, at a very basic level, the need for it. Laura did too. But she'd never actually *do* it. Or rather, Harriet would never ask her to. Laura was too nice and more likely to give séances away for free than to try to come up with a marketing plan.

"So, you're going to stay here? And you're really okay with me leaving?"

Harriet took a last look at the photograph before putting it back down on the table. "No offense, but it isn't like you're a huge help here anyhow."

"I know," I said. "I mean, I'm sorry."

"I just don't feel like this is where you're meant to be, Dec." She held my gaze, and neither of us missed the significance of her using my nickname for the first time in two years.

"But what about you?" I asked. "I mean, you're just going to suck it up and stay here?"

She took a deep breath. "Yes. For now."

I held her eyes. "Can you stop hating me for that?"

"I don't... Look. I know I'm hard on you. I get it. But this house and the business and..."

"Me and Laura?"

"Yeah. It just wasn't what I signed up for. I'm not Mom. But what did you really come up here for, anyhow?"

Harriet was always brewing something or flipping over cards and looking meaningfully over her shoulder. She'd bent over backward for the people who could pay. It was time, I'd thought, that she should do something for the family. Something for me. For Tristan. But now, it felt like she'd already done enough. Perhaps too much. "Like I said, I just came upstairs to see how you were."

It was a lie. We both knew it. But when she shared a smile I hadn't seen in two years, we both knew that was enough.

40

ANNIE

Enough. I pulled my hands away from the piano. Tried to push the Prelude out of my head. Now that I knew Tristan had never finished it, it was difficult to figure out whether Dmitry *had* wasted his time. Whether I was wasting mine. What would I even do now?

I needed a distraction, so I forced myself up the stairs. Knocked on Dec's door with hands cramped from playing.

He called for me to come in, but when I did, he did not pull the earbuds from his ears or even open his eyes. His hands were tight at his sides, his hair tousled in an alluring way that made me want to tousle it more.

I sat gingerly on the edge of the bed and reached out to touch his arm. His eyes opened slowly, and then he bolted upright, pulling the headphones out.

"Sorry," he said. "I thought you were Laura."

Something about that made me feel as though he had offered me a compliment. "I wanted to talk to you about what happened before."

His cheek twitched, and I was afraid he did not know what I was talking about until he said, "Please don't say you regret it."

"I do not. It is not that."

Dec knotted the cord in his hands and stared at it.

I took a deep breath. "I want you to understand that I do not go around kissing boys I do not know. I do not go around kissing boys at all. There is no time. I am never in one place long enough. And even if I were in one place, that is not who I am."

"I don't either," he said. "Go around kissing boys. Or girls. Kissing anyone."

Although that was not a huge surprise, it made me happy I had not misread things.

I took his hand. Unwound the headphone wire. His eyes widened in surprise, but I saw him try to hide it. I ran my fingers over his own. They were smooth and uncallused. They did not belong to someone who played the piano ten hours a day, and there was something soothing about that. Our fingers linked together naturally, and it was comforting, the warmth of his skin on mine.

"Why did you do it?" he asked.

"Because I believed you," I explained. "I have had fans show up at my home, well, Dmitry's apartment. They found me online, and...never mind. It is just, I play on these huge stages, and the lights are so bright, I cannot see anyone's face."

I knew I wasn't making sense and tried again. "You are real. And I like that my playing made things easier for you. I like *you*."

He shifted on the bed and leaned forward. My pulse fluttered. *Kiss me, oh please kiss me*, something trilled. I had kissed him without thinking last time, but now I needed him to be the one to act.

I closed my eyes, enjoying the sensation of his breath on my cheek, the anticipation of kissing him again.

"Daniel?"

My eyes popped open as Dec pulled away.

"Damn it, Tristan," Dec said. "How many times do I have to tell you not to do that?"

Tristan paled and stepped back, green eyes wide. "I didn't mean. I just. I was looking for Annie. And." His words slowed. "I guess I've found her."

Dec threw himself back on the bed with a strangled sound.

"Hi," I said and smiled an apology at Dec. "I am here."

"Yes," Tristan said, "I can see that. I was just wondering if maybe we might go down to the music room. I'd very much like to hear my Prelude played on this piano again."

I felt a lightness in my chest. Never in my wildest dreams had I imagined playing my signature piece for its composer. "Yes, of course," I said, standing. "Of course." Then I remembered what Tristan had interrupted. "I mean, if Dec does not mind."

Dec glared at Tristan and said through gritted teeth, "Why in the world would I mind?"

I had been interviewed approximately 137 times. Had any of those reporters asked what I thought it would feel like to play the Unfinished Prelude for the music's composer, I would have laughed self-consciously and skirted the question. The composer was unknown and dead after all, so the concept was not one worth addressing.

But now. *Now* as I played this strange, brilliant piano with Tristan sitting next to me, I discovered it was both the most nerve racking and amazing thing I had ever experienced.

As I played, Tristan alternately beamed, hummed, and once clapped with joy at my interpretation. Often, he stopped to give me suggestions on the phrasing of a particular section.

I could not remember being more in love with music than I was in that moment. The music, like my joy, filled me. Seduced me. *Oh, what bliss it would have brought Dmitry.*

I rode the wave of notes until next to me, barely loud enough to be heard over the piano, Tristan whispered, "I think I'm dying."

41

RUSS

"So, how do I get you and Alex together without destroying Dec's piano?" I asked. It was after 2:00 a.m., and my eyes were wrecked from reading the book I'd grabbed from Eaton Hall: *The History of Curses and Hexes*. Nowhere in it had I found a "cure" for a disappearing cursed boy. Instead, I'd found Ian sitting in my desk chair, thumbing through a book about possessed cats Dec had bought me as a joke.

Ian put the book down and smiled a slow, sly smile that made it completely clear what he was thinking.

"No," I said, unable to open my mouth out of a clench. "I'm not letting you possess me."

Ian shrugged. "Suit yourself. But I know Alex; that kid never gives up."

I wondered, for the millionth time, how I'd gotten myself into this mess. If I said no, I was all but giving Alex permission to continue to find new and more annoying ways to irritate Dec by trying to get at his piano. And if I said yes...

"Look, Griffin," Ian said, moving to the bed. "I get that it's your first time. I promise to be gentle."

"It isn't..." I realized too late what I'd walked into. "My first possession. Yeah. I've been doing all of this to avoid crap like that."

"But at least your first time would be with someone who cared about you," Ian said and winked.

I put my head in my hands. I needed to stop before this got worse. "Okay. Start over. You can't simply haunt Alex because...?"

"Because I may have lost my life, but I haven't lost my mind. There's a certain give-and-take in a haunting, you know. I need some...distance from him. A barrier, for lack of a better word."

"And you want me to be that barrier?" I asked, knowing the answer. "Never mind. So why can't we do this like a normal séance? You know, where Alex asks me questions and you give me the answers to relay?"

Ian smirked. "Okay, sure. And who are you going to get to sit in with you? Hampton sure as shit won't help you. Legally you need an adult, but then you'd be indebted to the Guild instead of the other way around. There are no specific rules for possessions. Of course, you could always just let Alex shoot you up again, but I'm not sure I'd advise that. Plus, you run the risk of him deciding that turning you in is the best option."

"And we can't just sit and talk because...?"

Ian leaned forward, all doe eyes. "Oh, we could. I mean, if

Alex gets wind of the fact that you can see me, he might be here every day asking you for something, but sure, if that's what you want. But really, I knew this would happen. I told him exactly how to contact me. I just didn't expect that damned instrument to put up such a fight. And I didn't expect him to lose my car."

I waited for an alternative idea, but none came. "Have you done it before?"

"Possessed anyone?"

"Yeah."

"You mean, like a *person*?" Ian cocked his head in an oddly familiar way that made me suspicious as well as slightly nauseous.

"What do you mean 'like a person'? What the hell else would you possess?"

Ian narrowed his eyes thoughtfully. "What's the quote? 'Outside of a dog, a book is a man's best friend. Inside of a dog, it's too dark to read.' It really is, you know. Dark."

It was impossible. But it was also Ian Mackenzie, which immediately rendered every fucked-up thing *possible*. "Garmer. You possessed your dog."

"It seemed like it would be a good way to keep an eye on things, but dogs' minds really *are* dark," Ian said. "I didn't try to take a bite out of you or anything, did I? It's kind of hard to get your bearings in there."

I leaned back on the bed and fixated on an errant cobweb in the corner of the ceiling. It was a small gift that Ian didn't remember being so affectionate as a dog. And it was a good sign that neither Ian nor Garmer seemed harmed by the experience. That didn't mean that I was itching to try it.

"How much harder can it be with a person?" Ian asked, obviously trying to be reassuring. "Look at all the stupid people who have ended up as ghosts and pulled it off."

I couldn't believe we were actually discussing this, that I was actually considering it. "Do you even know how that would work?"

"Sure." Ian grinned. "When a mommy ghost and a daddy ghost love each other very much..."

I didn't want to give Ian the satisfaction of laughing, but I couldn't help it. "So am I stuck with you now? I mean, can anyone I contact show up whenever they want?"

Ian crossed his legs languidly and ran a hand through his long, perfect hair. Vanity apparently didn't die. "Hate to break it to you, but, yeah; maybe this drug somehow makes you more susceptible to those you contact. And I'm kinda strong willed."

It made more sense than I wanted it to. There was always a price to pay for these things. Like I'd told Annie, nothing came for free, and dealing with Ian, it seemed, was the price I was going to pay for trying to prove myself.

Ian said, "We could practice. You know, give it a trial run?"

The kiss of fingers grazed the back of my neck. I pulled away and sat up. "Yeah, that's all good. Except for the fact that I don't trust you."

"I'm hurt." Ian pouted and stood. "But what exactly do you think I'm going to do? Besides, it would be good practice for when you go in front of the Guild? They won't give you a second chance."

"I thought we were talking about your brother. Besides, I'm not going to—"

"Save it. Don't bullshit a bullshitter. That's another thing I'm better at than you are." Ian slid to the floor, knelt on his heels in front of the bed, and leaned in close. His face was steely, chiseled, and no less intense than it was when he was alive. "So, go ahead. Ask."

I waited for Ian's breath to land on my cheek, but there was nothing. "Ask what?" I couldn't look away. I hated, *hated,* that Ian always seemed to know how to get to me.

"Ask me your questions. I can see them sitting right. Behind. Your. Lips." Ian leaned back. "I can read you better now that I'm dead, you know. If I tried. But I'd rather hear it from you. I'll tell you anything. Anything at all. All you need to do is ask."

Questions ran into one another like a pileup on the interstate. But more than anything, I was tired of fighting. Also, I knew that sometimes it was best to give in to Ian and get it over with. "Fine. How did it happen? And don't give me that song and dance about curiosity."

"Really?" Ian laughed softly, and almost sadly. "That's what you want to know?" He clasped his hands and rested them on his knees. My breathing sped up in an anticipation that felt like a betrayal. "I give you carte blanche to ask me anything, and you want to know how I *died?*"

I couldn't answer. It wasn't just morbid curiosity; it was a puzzle piece that didn't fit, a math problem that didn't add up. The idea that Ian would kill himself went against everything I knew about him, and I needed to understand what I'd missed. I needed to make sure there was nothing I could have done.

"Okay," he said. "I ate a bad piece of blowfish. That stuff can kill you if it isn't cut correctly."

I sighed. "Next."

"Would you believe that I was learning to fight bulls and got gored by a particularly long horn?"

I waited because I knew Ian would fill any silence that went on too long.

"Look," he said. "I turned eighteen and could see my entire miserable future laid out in front of me. Setting up shop in St. Hilaire and telling middle-aged women their high school crush really knew they existed. *God*. What a dreadful existence."

I tried to look at the oak tree outside my window, or at the books scattered around my desk, anywhere but into Ian's eyes, which were too close for comfort, and failed. "That's bullshit. You didn't have to kill yourself. You could have just gone somewhere else. There were still probably a lot of places on the map where you hadn't pissed people off yet." I'd asked for the truth. Now I wasn't sure what to do with what he'd given me. His words still didn't feel right.

"Oooh, burn. First off, killing myself was never my intention. And for what it's worth, I didn't kill myself. I simply decided not to do anything to keep myself from dying. And second, I would have been saddled with Colin and Alex *at least* until Dad got back from overseas, and frankly, I'm not sure that's ever going to happen. And third, I'd had just about as much of the almighty Guild controlling me as I could take, so no thank you."

There was something in Ian's eyes, now bluer than they'd been when he was alive, that made me believe he thought these might be reasons worth dying for. Perhaps I hadn't known him as well as I thought.

"What's it like?" I asked. "Being...?" I struggled to find the right word.

"Witty and charming and good in bed?" Ian chuckled.

"Dead."

"Oh, that." Ian rocked back, stretched out on the floor, and moved his arms up and down, making snow angels on my worn carpet. "It sucks, since you asked. Not something I'd recommend if you have other options."

His arms continued to move up and down, a gesture either childlike or anxious, neither of which were words ever used to describe Ian.

"Is that why you're sticking around?" I asked. "Because the alternatives suck?"

Ian froze, his arms at his side, and sat up. The heavy silence in the room made it clear he was taking my question seriously.

"No. Actually, I'm here because I was curious."

I cut him off, "I said don't give me that."

And then I was cut off by Ian saying, in turn, "About you."

There was no single set of rules when it came to ghosts. There were things we'd learned in school. All the acronyms (like Guilt, Hate, Obsession, Selfishness, Terror) for why ghosts ended up sticking around to haunt the living. But, as Dec's father used to say, "Ghosts are people too." Or were. But the point was the same; they were as unique as they'd been when they were living, each with their own goals and fears and motivations.

That Ian Mackenzie had any motivation involving me was unnerving. That Ian was sticking around in the afterlife because he was curious—*curious*—about me made me break out into a cold sweat.

I remembered Ian's comment that he found it easier to read me since he died and decided it wasn't worth trying to hide my feelings.

"You're sticking around because of me?" It was a question, but when I heard myself ask it, there was no question in the words. Perhaps I'd known Ian's answer before the words made their way to my mouth.

Ian sprung up, walked over to the desk, and began riffling through a stack of books. "Everyone thinks they want to be the best at whatever it is they're doing. But really, it's damned lonely to be the only one who knows how to do something." He turned around sharply, blue eyes narrowed. "Anyhow. I wanted to know what you're capable of. And now I think I do. Or rather, I have an inkling, and I want to see the rest."

"The rest?"

"Have you swallowed a parrot, Griffin?"

I felt a fluttering on my wrist and rubbed it. "What is this all about?"

"Haven't you been listening? I want you to go in and take over the Guild. I want you to change the way everything in St. Hilaire is done before the Guild destroys this entire town."

"Oh, is that all?" I asked, exasperated.

Ian leaned back on the desk and cocked his head, a small smile creeping across the right side of his face. "No, actually. It isn't."

The room chilled, and as I watched, Ian grew less opaque, more like the essence of Ian rather than a figure standing in my room. "I want to do it with you." Ian's voice came from some random point in space. "I want us to do it together. I know they want to talk to me. It isn't like I don't hear them. Some days they never shut up. And I'd like to have a word or two with them as well, actually. I just want to do it in my own time. In my own way."

I *knew* Ian was telling the truth just as I knew what it would mean if I went to the Guild and told them I could consult with St. Hilaire's most notorious and currently elusive ghost. "Why should I trust you?" I wanted to scream the question, but instead, my voice was soft, as if Ian had already won and this conversation was something we had to get through first.

I waited for an answer. And then I waited some more. But the only thing I heard was the wind howling outside the suddenly open window.

42

RUSS

I finally agreed to let Ian possess me after Alex showed up at my house and handcuffed himself to the Mustang.

My father was explaining how a replacement piece for the old train was being cast in Europe and would be shipped to St. Hilaire later in the week, when we were interrupted by an eerie howl. I'd peeked through the blinds to see Alex rattling the cuffs against the car and Garmer pacing back and forth whining.

I wasn't sure which was worse, Alex or the dog who might actually be Ian. Either would be trouble. I ran outside, closing the door tightly behind me, picked up a stick and threw it far into the woods. "Fetch."

The dog cocked its head before sticking its tongue out of the side of its mouth and running toward the trees.

One down.

"I'm not leaving," Alex said.

I was determined not to give in, but when Garmer came running back with the stick, his fur covered in burrs, and a drooling smile on his face that looked too familiar, I figured I had no choice.

Which is how I found myself in the Mustang at the edge of the woods near my house, waiting for the eldest and youngest Mackenzie brothers. I'd brought the vials, just in case, but was pretty sure I wouldn't need them this time.

I licked my lips and said, "Let's get this over with," to the empty car.

"You know, *they* say that patience is a virtue," Ian said, leaning his head in through the passenger door. "Don't you ever wonder who *they* are?"

The appearing and disappearing thing was as annoying as it was amazing. "Not really. And sorry if I'm not eager to continue spending time making sure Alex doesn't blow up St. Hilaire. Or himself."

"Yes, that could get messy."

"So, how do we start?" I asked.

"I think we just do it. I mean, unless you want to light some incense or bang a tambourine." Ian offered. "But then, I don't remember you being the type who needed atmosphere to perform."

I rolled down the window simply for something to do. Alex was supposed to meet me at noon. Since using the radio was no longer a possibility, we didn't have to be in the car, but I liked the idea of being able to escape, if escape was necessary.

And surprisingly, Alex was right on time.

Ian moved into the back of the car as his brother opened the front door and threw himself down in the passenger's seat.

"You better not be dicking me around," Alex said.

Ian laughed in the back seat. I suppressed an urge to throw both of them out into the woods.

"Look, Alex," I said. "Let's get this straight. I'm doing this to get you to leave Dec and his piano alone, not because this is my idea of a good time."

"Oh," said Ian. "This is definitely *not* your idea of a good time."

This was going to be more difficult than I thought.

Alex crossed his arms and slumped back in his seat. "Are we doing this or not?"

I glanced at Ian, nodded, closed my eyes, and took a deep breath. Allowing Ian to speak through me meant lowering every mental defense I had. It would have been a great time for a shot, just to take the edge off. And I wasn't sure what Ian could see or hear while he was in my head. I wasn't sure I wanted to know. But after so many years of keeping people at arm's length, I was disturbed and, I had to admit, almost excited, to let someone in.

I thought back to the short lesson we'd learned about possessions in school and imagined jumping into a frigid pool. Checked off the symptoms: breath burning in my lungs, limbs going numb, thoughts swirling like a funnel cloud. I saw Ian lift my arms. Stretch my muscles. Crack my neck. It was like watching a movie from the front row. Everything too close and intense.

"Hey A," Ian said and flicked Alex under the chin. "How've you been?"

Since the Guild didn't condone possessions, they didn't talk about it much. But one thing we *had* been taught was that mediums weren't "present" during possessions, although that wasn't necessarily true in this case. I couldn't hear Ian's thoughts, but I could hear their conversation as if it were taking place underwater. The younger brother's doubts. Ian proving it was really him by recalling exploits from their childhood. Confusion about Colin's newly intense and inexplicable relationship with Willow Rogers. But when Alex got to the real reason he'd been freaking out and started whining about his mother wanting to send him to reform school because now that Ian was gone, they didn't have enough mediums in the family to justify them staying in St. Hilaire, I checked out.

To distract myself, I classified my grandmother's plants. Angiosperms were plants that produced flowers. Gymnosperms were plants that did not produce flowers. Dicots had two seed leaves. Monocots only had one. On and on.

Eventually, I started feeling my fingers again. Smelled the leather seats. Was irritated by the grating sound of Alex's voice.

I shook my head hard enough to make sure Ian was out of it and glanced in the rearview mirror. The back seat was empty.

"What?" I asked Alex, who I was sure, had been saying *something*.

"I *said* that we need to do this again sometime. I knew Ian would be able to tell me how to handle Mom. But there are still some other things he wouldn't tell me."

"Speaking of answers." I hadn't meant to throw an additional price on top, but it never hurt to ask. "What did Sheridan have to do with all of this?"

Alex glared, wide and hungry. "Guess it doesn't matter now, right? I had the goods on him. David was hanging around outside Eaton Hall when Ian told Clive Rice he thought Dec's parents were going to bite it. I said that if he didn't help me, I was going to rat him out to Dec."

My breath caught. Dec would be devastated to find out anyone knew about his parents and did nothing to warn them. "The Guild knew?" I glanced at the still empty back seat. "Ian knew?"

"Yeah, but…the rules and all of that."

I spun in my seat and suddenly Alex's shirt collar sat bunched and twisted in my hand. "I'm only going to say this once," I whispered. "If you ever tell Dec, if *anyone* ever tells Dec, I'm going to hunt you down, and I promise you, you will never sleep well again."

Alex shivered and grabbed at his shirt. The red cotton looking too much like blood. "Get off me, you nutcase. If I were going to blab, I would have done that already. I just needed something to use on Sheridan so he'd take the fall for marking the cards in the poker game."

I inhaled. Something inside me shuddered with the effort. "Get out of my car," I growled. "Now."

Alex didn't wait for a second invitation. I gunned the engine and was off before the passenger door shut.

I drew the shades in my room and crawled into bed, sure that the pain in my head was more a product of Alex's confession than Ian's possession. The kicker was, for once, Alex was right. The Guild *did* have rules about telling people about their imminent deaths. And I had to agree those rules made sense in the abstract. We couldn't go around stopping people from dying like we were gods or something.

Those regulations were harder to stomach when I thought about Dec's parents specifically and what their deaths had done to my best friend.

I went back and forth about whether to be pissed at Ian for keeping his knowledge to himself. He had reached out to the Guild, so one point to him, I guess.

"Flower sperm?" Ian asked.

I should have been surprised he was suddenly in my room, but somehow it seemed fitting. I stared at him.

"Don't worry. I wasn't really listening. The subject matter just caught my attention."

"I'll bet." I pulled myself up against the headboard. "Did you honestly tell the Guild about Dec's parents?"

Ian flinched as if he'd been caught doing something illegal. "I thought they might consider getting off their thrones and doing the right thing for once."

"How did you know the Hamptons were going to die?"

"Hell, Griffin. How do you know anything? A feeling. A dream. Some freaking tea leaf out of place. I just knew."

There was a tone in his voice that was off. Defensive rather than cocky. "What aren't you telling me?"

"If you're ever going to join the Guild, you have to learn to ask more specific questions. Try again." Ian's eyes were hard and steely, testing me.

"What do you know about Dec's parents' deaths?"

Ian smirked. It was the smirk he used when he dismissed his brother Colin. My fists clenched. I tried again.

"I can feel it. You know something." I reached down inside myself and realized it was true. I might not to be able to read Ian anymore, but I *did* know this. "What is it?"

Ian paused for a moment. "So, I'll reward you with a little story. The Guild. Charlotte North specifically. She thought what St. Hilaire really needed was credibility. And spectacle. But mostly more money. A *lot* more money. The town had no obvious way of raising it, so she drafted me and the Hamptons to call the spirit of Sarahlyn Beck."

"What?" I thought of the statue in the square. Sarahlyn holding out her hands. Rocks in one, gold in the other.

Ian stood and placed the heel of his boot on the windowsill. He didn't look at me. "You'll remember from school that Sarahlyn was rumored to be an alchemistic. They said she could literally create gold. Who better than her to solve St. Hilaire's fiscal issues?"

"That's absurd."

"Of course. But it worked." Ian paused and turned, a mix of pride and regret merging in his eyes. For the first time, it seemed like being Ian Mackenzie was an exhausting thing to be. Knowledge had a weight. And Ian knew many things.

"What do you mean it worked?"

"I mean, the Guild formed a team. We contacted Sarahlyn. And we helped Charlotte North convince her to tell us where she'd stashed all the gold she made." Ian fiddled with the crank of the window, opening and closing it and opening it again.

I looked away, afraid that if I complained, Ian would stop talking. "Congratulations. What am I missing?"

"Don't be dense, Griffin. What you're missing is everything you learned in school. Ghosts don't just give you shit. There's a price for everything."

Before I could point out the obvious about Ian being a ghost and therefore having some ulterior motive himself, he sat on the bed and put his head in his hands. Talking in the direction of the floor, he said, "Rice and Norton were nonchalant; they'd gotten most of what they wanted. Where do you think the new gymnasium came from? Or the upgrades to that ridiculous old train? Just ask your father how much that thing costs to keep in working order. But Sarahlyn told us we would pay. I assumed she meant me, because, well, I just did. I never thought she was going to go after the Hamptons. At least not until I heard about the crash."

"You're saying Sarahlyn Beck killed Dec's parents?"

Ian's head snapped up. "I'm *saying* I believe the Guild was aware of the risks and asked us to help them anyhow without putting any of their own pretty little necks in jeopardy. And yes, I'm saying that Sarahlyn Beck somehow caused the accident that killed Dec's parents. Ergo, the Guild killed Dec's parents."

Knowledge had a weight, and this knowledge sat on my chest so heavily, I couldn't take in any air.

"And probably others," Ian said quietly.

Two questions played tug-of-war in my head. They both sucked.

I went for the hardest one. "You?"

Ian rolled his eyes, trying to look like he didn't care about the answer. He repeated, "Everything has its price."

I reached out a hand and forced myself to place it on Ian's back. His muscles rippled under my touch. I had to remind myself that he was a ghost. "Did she kill you too?"

Ian turned with a vacant and unreadable expression. Then he sprung up from the bed. "I shared my suspicions with the Hamptons that things weren't going to end well," he said, avoiding my question. "And they had the same feeling I did. Rice was climbing the walls because the numbers weren't matching up and things were getting strange."

"Strange?" I asked. "In St. Hilaire?" My head was spinning with all of this new information.

"Yeah, go figure." Ian waved me off as if he were talking to himself. I wondered if he'd ever shared this story with anyone else. "Things kept getting moved around town. Do you remember how Sarahlyn's statue kept turning green and no one could figure out why? And that wasn't all. My car was acting up. The Guild's whole computer system shut down for a week. I knew it was just a matter of time before she found a way to get her revenge."

He stopped and looked at me as if he'd run out of steam and suddenly remembered I was here. His voice softened when he said, "Anyhow, it was Dec's dad who told me to leave a note for Alex just in case I ever found myself *indisposed*. He was the one who gave me the information about Alex using the piano string in conjunction with the car radio. He said he got the idea from something his grandfather had told him about using a string from the piano along with some old family Victrola in order to talk to his dead wife. I knew Alex wasn't going to do well if anything happened to me. Not with Colin around, anyhow."

"So, back up. You warned the Hamptons?" I repeated, my brain latching onto the last lucid thing Ian had said.

"Yeah," he said. "But what were they supposed to do? Never leave the house?"

"And Dec doesn't know?"

"As he hasn't burned down Eaton Hall yet, I'm going to vote no."

My mind twisted and spun. "But Dec got the same letter I did about auditioning for Student Leader. Why would the Guild want him? Why not just let him skip town?"

"Where do you want me to start? However much he pretends to be the world's suckiest medium, he's descended from many generations of serious talent. They need him to keep that DNA going."

However much Ian's words made my stomach churn, I had to stifle a smile at the idea of the Guild trying to forcibly pair Dec up with anyone.

"Anyhow," he continued. "I said Charlotte North got *most* of what she wanted. Some of the gold didn't quite make it into the Guild's account, and I suspect they think the Hamptons might have told their son where it went. Or that I would have told Alex, not like there was a chance in hell of that."

I rubbed my eyes. "So where did it go?" I asked.

Ian looked away. *Hell.*

The sudden hopelessness I felt wasn't just about Ian, or Dec, or even Marian and Robert Hampton. It was also about every desire, every dream I'd had about joining the Guild. Even before I'd known of St. Hilaire as somewhere more than just the place where my grandmother lived, the place that my mother had left, refusing to return, I'd had yearned to be a part of something more, something greater. And now, when that desire—that *need*—was stronger than ever, here I was finding out that the Guild wasn't just corrupt, they were murderers who were trying to create some twisted sort of St. Hilaire master race.

"Ian," I said, needing the onslaught of information to stop for just one minute, so I could take stock of everything that was happening.

But Ian hadn't gotten that memo. He looked back at me and said, "Obviously you have to join the Guild and change it. You have to change it all."

I was certain he was joking, but no, his eyes were blazing in that way that made it so hard to look away and pretend I wanted to do anything other than just stare into them.

I thought about my promise to Dec, to do just what Ian was asking of me. But that was before I'd learned about the Guild's role in the Hamptons' deaths. Now I couldn't imagine how I could possibly join them. "You're out of your mind," I said carefully. "Can't you just return the money? Then we all move on?"

"That wouldn't change what happened. And what are you going to do? Show up at Eaton Hall holding a bag of money with a bright red bow on it? No, Griffin. You're going to need that cash as some point. Don't let yourself forget that we have dirt on the Guild that they don't want shared. But at the same time, we're young and talented and the perfect ones to save St. Hilaire. The only ones who can, really."

"You're dead," I reminded him.

"Minor issue," Ian shot back. "Outside of Norton and Rice, you're the only living person who knows what happened. I was there. They aren't going to be able to deny it. Rice and Norton are going to have to step down or something. Maybe not right away. You're going to have to prove yourself first. So stop looking for problems and let me help you."

Ian could guarantee my place with the Guild. He'd been their star pupil after all, and his death had been devastating for them. They couldn't reach him. Yet here he was, larger than life, offering me his help. His friendship. His honesty, if such a thing even existed.

Ian was smiling slightly with a look of naked anticipation on his face. I steeled myself, ready to accept his offer. I was suddenly certain I could handle whatever the cost would turn out to be.

But then...

But then...

Ian reached his hand out slowly. Had it been anyone else, I would have thought the action a tentative one. In the space of a breath Ian's hand was on my wrist. His fingers traced the wings of my owl tattoo, following each elaborately designed feather to its tip. My arm shook. Ian's touch felt like a drug. It felt like a violation. It felt awfully, terribly good. And it was the last of those feelings that made me pull my arm sharply away and avoid Ian's deep blue eyes when I said, "I think you need to leave."

43

ANNIE

"I don't have the flu. This is simply the truth of the matter," Tristan said sadly.

"But there must be something we can *do*," I said again. When Dmitry had been in pain, I had urged him to try different combinations of medications. When I was concerned I was not going to place in important competitions, I worked harder. In my experience, there had always been a way around a problem. Death, I was learning, was not a problem that could be solved. In Dmitry's case, there had been no chance to say goodbye. No chance to talk to him one last time. I was not going to make that same mistake again and watch passively as Tristan faded away into nothing.

I moved over on the piano bench, close enough to Tristan

that the velvet of his coat rested on my hand. His only reaction was to stare at his fingers as they hovered over the keys. "Do not think about the big concerns right now," I said. "Just focus on the things you still can do. What would you like to do, Tristan?"

He lowered his arms to his sides and looked at me as if no one had ever asked him what he wanted before. It was probably true; no one had asked him in a long, long time. I was glad I had.

"I suppose I'd like to try to play one last time," he said. "And sitting here, talking to you…" He stood and his cheeks flushed. "It's quite pleasant to have a normal conversation again."

I suppressed a laugh. "You find this normal?"

"It is." He nodded. "For me. I'm not sure how many such conversations I have left."

I shoved my hands under my legs to keep my fingers from running through the Prelude. This close to the piano, the urge to play was almost more than I could resist. "So, what would you like to talk about?"

Tristan thought for a moment and then said, "Music? I haven't been able to even discuss it in a very long time."

So much for avoiding the Prelude.

"In fact…" he said, eyes darting around the room. He stepped over to a low table, and stared at the computer that Dec and Laura shared. "This plays music, right? Could you make it work? I'd like to hear something new."

I hesitated, but Tristan's eyes pleaded with me, and I hoped Dec might understand the invasion of privacy.

"Well, maybe," I said. I opened a music program, connected the earbuds, and pushed play, half-expecting to hear my own music. But no, it was something loud and screeching. The screen read, *Iron Maiden*. That was unlikely to be to Tristan's taste.

I hit pause, and flipped through the artist list, landing on Dmitry Petrov. Dec had not been kidding when he said he was a fan. It was one thing to have my releases, but having Dmitry's seemed somehow more meaningful.

I selected one of my favorites. "Here," I said. I took the earbuds out and handed them to Tristan. "Tell me what you think." It was fascinating to watch as he put them in and listened to Dmitry. What started as confusion moved quickly to joy.

"Oh," he said. His hands moved by his sides as if they were re-creating the music he was hearing, suddenly free from the pain of his curse.

While Tristan listened, I walked around the room, trying out a variety of mismatched chairs. There were candles and electric lights, tapestries, and speakers. It seemed as if this room contained a bit of each era Hampton House had seen.

Behind me, Tristan coughed. The track had ended, the earbuds were in his hand, and tears were in his eyes.

"That was magic," he said reverentially. "Pure magic."

"That was my teacher, Dmitry," I replied, but really, they were the same thing.

I was about to share the highs and lows of Dmitry's miraculous career and heartbreaking downfall, but Tristan looked puzzled, so I stopped.

"He died," I said instead. "It had been coming for a long time. He was unhappy. The arthritis kept him from playing. He told me the medication made his head spin so much, he was unable to compose."

I sat in one of the flowered chairs. Before Tristan could respond, or I could give in to panic, I asked, "What is it like wherever Dmitry is now?"

Tristan's shoulders dropped noticeably. "Oh, Annie, I don't know. And I'm not being evasive. I realize that Daniel assumes I am, more often than not. But I really don't know. I am, it seems, in between things. And I hope, for your sake, that your friend is not. Do you think you and he left things unfinished?"

My question had been too large, my chance of success too unlikely. I thought back to the email Dmitry had sent, possibly—probably—knowing he was going to die. "I think he has already told me everything he needed to."

I stood and reached out to touch Tristan's shoulder. What I felt was not the velvet of his coat, but a whisper of velvet, like something that had once been there, but was no longer there.

He turned his head toward me, his expression unreadable. "Then you are fortunate, as well as free to enjoy your life. To move on and enjoy living."

It was a formal statement. Far more of a decisive one than I had heard him make, and, in it, I caught a glimmer of what he must have been like when he was still alive and still the boy composer whose music was praised in the highest circles.

I did not feel fortunate, however. I felt like missing Dmitry was a tangible thing that would fall out of the sky and crush me as soon as I left St. Hilaire. "I wish I could talk to him," I said, without thinking.

Tristan crossed his legs awkwardly and worried at a button of his coat. Not looking up, he asked, "What would you say?"

I thought about it. "I would tell him I love him. That I am grateful for everything he did for me."

"Do you suspect he was unaware of those things?" Tristan asked, his eyes still down.

My last meeting with Dmitry had been like a million others before. We had drunk too much coffee. Reviewed my upcoming itinerary. My set list. He had made me watch an episode of some ghastly TV show that he was binge-watching while I assisted him with the hot wax bath he used to ease his arthritic hands. "No." I shook my head. "He knew."

Tristan nodded and then raised his head, one eye visible through his mass of hair. I had the urge to put my arm around him, but I was afraid it would go right through. For the first time, he really did resemble a ghost, seeming to exist both in the room and outside of it.

"What about you?" I asked.

He cocked his head in an impossibly unnatural way. "I know too, Annie." Answering a question I had not specifically meant to ask, he said, "You love the Prelude, so therefore, I've been loved too."

I forced myself to nod and moved over, closer to him, imagining I could feel heat coming from Tristan's body, but really, shivering with cold.

DEC

How long had it been since I'd stood at the edge of my parents' graves? A month? Two? If I hated seeing the gray stones from my window, I really hated standing here staring at *Dear Father. Dear Mother.*

Tristan's coat rustled next to me as he shifted from foot to foot. Without his ever-present bidi, his hands roamed from the cuffs of his jacket, to the flowers we'd brought, to the collar of his shirt.

"Say something," I demanded.

Tristan flinched. "I *am* saying something, Daniel. I'm saying goodbye."

The edges of my vision narrowed until all that remained was a thin pinprick of light that bounced off the etched names on the stone. I blinked away the start of tears, but more followed.

"Tristan." I wasn't sure what I wanted to say. *Stay. Let's start over. We can fix this.*

"Don't be sad." Tristan bumped his shoulder into mine in an odd brotherly way. "This is all strangely freeing. I don't suppose I can explain that to you. Not to say I'm not somewhat"— he stopped, and half of his mouth flattened while he looked for the right word—"dismayed by this latest turn of events. I mean, I've been tethered here for quite a long time."

I ran a hand through my hair. It was getting long, and the air was getting chilly, and there was something wrong between me and Russ, only I didn't know what it was or how to fix it, and Annie had turned the world upside down, and I didn't know how to turn it right side up again or if I even should or wanted to. I just needed time to stop long enough for me to *think*. Long enough for me to make sense of things before they continued spiraling so miserably out of control.

Tristan lowered himself to the ground on the edge of the flowerbed across from the graves. It was odd how much he looked like one of the stone fairies so many people here kept in their front gardens as he steepled his long fingers and looked through them. "When I was a young child, my mother took me to a fortune-teller." He drew his fingers down and held them in his lap. "I can still see the blue caftan the fortune-teller was wearing. She told me I would travel great distances and would leave a very long legacy. I think she had a sense of humor, don't you?"

My chest tightened just like it had after my parents' funeral when Harriet told me and Laura she was going to accept guardianship of us. There were too many emotions fighting for any single one to get my full attention.

"That part didn't surprise me. I mean, obviously. I'd already had a piece performed by three major symphonies."

"Of course, you had," I said, only half joking.

"Then she told me I was going to change lives. When everything happened, I thought about her. It seemed as though I hadn't been able to change any lives for the better. Not my father's, certainly. And I don't know if my brothers cared or remembered me. Maybe a couple of musicians did."

I turned toward Tristan, putting my back to the graves. I couldn't look at them anymore.

"I'd like to think I've helped Annie," Tristan said. "And…"

I knew I was supposed to fill in the missing words. The problem was, to do that meant I had to accept that Tristan was, in fact, going away. For good this time.

I took a deep breath. "You saved my life. I know I've been a jerk to you," I said, hoping the admission would make me feel like less of one. It didn't work. "I actually liked hanging out with you when I was a kid. You know that, right?"

"It's okay, Daniel. You don't owe me an apology. You forget that I grew up with younger brothers. This is what happens in families. You sometimes spar even while you hold one another's hearts."

Tristan looked at me through his long lashes. Normally, I would have fired back some snarky, defensive comment, but for once, I didn't want to.

We all sat in the music room, even though Annie, Russ, and I were the only ones who could see Tristan. Harriet and Laura were able to listen to the music he was playing on the piano, though. I couldn't imagine how weird it was to see the keys moving on their own.

Tristan's face was tight with concentration as he fought to stay solid. Annie and I were both snuffling back tears.

I took Annie's hand and squeezed. She squeezed back. On my other side, Russ stared somberly at the base of the piano, his black clothing appropriate for once.

Annie had been playing the Prelude so often, I'd almost memorized the various new sections, but watching and hearing Tristan play them was unlike anything I'd ever experienced.

As Tristan hit the midpoint of the piece, his hands slowed, stilled, and then stopped. He rubbed his fingers. Pain shot across his face. Then he struggled to smile and said, "Thank you, Daniel. It was nice to do that one last time."

I stood, quick enough that my head spun. "Don't talk like that."

Tristan shook his head.

I slapped at the piano. "How can you be okay with disappearing?"

Harriet came up behind me and squeezed my arm before walking out.

Laura stared at the piano bench. "I wish I could see you, Tristan. But thank you. That was beautiful." Then she left too.

Then it was just the three of us. No, four. Or more like three-and-a-half.

Annie wiped her face on her sleeve and sat next to Tristan.

They exchanged a look that I didn't understand, almost as if they were having a conversation that didn't include the rest of us.

"How does it go?" she asked.

What little color there was in Tristan's face drained away. "No," he whispered. "You can't. I mean, I couldn't ask you to…" He looked around as if he were seeking help. Russ scrambled up to the piano before I even saw him move.

"Wait," I asked. "What's happening?"

Russ had been quiet up to this point. Too quiet. But now he asked Tristan, "The terms of the curse. What were they again?"

Tristan turned and caught my eye before answering. "I'd never rest until I finished the Prelude," he said slowly. "But it has to be completed on this piano. That's the part I remember, anyhow."

I moved to stand beside them. It was odd, this family that we'd become. Odd and fragile and it meant even more because we knew it wouldn't last. Not for much longer anyhow.

"Can you do it, Annie?" Russ asked.

Annie hesitated, but I could see her eagerness. She looked at Tristan and when he nodded, she said, "I think so. Will this allow him to stay?"

A chill went up my spine. "Wait," I shouted. "*What is happening?*"

Russ rubbed his wrist and paused long enough for the chill in my spine to turn into something hot and explosive. Then he said, "Annie is offering to help finish composing the Prelude on your piano in order to try to break the curse."

It seemed like this plan was a hopeful thing, but no one looked hopeful. "Break the curse? So, what, then Tristan will be okay? And what about Annie? Is she at any risk?"

Russ was silent in a way that meant he was weighing his words. "I don't know for sure. I can't answer either of those things. Not without knowing the exact words Tristan's father used and his intent. For instance, if his father actually used the word 'rest,' we'd have to know what that concept meant to him."

"Then she's not doing it." I knew my words were offensive, and that I didn't have the right to make any of Annie's decisions, but there was no way I could stand by and watch as St. Hilaire destroyed her too.

"Well, of course," Tristan started, just as Russ said, "It's likely..."

"Stop," Annie interjected. She looked around the room as if her words had even surprised herself. "Tristan," she asked. "Are you willing to allow me the honor of finishing your Prelude?"

Tristan stared at the keyboard for an impossibly long time. Then, although Annie had been the one to ask the question, he looked directly at me when he answered. "Yes. I think it's time, Daniel, don't you? I'm tired."

Acid ate at the back of my throat. I didn't want to take responsibility for this decision.

"There is one other thing," Annie said.

I saw it now, this other thing. It was a fear in her eyes, a tiredness of her own that I hadn't had time to notice. "Annie?"

She looked down at her hands. "I was unsure before, but I believe something might be happening. To me. This all sounds so silly."

"Go on," Russ told her.

"I am supposed to be practicing. For the Hull. And for my upcoming shows. It is just that I cannot seem to play anything aside from the Prelude. I have not been able to since I played it on this piano the first time." Her cheeks colored, and I stared at Russ, willing him to sort this out as he'd sorted out so many issues in the past.

"You mean, you aren't playing the other pieces well?" Russ asked, but I knew that wasn't what she meant.

Annie shook her head. "No. It is more as though I feel I *have to* play the Prelude. As though I can't stop. I am incapable of playing anything other than this."

I breathed in. "Is this part of your...?" I asked Tristan. I couldn't wrap my mouth around the word "curse." "Is that why Annie has been up playing in the middle of the night?"

She came up next to me. "I have been having problems sleeping. Playing the Prelude is the only thing that feels *right*."

Tristan looked pained. "I'd never want to hurt Annie. Is this my fault?"

We all looked to Russ for answers. He took a deep breath. "It isn't you," he said to Tristan. "It may be the curse, but it isn't you."

"So, what do we do?" I asked. If anyone was to blame for dragging Annie into this mess, it was me. I should have done the right thing and sent her away the night she showed up, instead of selfishly allowing her to stay.

Russ stood at the window, his back to us. I could see his shoulders rise and fall as his breathing sped up. When he turned, he said to Tristan, "If we're going to try to end the curse, I think you and Annie have to finish the Prelude while you still can."

"So, if we do this, Tristan will be okay?"

Russ shook his head slowly. "No. As I said, if we do this—and it works—Annie will be free of whatever it is that's making her play the Prelude and Tristan will be"—he hesitated—"at rest. Whatever that means."

"But it will be like it was with my dad, right? Like you'll still be out there somewhere?" I asked.

Tristan wrapped his arms around himself and stood next to Russ. Their silence said everything.

45

RUSS

Tristan stood behind Annie, placing his hands—the shadow of his hands because that's all that was left—over her own, guiding her through the music. It was an amazing thing to watch, but if there was one thing I knew, it was that the universe didn't simply hand you gifts. It wanted payment. In full. I had no idea what would be asked of her. Or Tristan. Or Dec.

When the last note stopped ringing through the cavernous room, Tristan whispered, "What happens now?"

"I wish I could tell you," I answered truthfully. This sort of stuff wasn't in any of the books I'd borrowed from Eaton Hall.

"We can't just sit here and wait," Dec insisted.

"Well, what?" I snipped. "Do you want to play a game or something because…"

"Wait," Tristan called out and slowly sunk to the ground. "I..."

Annie cast me a concerned look and leaned down next to him. Her hand hovered just above his shoulder for a moment before plunging straight through him as she tried to comfort him.

"No," Dec demanded. "No, not yet."

"Dec," I warned, stopping him in his tracks.

Tristan looked up at me and then to Annie. "Could you play something else please, Annie? Not the Prelude, but can you play something of your teacher's, perhaps?"

We all watched as she turned back to the piano and settled herself on the bench before launching into something that managed to be slow, sad, and somehow uplifting all at the same time. The notes seemed to take on a life of their own, swirling and swirling around us. Damn, she was good.

Tristan sat in the floor with his eyes closed, swaying slightly to the rhythm. I wanted to go over and hug him, but my feet were rooted where I stood, and I wouldn't have been able to touch him anyway. He was getting more and more transparent as we watched, or maybe it was a trick of light or a product of being tired. But probably not, because before the tune ended, he was gone completely without another word.

46

ANNIE

After the silence, and the tears, and the attempts to say something to take away our pain, and my proving I could now play the Tchaikovsky although it was rusty, and I could not work myself up to caring whether I won the Hull or not, Russ excused himself and went outside.

Dec had gone to speak to Laura about all that had happened. At a loss, I followed Russ and found him lying on the hood of the Mustang. Moonlight shone off the silver surface, the black of Russ's coat reflected in it like a dark cloud across its face.

I walked up to him tentatively, unsure if he wanted to be bothered. Sometimes people walked out because they wanted to be alone, sometimes because they wanted to see if anyone would follow. It had been like that with Dmitry. He would always test people's love for him by doing something outrageous and then wait to see who still cared about him after the inevitable explosion.

Russ sat up before I reached the car and moved over, making room on the shimmering hood.

"That sucked, and I feel as though it is all my fault," I said as I climbed up next to him. "Had I just flown to Canada like Viktor told me to, none of this would have happened, and maybe Tristan would still be here."

"That's possible," Russ said in a way that made the words not hurt as much. "But you have to reframe it. I think the reason he stayed around St. Hilaire so long was to help you. Not deliberately, of course. Maybe he knew, at some subconscious level, that you would come here someday. But either way, at the end, I think, you made him happy."

I had not known Russ long, but I had known him long enough to know he would not say something comforting if he did not believe it. "Thank you," I said.

In the half light, Russ looked younger and less imposing than he had previously, perhaps because his dark clothing blended so perfectly into the night. It felt like our shared experiences and shared concern for Dec had connected us as friends.

"I guess Dec will be free to focus on leaving now," I said, and immediately regretted it when Russ grimaced and pulled his coat around himself. "I'm sorry. I mean, it does not take a psychic. Um, medium... Sometimes it is easier to see things from the outside. And you obviously..." I was aware of myself rambling, so I stopped before I finished my sentence.

I could see the moon reflected in Russ's eyes as if it had taken the place of his pupils, wide and white.

"Does he know?" I asked. It was all too easy to conjure the feeling of Dec's lips on my own. It made me feel guilty for having had something Russ wanted for himself.

"He knows I'd do anything for him. Does anything really matter beyond that?" Russ kept his eyes on the moon. "And like you said, he's leaving. The sooner, the better, actually."

Russ looked at me, and suddenly I was not sure which would be harder, being the one to leave or being the one left.

He paused, rubbing his wrist, and then said, "I know we don't know each other well, and I'm not one for asking for favors, but is it okay for me to ask you for one?"

"Of course."

Russ's tone left no doubt that he was serious. "Help him leave. Help him get out of here as soon as possible."

Help Dec leave? Could I? Was it even possible that we could walk out of St. Hilaire together after all of this was over? My whole time here felt like something from a storybook. Was there any way to move our relationship into real life when I did not even know what I was going to do from here?

"It's what's right for him, Annie," Russ said. "He needs to get out of here."

"What about you?" I asked.

"I'm not going anywhere. I have a meeting with the Guild tomorrow, in fact," he said with the hint of a smile on his face. I stared at him long enough that the smile faded. "My mother," he began and then seemed to think better of it. "Doesn't loving people mean you have to let them do what they need to do?"

I pictured Dmitry, doped up on pain meds after the last time we played together in public. I had wanted to go to a quiet coffee shop to talk. Instead, he had pulled me aside in my dressing room and said he was going out and not to expect him back.

I had always tried to remember my place. Remember who Dmitry was and who I would have been had he not agreed to take me on. But that night, I was hurt. And now that childish hurt embarrassed me in light of Russ's comment.

"Even if you believe they are making a mistake?" I asked.

"Especially then." Russ shrugged and laughed sadly. "How come you never asked if I could contact him for you?"

"Dmitry?"

Russ nodded.

I tried to explain my feelings without divulging my conversation with Tristan. "I believe Dmitry would have spoken to me before he died if he had anything to say. He sent me an email asking me to find the Prelude. I have done that; for better or worse. I do not know that I have anything left to tell him."

Russ looked up at the sky and said, "I wish more people realized that. Sometimes you have to stop. Sometimes you don't get what you want when you try to force things."

I had a sudden urge to hug every inch of Russ's sadness away, but knew better than to try. "I believe you and Dmitry would have gotten along well," I said instead.

Russ pulled his eyes away from the moon and turned to me, but somehow the reflected light stayed in them. "What are you going to do now?"

I thought about the time I had lost and the events I already had scheduled. "I have shows, and this competition, and then…" I hesitated.

"And then?"

I made a decision that had been in the back on my mind for days. "Home. You said I should go home. For a minute, I thought that this place, that St. Hilaire might play a part, but now, well, now I have this bizarre idea that I need to go see my family. Before we get any further apart."

Russ nodded. "Families are tricky, regardless of whether they're the one you're born into or the one you create." He jumped down from the car and held out a hand. I took it and slid off the hood.

RUSS

Sometimes you don't get what you want. It was one thing to say the words to Annie, quite another to accept them myself. Dec was never going to care about me *like that,* and I'd never had any doubt about it.

That didn't make it painless.

On top of it, while I'd proven that my grandmother's solution would work and now had the opportunity to demonstrate my success to the Guild, it was becoming clear that the organization wasn't the creepy-but-benevolent group of elders I'd assumed them to be. They were not only corrupt but had allowed Dec's parents to die. So instead of rising through their ranks and being mentored, I was going to work my ass off because Ian Mackenzie told me that avenging their deaths and stopping the Guild's disturbing plans was my responsibility.

That also sucked.

I walked through the quiet house. My father was, of course, at work. The squeak of the floorboards under my feet was the only noise cutting through the silence. I tried humming. I let out a loud string of expletives to hear how they sounded. I recited Chaucer in Middle English because some teacher at some school had told me it would be an important thing to know. So far it hadn't been.

The living room was cold and drafty. The kitchen cluttered. I didn't go into my father's room because I was a firm believer in privacy. The bathroom reminded me it was my turn to clean this week. I didn't bother going up into the attic.

I went to my room and flicked on the bedside lamp. Flicked it off. Lit the candles that hung off iron sconces. I was waiting for something. I just didn't know what.

I was tired of waiting.

I pulled out my phone and scrolled through my few contacts. Annie's talk of home made me miss my mother. Dad insisted I keep her number in my phone, *just in case*. I was sure that meant I should call if my father was run over by a train or otherwise debilitated. Not because I was confused, sad, and lonely.

I threw the phone onto the desk and looked in the mirror. Spiked hair. Tired eyes. Mouth drawn in a thin line. Like always.

The closet door stood open slightly. Beckoning. I tried to look away. Failed.

I was in the closet without consciously walking over to it,

and felt the joke somewhere deep inside. Maybe Willow had been right after all. I was so tired of hiding from the things I wanted.

The black pack was in my hand before I knew it. I made my way to the bed. Peeled off my coat. Pushed up my sleeve. My arm pulsed. Hungry.

I stared at the owl on my wrist. It stared back.

I was alone. But then I was always alone and probably always would be. So what did it matter? I wasn't a drug user. I wasn't looking for some recreational high. I was a student, a scholar. But I was so freaking tired of it all. I simply needed a break.

I opened the pack and drew up a raindrop of liquid. It looked like a pearl in the needle. I mixed it with an equal-sized pearl of the second substance. I pushed it into my arm and my shoulders relaxed. My vision blurred slightly. I hadn't taken enough to see ghosts. Everything was shadowy. Insubstantial. I knew Dec would strongly disapprove of what I was doing, but that didn't matter. For once, nothing mattered. Not my mom. Or Dec. Or the Guild. Or anything. There would be time to worry about all of that tomorrow. I didn't have to be at my meeting with the Guild for another twelve hours.

I didn't remember the last time I'd felt so unburdened. Almost free. I smiled. *Smiled.*

I lay back on the bed. The room spun pleasantly. Nothing mattered.

"Are you done deliberating? Do you need a Magic 8 ball or something?"

The room was middle-of-the-night dark. Even the light of my clock was missing, so I assumed there'd been a power outage before I realized I could still hear the whirring of the ceiling fan. I squinted and realized that something was blocking my view of the nightstand. *Someone.*

I blinked. Then blinked again. Everything flooded back. Tristan. Annie. Dec. The Guild. Ian. Shit, Ian. "No. Not tonight. You are not doing this to me tonight," I whispered both because my throat was ripped and because I didn't want to wake my father.

Ian bent over and smoothed down my hair until I batted his hand away. He said, "I'll go away if you tell me to. Permanently, if that's what you want. *After* you hear what I have to say."

I struggled to sit. I could see the clock now. 1:00 a.m. I had to be up at eight to get ready to meet with the Guild. I closed my eyes, but Ian was still there when I opened them. "You have five minutes."

"Funny," Ian said. "You never seemed the type for a quickie."

"Make that four."

Ian sighed. "Fine, I'll skip the foreplay. But, I have a teeny bit of a confession to make."

Of course he did. My right arm ached where I'd taken the shot. Everything ached if I was honest. Something in me longed for a repeat, if I was being even more honest. "Then go find a priest."

"My. You do wake up grumpy, don't you?"

"Ian. I have to meet with the Guild. Just say what you have

to and then leave." I looked at the clock again. Three minutes. I could endure anything for three minutes.

I glared at him until he sat and bent forward, arms on his legs, his back toward me, his eyes on some unknown point in space. "You need to talk to me about that night in the woods."

I froze. "No," I insisted. "I'm not doing this. Not today."

"Chill, Russ." Ian's voice was strange, raw. "I'm not going to hurt you."

It was the first time I could remember Ian using my first name, and it twisted inside me, this presumption that I'd let Ian close enough to do any damage.

I buried my face in the bedspread, hoping Ian would be gone when I came up for air. The room was heavy with silence; certainly more than three minutes had passed. My thoughts tangled with my feelings. All of them felt jagged. New. Like something being woken.

"I know," I said. It had never been pain that scared me. Not exactly.

"Then trust me long enough for one conversation. Trust that maybe you're the best that St. Hilaire has, but that I know things you don't. Trust that I want to help you."

Perhaps Ian was telling the truth about helping. There was no doubt he'd helped Tristan. The thing with Ian was, he always meant what he said when he said it. Sometimes, though, that only lasted until the next time he opened his mouth.

"Tell me about that night," Ian repeated.

Whether I wanted to or not, I knew I couldn't answer Ian's question. There was a dark hole in my memories. I stared down at my comforter until my vision blurred—the blue swirls that

I'd often watched until I lost myself inside their movement weren't working this time. "You tell me," I said, looking up at Ian. "You tell me what happened that night."

Ian's blue eyes opened wide. For a minute, I was sure he was working on some snarky reply. But his voice was soft when he replied, "We met in the woods. Do you remember?"

"Yeah, we were..." I struggled to remember what we'd been doing there. My brain gifted me with the smell of moss, the sound of the rain, the prickle of my skin when my arm had brushed against Ian's. Nothing useful.

"You were looking for some of the plants in your grand-mother's book," Ian prodded.

"*Artemisia absinthium*," I said mechanically as parts of the memory fell into place.

"That wasn't..."

"Wormwood," I translated. "I was looking for wormwood."

"Right, that's it."

I shuddered under the weight of Ian's gaze and attempted to remember, attempted to picture us traipsing through the wet fields in the woods, looking at plant after plant. "You tried to stop me."

Ian nodded. "That stuff's illegal for a reason."

I stared at him silently. Not like Ian had ever cared about things like legality, and I was still unsure of the point of this conversation.

"You weren't ready for it, Griffin," Ian continued, his voice still careful. "And you proved my point by trying to punch me."

Now that he said it, I remembered finding the plant. Silvery-green, the fronds grew outward from a tight center. I hadn't had time to think or to process the collection and treatment of the leaves. My grandmother had written about smoking them, but Ian was there pulling at me, and I'd had to act quickly.

"Sorry," I mumbled. In truth, I hadn't *tried* to punch Ian. What I'd actually done was succeed in smashing my fist into Ian's sternum, forcing him back long enough to give me room to grab a handful of bitter leaves and swallow them.

"You stripped naked in the woods and said you were being chased by stars," Ian said, ignoring the apology. Gone was the tentative tone, the cautious approach. This was the Ian I knew. "It was either my lucky day or you were losing your mind. Much as I didn't want to, I assumed the latter."

My memory ran dry. None of these last actions registered anywhere in my head. My blood surged, studded with shame. I shivered and went to pull my coat tight.

Ian grabbed my wrist. "No. Stop."

I stopped.

"I didn't know what to do. You went ape shit when I said I'd take you to Eaton Hall, and I couldn't take you home. Your dad didn't need to see you like that. Lord knows, Hampton would have tried to kill me had I taken you there, but he seemed the best bet, so I dialed his number on your phone, stuck it in your hand, and hid in the woods until he showed. I didn't want someone from the Guild finding you first."

It was odd, this Ian who admitted such things. It made me want...but no. I shook my head, worried that the drug had stayed dormant in my system, waiting for something like this. My head didn't clear. "But that didn't. It doesn't." Speaking was difficult. Thoughts curled through my head, escaping my grasp.

Ian took my arm and flipped my wrist over and traced the faint white circles that made up the owl with his thumb, again and again. It felt like he'd been doing it for a long, long time when finally he broke the silence and said, "And then you stopped speaking to me."

I had to clear my throat, but honestly, I was surprised to have any voice at all. "It seemed like the safe thing to do."

"Safe?" Ian laughed, knowing that safety wasn't something I usually went looking for.

"Are you going to tell me what this is all about?" I asked.

Ian gave me his Cheshire Cat grin. "Are you going to agree to work with me to sort this shit out with the Guild?"

I took a deep breath, a cleansing breath, Dec's mom would have called it. Then I nodded slightly, which was as much as I had to offer.

"Stellar." Ian lifted an eyebrow. "But my point is..." He launched himself off the bed and scooped my backpack out of the closet, pulling out the black pouch of vials as if he owned them. "You need to ditch all this."

"No."

Ian stood over me, muscular arms crossed, glaring at me like he used to glare at Colin when he was chewing him out for some infraction. "I'm not your..." I started unsure of how to finish my sentence. *Brother. Lover. Sycophant.* None of them quite fit.

"I thought you were going to die that night. I'm not going to stand by and think that again."

"You're serious?" I asked. The possibility that Ian had been spying on me pushed into my head.

"I'm serious."

"Thanks for caring, but I'm not going to die. I know what I'm doing. You don't have to save me." I rubbed my eyes in disbelief. "Besides, weren't you the one telling me to use my 'unique abilities' to win over the Guild?"

"I'm not saying you don't know what you're doing. But sometimes, when you think you're using something, it's really using you."

Before I could formulate a response, Ian added, "Also, now you have *me*."

I didn't move a muscle, held in place by my anger. All except my jaw, which clenched tight. "You. Are. Not. My. Abilities."

Ian broke out into a wide, arrogant smile. "No, Griffin. I'm better. I'm what they want, only they can't have me without you."

"So now I'm a charity case?" My head was spinning. I was still having a surprisingly hard time latching onto words.

"I didn't say that either," Ian insisted. "*You* are the best that St. Hilaire has. *You* are going to take over this entire operation, straighten it out, and make it mean something. *You* are possibility."

"Possibility?" It was an improbable word. "What does that even mean?"

Ian put the pack of vials down on the bed and sat next to it. He smiled the snakelike smile that made my internal organs melt. "It means you're better than your grandmother." Ian slid the zipper of the black case open. "It means you're better than the mother who abandoned you." I watched in shock as he grabbed one of the vials I'd worked so hard to fill with serums.

The top snapped open in his hand with a terrifying *click*, and then he leaned over and poured the liquid into the dirt around the base of my ficus. "It means you're better than I am, although don't quote me on that." As we watched, the dirt bubbled up; one white shoot poked up through the soil, bloomed a flower as iridescent as Ian's Mustang, spun around three or four times, dropped off, and died.

Ian raised an eyebrow and looked at me. "You're better than this. And you're a fuckload better than you think you are." His voice was a whisper as sharp as a razor.

I couldn't look away from the plant. Something inside me echoed the life and death of the flower. I thought I might laugh. I thought I might be sick. The crook of my arm burned with desire for the substance Ian had spilled out. My hands clenched. I was shaking.

I still have one vial. I can make more. That realization was the only thing allowing me to hold it together. I had my grandmother's notebook. Her plants were still growing deep in the woods behind the house. I could make more. I'd be fine. Ian didn't understand. Of course he didn't, he was Ian Mackenzie. He didn't need to understand everything I'd gone through, everything I'd sacrificed, everything I'd hidden. Ian had never had to do any of those things.

Ian grabbed my chin and turned my head until I had no option but to look straight into his extraordinarily blue eyes. "You're on the brink, Griffin. I can feel it."

"On the brink of what?"

"Losing it. Believe me, I've known junkies. I get the pull. But I saw you in the freaking woods that night. And now you're one step from throwing away everything you have ever wanted because this"—he moved back and held up the other vial—"is going to become more important to you than anything else."

I wanted to reach for it, to safeguard the thin glass tube that Ian held too tightly. I wasn't a junkie. I knew exactly what I was doing. It was all for a cause, a greater purpose. Besides, it wasn't as if I *needed* the drug. I'd done perfectly fine before I moved to St. Hilaire, known things I shouldn't have known and occasionally talked to people that no one else saw. And I didn't need it now. But that didn't stop every molecule in my body from wanting it.

Ian continued, "The good thing is, you're also one step away from getting everything else."

Was I? Was it still possible that I could walk into the Guild's testing room and pass their tests clean? On my own? Was it still possible I could make my father's sacrifice worth it? Possible I could make sure that what happened to the Hamptons never happened to anyone else? Possible that Dec… No, *that* wasn't going to happen. In my heart, I'd had always known that would never happen. Now Dec was leaving; I had to accept it. It's just that accepting it would be so much easier if I had my grand-mother's serum, the option of a few missing hours when things got too much to handle.

"You have to want to succeed more than you want anything else. Do you?" Ian held the remaining vial out. It wavered in front of my eyes, the thin glass the only thing standing between me and the liquid. I could almost feel the serum crawling through my arm. My mouth was dry. I held the cuff of the bed-spread in clenched fists. It would take only one swift movement to grab the tube, another to conceal it safely in the pocket of my coat.

I licked my lips. Hesitated.

"Let me know when you figure it out," Ian said and vanished, taking the last vial with him.

48

DEC

Nothing came for free. Everything had a price. The universe wasn't the benevolent giver of unearned favors; it demanded payment. Even St. Hilaire elementary kids knew that. And now I was living proof.

I opened the window. The room smelled like lemons, even though the only scented thing here was a bouquet of flowers that mirrored the one Tristan and I had taken to the cemetery.

My phone buzzed. The Guild again. They hung up after two rings, not long enough to leave a voicemail.

I turned and stared at the photo of my parents. Marian and Robert Hampton would have done anything for the Guild. They actually *had* when they agreed to date and then gave up everything to stay in St. Hilaire and later forced me to pretend I

couldn't see Tristan in order to protect me. And not even knowing those things had changed the fact that my parents would be
disappointed in me for shirking my responsibility to our family.
Now that I was so close to leaving, I had to face that fact.

What kind of life would I have if I gave up and stayed here?
Would I even have one? I tried to picture myself serving in the
Youth Corps, following a Guild member around and running
their errands. I had to wonder who they might pair me up with
in their hopes of strengthening the next generation or whatever.
The idea alone made me nauseous.

Leaving was my only option.

I sunk to the floor, eyes still on the photo. "Please don't hate
me," I whispered, hoping my parents could hear me.

Wherever they were.

49

ANNIE

I was not surprised there had been a price to pay for breaking Tristan's curse. Or even that I was the one who had to pay it. I had been linked to the Prelude for years, more than I even knew. And it was right that I was the one who brought the curse to an end.

But that did not make it a lighter burden.

I shook my necklace and pressed the button again to make it play, but the gears were stuck and silent.

I pulled out my keyboard and tried to play the Prelude, but when I got to the end of the part I had been playing for years, I stopped; the notes that came next were nowhere in my memory.

The necklace. The notes on the mirror. The part that Tristan had hummed with me, the ending I'd played with him in the music room. It was all gone.

I ran downstairs to the piano and played the dissonant end piece, then played it again, trying to think of something else, *anything* else that might jog my memory of the melody. But my fingers were frozen, useless, on the keys.

I tried to hum the notes, but it was futile. The entire remainder of the Prelude was just gone.

Gone.

And with it went my plans for the Hull.

And possibly my career.

And Tristan's legacy.

And my promise to Dmitry.

50

RUSS

Balance. That was the thing at St. Hilaire's heart, really. Life versus death. Knowledge versus ignorance. Truth versus lies. Our plane of being versus whatever else existed.

Dec and Annie and I had thrown off that balance by breaking Tristan's curse, and I suspected I was going to throw it off a lot more in the future if Ian had anything to say about it.

I was surprisingly okay with that.

But it didn't bring me any comfort as I sat on the floor of my room, shivering. Even in my coat, my warmest sweater, the blanket off the bed, I couldn't stop the chill. I shook and tried to convince myself that I was experiencing some unknown part of Tristan's curse. Through it all, Ian's voice rang in my head and told me I'd done this to myself.

I crawled to my bookcase, looking for something distracting. I pulled out book after book, throwing each to the floor. Then I scrambled to pile them up in a messy stack before the pages crumpled. It was pointless. There was no way to trick my mind this time.

I leaned my head against the wall. The photo of my mother caught my eye, although it was the memory of Ian holding the tiny silver frame that held it there.

I bit my bottom lip to keep from crying out, but a wave of pain made me double over. Screw Ian Mackenzie. Screw the Guild. Screw everything.

I. Just. Needed. One. Damned. Shot.

51

DEC

I was on hold. *On hold.* Bad enough the Guild had assumed I'd *ever* be interested in working for them as a Student Leader. Bad enough I'd had to actually pick up the phone to call them. Bad enough Colin Mackenzie had answered the phone and chewed me out for not having the Guild flag up in front of the house and threatened to put us on some *list*, but now, I was on hold. It was wrong. Not to mention freaking annoying. On top of it, they were playing some sort of new age pan flute music that was going to make my head explode.

I put the phone on speaker and threw it onto my bed, but the music was even more annoying through the tiny amplifier. Then I took out the old hard-side suitcase I'd stashed in the closet and opened it. It smelled pleasantly musty. Laura and

I had always imagined it held air from trips our parents had taken. I wondered if my own journey would take their scent away.

I threw some things into it, clothes mostly, but it was hard to know what I'd need in my new life.

The music continued, but without the possibility of Tristan, my room held a smothering type of silence. I could still smell citrus in the fabric of the drapes, and it was hard to stop looking for him in the shadows.

I knew how grief worked, and I wasn't ready to drown in it again.

The pan flute music played on and then was punctuated by a knock on my door.

"Come in."

"They called," Annie said. She stared over at my phone and sat next to it. "The train company. The train has been fixed."

I studied her face, hoping to get some idea of how she felt about it, but I had no clue. "Oh?" I said. "I mean, congratulations. I guess."

A new type of sadness welled up in me. It was over. I'd had my chance and blown it, or been distracted by Tristan and Russ, and that was it. Annie and I would exchange emails or maybe postcards. Someday she'd write and tell me about the great guy she met in Switzerland or Greece, and I would have to pretend to be happy, like I was pretending now.

I sat next to Annie in time to see her swipe at her eyes with the back of her hand.

"I'm sorry," she said. "The Prelude is gone. All of it, even the necklace. It is just...gone."

"Gone?" What did that mean? How did something like music just disappear? But then I got it because while I could remember the music from the videos, when I tried for more, my memories were blank, empty.

Without thinking, I turned and hugged her as if somehow we could come together to recapture the notes between us. I allowed my hands to roam into her hair. "The curse? I'm sorry," I whispered into her ear. "I'm sorry you came here and got sucked into all of this."

Annie pulled back and took my hand in hers. "I am not. Really. It is just so hard. For a little while, I knew what was going to happen. How everything would work out. And I knew that Dmitry would be proud of me. That is the worst of it. That I failed him."

"But you didn't," I said. Everything I'd learned from my parents about comforting those in mourning came rushing back. "You did exactly what he asked. You found the Prelude. You found the composer. You did more than that. You freed Tristan. How many people can say that they've saved a soul?"

Annie hesitated. She wiped her face again, but I could tell that what I'd said had helped. She gave me a sad nod. "Wow, that is really annoying," she said, pointing toward the phone.

"I'm on hold," I said, without going into detail. "What are you going to do now?" I was half-afraid she would say she was staying in St. Hilaire, just as I was leaving.

"Well, I am going to have a large amount of explaining to do. Viktor will not understand; what could I tell him, anyhow? I guess I will practice the Tchaikovsky, even though it is too late. I have no chance of winning. Then there are the Dublin dates, and after that, I think I might take a break. Go home to see my parents; get to know my brother. Sort things out from there. What about you?"

"I can't stay here. I don't fit in. I don't have my parents' talent, and every single time I open my eyes, all I can see is that they aren't here. Laura and Harriet can keep the business going without me." I stared at my suitcase, wishing I had something concrete to share. "There's nothing left for me in St. Hilaire."

Annie took my hand again. I wanted to stop time. She said, "Laura and Russ both believe you would be happier somewhere else."

Tears stung my eyes. Russ and Laura knew I wanted to leave, but I had never been sure if they understood that I *had* to. That leaving St. Hilaire didn't mean leaving *them*.

"Where will you go?" she asked.

I looked into her eyes, which were as green as Tristan's in the light of my room. "I don't know long-term," I admitted. "I can take the GED from anywhere. I have a little money saved up, but not a ton. I'll have to get a job. I think I'll start in the city. Mom had a cousin whose floor I can probably crash on for a couple of nights. Maybe I can get a piano-playing gig?" Blood rushed to my cheeks. "God, I sound like a geek saying that to you. Never mind. I'll do something. You'd think I'd have sorted that part out by now, right?"

Annie smiled; it seemed like she'd moved ever so slightly closer. "I might be able to help. A little. Have you ever wanted to see Ireland?"

"Ireland?"

"Viktor is always complaining about having to do all of the

travel administration. It is mostly data entry and phone calls. You could do the tasks from here, but you are leaving anyhow. I can cover your plane ticket. In all honesty, I could use a buffer. This is all going to get harder before it gets easier."

I looked around my room at the ticket stubs and receipts that had belonged to other people with other lives. I stared at my passport, unused and waiting for me to get my shit together. "Are you offering me a job?"

"Come with me, Dec," Annie said. "Please? For a while?"

I stared at her and tried to see the person in front of me and not the girl on my computer or the inside of my closet door. She looked hopeful. Excited. A smile danced through her eyes while she waited for my answer. As if there was any doubt.

Before I could say anything, a voice came from my phone, "Ireland, Mr. Hampton? Isn't that a fascinating turn of events?" Clive Rice sounded amused, but then he always sounded vaguely entertained by life.

I ran over and picked up the phone, taking it off speaker. "Sir? Sorry, I—"

"No, no, no, Mr. Hampton. Apologies are unnecessary, even if quite understandable."

"Sir?"

"Travel is good for a young mind. Your parents traveled. Of course, that was before you or your sisters were born. I believe it made them better at their jobs. More empathetic. More open to those who needed them. I trust the same thing will happen for you. I will expect you to come in for your test tomorrow. Then we will have your position set up for when you return."

Tomorrow? Shit. I held on tight to the phone, worried I'd

drop it. Rice wasn't offering, he was insisting. "I'm not planning to come back," I said quietly. I knew I should be more confident; it wasn't like I hadn't been preparing for this in one way or the other for the past two years. But confidence was surprisingly difficult to come by with Annie staring out my window and Tristan gone and Russ doing everything he could to kiss the Guild's ass.

"I'm sorry? I didn't quite hear you," Rice said.

I cleared my throat. "I said I'm not planning to come back. I mean, I'll visit. Of course, I will. Laura is here and Russ Griffin. And Harriet." Harriet's name came out as almost a surprise to me.

Annie turned and watched, no judgment on her face.

There was silence on the other end of the line.

Then, Clive Rice said, "I'm not quite sure you understand the gravity of the situation, Mr. Hampton. Your parents were very important to us. To all of us." To my ear, the words sounded almost sinister. "Their legacy is important to St. Hilaire. We had hoped, well, we are counting on you to take your rightful place here where you belong."

I glanced out the window at the sun playing off the tops of my parents' headstones. I steadied my voice. "If you need someone, you should talk to Russ Griffin."

Clive Rice laughed softly. "Oh, we're well aware of Mr. Griffin's unique abilities, Mr. Hampton. Very aware."

"Then you know how much better he is at all of this than I am, Mr. Rice." The anger I'd been fighting for the past two years transformed into a type of resolve I'd never quite managed before. I smiled at Annie. I smiled at my bulletin board and the desk where Tristan had burnt circles into the wood. I smiled at the picture of my parents and Annie's Carnegie Hall flyer, which was still up on my closet door. I smiled at the thought of a future, *my* future, not one that had been chosen for me, but one I was choosing.

"Be that as it may, Mr. Hampton…"

I steeled myself. "I'm sorry, sir, but I have to go."

I hung up and stared at Annie.

It was done.

It was done.

I felt lighter. Relieved. Freed. I knew I should feel terrified. The Guild had long arms. I almost didn't care. It wasn't as if they actually hurt anyone. Those were all just rumors. Sure, I would have to leave right away. No more deliberating. I almost didn't care about that either.

Annie looked puzzled but calm. *Annie.* She was the key to everything. I took the step to where she stood, twirled her around, and laughed a laugh filled with sadness and shared knowledge and the loss of a friend. But still we laughed together.

And then I kissed her. That was done too.

52

RUSS

You are possibility.

I couldn't get Ian's words out of my head and couldn't stop wanting to argue and tell him it wasn't true. I wanted it to be me. I thought I could do it, but it was the drug that was possibility; *I* was just some fleshy conduit. That made me a failure regardless of whatever the hell Ian Mackenzie thought.

My neck ached. My jaw was stiff from clenching my teeth. There were small half-moons in my palms from where my nails had dug in. This wasn't the way I imagined meeting the Guild.

I went through the motions of dressing, of walking to Eaton Hall. My thoughts ricocheted with each step. *What if I can't do it without the drug? What if I destroy my best chance to work for*

*the Guild? To become who I need to be? What if the Guild is so
corrupt that I can't do anything to fix it? What if I try and fail?*

What if Ian Mackenzie is just fucking with me?

My thoughts were a Greek chorus of doubts that kept me
company as I approached the hall. Willow Rogers, a gold Guild
executive counsel pin on her collar, ushered me into a waiting
room.

I sat, restless, until the she called my name and walked me
to a tiny room.

"Say hi to Colin for me," I said as she was walking out. But
true to character, she didn't turn back or even hesitate. Not yet
even part of the Youth Corps, I was nothing in her eyes.

I looked around at four walls, a creaky chair, an even creak-
ier table. One of the walls had a speaker hung on it. There was a
spotlight on the ceiling. That was all. Ian had been right about
this, at least.

My future would be decided by a panel. Charlotte North,
Clive Rice, and Madeline Fisher weren't the entirety of the
Guild, just some of the executive members. I'd known them as
long as I'd been in St. Hilaire, but now they felt like enemies.
How could I look Charlotte North in the eyes after what Ian
had told me about her role in Dec's parents' deaths? And Ian's.
Possibly Ian's. *Crap.*

I ran a hand through my hair, the sleeve of my dad's dusty
black wool suit scratching against my wrist, as all of the lights
aside from the dim spot shut off.

The speaker crackled. "You've opted not to ask for materials
of any sort, so we trust this space is suitable?" asked Charlotte
North.

My hands clenched. Just hearing her voice set me off. There were so many things I wanted to say to her. But I said the only thing I was allowed to say. "Yes, ma'am."

The Guild had offered to provide whatever I needed, including alcohol, despite the fact I was underage. They really didn't care how you contacted a spirit, just that you did. But I wasn't going to tip my hand and tell them about my grandmother's serum. If there was one thing Ian taught me, it's that knowledge was power. I wasn't going to be quick to give mine away.

"Then let's get started," she said. "For your first task, we'd like you to tell us what playing card is lying on the table in the foyer. Just press the red button on the speaker to talk and release it to hear us when you're ready."

I nodded, though I knew no one could hear it. I tried to quiet my mind and forget everything Ian had told me about the Guild. Harder, I needed to ignore the betrayal of my body, the craving I still felt for a shot.

In my mind, I pictured clouds moving through a blue sky, a meditation tool my grandmother had written about working for her. I allowed myself to remember the smell of incense. A familiar buzzing ran up the base of my spine. I pictured the lobby, the green moss-colored paint, the stained wood floors, the half-moon tables carved with patterns of fruit. On one of those tables, I imagined a playing card. Ordinary. Red diamonds crisscrossing the back.

There were fifty-two cards, two more if you included the jokers. Those weren't insurmountable odds. I willed the card to flip over, but it wouldn't budge. I was bad at this sort of thing.

I wasn't a psychic. This wasn't how St. Hilaire worked. It was an unfair task unless…

We weren't psychics. But we *were* mediums. We talked to the dead. *I* talked to the dead. I had to believe that's why I was here.

There was only one ghost I could summon on short notice.

"Ian," I whispered. My chest tightened. It would be like Ian to ignore me today.

It took a minute. A very long minute, but then Ian was in the room next to me, looking me up and down. "Ace of spades. And by the way, you look hot in that suit."

I pulled at the collar of my shirt, which was suddenly tight. I counted to three, waiting to see if Ian was going to change his answer. When that didn't happen, I reached over and pressed the button on the speaker. "Ace of spades," I said into it.

There was muttering from the other side.

"Very good, Mr. Griffin."

Ian stepped close, bent, and whispered in my ear. "You also look a little rough around the edges. Hard night?"

I pushed him away.

Over the loudspeaker, the voice switched to Clive Rice's. "Melody Thorne has a message for you, Mr. Griffin. Please deliver it to us." The speaker clicked off.

I took a deep breath and sent out tendrils of thought. I'd tried, time and again, to explain the process to Dec, but in words, it made no sense, not even when I said it to myself. Still, it worked. Most of the time.

Melody was stronger than most of us; now I just had to *find* her.

"Boo!"

I jumped and turned around to see Ian doubled over in laughter. "If this is your idea of helping, get another one," I spat out.

"Come on, Griffin," Ian said. "Melody looooves me."

I shook my head and then winced from the sudden movement. "Yeah, sure, she does."

"The first day of withdrawal is the hardest," Ian said, placing a hand on my neck. "So I'm told, anyhow."

I pulled away, even though Ian's cold hand had felt surprisingly good.

"Can we not do this now?" I hissed. "I'm kind of busy."

Ian shrugged. "Oh, sure. See you later." He started to walk toward the door as if he needed to open it in order to leave.

"Wait. What about Melody?" I asked.

Ian stopped. "Oh, right, almost forgot." He dug into the pocket of his skintight jeans. "I ran into her on my way here. She sends her regards."

"Ian…"

"Deep breath, Griffin. She also sent this. Said you'd recognize it."

Ian pulled my hand up and deposited a tarot card onto my palm. It was judgment, the tarot card Willow had drawn for me in the woods.

I stared at it, wondering how it had survived being crammed into Ian's overtight pocket intact.

It was hard to know what to trust. Still, I leaned over, pressed the button, and said, "It's the judgment card. The card of new beginnings," I said.

For a minute, there was silence. Then a crackle, and then Madeline Fisher. "We like to give our candidates some amount of latitude to show their individuality. For the final test, we'd like you to call upon any spirit you choose, to deliver any message it would like to send. And we'd like to remind you that this is the most crucial area of our testing."

I nodded at the speaker. I'd seen ghosts all of my life; but I'd always had a problem with supply and demand. Ghosts spoke to me when they wanted to, not necessarily when I needed to begin the conversation. Hence Grandmother's serum. Even thinking about it made my arm itch. Still, for better or worse, I had to do this straight.

"Tell them you can summon me," Ian said.

I looked around the empty room and wondered if I was hallucinating and should just make something up. *No, this is the Guild, and corrupt or not, they'd recognize a sham.*

I looked up at the ceiling tiles and started counting the pinprick-sized holes to quiet my mind.

From the corner, Ian's voice said, "There are four thousand two hundred eighty-four. Now tell them we're in touch."

I didn't want to. I wanted to do this one thing without Ian Mackenzie even as I realized he was my salvation.

"You have all the time in the world to impress them with your finesse, Griffin. But if you don't give them something big now, none of that will matter."

I stared at the space where Ian should have been. He was easier to deal with when he was being an arrogant shit. *This* was the Ian who got under my skin, the one Dec had never seen, the one I'd never quite been able to break free from. We were on some emotional teeter-totter, even now that Ian was dead, and I was never sure if I was the one with my feet on the ground or the one dangling up in the air.

The Guild's speaker crackled.

"Damn it, Russ." In my ear, Ian's voice took on an urgency I wasn't sure I'd heard in it before. "Don't make me possess you again. Do it."

I hit the button. Leaned my head back until it hit the top of the chair, felt for the owl at my wrist, tracing the outline although I couldn't see it through the heavy cloth of my jacket, and between clenched teeth, said, "I've been in touch with Ian Mackenzie. He... I thought you might want to know."

There was a heavy silence, though I knew the speaker connection was open and that the testing committee had heard what I'd said. There was a pause, and then I heard the connection click off. I was alone.

"Please," Clive Rice said, pointing to a dark hallway. "Come join me."

I followed him to a room filled with plush carpet, gold lamps, and deep sofas. There was certainly no sign of St. Hilaire's financial troubles here.

It wasn't until Clive Rice had closed the door behind us that he said, "Good job, Mr. Griffin. Good job."

"Thank you," I said as I took a seat next to the crackling fire and pulled at my collar. The warmth was nice, but it made the suit jacket even itchier.

Rice tapped on the face of his watch. "Infernal thing, never works when I need it to. Be that as it may, I'm going to get to the point, if you don't mind."

My pulse raced.

Rice said, "For better or worse, it has not, in the past, been the way of the Guild to oversee the personal lives of its members. But there has been some talk that you had a certain 'relationship' with Ian Mackenzie, did you not?"

Fire rose to my cheeks. I rubbed my wrist, wishing I could make myself disappear. "We knew each other," I admitted. St. Hilaire was a small town. Ian had been a large personality. He'd always made sure to stand out in a crowd. Perhaps it had been too much to hope Ian had been discreet about this one thing.

"Yes, well." Rice cleared his throat. "As I'm sure you're aware, we've been trying to contact him for some months with no success. It comes as a bit of a pleasant surprise to hear that you've managed to entice him into speaking with you."

"Yes, sir."

Rice poured himself a drink but didn't offer me anything. The ice clinked against the crystal as he tilted the glass back and forth. "I'm going to be straight with you, Mr. Griffin. I get the impression you are someone who might value the truth?"

How was it possible that Rice didn't choke on the word? Allowing Dec's parents to die made him a hypocrite of the worst sort.

When I didn't reply, Rice continued, "Ian Mackenzie's younger brothers are not nearly as accomplished as you. And some of our members thought, well, that you might have had contact with him. On the other plane," he said to clarify. "But, frankly…"

I clenched my fists, jolting at the pain.

Hold it together, Ian whispered in my ear. I was impressed that he was strong enough as a ghost to keep the president of the Guild from seeing him.

"Well, that wasn't why we called you in to audition, it certainly aids in your case," Rice continued.

"Well, sir, as you know, I'd very much like to work with the Guild." I hated how much I sounded like a suck-up. "I mean, I'd like to carry on my grandmother's work."

"Your grandmother? Of course, of course," said Rice, jotting down some notes. "But we will, of course, have to speak to Mr. Mackenzie to verify your claim. First, though, we'd like to have a look at his car. My understanding is that it is currently in your custody?"

Don't, Ian hissed.

There was no time to deliberate. I either had to trust Ian or not.

"My father is doing some work on it, sir. I'll have to ask him when it will be done," I said, holding Clive Rice's gaze until the man looked away.

This time, it was Clive Rice who sighed.

53

RUSS

"You can't give them my car." Ian leaned back against my desk, arms crossed, emphatic.

"You said you were going to help me."

"I *am* helping you. And I'll continue to help you. But you can't give them my car." Ian stretched and pulled his long hair into a ponytail. Then he let it fall, flow like water over his shoulders. He smiled, more with his eyes than his mouth.

I stood, which made my head swim. I would have had that last vial of serum if it weren't for Ian. "Why? And remember no bullshit."

Ian took a step forward. His legs were long, and the room was small, and one step was all it took to place him directly in my face. "Look. You know the car was a collection of 'found' objects. Well, hypothetically, imagine that some of those objects were *found* in places the Guild might not have wanted me to look."

"Like where?"

Ian took a deep breath. "Let's just say there's a reason Clive Rice's watch doesn't work. And man, Griffin." Ian's eyes bored through mine. "You don't need to know either."

"At least tell me what they want it for," I insisted.

Ian stepped over to the desk and picked up an antique letter opener that had belonged to my grandmother. "It *might* be they want to figure out how I built it," Ian said, brandishing the opener like a sword. "It *might* be they want some of those objects back, and it *might* be I stashed Sarahlyn's gold under the intake manifold." He stabbed the base of my fern with the opener. It stuck in the soft dirt like Excalibur. "And it doesn't matter because you aren't going to give it to them."

This time, it was me who stepped forward. Being this close to Ian had the same effect as four quick shots of espresso; energizing and disorienting. Unlike most ghosts whose personalities were muted by death, Ian retained the intensity that I'd always found unsettling.

I removed the letter opener from the dirt, wiped it off on the bottom of my shirt and stashed it in a desk drawer. "God, Ian. I don't even know what to address first. You stole money from the Guild and hid it in your impossible-to-hide car? Are you out of your mind? Never mind, don't bother answering that. But you're dead. Aside from the money, why do you care if they examine your car?"

Ian's eyes surged black. "I still have a reputation."

342

"A reputation," I echoed. "You're shitting me, right? What am I supposed to tell them?"

Ian folded his arms. "Tell them you don't have it."

"But I do," I said.

"But you won't."

"And why won't I?"

"Because you're going to give it to Hampton."

"I'm going to give Dec the Mustang?" The only thing that stopped me from laughing was the serious expression on Ian's face. "Why the hell would I do that?"

I turned and faced the bed, hoping the change of view would be enough to allow me to make sense of Ian's plan.

Ian pushed his way between me and the bed and sat, his long legs pressing down on my ankles. "We have to talk about you trusting me," Ian said.

"No, we have to talk about boundaries," I replied, stepping back.

"Griffin, that's the same conversation."

My skull hurt. *I'm in over my head. Worse, it's too late to do anything about it.* "First, you have to stop barging into my house, into my *room* without asking. It's creepy."

Ian stood.

"Second, if you're going to insist I do ridiculous things, you're going to have to come up with better reasons."

Ian didn't move, but somehow the space between us had diminished.

"And third..."

I couldn't finish speaking the third thing because somehow Ian's mouth was on mine. His lips were frostier than I remembered, but the urgency of them was like always. Ian's kisses were cold steel, dark alleys, the thumping bass of a night-club, the surge of serum through my veins. There was nothing gentle in Ian's wanting, and I wished I minded, but I didn't. It had been so long since I'd allowed myself to be touched that it was as if I were being possessed all over again.

Ian began to pull away, but this time I reached up and pulled him close. I didn't know if I did it because I wanted the kissing to continue or because I was terrified of having to *say* something once it ended.

Words evaporated. There was the momentary dissolution of every carefully crafted defense against the world I'd had created. Ian's cold hands cupped my neck, and I felt myself became as insubstantial as a spirit.

I was drowning in sensation, and when my lungs were as empty of air as Ian's, I dropped my hand, stepped away, turned my back. The room was cold and despite the warmth of my coat, I shivered.

Ian cleared his throat, but his voice was hoarse when he said, "What was your third thing?"

I tried to remember what the third boundary item was, but my mind was blank. "You can't…" I exhaled in resignation, but that was a lie. I knew it, and Ian knew it. Ian Mackenzie could do whatever he wanted. He always had.

Ian stepped up behind me, not touching, but near enough that his ghost-chill made the hair on my arms stand up. Quietly, he said, "Give Hampton my car, the Guild wants him and he needs to get out of here while he still can. Before they stop him. And they *will* try to stop him."

"That doesn't even make sense," I protested, still not looking at him.

"Anyhow," Ian said, his fingers landing flat and sure on my shoulder. "It doesn't matter what the Guild wants. It matters what the Guild *has*, and the Guild *has* us."

Ian's last word rang in my ears. His hand felt heavy and solid through my coat. I tried to ignore it and process things rationally. Dec could have the car. I might not be ready for Dec to leave St. Hilaire, but withholding the car wouldn't change that. I'd wanted that car more than I'd ever wanted anything. Still, if I didn't give it to Dec, the Guild would take it anyway, and the realization that maybe it wasn't the car that mattered to me, but the car's creator, crystallized in the pit of my stomach.

I nodded in defeat.

Ian stepped around in front of me, too solid, too intense, too real to fit the description of "ghost" that I'd been taught. He reached out and wrapped a hand around each of my wrists.

"I know it's your favorite toy, and I'll help you build another one," Ian said. My pulse raced against his fingers. I was so fevered, I could imagine that my own heat was warming Ian's ghost-touch. "I'll help you build a hundred. A whole herd of Ian Mackenzie Mustangs."

"Why would you do this?" I asked with my last remaining shred of resistance. I knew Ian understood that I wasn't speaking about the car.

Ian didn't loosen his grasp or avert his eyes. I struggled not to look away even as I considered reminding Ian not to give me some bullshit answer.

But there was nothing aside from sincerity in Ian's words

when he answered, "Because you talk about changing the Guild like it's something you actually give a damn about. Because you've spent the last three years sorting out everyone's troubles except your own. Because you wear that stupid coat even in the dead of summer, and because I think it's worth haunting this ridiculous place just to see what it takes to make you smile."

He let out a puff of cool air and despite myself, I felt my muscles relax. I had no way of answering Ian's words, no words of my own to explain my churning emotions, so I leaned forward and did the only thing I could think of, I kissed Ian. And Ian kissed me back. And we kissed again and again until it was no longer possible to tell who was doing the kissing and who was being kissed.

54

ANNIE

I did not cry when, as a six-year old, I left my parents' house. The night before, as my mother packed my few belongings into a suitcase and my father stayed late at work, I played scales over and over on the old piano in our front room. I played because I did not know what else to do. I played because it was easier to play than it would have been to stop.

I had seen Dmitry perform once, and it had been the most riveting experience of my young life. I wanted to do what he was doing, although I could not possibly have dreamed of what was to come.

As I prepared to leave my home, I worried about who would braid my hair before performances, and who would help me with my mathematics homework. Yet I remember being consumed with both excitement and guilt for being excited at the prospect of leaving everything I had known for the world of music. I had no way of understanding the importance of the things I was forsaking.

In contrast, as I packed the few belongings I had brought with me to St. Hilaire, I was very much aware of what I was leaving behind. The Prelude was gone, and I knew I would never get it back. Despite Dec's reassurances to the contrary, I had failed Dmitry and failed Tristan and I wondered if either of them would think it a worthy trade for offering Dec a pathway to a new future.

"Oh, get a grip," I said to myself as I wiped away a tear. It was odd really, how I had allowed myself to become attached to this place in such a short time. I had spent most of my life traveling and staying a week here, a week there. Yet, somehow, this was different.

I wandered downstairs to the music room. Even though it was the middle of the night, Laura was sitting in the window seat, staring out the window, turning something in her hand.

"You're up late," I said. "Or early?"

Laura looked up and me, and I could see the exhaustion in her eyes. "I was just sitting here thinking," she said. "Everything's changing."

I sat next to her, feeling as if it were all my fault. "I am so sorry," I said. "If my being here caused any problems."

She shook her head. "Oh, no. I haven't seen Dec this happy in years. That's worth everything."

I had the same feeling of longing I had when I was in Laura's room, looking at the photo of the two of them as little children. "You are a very good sister," I said. "I have not been as good."

Laura smiled again tiredly. "Well, you still have time."

She was right. I had to stop assuming the past and the future had to be the same, that I had no choice but to keep repeating the same mistakes.

The movement of her hands caught my eye again. Her fingers drummed on a thin black device. "What is that?" I asked.

She held it up and scowled at it. "Colin Mackenzie delivered it today. It's a recorder. Some new rule of the Guild's says that all séances need to be recorded and kept on file in case they need to review them later."

I raised an eyebrow. "Wow, Big Brother lives."

She sighed. "I'm sure there's a good reason, but...I can't say it feels right. Sometimes ghosts get really personal. Like that old woman." She stopped, and I could tell she had said something she felt she should not have.

"What old woman?" I asked.

She sighed again, only this time there was more exhaustion and less confusion in it. "Before you came downstairs, there was a woman here. She was wearing a necklace shaped like tree branches."

"What?" I wasn't sure whether to be happy or terrified. "My *babulya* was here? My grandmother? She died the year after I left Russia. I never got to see her again."

Laura put her hand on mine. "Her English wasn't very good, but I did understand the part where she said she's proud of you, Annie. I know that's a super-generic message, but I think you need to listen to it."

I felt the tears come. I knew it had been my *babulya* when Laura mentioned the necklace. My father had made it for her, and it was too obscure a detail for Laura to guess at. I had not seen my grandmother since I was six and hanging on to her skirts as I watched her bake bread. Her kitchen had been cramped, but it had been a place of magic and peace for me growing up; spending time with her was my reward for a day of dedicated practicing.

Laura squeezed my hand and stood. "I'll give you some time alone. It can be hard to hear stuff like this the first time. But after you leave, don't let Dec fool you about having no talent as a medium. He sees more than he lets on."

I squeezed back, part of me wishing I could stay here forever.

55

DEC

"I guess I always knew you meant it," Laura said as she stood in the center of my room, looking lost. When I tried to see the room like she did—our parents' suitcases in the middle of the floor, the walls bare, my bulletin board cleaned off except for the poster of Annie, which I'd stopped hiding on the inside of the closet door, and a small wooden turtle ornament that had been in the pocket of a jacket I'd bought at the consignment store in Buchanan—I could see why. "But what about school?"

She kept pulling on her sleeves, straightening the hem of her skirt. She was grasping at straws, and before I could explain, she had it figured out. "That's why you were always running to the library, isn't it? You were planning something."

"I'm taking the GED," I said, and quickly added, "You

could too. You could come with me," even though I wasn't sure how, or if, that would work.

She shook her head. "I'm sure Harriet would love that. But, I like St. Hilaire. I'm happy here."

"I know." I glanced out the window. It was dark. Middle-of-the-night dark. About to storm. Annie and I needed to leave before the Guild decided I couldn't.

"You could stay. I mean, Mom and Dad would want us to stick together." Laura ran out of steam and hugged me instead. "Oh, hell. Don't forget us, okay? I expect postcards, not just emails, promise?"

"I promise," I said just as Annie came in.

She stopped short when she saw us. "Oh, I will come back."

We pulled apart and said, "No, it's okay" at the same time.

"Don't you forget us either," Laura said to Annie.

"That would be impossible," Annie said. I watched her eyes play along my desk and make their way to the burned circles. It felt like Tristan was still somehow here.

"I'm a jerk for missing him," I admitted.

Annie came up along one side of me and Laura the other. "Somehow, I will make sure his name will not be forgotten," Annie said. "Everyone will know he wrote the Prelude. What there is of it anyhow."

I sighed. There was nothing left to say. We all understood what we'd lost.

My phone buzzed with a text from Russ. **Come down. I'm outside.**

It was 2:00 a.m. I wasn't sure how to face Russ. My plan had been to call him from the road. Annie and I were going to head to Buchanan, and she was going to buy a ticket out of the machine for each of us on the morning train to the city. With any luck, we'd never see Russ's dad.

Of course, Russ knew I was leaving, just like Russ knew every other major event in my life. Our friendship had changed, but I guessed some things stayed the same.

"Go," Annie said. "I'll bring the bags down."

I nodded and made my way down the stairs.

It was odd not knowing what to say to your best friend. For a minute, we kind of stood there, looking at each other like we'd never met. I tried to commit this Russ to memory: worn, unseasonal coat, dyed hair, the way he stood, spring-loaded, looking like he was prepared to fight.

I wondered what Russ saw when he looked at me. Just a guy who couldn't wait to get the hell out of town, probably.

"Look, about Ian…" I said. I wanted to get the whole topic out of the way before I had to figure out the right words to make saying goodbye to Russ not hurt like hell.

Russ shuffled slightly.

"I just wanted to say that I'm sorry I gave you a hard time. You don't owe me an explanation." There wasn't much I could leave Russ with. This felt like all I had to offer.

He turned and took two steps away. Then a third. Then he turned back, his face betraying all the emotions he usually kept hidden. "I think I do, actually. I owe you that," Russ said, voice low. "He's helping me. With the Guild and with…everything."

Muscle memory almost made me remind Russ that Ian was a manipulative jerk, an egomaniac, a *ghost*. But Russ knew all of that. And really, who was I to tell anyone else what to do?

"You'll be careful, right?" I said. "I mean, just remember he's a ghost, and you know what they're like."

"I'm not sure there's all that much difference between live Ian and dead Ian." Russ flushed, and for some reason that made me so uncomfortable, I had to look away. "The funny thing is, I'm not sure I care."

Now I had no choice but to glance back. Russ looked odd. Almost happy. That was it. Oddly happy. For years, I'd fought against his friendship—or whatever it was—with Ian. That had always felt justified. But what if?

"You and Ian?" I asked, already guessing the answer.

Russ couldn't hide a hint of a grin. "I'm still wrapping my head around it. Look, there's something else," Russ said. He flipped up the collar of his jacket, revealing a Guild pin. "I got in. I'm going to be Student Leader this year."

Russ's success with the Guild certainly wasn't a surprise. It had never been a matter of *if*, just *when*. "Congrats. But promise you'll be careful with that too?"

Russ nodded and his shoulders relaxed. We wouldn't fight tonight. That was good. Then Russ reached around into his bag and pulled out a manila envelope. "And I brought you something."

I reached out for the lumpy envelope, which was heavier than it looked. "You didn't need to get me a card," I said, turning it over in my hands. "I know you love me."

Russ swallowed hard and pasted a sort-of smile on his face. "Maybe you have more ability than you thought."

I breathed out, feeling more relieved than I had in a long, long time. "I think I'll leave that to you from now on, actually."

We both stared at the envelope in my hand. I pulled the red tab and dumped the contents out into my hand; a jumble of metal and plastic.

It was impossible.

"No," I said. "You are not giving me the car."

Russ tapped his firm stomach. "You know, I need to take a couple of pounds off. Walking is sounding like a good idea."

"I'm not. I can't," I protested. "What about the Guild? I'm sure part of asking you to work with them was…" I stopped myself. "How many rules do you think this breaks?"

"At least six that I can think of off the top of my head."

I spun around. I'd bet it was breaking at eight at minimum. The car wasn't just a product; it was a product of St. Hilaire. And if the rumors about the car's DNA were to be believed, stolen goods were the least of it. The Guild revered the car as if it was the town mascot. They weren't going to let it just drive out of town. But then they weren't going to be happy I was leaving either.

Perhaps it made sense. The car and I were both going to be on the run from the Guild.

"And what about Ian?" I asked.

"Actually, it was his idea, and Ian can be very persuasive."

I resisted sharing any of the snarky comments that came to mind and thrust the keys back in Russ's direction. "I can't take them."

Russ linked his fingers together and took a step backward, leaving the keys hanging in my hand like a bunch of grapes.

"I'm going to miss you, Dec. Really. But you need to get going." He pointed at the keys. "Your future awaits."

Russ was right. He was always right about these things.

"Sure you don't want to join me?" I asked.

Russ looked away and for a minute, I thought he'd say yes. But then he said, "What do you think I'm going to do, get a real job? I'd rather not. Thanks."

Annie came down with the suitcases and took the keys. I was happy to let her drive. Cars had never been a big deal to me, and the wide-eyed look she gave me when she saw the keys was worth being demoted to passenger status.

"I parked outside the gates." Russ's voice was careful. "Near the planetarium."

It was a relatively short walk to the Buchanan Planetarium, but I couldn't imagine why Russ had taken the car there. "Why?" I started to ask, and then it became clear when I saw Clive Rice coming up the walk.

"Leaving so soon, Mr. Hampton?"

I'd known Clive Rice all my life. While I never would have called him warm, he was someone I'd always considered odd rather than menacing. But something about the set of his jaw and the fact that he was in front of my house at 2:00 a.m. for no good reason I could think of, made me nervous.

"I couldn't sleep," I said. "We thought we'd go for a walk."

Russ took a step closer so that Annie was sandwiched between us. There was no way we looked like we were going for a walk. Not with our bags and suitcases on the stairs behind us.

"Yes," Rice said. "Insomnia. It afflicts many in St. Hilaire." Then he turned toward Annie, and something in my spine shuddered. "And you, Miss Krylova? Have *you* had sleep issues since you've been a guest here?"

I could almost hear Annie searching for the right words. "A bit," she said softly.

"Well," Rice said. "It does seem like a nice night for a stroll, so I'll let you get on with it." His eyes flicked to Russ. "I expect to see you Monday morning, Mr. Griffin. We have much to discuss."

Russ nodded, but didn't say anything. Even though Rice had dismissed us, no one moved until I worked up the guts to take a few steps forward.

"Oh, Mr. Hampton. One thing I forgot to mention," Rice said to my back. I turned to look at him just as Annie grabbed for my hand. "Your parents." I froze. It was so quiet that I could hear Russ's breathing and a coyote or some other animal rustling in the woods.

It felt like hours before Rice continued. "I was thinking how much they'd given to this community. How much we miss their valuable input. I thought we might break with usual protocol and reach out to them. Next week at our fundraiser. Or perhaps it could be an assignment for the Corps. Your parents were always so good with children."

I trembled. The night air blew the scent of my mom's wildflowers around us. All the things I wanted to say to her and my father raced through my head. I wanted to know they were okay and to let them know that I finally was too. Despite how it probably looked, I wanted to talk to my dad about Tristan and hear all of the stories he had always kept hidden about his own childhood. And of course, I wanted to ask about the accident, but that was suddenly last on my list.

I imagined my mother's arms around me and the way my father's face would light up when he met Annie. For a single minute, the pain, the longing, the loss of the past two years lifted in a sense of possible comfort.

Russ turned to face me, his back to Clive Rice. His eyes caught mine and he mouthed, "No."

I was at war with myself. Stay for this chance or leave right now and turn my back on my parents, and Laura, and Harriet, and all the Hamptons who came before me.

I turned and looked at the house, and my entire childhood seemed to envelop me. What if I left and wasn't allowed to return? What if the Guild got more and more out of control and went after Laura and Harriet?

Russ coughed under his breath and drew my attention. I wanted the time to discuss this choice with him, but Clive Rice was standing there with an expectant and smug look on his face that demanded a response.

Under his breath, Russ said, "Remember our conversation," as if I could have forgotten it. Nothing had changed. Even if we could talk to my parents, they probably wouldn't be the people I remembered or wouldn't be able to answer my questions. And if I wasn't going to go through that with Russ, there was no way I was going to jeopardize everything with Annie and my future on the chance that Clive Rice, or *worse,* the Youth Corps could pull it off. Even with Russ as their leader.

I squeezed Annie's hand and looked Rice in the eyes. "Thank you," I said, voice unsteady. "I appreciate the offer, but no. I don't think my parents would want that." I prayed I was right. That I wasn't making the biggest mistake of my life.

Annie squeezed my hand back and nodded.

"Get going, you two," Russ said with a tone of false cheerfulness. I nodded at him, grabbed our bags, and started to walk toward the path that would take us to the gates.

"Yes, Mr. Hampton, safe travels," said Clive Rice. I turned back for a second and saw him tapping his watch. "You have but six hours before your flight. You don't want to be late."

"How do you know that?" I asked. I knew I'd never mentioned specifics on the phone. Or had I?

His stare was unwavering. "Oh, we made it our business to know. And don't forget to remind your sisters to put up the Guild flag. I would hate to see any trouble come to them."

Russ coughed and nodded toward the path. I nodded back and started walking, although I could feel my legs shudder. The sting of tears behind my eyes was blurring my vision.

Annie and I stayed quiet as we walked through the gates and down the block to where Russ had left the car. Neither of us had turned to look back.

"Are you okay?" she whispered.

I nodded. I wasn't sure I could speak.

"That was very unnerving, but is it odd," she asked, "that I feel like I'm leaving *my* home behind too?"

I thought about her question as we reached the car. It looked dark and imposing on the mundane Buchanan street.

After we got in, I pulled down the visor and looked at St. Hilaire reflected in the mirror. The steeple of Eaton Hall, the intricate iron scrollwork in the gate. Those were the only things I could see from here, and had it not been for Clive Rice, the view would have made my running away seem like an overreaction.

"No," I answered finally. Perhaps I hadn't even appreciated St. Hilaire until Annie showed up. In a way, she'd returned my home to me as well. "It's not odd at all."

Annie asked, "They *will* let you come back, right? To visit?"

I looked back at St. Hilaire through the mirror again. Of course, I wanted to come back to see everyone, and the graves of my parents would always pull me back. And Tristan. I couldn't let his sacrifice be for nothing.

And Russ. Of course, Russ. To make sure he and Ian… The fact that I had to think of Russ and Ian in any way connected *again* ate at me, but less than it had in the past, so maybe that was progress.

"Russ," I said. "He's working with the Guild now. I'm sure he'll make it okay." Maybe that was part of why Russ wanted the position so badly. Maybe it was part of why he'd given me the Mustang. Could I dare drive it back through St. Hilaire's gates? I'd have to cross that bridge when I came to it.

I rolled down the window and heard a whine coming from the field across from the planetarium. Alex Mackenzie's dog sat with its tongue hanging out of its mouth and a strange non-canine expression on its face. There were definitely some things I wasn't going to miss.

I turned around and looked at St. Hilaire. Saw it as Annie must, as Tristan might have with all of its hope and possibilities. I imaged Hampton House and the graves of my parents and grandparents and every generation before that. Then I looked at Annie, at her soft smile, all the while listening to the Mustang's purr-like hum.

"Of course," I said aloud to her. But under my breath I

muttered "thanks" to all of them. It was such a small word. One that couldn't convey the mix of gratitude and wonder and sadness that was suddenly boiling up inside me. But it would have to do.

56

RUSS

It was starting to rain, so I pulled up my collar.

Clive Rice seemed oblivious to the weather. He simply stood in the drive, arms folded, a bitter look on his face. I'd won this round, but I suspected it would be war from here on out.

"Monday," he said. "8:00 a.m. And I expect Mr. Mackenzie's presence as well. We have questions. Many questions." Then he turned and walked off.

I waited in the rain until I saw him turn in the opposite direction from Buchanan. Dec and Annie were free to do as they pleased for now.

Much as I tried to block it out, something screamed so loudly in my heart that I feared it might never again be silenced. Every muscle and every drop of tainted blood in my body urged me to say yes and go with Dec and Annie. My father would have understood. My mother wouldn't care. Ian would…well, who ever knew anything about what Ian would feel.

But it was my grandmother's voice, her warning that sang sweetly in my ears. *Don't forget what you are.*

Now that I knew what I was capable of, her words were almost laughable. Forget? That was like forgetting to breathe or forgetting to bleed. I had a responsibility that went so much further than my own desires. I was a conduit. A door. And doors couldn't simply pick up and move.

For all of Dec's talk, somehow I had never quite believed he would go. But he had, and St. Hilaire felt far emptier, even more than when I'd first arrived three years ago. Then, I'd stood on the front porch of my grandmother's house and watched my mother drive out of my life. I tried to remind myself this wasn't the same. Dec wasn't deserting me. He'd come back. I'd make sure of it.

"Our little boy has grown up and flown the nest," Ian said, suddenly next to me. The time would come when I'd need to talk to Ian about the appearing and disappearing thing, but today wasn't that day; today I was glad not to be alone.

I narrowed my eyes at him. "You smell like wet dog."

"Professional hazard," Ian said and placed a hand on my back. I flinched but didn't pull away.

"So, what do we do now?" I asked.

Ian's expression was carnivorous, his eyes greedy. "Oh, you just make it too easy."

I shook my head, but allowed myself a shadow of a real smile. That was something. An improvement of sorts. A promise that life would move on.

Then I thought about everything we still had to do and said, "*This* isn't going to be easy, is it? Challenging the Guild? Changing them? Making them pay for what they've done?"

"If it were easy, you wouldn't need me."

"I don't—" I began to protest and then thought better of it. I'd filled Ian in on everything that had happened with Tristan and it made for an easy change of subject. We'd have plenty of time to talk about the Guild later. "Do you think we'll ever see Tristan again?"

Ian shook his head. "I don't think so. He did what he had to do. He deserves to rest now."

"And what about you?"

Ian gave me a look that began as arrogance and ended as something I couldn't name. My heart pounded hard as Ian leaned in close, breath cold on my cheek, words steaming in the rain.

"I used to say, 'I'll rest when I'm dead.' But, you know?" Ian's voice was low and hungry. He reached over and undid the top button of my coat. "There are still many things I want to do first."

That one unfastened button made me feel exposed, but perhaps that wasn't completely a bad thing. Change, I knew, was often painful, even when it was for the best.

I lifted my face into the drizzle and pushed my left hand into my coat pocket. My fingers rubbed a wormwood leaf; it was almost time to harvest more, and then I'd make another couple of vials of Grandmother's serum and stash them in my closet or somewhere else where Ian wouldn't find them. I didn't have a definitive plan; I certainly didn't need a shot to contact

Ian anymore. But no way was I going to leave my career with the Guild up to chance.

In the meantime, I'd found a notation about making a tea in grandmother's notebook. I had to take the edge off this day. Had to find a way to stop the ache inside me from swallowing me whole. Had to find a way to feed this overwhelming hunger for *more*. My arm pulsed with the thought of it, the taste danced on my tongue. My thumbnail sliced into the leaf, and I could smell the medicinal odor. Soon, I thought, trying to quiet my jagged pulse. *Soon.*

Next to me, Ian was silent for once. Oblivious. I wondered if we'd always have secrets from each other. I wondered if Ian would really stand by me as I tried to change the Guild, or if, like so many of Ian's past endeavors, this one would lose his interest over time. I wondered what it meant to be falling for a ghost.

Then I forced my finger to release the leaf and reached up to rub my Guild pin between damp fingers. This wasn't the future I'd envisioned, but it was, in a way, the future I'd asked for. For now, that would have to be enough.

ACKNOWLEDGMENTS

The idea for this book drove out of an episode of *Mysteries at the Museum* that focused on the spiritualist community of Lily Dale, New York, and then, like Ian's Mustang, it quickly veered left as it sped out of town to become its own thing. Aside from that initial concept, no connection between St. Hilaire and Lily Dale is intended.

To Macon St. Hilaire, for lending me the perfect name for my own spooky town, and to Laurin Buchanan, for lending me the perfect name for a not-so-spooky one, I am grateful.

Many thanks to:

The usual suspects: Beth Hull, for the days of our Friday shares, for brainstorming, quippy lines, and for being able to hear Ian in your head as clearly as I hear him in my own, and for generally putting up with me. Shawn Barnes, for gleefully sharing your keen political and cultural knowledge. You will always be my go-to source when I need to add more corruption to my books (and I mean that in the best of all possible ways).

My agent, Lauren MacLeod, for battling monsters under the bed and shining a light in all the dark places.

The whole Sourcebooks team, for creating some of the most visually lovely books in the history of visually lovely books (including this one!). Particular gratitude goes out to my editor Annie Berger; editorial assistant Sarah Kasman; senior production editor Cassie Gutman; copy editor Christa Desir; Beth Oleniczak and Heather Moore for marketing and publicity magic; and Trisha Previte for the perfect cover design. Special thanks to Margaret Coffee and Michael Leali for getting books into the hands of librarians and educators and for making trade show events so meaningful.

To Fiona McLaren, Shyla Stokes, Suzanne Kamata, Lisa Maxwell, Rachel Lynn Solomon, and Tom Wilinsky, for comments given at one point or another in *Prelude*'s varied history, as well as to anyone else who read an early draft oh-so long ago.

To my dad, Harold Baker, for always believing in me. I'm mentioning Frank Sinatra here since I couldn't work him into this book. Next time, I promise.

And to John and Keira, who have to live with the music and in the worlds of my various books, I hope you're enjoying the ride. I love you both.

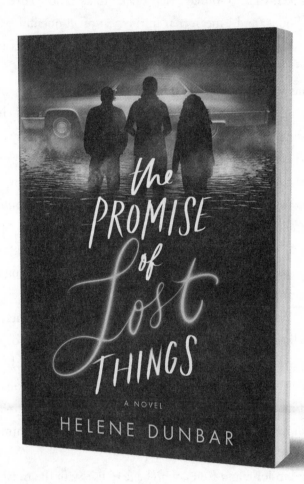

chapter one

RUSS

In St. Hilaire, New York, everyone talked to the dead.

If you were lucky or talented, or both, the dead might listen. Sometimes they talked back. Sometimes they made sense. Sometimes they were just a pain in the ass.

I knew it was odd to live in a town filled with mediums whose primary business involved séances, healing sessions, and ghost walks. It was odd to live behind a gate that only opened to visitors—for a price—during the summer when they'd converge on our town seeking answers, comfort, and forgiveness from those who had passed on.

And perhaps it was equally odd to embrace the idea that death wasn't an end point. Even though, maybe, in most cases it should be.

But, odd as it was, I loved it. I loved the history of our town, which was founded by a group of talented mediums over a hundred-and-fifty years ago. I loved the weirdness of séances and fairy trails and people coming to walk the huge labyrinth on the other end of town. I loved feeling like I was part of something big, something that mattered, as well as the fact that I could bring hope and closure to the people who came here. And I *really* loved being chosen as leader of the Youth Corps, made up of all the high school seniors. The role put me on the path to an actual job with the town's governing body, the Guild, assuming I survived high school and some extra training courses, first.

Today's lesson started the way most spirit-related activities did, with a voice in my ear and a feeling I was being watched, a slight vibration under my chair and a chill in the air.

I shivered in my wool coat. The chill, which seemed to settle somewhere in my spine and radiate through my body like a spiderweb, was a reaction to ghosts that most mediums outgrew, but one I guess I was stuck with. I tightened the muscles in my shoulders, locked my knees in an effort to stay still, and hoped Willow Rogers didn't notice, which was ridiculous because Willow Rogers noticed everything.

"Tell me, Russ," she commanded. She sounded bored as if she'd rather be manning an off-season phone line or working the research desk at the town archives than mentoring me in conjuring the dead. More than that, she *looked* bored, her green eyes dismissive and clouded as if her thoughts were far away.

I tilted my head and searched the air around her. "There's a woman," I said. "Standing over your left shoulder." I examined the ghost's clothing: over a hundred years out of date. Her hair: a messy blond ponytail. This lesson was so easy; it was no wonder Willow was bored. The spirit could have walked out of my freshman-year textbook. "Melody Thorne," I said, identifying one of our town's founders and most frequent ghostly visitors.

Willow stared at me, perfectly still and unblinking, her lips red against her skin as she said, "Continue."

I tried to tune out the sound of my heart beating in my ear. Narrowed my eyes to focus on the syllables formed by the ghost's barely there mouth. "You have a"—I leaned forward to listen more closely to what the spirit of Melody Thorne was saying—"a class. No, a meeting. You have a meeting at four o'clock and she's worried you'll be late."

There were no clocks in the room, so Willow glanced at her phone. Her face flashed with annoyance and then cleared before she stood and smoothed down her straight black skirt. "That's all for today," she said, which meant I hadn't done anything she could find fault with. Willow was notoriously generous with her criticism.

I stood and stretched. The muscles in my neck were taut and sore. These weekly lessons were required to help me strengthen my skills as a medium, but they were dull, exhausting, and it was clear both of us were only here out of obligation. I could do this sort of thing in my sleep.

Willow walked to the door of the classroom, her high heels echoing on the parquet floor. Then she turned back abruptly, as if she were trying to catch me off guard. "I overheard Father talking..." she started, her face animated for the first time since she'd walked into the room. "Is it true that Ian Mackenzie speaks to you?"

I inhaled sharply. Willow and I never spoke directly about our lives. We'd talk about school or the Guild or general current events: the museum got a new collection of dowsing rods from the early 1920s, or did you hear Miranda had something strange happen during a reading she was conducting? But never anything more personal and for me, it didn't get any more personal than Ian Mackenzie.

I didn't talk about Ian with anyone. I hadn't talked about him when he was alive and considered St. Hilaire's hottest, young medium, even though we were friends with benefits. Or enemies with benefits. Or whatever you call it when you kind-of-sort-of like someone and kind-of-sort-of hate them at the same time and yet can't seem to stay away.

I *really* didn't talk about him now that he was dead and haunting me (and only me) and now that we actually *did* like each other. Maybe more than liked each other. When it came to Ian, the specifics were always hard to pin down.

I answered her question with a tentative nod and waited while she looked me up and down. She had a piercing stare, one I'd often emulated with some success. I knew she had to be irritated that Ian would talk to me and not her. After all, she and Ian had gone to school together and served on the Youth Corps together. And even though she was only a few years older than me, she was already a member of the Guild. More than that, she'd actually been raised by them as a type of collective adopted daughter. She even called Guild President Clive Rice "Father."

And Ian? He was a Guild legend. That hadn't changed just because he was dead.

I was only a high school senior. A senior who was currently student leader of the Guild's Youth Corps, but still, that was nothing in comparison to either of them. She had to be pissed I had a line to St. Hilaire's most elusive ghost.

"I suppose it makes sense," she said, narrowing her eyes and letting contempt bleed into her voice. "Ian was always motivated more by what was in his pants than what was in his head."

I winced. She wasn't wrong, and despite my determination to stay in control, I felt myself flush. But it was one thing for everyone to know that the ghost of Ian Mackenzie, one of the best mediums St. Hilaire had ever seen, spoke to me. It was another for them to know…assume… Hell, *I* couldn't define what my relationship with Ian had been when he was alive—much less what it was now—so there was certainly no way Willow and the rest of St. Hilaire could have a clue.

But Ian and Willow were more alike than either would have admitted, and the number one rule for dealing with both of them was the same: Don't show fear.

I coughed, regrouped, and said, "I'm sure he'd want to send his best to Colin. How is your boyfriend, anyhow?" I had to restrain myself from putting air quotes around the word *boyfriend*. Colin was Ian's younger brother. He and Ian had hated each other when Ian was alive, and Ian's death hadn't changed those feelings. Rumors about Colin and Willow had been swirling around for ages, though "boyfriend" was probably putting a pretty spin on it.

Willow's eyes flashed, but when she turned back to the door, she didn't answer. All she said was, "Be here the same time on Wednesday to continue your training." Then she walked out.

———

When I got home, I booted up the brick of a laptop I'd been using for over five years despite numerous crashes, stuck keys, and burned-out pixels on the screen. My browser opened to the *Buchanan Sentinel*. Buchanan was the town that sat just outside St. Hilaire, and their big news usually involved some sort of high school sportsball or a debate on mailbox colors, but sometimes I needed to see what was going on in the rest of the world.

Today's headline read: GHOST KILLERS TEAM TO RE-FORM AND AIR 2-HOUR SPECIAL ON ST. HILAIRE.

I vaguely remembered the show and its mission to visit supposedly haunted places and debunk them. It had been a hit for a while and had changed casts multiple times before it just seemed to stop, but I'd never watched it when it was on and hadn't paid much attention to it ending.

I skimmed the article, most of which discussed St. Hilaire's founding as a home for spiritualists and described how we opened for business to the public in the summer, offering to contact the dead relatives, lovers, friends, and coworkers of the often-desperate customers who came through the gates for a mere fifteen dollars a head. Stock photos showed the painted Victorians and the old-growth forests, the wishing rock and the bronzed statues of our founders.

A paragraph at the bottom touched on the always-contentious topic of how, since spiritualism was classified as a religion, St.

Hilaire received tax breaks not offered to adjacent towns and how that had pissed people off in neighboring Buchanan who felt as if they were picking up our slack.

My father and I had never had enough money to worry about tax breaks. And it was hard to get worked up about Buchanan residents being irritated, since they always seemed bothered by something we were or weren't doing.

There was little concrete information in the piece about the show. No air date or cast list or rationale other than that St. Hilaire was *Ghost Killers'* next target and that it was a "breaking story."

"Welcome to small-town America," I muttered to myself. "But it didn't even mention the Guild. How can you write an article about St. Hilaire without mentioning the Guild?"

"You know what they say about people who talk to themselves, right?" a voice behind me asked.

"That they have a captive audience?" I tossed back.

Ian Mackenzie choked out a laugh. No. The *ghost* of Ian Mackenzie choked out a laugh, but really, there was little difference between the two. Even as a ghost, Ian was bigger than…well, life.

He leaned over my shoulder to read, and I could feel a cold whisper of something like breath land deliberately on my neck. I shivered.

"Need I remind you they didn't mention the Guild because the Guild is obsolete?" he asked. "Or at least it will be once we get through with them." Then he pulled back and said, "Although they could have interviewed me. And maybe you, I guess."

I couldn't help but laugh at Ian's indignation. Aside from one conversation I'd facilitated with his youngest brother, Alex, Ian hadn't spoken to a single living person aside from me since he'd died, and here he was, wondering why the press wasn't calling and asking him to do the late-night talk-show circuit. *Typical.* "Good thing you don't have an agenda."

"No," Ian corrected me. "*We* have an agenda."

"Okay, fine." I admitted. "Technically, he wasn't wrong. The Guild had always been secretive and controlling. But Ian had told me about rumors of them actually *killing* people during the time he'd run the Corps. Plus, lately, they'd been doing ridiculous things like making all the houses put up Guild flags and running people out of town for refusing to follow some arbitrary rules. Something had to give, and we were going to make sure it did. We just didn't know how we would do that yet.

"I thought my being chosen to lead the Youth Corps would give us inside information we could use against them, but so far most of my time has been sucked up with these." I gestured to the piles of reports that threatened to take over the room.

And it was true. All high school seniors had to serve in the Guild's Youth Corps. And most years, one student was chosen to lead the Corps and possibly jump straight into a Guild-shaped career. When I'd originally dreamed of being chosen student leader, I'd assumed the role would include many things: the chance to learn everything I could from the town's most esteemed mediums, an opportunity to hone my talents, and a chance to prove I was Guild material.

I didn't think it was going include trying to take down a corrupt organization.

Or communing with Ian who, through sheer willpower, was keeping himself tethered here instead of doing…well, whatever those who have passed on beyond the ghost state normally did.

Unfortunately, neither of us were getting very far. Not with *that* goal, anyhow. Aside from my weekly lessons with Willow, my three months as student leader had included one thing: paperwork. Stacks and stacks of reports the Guild expected me to read, verify, catalog, and input into their databases. My entire position was turning into nothing more than a hellish internship.

Ian picked up the top half of a mountain of séance reports, riffled through them, and then before I could stop him, he tossed them dramatically across the room. "Why not make them go away," he said.

I watched the papers fall like snow, one after the other, the staples making tiny clicks as they hit the worn wooden floor.

Then I watched Ian watching the papers. He was more solid than most ghosts, smugger than, well, anything.

"Are you telling me they didn't make you do the reports when you were leader?" I asked, already able to guess his answer.

Ian raised an eyebrow.

"What?"

"Wake up, Griffin. This is a waste of your time." Ian crossed his well-defined arms loosely in front of him, relaxed and in control. As usual.

I considered asking how he'd gotten out of having to do the Guild's grunt work but thought better of it. It was foolish to assume I'd be treated the same way Ian had been. And even if he told me his secrets, I was too sensible and not charming enough to resort to whatever tactics he'd used to bend the Guild to his will.

"I suppose you have a better idea?" I asked.

He cocked his head and smiled a smile full of innuendo. "I have many better ideas."

If "Don't show fear" was rule number one when dealing with Ian Mackenzie, rule number two was "Don't take the bait."

Even when part of me wanted to. *Especially* when I wanted to.

"No doubt," I said and quickly began to distract myself by gathering the papers. "Weren't we going to discuss you not bursting into my room anymore?"

"I'm dead. Where would you send the engraved invitations?"

I rolled my eyes and moved the now-ordered stack out of Ian's grasp. Boundaries had never been his strong suit. "Can't we just… I don't know. Set up a time to meet?"

"Like a date? Do I need to bring flowers and make dinner reservations, too?" Ian leaned back against the bed and smirked. "Funny enough, my watch doesn't exactly work in the great beyond. What's your problem, anyhow?"

What was my problem? I didn't know where to begin. Willow had gotten under my skin, and these days, Ian seemed to live there.

But most of all, I was struggling with the fact that I'd spent years working my ass off to prove myself to the Guild and now I was doing everything I could to find a way to destroy them. It was stressing me out.

"I don't have a problem," I said.

Ian ignored my bullshit answer as he wandered around the room and, from somewhere, sourced a marble. He rolled it back and forth on the desk.

The cat's-eye rolled left, then right. I wasn't sure where it had come from. I wasn't sure why this act was worth Ian's limited reserve of energy. I wasn't sure why I cared. Except…

Ian Mackenzie was a complicated thing to be. He'd been the

darling of St. Hilaire when he was alive. He was their darling now. Or would be if he'd agreed to speak to anyone other than me. But now that he was dead, there were times when I could see cracks in his characteristic cockiness, times when he seemed oddly anxious. And, despite my better judgment, I found that, in those times, I had an overwhelming desire to do something to relieve his anxiety.

When Ian rolled the marble toward me a fourth time, I bent over and grabbed it. As if it had been his plan all along, he leaned forward and kissed me. The marble was icy where it lay clenched in my fist. Ian, too, was cold. I always forgot Ian would be cold and therefore I was always surprised. But then Ian had always been unexpected. He was an open window where I was sure I'd shut it, a road out of town that didn't exist on a map.

I pulled away to catch my breath and clear my head and remember my name. But Ian was a drug, and I couldn't help but want more.

This time he placed one cold finger on my lips.

I waited. Waited. Waited. My breath came in fits and starts, my traitorous heart pounded, looking for escape. My focus was equally divided between the marble in my hand and the strip of icy flesh against my lips. I waited as if waiting were the only thing I knew how to do. And around Ian, that wasn't far from the truth.

"Trust me," he said, holding my gaze. I found it impossible to look away and equally impossible to remember what I was supposed to trust Ian *with*. I was still wrestling with this new understanding between us after I'd refused to speak to him the entire year before his mysterious death.

My phone buzzed and broke the spell. Grateful and annoyed in equal measure, I blinked, pulled away, and stared at an unfamiliar local number before letting the call go to voicemail.

Ian reached toward my cell phone, but I slapped his hand away. "You gave up things like phones when you…" I was going to say *chose to die* because that's what everyone believed had happened. That Ian was too good of a medium, too good looking, too privileged and special to do anything as uncivilized as to just *happen* to die young. His death must have been a deliberate choice, everyone said, caused by Ian being wild and reckless and too consumed with being Ian to bother staying alive.

I'd bought into the story, too, at the time. But something about it had always unsettled me, and Ian always skirted around the subject like a spider. "Sorry. I didn't mean…"

Ian didn't look away.

"Sorry," I said again, forcing myself to glance down.

I reached over and grabbed another stack of papers, aiming to line up the staples in the upper-left corner. As I did, something caught my eye. I sorted through the pile in my hand and then looked through the ones on the table. Then I looked again.

"Seventeen?" I asked Ian. "They held seventeen séances to try to reach you in a single season?"

I knew the Guild had been oddly obsessed with contacting Ian. But I hadn't realized they had been *this* bent out of shape. In all that time, Ian had never thrown them a single bone.

"Never let it be said I don't know how to play hard to get," he said. "Give me those." He reached over for the stacks and skimmed the forms, turning pages, and turning them back.

I studied him. Ian was so present, so focused, that I rarely had the chance to watch him without him watching me back. But now he was captivated by the reports and I had the chance to take in the straightness of his back, the way he distractedly narrowed his eyes as he considered what he was reading, and I had the chance to think about how much easier my life would be without this connection to him that I couldn't seem to shake. And how much duller.

"Willow Rogers," he said, looking up so quickly I felt as if I'd been caught watching porn in the library.

"What?"

"Willow Rogers was part of…" Ian thumbed through the reports. "Shit. Over half of these."

"Okay. And?"

"I thought they kept trying to reach me because they were worried about marketing St. Hilaire to tourists and wanted me to be their poster boy. But now I wonder if the reason wasn't something else."

Ian's expression was unusually distorted for someone who was always concerned about appearances. I would have loved to believe that this lapse in control, this letting down of his guard, was due to us spending more time together, but like everything with him, it was hard to know for sure.

"Something else like what?" I asked, but when he didn't answer and didn't meet my eyes and the room got perceptively colder, I felt my anger rise. "Ian?"

"Just keep your distance from her," he said, still looking away.

"That's gonna be a little difficult given that she's mentoring me, don't you think?"

He rubbed the back of his neck. "Maybe you can ask for a new mentor?"

"Who did you have in mind since she's pretty much the best here, now that you're..." I paused when Ian narrowed his eyes. "Anyhow, stop being so...cagey," I demanded, although I easily could have said, *Stop being so...Ian*. "There's no point to us trying to get anything done if you aren't going to be honest with me."

Ian tilted his head at an odd angle, which was something he'd just started to do. It was a ghost thing, I guessed, and the awkwardness sent shivers racing up my spine. "You want to play that card? Really?" His voice had an edge that did nothing to put me at ease. I could bleed out from the sharpness of that tone alone. "Then let's see your arm."

"What?" I flinched against my shirtsleeves. Ian always had a special way of making me feel exposed.

He turned away.

"Ian..." I started, searching for a way to avoid an argument. Lately, I'd lost my taste for battle. I looked for loopholes in Ian's argument, but we both knew I'd deliberately done the one thing I'd promised him I wouldn't do—continue to mix up potentially lethal batches of potentially lethal herbs as directed by a crumbling old book of my grandmother's, and inject them into my arm in order to have the ability to visit with ghosts without having to hold a proper séance.

There was no way of getting around the lie; that serum had been the only way I could talk to Ian in the beginning without the whole dog-and-pony show of an illegal formal séance, since I was technically under age for holding one on my own. I had a hard time believing he could hate it that much. "I don't want to fight with you."

"That isn't a denial," Ian observed, thankfully bringing his head back to a more normal angle.

"No," I admitted. "No, it isn't a denial. But it also has nothing to do with you."

I could see Ian's shoulders tense, feel the temperature drop in waves. Although he'd never done it, it was a fair bet he had enough energy or presence or whatever-the-hell it was to damage the house. It was amazing the amount of power a pissed-off ghost could harness.

Instead, Ian stuck his hands in the pockets of his painted-on dark jeans. "Right. It's your life," he said. "I'll keep in mind that it has nothing to do with me."

"Ian," I said, but he was gone before I got the word out.

The passive-aggressive disappearing-in-the-middle-of-an-argument thing drove me nuts, and he knew it.

I sat down and tried to parse the silence. Ian was a black hole of sound and vision, noise and expectation. It always took a few minutes after he left for me to return to myself, not unlike waking up from a realistic dream. Sometimes it took a few minutes before I could tell what was real and what wasn't.

My phone lit up with a reminder of the earlier voicemail. I played the message back and then played it again, oddly relieved.

The message had nothing to do with ghosts. Nothing even to do with St. Hilaire. The real world was calling, and for once, I was more than happy to answer.

ABOUT
THE AUTHOR

Helene Dunbar is the author of *We Are Lost and Found* and *Prelude for Lost Souls*, as well as *Boomerang, These Gentle Wounds*, and *What Remains*. Over the years, she's worked as a drama critic, music journalist, grant writer, and marketing manager. She lives with her husband and daughter in Nashville, Tennessee. Visit her at helenedunbar.com, on Twitter @helene_dunbar, or on Instagram @helenedunbar.